Emily Forbes is an award-winning author of Medical Romance for Mills & Boon. She has written over twenty-five books and has twice been a finalist in the Australian Romantic Book of the Year Award, which she won in 2013 for her novel *Sydney Harbour Hospital: Bella's Wishlist*. You can get in touch with Emily at emilyforbes@internode.on.net, or visit her website at emily-forbesauthor.com.

Annie O'Neil spent most of her childhood with her leg draped over the family rocking chair and a book in her hand. Novels, baking, and writing too much teenage angst poetry ate up most of her youth. Now Annie splits her time between corralling her husband into helping her with their cows, baking, reading, barrel racing (not really!) and spending some very happy hours at her computer, writing.

D0754818

RESCUED BY THE SINGLE DAD

EMILY FORBES

THE DOCTOR'S MARRIAGE FOR A MONTH

ANNIE O'NEIL

MILLS & BOON

First Published in Great Britain 2019
by Mills & Boon, an imprint of HarperCollins*Publishers*
1 London Bridge Street, London, SE1 9GF

Rescued by the Single Dad © 2019 by Emily Forbes

The Doctor's Marriage for a Month © 2019 by Annie O'Neil

ISBN: 978-0-263-26962-8

MIX
Paper from
responsible sources
FSC™ C007454

This book is produced from independently certified FSC™ paper
to ensure responsible forest management.
For more information visit www.harpercollins.co.uk/green.

Printed and bound in Spain
by CPI, Barcelona

RESCUED BY
THE SINGLE DAD

EMILY FORBES

MILLS & BOON

For Beck.
Thank you for many years of fun, laughter
and fabulous friendship.
Wishing you a very happy and very big birthday!
I look forward to celebrating this one
and many others with you.
Love, Emily

10 March 2019

CHAPTER ONE

CHARLI SLID OUT from the booth as a waitress delivered pizzas to the table. She had only been in Australia for two days and was still suffering the effects of jet-lag after the long flight east. Her body clock was telling her she'd been up all night and her stomach heaved at the thought of pizza for breakfast, even though it was just a little after ten p.m.

Her sister and her friends looked as though they were preparing to kick on and Charli needed something soft to drink if she was going to last any longer. Amy and her fellow ski instructors seemed to be able to hold their drinks far better than Charli ever could. She'd heard the Australians partied hard and she doubted she'd keep up even if she wasn't exhausted.

She couldn't remember the last time she'd had a decent night's sleep. It felt like years ago. She'd spent the past seven years studying hard and working part time in her hours off. While she'd had plenty of late nights, very few had been because she'd been out having fun. Medical school had been hugely demanding of both her time and effort, and her two years of Foundation Training had been even more exhausting. Sleep had been hard to come by for many years and, most recently, it had been thanks to her lousy ex, but she'd come to Australia to forget about him and she refused to waste any more time thinking about past mistakes. She'd make a trip to the bar and order a round of drinks and then maybe no one would notice if she sneaked away early.

The bar was crowded, the crush of the *après-ski* crowd several people deep, and Charli could feel herself swaying on her feet as she waited to be served. Her eyes drifted closed, just briefly, but it was long enough to cause her to lose her balance and stumble. She staggered backwards, bumping into the person behind her. Large hands grabbed at her elbows, steadying her.

'Whoa, are you okay?'

She heard a deep voice in her ear. She turned around and looked up into a pair of very dark eyes.

She blinked as she tried to clear her head. She felt foggy, disoriented and she focussed hard. Her first thought was that this man who had her by the elbows was cute. About her age, several inches taller than her, maybe a smidge over six feet, with messy dark hair to go with his dark eyes.

'Are you okay?'

She could see his lips moving, she could see his teeth, which were even and white in contrast to the shadow of a beard on his jaw. She heard him speak but the combination of jet-lag and his broad Australian accent meant it took her a few moments to translate his words into something she could make sense of. She nodded. 'Yes, sorry about that.'

'Are you sure you should be ordering more drinks?'

'They're for my friends.'

He raised one dark eyebrow and she noticed he had a small scar just under his left eye. She must be standing way too close if she could notice that but the crowd around her, coupled with the fact that he was still holding onto her, meant she couldn't move away. His hands were warm and gentle and she found she didn't actually want to step away.

'I promise,' she said. 'I'm having a lemonade. I'm just jet-lagged.'

'In that case, let me order for you. What else can I get you?'

'A jug of beer—'

'And a lemonade,' he added as he dropped his hands and turned towards the bar.

Charli nodded as she pulled her purse from her handbag, wishing he hadn't let go of her. She still felt a little unsteady but this time she didn't think it was solely because of the jet-lag. She studied his back as he placed the order. Her eyes took in the breadth of his shoulders and the way his hair curled over the collar of his T-shirt. His shirt fit him snugly, showing off his muscular physique. She lifted her eyes up to his as he turned back from the bar. 'How much will it be?' she asked.

'Twenty bucks should cover it.'

'Twenty? What colour is that again?'

'Orange.'

'I'm still getting used to your money,' she said as she fished in her purse for the colourful note. 'It's pretty.'

'You're English?'

She nodded. 'Just arrived. Hence the jet-lag,' she said, holding out the note. He reached for the money with his left hand and her fingers tingled as she placed the note in his hand. She noticed he wasn't wearing a wedding ring. Maybe her jet-lag wasn't as bad as she'd thought.

'Whereabouts are you from?' he asked her.

'London. Have you been there?'

'I have.'

'Did you like it?'

'To be completely honest, I prefer it here. Fewer people, better weather.' He smiled at her, softening his words, but she wasn't offended. He'd probably be able to say anything that he liked without upsetting people as long as he said it with a smile. His smile was wide, making his eyes crinkle at the corners and his mouth turn up at the edges. It suited him.

'In case you haven't noticed,' she said, 'you're in the snow. Snow is snow all around the world.' Somehow, she managed to continue the conversation even though she was distracted.

'Yes, but in Australia we choose to go to the snow, we don't have to put up with it unless we want to, and even in the snow we get our fair share of sunny days. There's nothing better than wearing a T-shirt and getting a sun tan while you ski.'

'You ski in a T-shirt?'

Her eyes roamed over him again, taking in the view from the front this time. It was even better than the back. His chest was broad, his stomach flat, his arms were tanned and muscular, lightly covered with dark hair—enough to be masculine, not enough to be off-putting—and his skin was olive. His T-shirt hugged his chest and abdominals and was tucked into a pair of red ski pants that had some official-looking emblem on them, but she couldn't make out what it said in the dim lighting of the bar.

'You bet.' He spoke in the same laid-back, friendly manner that Amy's friends used. Unhurried, relaxed. She'd have to get used to the Aussie way of speaking.

He paid for their order but made no move to pick up his drinks and leave the bar.

'Hey, Reeves, a man is not a camel!'

Charli saw him turn his head at the comment. She followed the direction of his gaze and saw a group of men, all wearing the same navy and red uniform, standing around a tall round table. 'Are they talking to you?' she asked.

'Afraid so.'

'I'd better let you go,' she said, hoping he'd say he'd stay. 'Thank you for your help.'

'It was my pleasure…' He paused and she knew he was waiting for her name.

'Charli.'

'Charli,' he repeated. She liked the way it sounded when he said it. 'Maybe I'll see you around.'

She hoped so, she thought as she took the jug of beer and her lemonade back to the booth, sliding in next to her sister.

'Who was that?' Amy asked.

'I don't know,' she said, realising belatedly that she had no idea. She had a name but no idea if it was his first or last.

'I bet he could take your mind off your troubles for the next few days,' her sister added.

Charli smiled but shook her head. She'd decided she was a terrible judge of character but even she could tell he had trouble written all over him. He was cute and confident and his smile had made her knees wobble, but she suspected he had that effect on a lot of women and she wasn't about to let him add her to his list. 'I'm not looking for someone from ski patrol to take my mind off things.'

'You should be, he was hot. But he's not ski patrol, their uniform is red and white, not red and navy.'

'Do you know what he does?' She should have got more information, she thought, even as she tried to tell herself she wasn't interested. The last thing she needed was a rebound fling with a hot stranger. But she couldn't deny he'd caught her attention.

Amy shook her head before she was dragged back into conversation with one of the other ski instructors, a handsome, blond Canadian. It looked as though Amy might get her own distraction tonight.

Charli scanned the room but she couldn't see the cute guy or his friends from where she sat, and she wasn't about to go looking for him. She needed to clear her head, not complicate it, but if she *had* been looking she suspected he was just the type she would have fallen for. It would be safer if she just took herself back to Amy's apartment and got a decent night's sleep. Tomorrow was another day.

She leant over to Amy. 'I think I might call it a night,' she said as she picked up her jacket.

'Really?'

'I'm tired.'

'I'll come with you,' Amy said as she started to stand.

'No, no, don't leave on my account.'

But Amy was already up and had tucked her arm through Charli's elbow. 'You've come all this way to see me, Canadian Dan will understand.' She smiled and raised an eyebrow. 'Unless you're going to find that hot guy and don't want me cramping your style?'

Charli shook her head. 'No, I'm going home to bed, alone. I'm tired of being disappointed by men, I'd rather just go to bed with my fantasies than find out that the reality isn't what I hoped for.'

'Oh, Charli.' Amy sighed as she hugged her younger sister close. 'I know Hugo hurt you but not all men are bastards.'

'Maybe not, but I'm not game to find out tonight.'

'Well, let me know if you change your mind. There are plenty of cute guys here who will happily let you try out your fantasies on them.'

Charli laughed. 'Seriously, I'm fine. I'll go and tuck myself into bed and I'll see you in the morning.' She kissed her sister's cheek and gently pushed her back into her seat. 'There's no need for both of us to have an early night. Stay, have fun.'

She'd meant it when she'd said she wasn't looking for a man to take her mind off things but, even so, she couldn't resist one last glance around the bar on her way out.

He was still there.

He was leaning against the wall, surrounded by his mates, but he was watching her. Her heart skittered as his eyes locked onto hers. He straightened up and her step faltered as he put his glass on the table and moved towards her. Somehow she managed to keep walking but her eyes didn't leave his. He weaved through the crowd, his path at an angle to hers, and she knew he would reach her before she got to the door.

He waited for her and she stopped beside him, her feet deciding her course of action for her.

'Are you leaving?' His voice was calm and his dark eyes held her gaze, making her feel as though he could see into the depths of her soul.

She nodded.

'Will you stay and have a drink with me?'

Should she? She wanted to but she really didn't trust herself to make good decisions. Even when she wasn't jet-lagged, she made terrible ones. 'I don't even know your name.' She stalled for time.

'It's Patrick. Patrick Reeves.'

He continued to watch her closely and the rest of the crowd faded into insignificance as she hugged the sound of his name to herself. It was a nice name and he had an even nicer face and a fabulous smile. She was tempted, very tempted, but she was also exhausted. 'I don't think I'll be very good company,' she said, barely able to string two words together, although whether that was the effect of jet-lag or Patrick's intense gaze she wasn't sure.

'May I walk you home, then?'

She hesitated, but only briefly. She knew she'd regret it if she walked out alone. She nodded. Decision made. 'I'd like that.'

He held her jacket for her, helping her into it. 'Where are you staying?' he asked as they left the bar and he shrugged into his insulated jacket.

'At Snowgum Chalet, with my sister.' Her boots slipped on the icy path and Patrick reached out to steady her, wrapping an arm around her waist, catching her before she could fall. He lifted her slightly, settling her back on her feet.

'Thank you.' He still had his arm around her and her tongue felt too big in her mouth, making her stumble over the words. 'I seem to have trouble keeping my feet around you.'

He knew the feeling. She was looking up at him with big blue eyes. His heart missed a beat and he felt like he was falling too. 'I'll have to remember to watch out for you on the slopes,' he said as he took her hand. It was small but fitted perfectly into his grip and he tucked it into his elbow. 'I have a feeling you could be dangerous.'

'I'm usually okay on skis,' she replied, completely missing his meaning, 'but I am very wobbly today. I'm sure I'll be all right after a decent sleep. Are you skiing tomorrow?'

He shook his head. 'Unfortunately not.'

'Do you work here? I saw your friends were all wearing the same uniform.'

'Not exactly,' he said as he changed direction, taking a path to the right that turned past Ironbark Lodge and headed down the hill to Snowgum Chalet. 'We're all paramedics, we've been doing alpine training exercises here. We're part of the High Country Special Operations arm.'

'That sounds exciting. What did you have to do?'

'Avalanche training, helicopter drops into the back country, abseiling down cliffs, that sort of thing.'

'Exciting *and* exhausting.'

He supposed it was both but there was nothing unusual in the hectic pace of his life. Working as a Special Ops paramedic meant his life moved rapidly from one disaster to another and he embraced the pace, especially over the past two years. Being busy meant he didn't have time to think. Didn't have time to dwell on things.

'It's been challenging,' he admitted as they reached the front door of her lodge, 'but it's exhilarating too.'

It had been busy and he was knackered. He should be going home to bed, not chatting up pretty strangers in the snow, but he'd been powerless to resist her. He could count on one hand the number of women he'd bothered to look at twice since losing his wife two years ago. There had been no shortage of offers, plenty of women seemed to find the idea of a widower romantically attractive, but he had barely given any of them the time of day. Initially he'd been too grief-stricken, then he'd felt as if he was being unfaithful, and lately he'd been too busy. But something about Charli had struck a chord with him; something about her had made him sit up and take notice.

He was getting lonely. Shift work and a three-year-old daughter occupied a lot of his time but there were nights when he was home, alone on the couch while his daughter slept, and he missed adult company. Female company. He wanted a connection, it didn't need to be permanent, but finding someone attractive was an unusual experience for him and that flutter of anticipation, that curiosity, that tremor of excitement, had been enough to galvanise him into action. When he'd seen her heading for the door he'd known he couldn't let her leave without talking to her once more. He knew that if he let her walk out of the bar he would never see her again.

Charli let go of his hand as she searched in her bag for the key. She turned to him and for the briefest of moments he thought about what he'd say if she invited him in.

He was leaving tomorrow. At best, they could have one night together. But he didn't get the impression that outcome was on the cards and he didn't know if he would accept the invitation if it was forthcoming.

'Do you think we could have that drink tomorrow night?' she asked.

He should have been relieved that her words weren't

the ones he'd half hoped to hear. A lack of an invitation meant he didn't have to wrestle with his conscience, didn't have to remind himself of all the reasons why he should say goodnight and go home to his own bed. She'd made the decision for him. He should be grateful but he couldn't help feeling disappointed.

'I'd love to but I have to go back to Melbourne.' He was due to leave first thing in the morning but the disappointment left a sour taste in his mouth. Maybe he could postpone his departure for just a few hours? He'd have to make some phone calls, ask for more favours, but it would be worth it. He had to try. 'Could I take you to brunch instead, or are you planning to be out skiing bright and early?'

'No, brunch sounds lovely.' She smiled up at him and made him wonder if it was too soon to kiss her goodnight.

He'd known her less than an hour. He figured it probably was too soon.

'Great,' he said as he resisted temptation and waited for her to unlock her door to her ground-floor apartment. He had no reason to delay the farewell any longer. 'I'll meet you here at ten.'

He headed towards his bed, feeling unexpectedly hopeful and positive.

Snow blanketed the ground beneath his boots but the evening sky was clear and dark. There were no clouds and no moon but hundreds of tiny stars studded the darkness, relieving the blackness. He stopped outside the bar and the background hum of the alpine resort village faded as he closed his eyes and breathed deeply, inhaling the fresh mountain air. The scent of snow gums, wood smoke and barbeque filled his nose.

He stood still for a moment longer, soaking up the atmosphere.

The lights reflected off the snow as the machine operators traversed the slopes, smoothing out the ski runs ready for tomorrow, but he turned his back on the runs and looked instead past the chalets and buildings of the Wombat Gully Ski Resort and further up the mountain where the stately snow gums lined the ski runs. They stood sentinel, their trunks smooth and ghostly white, lit only by the light coming from the lodges. There was no wind to rustle their leaves, the air was still and so was he.

He knew he was okay. He'd kept things together for two years and had come through the worst of it. He was managing as a single parent. It wasn't easy, far from it, but it was getting better. He had a routine, he had good support and he and his daughter had formed their own duo. Three had become two but two was okay. They were doing all right. Two was better than one. And he had a career he loved. He knew it could be all-consuming but it had saved him from depression and misery and had given him something else to focus on. Between his work and Ella, he had everything he needed. Not everything he *wanted* but life was good. He was doing okay.

Opening his eyes, he took in the natural beauty that surrounded him and thought, for the first time in years, that it was good to be alive. No, not thought but believed. There was a difference.

He breathed out and his warm breath condensed into white puffs of steam in the frigid air. He'd put his life on hold since Margie's unexpected death, concentrating on his daughter and on his career, and his personal life had been largely ignored. Perhaps it was time to look to the future.

Patrick ignored the drone of the snow groomers and the constant thrumming of the snow-making machines and the music drifting into the night from the bar behind him—none of that was anything to do with him—as his thoughts drifted back to Charli. He would meet her for brunch. It felt odd to be organising a date but also exciting. After that he would return to Melbourne but at least he would have taken a step forward. A step towards a future. He and Ella couldn't remain a pair for ever, he didn't believe that was healthy. To move forward he had to get back into the dating game. But he wanted to do it on his terms. He wanted to wait until he felt a connection with someone. Charli was a promising start.

'Hey, Pat, you calling it a night?'

Pat turned, his self-reflection interrupted by Connor Green, one of his colleagues, who was headed his way.

'Yep.' He waited to see if Connor had been sent to try to persuade him to return to the bar. He was out of luck if that was his mission. The team was close-knit and Pat had become good friends with his teammates over the years. They'd provided great support to him, but he wanted a clear head for tomorrow.

'Me too,' Connor replied.

A sudden gust of wind swirled around Pat as Connor spoke, startling him after the extraordinary stillness of the night. A noise similar to that of a jet engine roared behind them, its sound swallowing the background noise, and the ground shook beneath their feet. Pat looked up but the sky was just as dark as before. He could see nothing untoward but the rumble continued, the ground unsteady, testing their balance. He felt his heart rate accelerate as he turned around, his eyes glued to the mountain, searching for the source of the noise, his gut telling him it wasn't a plane.

Was it an avalanche? Even though they'd spent hours on avalanche training he'd never heard, or seen, one. They were a rare occurrence in Australia.

His eyes scanned the slopes, glancing over the buildings as he looked towards the tree line. Ironbark Lodge sat highest on the mountain and he could see it silhouetted against the snow, its windows lit up against the night sky. He saw the lights waver and flicker as though candles illuminated the glass instead of electricity. And then the lights disappeared, leaving the lodge in darkness.

Pat looked down the mountain, expecting a complete power outage, but the other buildings remained bright. Movement in the corner of his eye drew his gaze up again.

He blinked.

Ironbark Lodge looked as if it was moving.

He must be more tired than he thought. He shook his head and rubbed one hand across his eyes before opening them again. He must be seeing things.

No. He wasn't. The lodge was definitely moving.

'Bloody hell!' It took him a moment to process what he was looking at and meanwhile Ironbark Lodge continued to move. He watched on in horror and disbelief as the lodge slid down the side of the mountain.

Snowgum Chalet sat directly in its path.

He took off, sprinting along the icy paths, retracing his steps from moments before, running right into the path of the disaster.

CHAPTER TWO

'AMY?' CHARLI CALLED from the darkness of the bedroom.

She'd fallen asleep quickly with a smile on her lips as she'd thought about having brunch with Patrick but had been woken abruptly by the wind. 'Amy, are you there? Can you hear that?'

The wind was loud. So loud it sounded like it was rushing through the apartment. At first, she'd thought the noise was the bathroom fan but as it continued to increase in volume she realised it wasn't coming from the bathroom but was moving closer. It sounded like it was coming for her. She sat up just as a loud explosion split the air and her heart leapt as the unexpected sound shattered the night.

What was that? A gas cylinder exploding? A car backfiring?

The windows of the apartment rattled as she reached for the bedside lamp. The whole bed was shaking and it took her two attempts to find the switch. A backfiring car wouldn't shake the bed.

But an avalanche might.

'Amy?' she called again, louder this time, as she finally turned on the light.

Was Amy home or was she still in the bar? Charli was

about to get out of bed to look for her when the lights went out, engulfing her in darkness.

The noise hadn't stopped, it had only intensified.

It was incredible. It sounded like a freight train, which was impossible as there was no train on the mountain. Her next thought was perhaps it was one of the snow-grooming machines. Had someone lost control? And then, cutting through the noise, she heard screams.

'Amy?'

She leapt out of bed, stumbling in the darkness.

The noise was deafening now. Windows shattered and she heard glass hit the floor. Timbers were crack-ing and metal twisted and screeched, hurting her ears. She could hear bricks falling and over it all the noise of the wind and the screams continued.

Instinctively she threw her hands over her head as she took another step forward before her legs gave way beneath her. She didn't realise that it wasn't her legs but the floor that had disappeared from under her, and then there was nothing.

No light. No sound and only very slight vibrations. The wind had stopped as suddenly as it had begun and the room was no longer shaking violently, but she still couldn't see and, much worse, she still couldn't hear a sound. Even the screams had been silenced.

'Amy?'

She coughed as she inhaled a mouthful of dust and it stuck on her tongue.

'Are you there?'

There was only silence. Had Amy come home? Was she there?

Charli had no idea. It was awfully quiet.

Deathly quiet.

The room had stopped shaking and was now resting quietly in the dark. But the sudden silence wasn't peaceful or calming, it was frightening. What had happened?

The air was frigid. The temperature had dropped and the floor beneath her legs was cold and damp. The bedroom was carpeted but the carpet was now flooded and icy water swirled around her. She could feel it and it chilled her to the bone, but she had no idea where it had come from.

'Hello. Is anyone there?' she yelled, choking on the thick dust that seemed to be hanging in the air.

She tried to stand up but smacked her head on something hard before she could fully straighten her knees. She swore out loud and rubbed her forehead above her left eye. A lump was already forming from the collision. She crouched down and reached up with one hand. She felt concrete under her fingers. Was that the ceiling? Why was it so low?

She squatted on the floor as she tried to figure out what had happened. Had the ceiling collapsed? God, she hoped not. Amy's apartment was on the ground floor of a four-storey building.

What had happened? It was impossible to tell. The darkness made it impossible to get her bearings, impossible to work out what had happened and what was going on.

She reached out carefully, not knowing what she might find.

There was nothing in front of her so she crawled towards the door, or to where she thought the door was. Her hands were immersed in the freezing cold water and her fingers were going numb. She was dressed only in a T-shirt and knickers, clothes that were warm enough to sleep in while the central heating worked, but it offered no protection in her current situation.

She stretched her hands out and shuffled forward on her knees. There was an overpowering smell of diesel fumes and overflowing toilets. She didn't want to know what she was crawling through.

Something sharp grazed her calf but she pressed on, hands outstretched in front of her.

It felt like she'd gone no further than a few feet before she ran into a wall. She was sure the door had to be there somewhere. She moved sideways, still calling Amy's name, as she felt for a gap, her fingers searching for the door frame. She cried out as something pierced her palm, slicing into the flesh beneath her right thumb. The wound throbbed and she could feel blood running down to her elbow. She ignored the warm blood as she felt more frantically for the doorway but there was no gap. Instead she found herself wedged into a corner.

She was confused, disoriented but she continued to inch her way around the room.

She kept her hands outstretched, fearful of hitting her head again in the darkness. She breathed in the putrid, frigid air as she crawled through the darkness.

Her hands met more cold concrete. It was rough under her fingers, the smooth walls obliterated, leaving what felt like a pile of rubble. The ceiling pressed down on her head, making her feel claustrophobic. She fought back a wave of panic. Where was she? Nothing was familiar.

'Amy? Are you here?' She was sobbing now, crying salty tears that ran down her cheeks and mingled with the dust that caked her mouth.

She forced herself to keep moving. She couldn't stay

still. She had to find a way out of there before she froze to death.

She moved a few more feet and her fingers made contact with smooth metal. Was that the bed frame? Had she done a full circle? The bed had a high metal bed head. She traced the frame. The poles were bent, the frame leaning in towards the centre of the bed. She reached up and felt the ceiling. Somehow the metal bed head was supporting the ceiling. A concrete ceiling that should be five feet above her head, not several inches.

How had the bed not collapsed completely?

She was lucky she hadn't been crushed, she thought, before she had a more terrifying realisation. But what about Amy? Where *was* her sister? What might have happened to her?

'Amy?' she whispered. Scared now of what she might *not* hear. Listening in hope for her sister's voice.

Still nothing.

The carpet was sodden and sludgy under her knees. Crawling through freezing mud and water in the dark wasn't getting her anywhere. She needed to see. She needed light. She felt for the bedside table, reaching for her mobile phone that had been resting on top. She desperately needed the flashlight function, but her hand met empty air. There was no table and she could only assume her phone now lay submerged in the vile water that lapped at her thighs.

She moved around the other side of the bed, only to find herself in another dead end. There was no way around this. She was trapped in a windowless, flooded tomb.

How had she ended up here?

What had happened?

Had a snow groomer crashed into their apartment? What had happened to the apartments above?

She had no idea.

All she knew was that she was trapped, buried alive.

She wanted to scream but the air was still so cold and so thick with dust she didn't want to breathe it in.

Stay calm. Think.

She wanted to be warm.

Crawling back to the bed, she curled into a ball and tucked her injured hand under her armpit in an attempt to stop the bleeding and to warm herself up. She tugged the quilt over her, it was cold but dry and although she still wasn't warm at least she wasn't sitting in that filthy water.

She closed her eyes as she tried to figure out what to do. She wanted to get out of there but had no idea how she would achieve that.

Amy would know.

She let her tears flow as she lay in the darkness.

She wanted her sister.

Pat only had one thought as he ran towards Snowgum Chalet.

Charli.

He had to warn her. Had to get her out.

He skidded to a stop and gulped a lungful of frigid air as he tried to comprehend what he was seeing.

Ironbark Lodge was sliding almost gracefully down the slope, seemingly with no great urgency, keeping pace with the eucalyptus trees that were falling alongside it. It left a dark smear of mud in its wake as it pushed the snow ahead like a gigantic snowplough. The bottom floors of the building were pushed out as it gathered momentum and the upper levels toppled backwards. The accompanying sound was an agonising, horrific cracking of timbers, an explosion of glass, a high-pitched shrieking of twisting metal and devastating human cries, but still the lodge continued to slide down the slope in front of him, heading straight for Snowgum Chalet. And Charli.

There was nothing he could do and he watched helplessly as the disaster unfolded before him until, with a sickening crash, the two lodges collided. Pat took a step forward, hopelessly, helplessly, as Snowgum Chalet collapsed like a deck of cards and the third and fourth stories crushed the floors below and sent a cloud of white concrete dust into the air.

Car alarms were blaring and, over the top of all the noise, the village distress siren wailed. The noise of the disaster brought people out of the buildings. They poured out of the surrounding bars, restaurants and lodges before stopping in their tracks, staring in disbelief at the site that confronted them. A dark muddy scar bisected the snow-covered mountain and an enormous pile of rubble, which moments before had been two buildings, dominated the landscape. They stared, momentarily frozen, at the ruins of the buildings that had, God only knew, how many people inside.

Pat could hear screams and calls for help coming from underneath the rubble. He had no idea how people had survived this disaster but clearly they had. He desperately hoped Charli had been one of them but he couldn't imagine how. Her apartment was—had been—on the ground floor. Unless she had somehow, miraculously, managed to escape, she was now buried under tonnes of concrete, bricks and steel. He fought back a wave of nausea as the dust cloud settled and he surveyed the scene. Everything had changed in an instant.

A few bystanders had already gathered their wits and were trying to move debris. There wasn't any discussion or any system to the recovery attempt, people simply started at the area closest to them. They stood in the mud, pulling at bricks and window frames, blocks of concrete and pieces of broken furniture. They looked like scavengers sorting through a rubbish tip. Nothing in front of them resembled a building.

He had to help. He pulled his gloves from the pocket of his jacket and shoved his hands into them as his feet began moving, propelling him towards the devastation. Muddy water continued to flow down the hill, making conditions underfoot slippery and treacherous. He could smell diesel fuel and sewage and gas but he couldn't stop. Charli's life might depend on him.

'Charli! Charli?'

For a split second he thought it was her voice he could hear. He turned around and saw a young woman flying down the path, her blonde hair streaming behind her.

Was it Charli?

She ran past Connor and Pat saw him grab at her. He held onto her, restraining her. Pat knew if he hadn't caught her she would have kept running.

She beat at his chest with her fists. 'Let me go. My sister is in there. I have to find her.'

His heart fell like a stone into his stomach, the last vestiges of hope shattered. It wasn't Charli. It was her sister.

He left Connor to deal with her as he stepped cautiously onto a teetering slab of concrete before thinking better of it when it wobbled under his feet. He didn't want to upset the balance. Who knew what lay beneath his feet.

He lay on his stomach and inched along the slab, listening to the cries for help and trying to work out where they were coming from. Sound bounced off the hard surfaces and off the mountain, distorting the voices and making it difficult to judge direction.

The darkness wasn't helping matters either. He couldn't see clearly, he couldn't tell if there were gaps in the rubble, any way in or out. He couldn't see survivors but he could hear them. He needed better light so he could tell where to start. He pulled his phone from his pocket, swiped the screen and pressed the flashlight icon but the light it gave off was pathetic.

'I need some light over here. Does anyone have a torch?' The lights of the village had been bright enough to see the buildings topple but they weren't bright enough now. He needed stronger beams, much stronger. The headlights from a car or a snowplough.

'Pat, what the hell are you doing? It's not safe, man.'

He heard Connor's voice from behind him. He turned his head. He could see dozens of people gathered in the semi-darkness, torches and phones causing multiple circles of light. 'Pass me a torch.'

'No. You need to come back. We need to assess the situation. It's too dangerous.'

'I can hear people. I need to see if I can reach them.'

'And what if that slab gives way under you? We could lose you along with anyone trapped under there,' Connor responded. 'We need a plan.'

Pat ignored him. He knew Connor wouldn't risk coming out after him. Two people on this teetering slab would be asking for trouble. Pat could stay out there safe in the knowledge that no one could drag him back. He knew he was taking a risk but what choice did he have? People were trapped. They needed his help.

'Hello? Can you hear me?' he called out.

'Yes.'

'I'm trapped.'

'Help us.' One, two, three different voices called back to him.

But none of them belonged to Charli.

He didn't want to stop but he couldn't ignore these cries for assistance. 'Are you hurt?'

'My wife. You have to help me. I can't reach her.'

'I'm stuck, my leg is caught. There's water coming in. I can't move. Help me, please, help me.'

There were only two replies to his question.

'Who is there? Can you tell me your names?'

'Simon.' The voice was faint and Pat strained to listen. Where were the other voices? Where was the husband? His wife?

'Pat, you need to follow protocol. It's not safe,' Connor called out, urging him to rethink his position.

Pat knew he was right. But knowing Connor was right wasn't enough to get him to pull back. He could argue that this wasn't a training drill or an official rescue. Not yet. He was effectively just a bystander, a good Samaritan, and his first instinct was to help. He would be careful. If he thought he was in danger, or there was a risk of causing further harm, he'd pull back.

'Think about Ella,' Connor called to him. 'What happens to her if something happens to you?'

Pat hesitated, knowing Connor had won this round. He was being foolish, he wasn't just risking his own safety, he was risking more than that, he was risking

Ella's life as she knew it. Ella was all he had left and he had to stay safe for her.

Connor hadn't needed to come after him at all. He had won the battle of wills with a few well-chosen words.

'Simon?' Pat called out. 'I'll be back, I need to get help.'

'Don't leave me here.'

Simon's voice called back to him, begging him not to go. One voice only. What had happened to the others? Had they lost consciousness? Or worse? Could they hear but not respond? Would Simon notice the silence?

Pat wanted to stay but he knew it was impossible to perform this rescue without equipment and help. 'I promise I'll be back.'

But he couldn't promise he'd be back in time.

He closed his eyes and pictured Ella's face and knew he had no option. It ripped him in two to leave but he had no choice.

He turned and began to inch his way off the slab. He had moved less than a foot when the ground wobbled and shifted and the concrete under him trembled and vibrated. His heart was in his throat as adrenalin surged through his body and he fought to keep his balance.

'Reeves,' Connor yelled at him. 'Get back here!'

CHAPTER THREE

CHARLI WOKE WITH a start. Something wet dripped from the ceiling, hitting her forehead.

She frowned, perplexed, and lifted her hand to wipe the moisture from her skin. She winced as her fingers brushed across her hairline. There was a large bump over her left eye and her skin felt tacky. And then she remembered where she was and what had happened.

She was freezing and her hand was throbbing. She'd torn a strip of fabric off the bedsheet and wrapped it around the base of her right thumb to stem the bleeding, but she hadn't been able to see how bad the wound was and her fingers were too cold to be able to give her any sensory feedback but she thought it had stopped bleeding.

The room was still pitch black, giving her no clue as to the time. She hadn't meant to fall asleep. She was thirsty and freezing and worried. She'd never treated anyone with hypothermia but she knew it was a real danger. She was curled in a ball on the bed, nestled into the small gap between the collapsed roof and the crushed bedhead. The quilt covered her but it was doing little to keep her warm.

Moisture continued to drip onto her head. She cupped

her hands and let it gather in her palms. She lifted her hands to her face, wrinkling her nose in disappointment and disgust as she smelt the tainted water. It was undrinkable.

She tucked her hands under her armpits in a vain attempt to increase her body heat and lay in the dark, straining her ears to hear signs of life from anywhere around her. Was Amy in the apartment too? Had she fallen asleep and not heard Amy come home? Maybe her sister was there somewhere. Maybe she'd been knocked unconscious?

'Amy?' she whispered into the dark. In hope. Just in case, by some miracle, her sister was there.

Was that the sound of someone breathing?

Her heart rate spiked and she waited, listening carefully, before realising it was her own breathing she could hear, loud in the silence.

But then, in the distance, she heard another noise. A voice. People calling out, talking to each other. There *were* other people here, she wasn't alone!

'Hello? Can you hear me? *Hello?*'

There was no reply, the voices simply continued in the distance. They didn't stop or change or show any sign that they had heard her. No one replied to her and the words were indistinct. She knew they weren't close.

Her voice was hoarse, her throat parched and sore. No one was going to hear her. She needed to make more noise. But how?

She sat up slowly, uncurling herself like a fern frond, and hesitantly felt for the floor with her cold, bare feet. Her toes were tiny blocks of ice, she had some sensation in the two biggest toes but nothing in the rest. How many hours had she been trapped here?

She should have stayed in the bar with Patrick. She should have had another lemonade. She couldn't remember now why it had been so necessary, so important that she get to bed. Maybe just a few more minutes' conversation would have delayed things enough so that she wouldn't have been in the apartment. But it was too late for those regrets now, she was in the apartment and she was alone.

She couldn't lie on the bed and wait to be found. She needed to *make* it happen. She needed to *do* something. Anything.

The carpet was sodden but no longer under water. She crawled across the damp, muddy floor as she felt around cautiously in the dark, searching for something she could use to create noise. Her hand throbbed where she had cut her palm but she ignored that. There were more important things to worry about. Her eyes hadn't become accustomed to the blackness, which she knew meant there was no light coming in. Did that mean there was also no fresh air? Would she suffocate before she was found?

Her thoughts lent urgency to her search. There were people out there, out beyond this tomb she was imprisoned in, and she needed them to find her. She couldn't contemplate dying in here. Someone would find her. She had to believe that. She wasn't ready to die. Not yet. She needed to alert people to her existence.

Lost in her thoughts, it took her a moment to realise her fingers had closed around a slender object. A pole of some sort. It was cold to the touch, metal, not wood. It felt like a ski pole but she knew there weren't any in the room. It could be a piece of the bed, the rail from the wardrobe, part of the bedside lamp. She didn't know what it was or how it came to be lying on the floor. It didn't matter. All that mattered was that it would make more noise than she was capable of by yelling.

She crawled back to the bed. She could still hear noises from above but the voices were being drowned out by mechanical sounds now. She could feel her anxiety increasing with every passing second. What were they doing with those machines? What if they were bulldozers? What if they pushed more debris down on top of her? Her breaths came in short, rapid bursts as panic set in. She had to make some noise. They *had* to find her. Her panic gave strength to her cold, lethargic muscles and she hit the pole against the metal frame with as much energy as she could muster.

Her arm tired easily but she forced herself to continue.

One minute, two, she wasn't sure.

Lactic acid burned in her muscles and she stopped briefly, giving her arms a chance to rest. Her ears were ringing but she listened for noises from above. Something, anything, to let her know she'd been heard.

'Hello? Can anyone hear me?' she called, but her voice sounded faint even to her ears.

She heard a whistle, one long blast, that echoed around the mountain.

When it ceased, so had all the noise. Everything was silent.

What did it mean? Was it a warning whistle? Was there danger? Why was it so quiet?

She waited, the pole heavy in her hand. Where was everyone? Where had they gone?

Her heart beat furiously in her chest. She breathed deeply, trying to quell the rising panic that threatened to overwhelm her, but all she got was a lungful of stale, putrid air. The smell was vile and made her feel nauseous.

She let the pole fall from her fingertips.

What was coming her way now? More water? More mud?

Death?

She didn't know how much more she could take. Her reserves were running low. She was exhausted, thirsty, hungry, sore, filthy and alone. Maybe it was easier just to let go.

She put her head down and cried and the tears gathered in the corner of her mouth. Ignoring the knowledge that her skin was covered in dust and who knew what else, she licked the tears from her lips. They were the only moisture she could get.

What would she do when her tears dried up?

She lay on the damp mattress in the dark and imagined dying alone. Buried here on the wrong side of the world.

Pat was exhausted. Since the landslide he'd slept for a total of eight out of the past thirty hours. He'd taken his assigned breaks but no more and, like all the search and rescue personnel, he was surviving on coffee and adrenalin.

Sixteen people had been listed as missing. In the past thirty hours, nine bodies had been recovered but not one survivor had been among them.

And Charli was still missing.

He had to believe that was good news. There was still hope. Though he knew that the more time that passed the lower her chances of survival were, he wasn't going to give up. He'd made a silent promise to Charli that he wouldn't stop until he found her. It wasn't in his nature to give in and he refused to, even though hope was fading rapidly. There were still seven people to be found and he wasn't stopping until they'd all been accounted for.

Close to two thousand people were involved in the search and recovery effort but he'd made certain that he was assigned to the search zone that included the remains of Snowgum Chalet. The noise level on the mountain was high. Concrete drills and bobcats were the background noise to the sound of thousands of voices. At regular intervals a signal whistle blew and everyone downed tools and the mountain fell silent as they all held their collective breath and listened for any sound of survivors.

But the site remained eerily quiet. There was nothing at all to hear.

Even a concrete X-ray machine and thermal imaging equipment had so far failed to detect any trace of survivors.

Perhaps today their luck would turn.

At times he felt as though they were taking one step forward and two back. Between the fatigue and the lack of progress it was getting increasingly difficult to keep morale high. It was falling with every hour that passed but Pat knew that all it would take to lift everyone's spirits would be to find just one survivor. Just one. But low temperatures and exposure to the elements, combined with potential injuries, meant they didn't have a lot of time. Hypothermia, blood loss, fractures, organ damage—all of these could be fatal.

He tried to focus on the positives. There had been no further landslides and the skies remained clear. They didn't need snowfall to hamper their efforts.

He knew the negatives still outweighed the positives but despite the negative outcome of their efforts so far he refused to give in. Someone *must* have survived.

He swallowed the last mouthful of his breakfast before strapping himself into a harness in preparation for his stint working on the precariously steep slope. The mountain was wet, slippery and treacherous. His movements were slow and deliberate. It was imperative that he didn't dislodge the earth or other debris beneath him as there was the risk of the rubble giving way and sending him, and others, plunging down the mountainside. The process was like a game of Jenga or pick-up sticks. Moving or even touching the wrong piece could cause other pieces to fall and the result could be disastrous.

He'd been working for several hours with just a short break when the Sunday morning chapel bells rang out over the mountain. They'd been advised that today's service would give the volunteers, search-and-rescue crew and people who hadn't been evacuated from the mountain an opportunity to say a prayer for the dead and the missing, and anyone who wished to could put down tools and attend.

The site gradually went quiet as equipment was abandoned, machines switched off and work ceased as people made their way to the chapel.

'Did you want to come to the service?' Connor asked from his position alongside Pat.

Pat shook his head. 'You know I don't believe in God.' He'd given up on his tenuous belief two years ago when his prayers had gone unanswered. 'I think my time is better spent here, searching, doing something more practical.' He had a feeling something was about to happen. Something told him it was important to stay on site.

'Fair enough. But you can't search alone,' Connor said as he carefully shifted another piece of concrete. 'I'll stay too.'

Pat suspected a number of people were going to the chapel because they thought paying their respects was the right thing to do. He could understand their reasons but, in his mind, their attendance implied that they didn't expect to find anyone alive. He wasn't prepared to give up hope. Not yet. It was still possible. Each passing minute made it less likely but that was why it was so important to keep going. Until every missing person was accounted for, he wasn't going to give up. He nodded briefly, acknowledging Connor's offer. He wasn't going to try to talk him out of it. Protocol dictated that they work in pairs. He needed Connor if he wanted to continue.

The bells stopped ringing as the search zone was vacated, leaving Pat and Connor alone in their small section. They worked in silence, their movements methodical as they continued to clear their small area. As Pat pulled at a piece of broken and twisted window frame he heard a metallic ping. He threw the debris over his shoulder, assuming his movements had made the noise, but as the metal flew through the air he heard a second ping.

He looked around the site. There were a few people still working but no one nearby. He knew that sound on the mountain carried long distances and echoed. The sound could have come from anywhere but in the silence that had descended on the site he felt his hopes lift.

'Did you hear that?' he asked Connor.

'Hear what?'

Pat was kneeling on the rubble but went completely still as he listened again.

'What was it?' Connor said.

Pat held up a hand. 'Hang on a minute.' But there was nothing more.

'Hello? Can you hear me?' He called out across the site. He could hear the expectation and excitement in his voice. He waited, still and silent, and his heart skipped a beat as he heard a reply.

'Can you hear...?'

'There! That.' He turned to look at Connor but his friend was shaking his head.

'It's just an echo.'

Was it his imagination playing tricks? He was tired, they all were, but he knew it was something important. 'I don't think so.' He called again. 'Hello?'

'Please. Help me.'

Pat turned back to Connor. 'Tell me you heard that?'

Connor's eyes were wide with surprise as he nodded.

Pat grinned. He could feel his smile splitting his face in two. 'We've got someone!'

CHAPTER FOUR

PAT INCHED CAREFULLY across the concrete slab that might have once been a ceiling or a floor or even a wall. He reined in his eagerness, making sure his movements were slow and deliberate. The engineers had deemed the site safe but still he was cautious.

'Hello?' he called again as he pushed himself further out onto the collapsed building. 'Can you still hear me?

'Yes.'

The voice was faint and raspy but it was real. And it was female.

She was real and she was alive!

Excitement rushed through his body, flooding his muscles with adrenalin. Finally, they could mark another name off the list and this time they had a survivor.

'Can you tell me your name?'

'Charlotte. Charlotte Lawson.'

Could it be?

'Charli? Is that you? It's Patrick.'

'Patrick?'

'I've been looking for you.' He couldn't believe he had found her, that she was alive. It was a miracle. But he didn't believe in miracles. 'Are you hurt?'

'No. Not badly. But my sister, Amy… I don't know

where she is. It's pitch-black in here, I can't see anything. The walls have collapsed and I'm trapped. Please, help us.'

'Charli, Amy is okay. She wasn't in the building.'

'Are you sure?'

'Positive. I've seen her. I've spoken to her. I'll get her here and you can talk to her.' He could hear Charli sobbing with relief.

'Don't leave me.'

'I won't leave you. I promise. I'm going to get you out but you need to listen to me. It's going to take time but I give you my word we will get you out.' He did his best to sound reassuring but he had heard the wobble in her voice. He could only imagine what she was thinking, how she was feeling. It was a miracle that she'd been found and that she was, apparently, unharmed, but Pat knew they'd need another miracle to get her out before anything untoward happened.

There had been other casualties who had survived the landslide only to perish before they'd been able to rescue them, and those deaths weighed heavily on his conscience. He'd talked to those people but hadn't been able to save them. He wasn't going to let the same fate befall Charli.

He turned back to Connor and saw he already had his radio in his hand and was putting the call out. Within seconds their team was reassembling, along with the medical specialists and engineers who had been flown in to Wombat Gully. The chapel bells were ringing again and the noise level intensified as people poured out, buzzing with excitement as the news spread.

A survivor!

Pat could hear Connor briefing the teams. The site

had been cordoned off but he knew that once news broke that a survivor had been located, the media would be pressing in as close as possible. Connor was issuing instructions to the police to expand the cordon to give them more privacy. They needed to be able to communicate with Charli and extraneous noise wasn't going to be helpful.

Pat was handed a headset and a search cam, a thin, flexible pole with a camera on the end that could be fed through small gaps. 'All right, Charli. We're going to send a camera down to you. It'll have a light on it and a microphone. I'll be wearing a headset so you can talk to me. I'll be listening.'

A hole needed to be drilled through the concrete in order to feed the camera through. The engineer tried to convince Pat to leave while he worked, worried about the slab taking their combined weight. 'No. I'm staying,' Pat argued. 'Connor and I were both on the slab and it held. I need to be here.'

'Charli.' He spoke to her, letting her know their plans. 'We need to drill a small hole to get the camera through. It's going to get noisy for a few minutes but I'll still be right here.'

The engineer used a diamond-tipped drill and made a small opening. Pat pushed the pole into the gap but the camera showed nothing. There was a small space but it was empty. There was no one in it.

Disappointment and frustration flooded through him. He'd been sure they were in the right place.

Pat spoke over his shoulder to the site engineer. 'How many apartments were in this building?'

'Twelve, four floors, three on each floor. You should be right above her.'

Pat checked the surroundings. Was there another floor under this slab? There didn't look as though there was enough space. The concrete slab they had drilled through and the space he was looking at through the camera must only be a few feet off the ground. Where was she?

'She's got to be here. There must be a second slab. We'll have to go through the next one.' That had to be the only solution.

The engineer nodded and issued directives to Pat to pass on to Charli.

'Charli, I think we're right above you. We're going to drill carefully through more concrete. It could be close to you. We'll go slowly and stop regularly to check in with you. I need you to tell us if you're worried about anything.'

'How will I know? I can't see.'

Pat knew that was a problem. They had to be careful and had no way of knowing where she was. They could be drilling right above her head. 'Charli, are you sitting up or lying down?' he asked.

'I'm lying down, there's not much room here.'

They needed more information. 'Can you reach your hand above your head? How much space is there?'

'Maybe a foot.'

'What about around you?'

'I'm on the bed. There's a wall to my left and maybe a few feet to my right and at the foot of the bed. I think the frame of the bed head is holding up the ceiling.'

'Okay. That's great, Charli, you're doing well.'

He couldn't continue the conversation while the engineers were drilling but they stopped every couple of minutes, giving him an opportunity to check in.

'How are you doing, Charli?'

'I'm okay. Cold and thirsty.'

'I'll buy you a hot chocolate when we get you out of here.'

'Is that a promise?'

'For sure.' He should have insisted on buying her a drink on Friday night. Maybe then she would have still been in the bar when the landslide had occurred. Maybe then she would have been safe. He knew he couldn't keep everyone safe but he wished he'd followed his heart. He promised himself he wouldn't take the safe option next time. 'You must be hungry too.'

'I am. How long have I been stuck in here?'

'About thirty-six hours.'

'*What?* What day is it?' she asked.

'Sunday.'

'*Sunday!* What time is it?'

'Almost eleven in the morning.'

It had been nearly four hours since he'd come on shift. He wondered if he'd be made to leave when his shift ended. He knew that protocol dictated that he should, but he also knew he would argue against it. There was no way he was leaving the site until they'd got Charli out of there.

'Okay, I think we're almost there,' he said. 'The drilling's going to start again.'

Another couple of minutes was all that was needed before the engineer gave Pat a thumbs-up.

'I can see a tiny bit of light!' Charli's voice carried up to him.

They were through.

Pat fed the search cam through the next layer of concrete. When it emerged into the next space he could see a figure curled on a bed. They'd done it!

She was hugging her knees to her chest and she looked cold and vulnerable, but they'd found her and she was alive.

She was looking up into the camera and Pat barely recognised her. In the bar he'd been completely blind-sided by her beauty. She'd had the kind of face that stopped men in the street, a perfect oval framed by thick blonde hair, she'd had flawless skin and enormous blue eyes, but now her hair was matted and filthy, her face smeared with mud, and he could see a darker stain on the left side of her forehead. A bruise. Or maybe blood. Her eyes were pale and huge in her face and she looked terrified. He wanted desperately to get in there to comfort her. She looked as though she needed it.

Everything was covered with mud. Including Charli. The space was a mess, the bed was buckled and Pat could see a crushed wardrobe and what was possibly the remains of a bedside table. A lamp lay on the floor in the mud.

Charli was looking around and Pat wondered if the light was a mistake. Was it giving her more of an idea about the predicament she was in? Would seeing her surroundings add to the trauma?

'Hey, there.' Pat spoke through the microphone. 'Can you hear me clearly?'

Charli turned her head back towards the camera. She couldn't see him but it was obviously an instinctive move to turn towards the sound.

'Yes.' She nodded. 'Can you get me out now?'

'Can't wait for that hot chocolate, hey?'

'I'm cold.'

She gave him a half-smile and his spirits lifted. She was tough. He knew she'd pull through but he vowed to be there to help her. 'We'll get you out as soon as we can.'

Retrieving her was going to be a slow process but Pat was feeling truly positive for the first time since the disaster.

'Is Amy there? Can I talk to her?'

'Yes, of course.' He'd seen Amy arrive on the scene. Someone had tracked her down. 'Amy can't come onto the site but I'll take my headset to her. Give me a moment.'

He found Amy and passed the headset to her. It was probably a good idea to let her talk to her sister. While he didn't want to think about the worst-case scenario there was no denying this whole exercise was risky and Pat knew it could go horribly wrong. He wasn't going to deny the siblings the opportunity to talk. Who knew what could happen next?

Amy had tears streaming down her face as she put the headset on. 'I'm sorry, Charli. I should have come home with you.'

He could only hear one side of the conversation but it was enough to give him the gist of it.

'But at least we would have been together.

'Are you hurt?

'You're sure?

'I know. Okay. I'll be waiting for you. I love you.'

Amy removed the headset and passed it back to Pat. 'Promise me you'll get her out,' she pleaded. 'She's the only family I've got.'

'I promise,' he said as he signalled to one of his team members to swap places with him as he spoke again to Charli. 'The engineers are going to continue to enlarge this opening and I'm going to hand over the communication to Dave, who's also a paramedic, while I see what I can do about getting you warmed up.' He knew she would be frozen. Everything looked wet or at least damp and there had been no heating. 'Is that okay?'

'Will you be back?'

'Before you know it.'

Pat switched places with Dave. He wanted to have a discussion with Melissa Cartwright, the ED doctor who had been choppered in to Wombat Gully to co-ordinate any medical care. They needed a plan. A triage and stabilising centre had been set up in the resort medical centre but the first step before they could treat Charli was getting her out of there safely.

'How do you think she's doing?' Melissa asked.

'She seems lucid. No significant injuries. Cold and thirsty.' Pat summarised what he knew so far. 'It's going to be a tricky extraction. There are two slabs of concrete above her and the engineers don't think we can get in underneath without the risk of the whole structure collapsing. We'll have to go through the slabs. It's going to take time.'

'Hypothermia is a risk,' Melissa said. 'We need to warm her up, get fluids into her, and we need to be able to monitor her condition.'

'Okay, we'll get some leads through as soon as possible.' He turned to Connor. 'Can you organise a bearhugger?'

He waited for confirmation before he crawled back out onto the slab. He tapped Dave on the shoulder and slipped the headset back on, restoring communication with Charli.

'Hey, there, Charli, it's Pat. I'm back.'

* * *

Charli closed her eyes at the sound of Pat's voice. Dave had tried to have a conversation with her but she didn't have the energy to start over. She only had enough energy for Pat and she could feel herself relax now that he was back. She'd been edgy when he'd left. Even though another paramedic had taken his place she'd felt as though she'd lost the lifeline that tethered her to the world above. The world outside her tomb. She took a deep breath and opened her eyes.

'You still doing okay?' he asked.

His voice was deep and mellow and soothing. He sounded in control and that calmed her nerves. His voice made her feel safe.

She pictured his face, his smile that had made his eyes crinkle at the corners, the little scar under his left eye, and his messy, dark hair. She remembered the warmth of his hands on her elbows and wished he was with her now. She longed for some warmth and she longed for the touch of another person. More specifically, she found herself longing for him.

'I'm good,' she replied, which was a ridiculous thing to say given she was buried under tonnes of rubble. But at least she was alive. 'But I'll be better when you get me out of here.' She knew he'd get her out. She trusted him.

'That's the way.' She could hear the smile in his voice and knowing she'd made him smile lifted her spirits. 'All right, the engineers have made a hole large enough through both slabs that I can start passing some things down to you.'

The hole was above her chest. She could see light coming in but she couldn't see out. She wriggled around on the bed so her face was underneath the hole. She could see blue sky. She winced and closed her eyes. The sky was far too bright after hours of darkness but she couldn't resist slowly opening them once more because she had wondered if she'd ever see the sky again.

The sunlight dimmed as Pat's face appeared in the hole, illuminated from below by the small light on the search cam.

'Hello again.'

She smiled at the sight of him, pleased that his face was the first she would see. His dark hair was sticking out in all directions, wild and unruly. His jaw was covered in dark stubble and he was smiling at her, his teeth white against the darkness of his beard. His eyes crinkled at the corners and she was struck by the life in them and by their colour.

'Your eyes are green!'

'You do remember me, don't you?' he teased her, and she felt herself smiling properly in return. She hadn't thought she'd ever feel like smiling again.

'Yes, of course, but in the bar I thought your eyes were brown.'

His face disappeared all too suddenly. She wanted to call out and ask him to come back. She wanted to keep looking at him. She wanted one last chance to burn his face into her memory just in case things went wrong. But she was too slow. His face was gone from sight and her heart plunged in her chest. It was a stupid thing to be disappointed about as she knew, given her situation, that there were more important things for her to think about, but she really liked his face.

His hand was reaching down through the hole. The hole was small and it was a tight fit. His forearm filled the space. He could almost touch her. He was still within reach. All she had to do was lift her hand and she would have that connection. She reached up and held onto his fingers. He wasn't wearing gloves and his hand was warm. Hers was freezing by comparison. He must have just removed his glove and she was grateful. She craved warmth. Her body craved the touch of another person. She remembered how she'd felt when he'd held her before. Twice he'd caught her, supported her and made her safe. She wished he was there with her now. Tears sprang to her eyes and she wiped them from her face with her other hand, pleased he couldn't see her reaction through the tiny gap that his arm had filled.

'Hey, what's wrong?'

His voice came through the microphone. She'd forgotten about the tiny camera that had been fed into her space. She could see the thin pole running along the length of his arm. Just because she couldn't see him didn't mean he couldn't see her.

'I wasn't sure I'd ever see another person again,' she answered honestly.

She held onto his hand for several seconds before letting go. She didn't want to let go, she felt safe with her hand in his, but she wanted to see his face again. She needed to see his smile.

He removed his arm and suddenly there he was, grinning down at her again.

'Sorry, it was my face you got.'

'I'm glad it's you. You have a very nice face.'

She wondered what had got into her. She never volunteered her feelings. She'd learnt to bottle them up since her mother had died. Showing your feelings gave other people a chance to hurt you, but for the first time in hours her fears were receding and it was all to do with this man.

'Are you positive you're not injured? Concussion, perhaps?' He was still grinning at her.

'I might have a slight concussion,' she admitted, and then she smiled. 'And my eyes might need a bit more time to get accustomed to the light.' A little levity made her feel much better. Much more positive.

'That would explain it. I'll make a note to get your eyes tested when we get you out of there.'

'You will get me out, won't you?'

'We will. This is what we've been hoping for. *You're* what we've been hoping for.'

'What do you mean?' She saw a little crease appear between his dark eyebrows. There was a worried look in his green eyes and Charli felt a flutter of panic. 'What is it? What's wrong?'

'We've been searching for two days. You're the first person we've found.'

'The first person? Are other people missing?' For some reason she'd imagined that whatever had gone wrong had only affected her apartment. She hadn't considered other people for one minute. She hadn't had room in her head for those thoughts but now she really needed to know what was going on. 'What happened?'

'There was a landslide. It started on the mountain above you.' He paused and she sensed he was figuring out how much to tell her. How bad could it be? 'Two lodges collapsed and sixteen people were missing.'

'Sixteen! How many have you found?'

'Ten. Including you.'

She knew she should be grateful that she'd been found but she was struggling with the horror of the situation. It was hard to wrap her head around. A landslide. Whole buildings collapsed. Six people still missing. She was too scared to ask how many others had survived.

'All right, time to get to work.' Pat's voice jolted her back to the present. 'We have a team of people up here—Dave you've met, Dr Melissa Cartwright, an ED specialist, engineers, mining experts and lots of pairs of hands all working to get you out, but first we need to check your condition. I'm going to start sending a few things your way. We're going to pump some warm air in and also set up a tube with some warm fluids to rehydrate you, but I'll also send down an oxygen mask and some leads to monitor your condition. Obviously, I can't get down to you yet but I'll talk you through it all.'

'I know what to do.'

'You do?'

'I'm a doctor.'

'You're a doctor?'

'Yes. I've just finished my Foundation Training. I'm about to start GP training.' She couldn't remember if she'd told him that. She couldn't have.

'That'll make things easier,' he said as he passed a thermometer down through the hole. 'Are you able to take an axillary temp for me?'

'Yes.' She was willing to do just about anything for him at this point in time.

She reached up for the thermometer, preparing herself for his touch this time, telling herself not to hold onto him, but her loneliness, fear and despair were still so close to the surface of her emotions that the touch of his hand brought tears to her eyes once again. The warmth of his fingers set her nerves alight, sending sparks shooting up her arm. She would have thought it was just because of the contrast in temperature between his skin and hers except for the fact that his touch set her heart racing. She fought to control her breathing, to control her heart rate, knowing she needed to stay calm, but it was difficult when all she wanted to do was cling to Pat and never let go.

Deciding she'd have to figure out how to cope with his touch, she put the thermometer under her armpit and clamped it in place. She didn't want to send them all into a panic when her pulse was taken.

She passed the thermometer back up through the hole, disappointed when Pat held it by the end, meaning she missed his touch. She could hear them discussing the reading. She knew her temperature was low as she'd read the numbers before passing it back. It was thirty-three point five degrees, and even though an axillary reading could be a degree out it was still well below a normal temperature of thirty-six point eight. But she was reassured by the fact that, despite the quilt, she was still shivering. That was potentially a good sign. She was possibly only mildly hypothermic.

Pat's hand appeared through the hole once more as he passed down some warmed blankets, some chemical heat packs, an oxygen mask and a pulse oximeter.

As she looked at the assortment it hit home that, as Pat had told her, it would take a while to get her out of there. She wrapped the blankets around her and then tucked the heat packs underneath. Fortunately Pat had already broken them to start the chemical reaction as she doubted she'd have the strength or dexterity in her cold, stiff fingers to do it herself. She bent her knees to hold one in her groin and another against her stomach. She'd love a pair of socks for her frozen feet but she knew the dangers of warming her extremities up too quickly. Forcing cold blood away from her hands and feet and back to her heart was highly risky and could be fatal.

Next through the hole was a long plastic feeding tube. Pat's voice came through the microphone. 'This is warm fluid, sip it slowly.'

She clipped the pulse oximeter onto her forefinger and sipped on the electrolyte and nutrient mixture. She thought it was possibly the best thing she'd tasted, ever. She took a couple of sips and then put the oxygen mask on.

'Keep the tube close,' Pat told her. 'Take a couple of mouthfuls at regular intervals, I'll tell you when. And one more thing, I'm going to pass a pipe down through the hole. It's called a bear-hugger and it looks like a vacuum-cleaner hose, but it's basically a heater. We'll blow warm air into your space and slowly increase the temperature. You're not going to be able to see out through this hole any more and the engineers are going to start drilling to my right, above your feet. Okay?'

Charli nodded. She closed her eyes and held the kindness in his eyes and the warmth of his smile in her heart.

She flinched as the engineers began drilling again. The noise startled her and the vibrations rattled and shook her surroundings, just like during the landslide. It was frightening. She tried to slow her breathing, knowing her respirations and heart rate were being monitored for signs of stress, but she knew she was failing. She could hear herself sucking in lungfuls of oxygen through the mask. But at least it went some way towards blocking out the smell of diesel fuel, sewage and mud.

Finally the noise ground to a halt and she felt herself

relax. She opened her eyes. Had they made it through already? That hadn't been too bad.

But she saw no difference in her surroundings. A hole had not miraculously opened up at her feet. She was still entombed.

'How're you doing, Charli?'

'It sounds as though the ceiling is going to collapse.' She found it difficult to talk, her accelerated heartbeat making her breathing shallow.

'I promise we know what we're doing. Would you like to listen to some music? That might block out some of the noise. Who do you like to listen to?'

'Adele.'

'Who?'

'Adele. She's an English singer. You haven't heard of her?' Charli could feel her breathing and heart-rate return to normal as Pat's voice calmed her down. If only he could be in her tiny space with her, she knew she'd feel better. She thought she could cope with anything if he was beside her. 'I thought she was big all round the world.'

'She probably is. I spend most of my time listening to *The Wiggles*.'

Charli had vaguely heard of *The Wiggles*. She thought they were a children's music group. 'You have kids?'

'A daughter. She's three.'

Of course he had a family. Disappointment flooded through her. She hadn't realised she'd been building a whole fantasy world for him to exist in, and it hadn't included a wife and family. She closed her eyes and sighed. He hadn't been wearing a wedding ring but that didn't mean he didn't have a partner. But if that were the case, why had he offered to buy her a drink and take her to brunch? She knew the answer to that one. Because all men were bastards. She certainly knew how to pick them. Or did they pick her? Was there something about her that attracted unfaithful men?

'Charli? Are you still with me?'

CHAPTER FIVE

'CHARLI? CAN YOU still hear me?'

Pat watched her through the monitor, his heart racing as panic gripped him. Her eyes were closed, dark eyelashes resting against pale cheeks. Was she conscious? Hypothermic? Was she all right? He couldn't see if her chest was moving and his concern escalated as the silence stretched on.

'Charli?'

'Are you married?'

He breathed out a sigh of relief as Charli opened her eyes and spoke to him. He hadn't realised he'd been holding his breath, anxiously waiting to hear her voice.

'What?' It took him a second or two to process her question. 'No, I'm not married.'

Margie had been dead for two years. He'd come to terms with the fact that she was gone but even though he still thought of her as his wife he didn't think of himself as married. He was very much alone.

'But you have a daughter?'

'Yes.' Alone except for Ella.

'Where is she?'

'In Melbourne.'

'Do you live in Melbourne?'

'Yes.'

'You were supposed to have left Wombat Gully by now, weren't you? You told me you were going to Melbourne on the night we met.'

'Yes. The landslide changed my plans somewhat.'

'It's lucky for me that you're here, though. I don't suppose anyone expected a real drill. Have you trained for this?'

'Are you asking to check my references? I promise I know what I'm doing. I've been a paramedic for ten years and part of the Special Operations team for five.'

'Is your Special Operations involved in rescues like our Hazardous Area Response Teams? You said you jump out of helicopters and abseil down mountains?'

'We don't do that every day.' He smiled. 'But, yes, it's the same as your HART teams.'

'How did you get into that?'

'These mountains are my back yard. I grew up less than an hour from here and spent all my spare time skiing, mountain biking, rock climbing and generally getting into trouble that I had to get myself out of. I joined the ambulance service and it was a natural progression to Special Ops for me. Did you get to work with the HART teams while you were studying medicine?'

'No,' she said. 'I'm not sure that I'm an emergency medicine type of girl. I like to play it safe. Amy is the adventurous sister.'

'Is she a professional ski instructor?' He wanted to keep her talking. Wanted to make sure she stayed conscious and alert, and if she wasn't going to listen to music then talking to him might help keep her mind off the extraction process.

'Amy trained as a primary teacher but she hasn't spent

a lot of time teaching. She spends most of her time travelling, working around the world. She always does kids' ski school lessons so I guess she is using her teaching degree. She's done a bit of teaching in developing countries but I think she likes the freedom of the ski fields. This is her third winter here.'

'But your first visit? We're not giving you a very good impression, are we?'

'I'll admit it's been a bit more dramatic than I like my holidays to be.'

They were an hour into the process when Pat's stomach started to grumble. It was time for another break in the drilling and he hoped no one else heard the rumbling. He knew he was overdue for a break but he wasn't going to leave Charli. She wasn't having anything more than warmed fluids and he felt it would be unfair of him to be too comfortable. Why should he get to have a full stomach, toilet breaks and showers? He wanted to feel what Charli was feeling and keeping a level of discomfort allowed him to do that.

He wanted to stay close by, wanted to be able to talk to her. It was about more than just keeping her calm. He wanted to be the one who was there for her, wanted to be the one to talk to her in the five-minute break between drilling. Having built up rapport and trust, he didn't want anyone else taking over. He suspected their conversation was as important to him as it was to her. Despite the circumstances, their conversation flowed easily. He couldn't remember feeling so comfortable with someone who was a virtual stranger. The dates he'd been on in the past two years had mostly been dreadful. Awkward and difficult. But there was no awkwardness with Charli.

The situation lent itself to honesty. If she asked him a question he felt obliged to give her an honest answer. Perhaps it helped her that she couldn't see him. Maybe it was a bit like being in a confessional box or being given the last rites. He wasn't religious, not at all, but he thought there was probably something to be said for being able to get things off your chest, admitting to your sins and so on. Not that he was prepared to entertain the idea that Charli might not survive this. He wasn't going to be the last person she spoke to or the last person she saw, but he could be the person she talked to at this moment in her life. He could be the one who helped her.

'Charli, did you want me to see if there's any mobile phone service? Maybe put a call in to your parents?' Charli had spoken to Amy but he was sure she'd like a chance to speak to her parents. They'd managed to keep her identity from the media. Amy wasn't speaking to the journalists but Pat knew the disastrous event was getting global coverage.

'No, there's no one I need to speak to.'

'We haven't released your name yet but, at some point your name will hit the headlines. It might be wise to give your parents a heads-up. Perhaps Amy could call them and break the news and then you could speak to them? You don't want to speak to your mother?'

'My mother is dead.'

Too late he remembered that Amy had told him Charli was her only family. *Way to go, Pat, great choice of topic.* Maybe he should let Charli ask the questions, that way he wouldn't be hearing answers he wasn't expecting and didn't know how to react to.

'I'm sorry to hear that,' he said.

Through the search cam he could see Charli shrug

her shoulders. 'It was a long time ago,' she said. 'It's been me and Amy, just the two of us, for almost as long as I can remember.'

'Is your father alive?'

'Yes. But I don't need to talk to him. I don't think he even knows where we are. He won't miss either of us.'

Pat frowned. That seemed like an odd thing to say. Why wouldn't he know, or care, where his daughters were? If Ella was in trouble halfway around the world, he knew he'd want to know. But he would save his questions for another time as he sensed he wasn't going to lighten the mood any by delving further.

'There's no one else?'

'No.'

Surely she had someone? Pat didn't understand. Everyone had somebody, didn't they? He had his parents and a younger brother, he'd had Margie and now he had Ella. He'd never had no one.

'Just Amy.'

Her voice was quiet but he realised as she spoke that of course she had someone. Amy was her someone. That was okay. He'd talk to her about Amy, that would keep her mind occupied while they worked to get her out.

'So, you're here on holiday but Amy is working here?' He had learned that Snowgum Chalet was used as accommodation for Wombat Gully resort staff.

'Yes. I came on a bit of a whim. She's been telling me for years how fabulous Australia is—I'm not sure that I believe her given the situation I'm in, but anyway I needed to see her, so here I am.'

'Why did you need to see her?'

'I had a fight with my boyfriend.'

'It's a long way to come after a fight.'

'It was a big one.' He heard the smile in her voice and saw the corners of her mouth lift. That was better, she had a much more positive tone.

'Big enough that you don't want to call him? Let him know what's happened?'

'He's now my ex. I don't want to call him,' she said with a shake of her head. 'He doesn't deserve to know what has happened. I don't want to talk to him, see him, have anything to do with him. That's one thing I'm sure of after all this time in here. I've had plenty of time to think about what really matters to me. And he isn't on my list.'

'That sounds like a doozy of a fight.'

'It was.'

'Do you want to talk about it?'

'I haven't told anyone about this except for Amy.' He thought that was the end of it but then she continued. 'I was in Spain with a girlfriend. We were celebrating the end of our Foundation training when Jane's father had a stroke. Jane wanted to fly back to the UK so I went with her. When I walked into my flat I found my boyfriend in bed with another girl. I don't know who was more surprised. Hugo, her or me.'

Pat wasn't sure if she was laughing or crying.

'I couldn't stay there and I was too shocked to think about kicking him out so I fled. I was still on holiday before I start the next stage of my training, so I came here. For almost as long as I can remember Amy has been the one I've run to when things haven't worked out.'

'Do you want to work things out with him?'

'Are you kidding?' Her voice regained some strength and volume. 'I'd never be able to trust him again. And he was either unhappy in the relationship or less invested in it than I was or just a complete arse.'

Pat was surprised how pleased he was to hear that Charli was definitely single. He was also pleased to hear some fire in her voice and to see a spark return to her eyes. There was still some fight left in her and he knew she was going to need it.

The next time the drilling stopped Charli tried to steer the conversation towards Pat. She was tired of talking about her life, nothing in it was going according to plan and she'd rather forget about it for a while. She didn't have a high opinion of men at this point in time but Pat seemed like he might be one of the good guys. The world could do with more men like him. *She* could do with a man like him.

'Tell me something more about you,' she said to him the next chance she got. 'How did you get that scar under your eye?'

'That's what you want to know?'

'Mmm-hmm, I've been wondering about it since I first saw you.'

'Is that a fact? And here I was, thinking that in your jet-lagged state, you'd barely remembered me.'

She still couldn't see him but she could hear the smile in his voice. She wished she could see it again but just thinking about his smile was enough to lift her mood. 'I remembered you. So, how did you get the scar? Were you rescuing someone else or doing something dangerous?'

'None of the above. Doing something stupid, more like it. My brother and I were practising our whip-cracking skills. I was holding a stick in my mouth and he was trying to crack it out. Needless to say, he missed the stick and got me under the eye. Our mother confiscated the whip and we were grounded for weeks.'

He was laughing and she'd bet he and his brother had given their mother plenty to worry about. 'Are you and your brother close?' It sounded as if they were.

'Yeah, we are.'

Lost in her thoughts, it took her a moment to realise that everything had gone silent above her. Immediately she thought the worst. 'Pat? Are you still there? Is something wrong?'

'No, everything's great.' His voice came down to her, reassuring and calm. 'The engineers are just about to remove the final piece of concrete. It's time to get you out.'

'Really?'

She started to sit up, forgetting once again that he could see her.

'Don't move! We need to take this slowly.'

Charli put her head down and watched as a backpack was lowered to the floor through the hole that the engineers had made at the foot of her bed. The bag was followed by a pair of boots and then legs in bright red trousers appeared followed by a body in a jacket and, finally, Patrick's head and face emerged.

He had a hard hat on with a bright light shining out from the front straight into her eyes.

She winced and he angled the light up. 'Sorry,' he said as he squatted on the floor and looked around.

'Don't apologise. I don't think I've ever been as glad to see another person in my life.'

He grinned.

She couldn't believe that he was there, that she wasn't alone any more.

She couldn't take her eyes off him. Her knight in rescue gear. He was tall and muscular and broad shouldered and took up a lot of the minimal space but she didn't mind. She was more than happy to share her space. Finally she could let herself believe she was going to get out of there.

Tears threatened as she realised she was actually going to make it out alive.

'Hey, it's all right, you're okay. Everything's going to be okay.' He was beside her now, his voice confident and reassuring as he leant over her and gathered her into his arms. She didn't think she'd ever felt anything as wonderful as his embrace. After more than forty hours trapped and alone, to have someone close enough to touch, close enough to feel the warmth of his breath on her cheek, was overwhelming. 'We'll do this together, okay?'

She nodded. 'Okay.'

'We're going to take it slow.'

'I just want to get out of here.'

'I know you do and don't worry, that's the next thing on my list, but we don't want to move you too quickly. Trust me.'

Charli knew there had been cases of hypothermic patients suffering cardiac arrest caused by toxins in the bloodstream. He was right to go slowly, she didn't want to have survived this long only to encounter another trauma. She bit back her impatience and chose to follow his instructions. He'd got her safely to this point. She chose to trust him.

He was still holding her hand and his dark green eyes didn't leave her face as he waited for her to agree.

She nodded.

He let go of her and reached for the backpack, dragging it towards him. The backpack contained a medical kit and he searched through it, pulling out a small torch.

'Close your eyes,' he told her.

She did as he instructed and waited for him to lift her eyelids as he shone the torch in her eyes. The light was bright and she was certain her pupils contracted in response but his expression gave nothing away. He was thorough and gentle as he checked her injuries. He unwrapped her makeshift bandages from her leg and hand and rinsed the wound on her leg with saline before quickly rewrapping her calf with clean dressings. His hands were warm and gentle. She closed her eyes and held her breath as he held her calf.

'Am I hurting you?' he asked.

She opened her eyes and shook her head. She had no pain but his touch was doing funny things to her insides. Making her quiver.

He wrapped another blanket around her shoulders.

She should tell him she wasn't shaking from cold but she couldn't speak.

She lay still and silent as he cleaned and checked and re-dressed the wound on the palm of her hand. She was aware of how filthy she was. Her hair was matted and she was covered in mud and blood and who knew what else after being entombed for hours. She wished she was cleaner, wished she smelt better, wished she could have a warm bath, but all of that would have to wait.

She flinched when she felt a sting in her elbow.

'Sorry,' he said as he inserted a bung. 'I want to get that in now so we can attach a drip and get you straight into the ambulance. There are a lot of news crews up above and we really don't want to treat you in full view of them.'

He brushed her hair from her forehead. Their faces were close. Close enough that she could see the individual hairs in the stubble of his beard. Close enough that she could feel his breath on her cheek. Close enough that she could press her lips to his if she chose.

She closed her eyes again as she imagined his lips brushing over hers. Imagined him leaning in to kiss her, even though she knew he was only inspecting the cut on her forehead.

She flinched as he rinsed the wound with saline and she reminded herself that he was taking care of her because that was his job. Kissing her would be the last thing on his mind. 'We'll do it properly up above but that will do for now,' he told her, before calling out to the crew above them.

Charli watched as a spinal board and harness were lowered through the hole. Pat undid the straps and laid the board beside her. 'I'm going to harness you to the spinal board to take you out.'

His arms encircled her as he slid the harness straps under her chest. They were pressed almost cheek to cheek in the confined space and she wanted desperately to burrow into his embrace.

'I'm going to roll you onto the board now.'

He rolled her away from him and she felt the hard edge of the spinal board against her back. She could feel the warmth of his hands through the thin latex of the surgical gloves that covered his fingers as he rolled her back onto the board. In contrast to his fingers the board was cold and uncomfortable under her spine.

'Slowly straighten your legs.'

Her legs were stiff and her knees felt locked.

'Take your time.' He waited until she was able to lie

flat. He reached up and clipped two carabiners to her harness and the spinal board before covering her legs with a blanket. 'Okay, here we go.'

He called out to the team of people on the surface, 'Ready!'

And Charli felt herself being lifted out.

Pat was left below her and she almost wished she was still there with him. She wasn't ready to leave him.

Her stretcher was put on the ground and she was surrounded by the rescue crew. She was in the centre of a circle, shielded from view as people double-checked her vital signs.

A woman leaned over her, introducing herself as the ED doctor, Melissa, but Charli wasn't registering much more than that. She was looking for Pat.

She heard someone comment on her heart rate and her respirations. She was aware that her breathing was fast and that her heart rate had accelerated. She knew it was important to stay calm but she needed to see Pat. She needed him to tether her, to slow her panic, to make her feel safe, even now that she was out.

And then she saw him. He'd followed her straight out of the hole. She could see his unruly dark hair as his head emerged from the rubble, half-hidden behind the rest of the people, but it wasn't until he was kneeling beside her, until she felt the weight of his hand on her arm, that she could breathe normally again.

'Look at me, Charli, breathe with me,' he said. 'You're okay…everything is going to be okay.'

Again, he held her gaze, watching and waiting for her to calm down. Again, she had the sense that she could trust him. That he wouldn't leave her.

'Look at the sky,' he said as she got her breathing under control.

She looked past him now, over his shoulder.

The sun was beginning to set and the sky was streaked with pink and orange. It looked like someone had pulled swathes of fairy floss across the sky. The mountain across the valley was covered in snow and the sunset was turning it pink. There was no wind, the air was still.

'It's beautiful,' she whispered, scarcely able to believe she was actually out and able to see the sky.

She was aware of cheers now and of a flurry of flashes and bright lights. Pat had warned her that the media had been covering the situation twenty-four seven, reporting on the bad news and hoping for some good.

'They've been waiting a long time for this moment. You'll be the headline on the evening news.'

She'd known they would film her extraction but she didn't care. She brought her eyes back to Pat. He was all she could see. All she *wanted* to see. In the evening light she could see that his dark green eyes had a lighter hazel ring around the edge. His smile was white and his jaw was darkened by that five-o'clock shadow. She couldn't remember if he'd started the day with stubble. Was it designer or was it just because of his dark colouring?

'On the count of three,' she heard someone say. 'One, two, three.'

She felt her stretcher being lifted. Pat took one side, next to her head. She didn't look to see who the other stretcher bearers were. Charli kept her eyes on Pat as she was carried across the rubble. She saw the open doors of an ambulance and felt herself being lowered onto the ambulance stretcher.

She saw Pat let go of her and her heart missed a beat as panic rose in her chest.

'Are you coming with me?' she asked.

'Don't you want Amy to go with you?'

'Can't you both come?'

He shook his head and her heart plummeted.

'Do you have to go back out there?' she asked. He'd spent hours with her, talking to her, comforting her, helping her through the process. She wondered how he coped with the pressure and couldn't imagine how he would be able to go back and do it all over again.

'No. My shift is finished, I'm due a break,' he said, 'but there's not enough room in the ambulance for Amy and me. I'll meet you at the medical centre.'

CHAPTER SIX

'Okay,' Charli replied just as Amy was ushered through the crowd of medics and rescue workers. Her face was tearstained but she was smiling. She leant over and hugged Charli, somehow managing not to dislodge the myriad tubes and monitor leads that the paramedics had already attached to her.

'Charli, thank God,' she sobbed. 'I thought I'd lost you.'

Amy's voice was thick with emotion and Charli fought back tears of her own as she hugged her sister. She'd had exactly the same thoughts while she'd been buried alive before Pat had put her mind at ease. 'Are you going to be okay?' Amy asked as she released her.

'I'll be fine,' she replied as she was loaded into the ambulance. Amy climbed into the back too and knelt beside her.

Charli flinched as the doors were slammed shut and Patrick disappeared from her view. She wasn't ready to say goodbye. He'd got her through her ordeal, he'd been with her every step, and she needed him.

She lifted one hand in a silent farewell. 'What do you need?' Amy asked her, misinterpreting her gesture.

'Nothing.' Amy would never understand if Charli

asked for Pat to accompany her in the ambulance instead. She couldn't do that to her sister. She was still the most important person in her life. Amy was still her someone.

Charli closed her eyes as it was easier to pretend to be tired than to talk. Not that she was pretending. She was exhausted, emotionally and physically drained, and she missed Pat's calming presence already. When she'd been trapped she'd wanted her sister. Now Amy was beside her and she wanted Pat, but she knew she couldn't put that longing into words without hurting Amy. So she kept her eyes closed and her mouth shut. It was fortunate that no one seemed to expect much more from her.

Amy held her hand while the ambulance drove slowly through the resort but Charli only opened her eyes when the ambulance stopped moving. The journey lasted only a few minutes before her stretcher was unloaded and she was wheeled into the resort medical centre. Screens had been erected to block the inquisitive journalists and news cameras but they worked both ways, Charli realised, as they prevented her from seeing if Patrick had followed her, as he'd promised. She was pushed into a treatment room but not moved from the stretcher.

The doctor was already there. Charli thought her name was Melissa, and she heard her issue instructions to the other staff who darted in and out of the room. She gave up trying to keep track of all the comings and goings—the movements combined with the bright fluorescent lights overhead were starting to give her a headache. She turned her head and looked at Amy, who still hadn't let go of her hand, as the medical staff poked and prodded her and discussed her condition—which they announced was surprisingly good—and her injuries—

relatively minor considering everything that had happened. She had three frostbitten toes, a cut to her head and two further cuts, one on her hand and another on her calf, that would need stitching.

'I'm going to attach a drip and start a course of antibiotics,' Melissa told Charli. 'And then I'll clean and suture your wounds.'

Charli could feel her heart rate and respiration rate accelerating and she watched the numbers rise on the monitor, which was completely counterproductive and just made the numbers rise more rapidly.

Melissa glanced at the monitor. 'Amy, would you mind waiting outside for a minute?'

The treatment process wasn't bothering Charli but she didn't mention that it wasn't the idea of stitches that was making her nervous. She was wondering where Pat was. He'd said he'd meet her there and she wondered if he was waiting outside. Being without him was making her anxious.

A sharp prick in her leg drew her attention back to the room and to what was going on around her. She looked down at her leg. Melissa had injected a local anaesthetic into her calf and was about to start cleaning and stitching her wound. She moved onto Charli's hand next and once her hand and leg were numb she became aware of pain in her feet. She wriggled in the bed, trying to find a comfortable position, but the pain didn't abate.

Melissa looked up at her. 'What's the matter, Charli? I need you to stay still.'

'My feet.' Charli gritted her teeth as she tried to ignore the pain long enough to speak. She didn't think she'd ever been in as much pain as this before. 'They feel as if they are on fire.'

'That's a good sign,' Melissa said as she looked down towards Charli's toes. 'It means the circulation is working. Blood is reaching your feet and toes as you warm up. Colour is returning to your toes. We should be able to save them. I can give you something for the pain.'

Charli nodded and concentrated on attempting to breathe through the pain, while Melissa ordered intravenous pain relief.

'Has that pain relief worked?' the doctor asked as she finished suturing the wound in Charli's palm.

Charli's feet felt like two enormous soccer balls at the ends of her legs but the burning sensation had decreased slightly. Her feet still felt hot but it was better. Almost bearable. She nodded.

'Do you need anything else,' Melissa asked, 'before we get ready to transfer you?'

She was exhausted, overwrought, hungry and filthy. She wanted a hot bath and some clean clothes, something to eat and for people to stop poking her and sticking needles into her. But what she got was a drip in her arm, some antiseptic wipes and a hospital gown.

She wanted to sleep.

She wanted to wake up somewhere familiar and safe.

She wanted Patrick.

Charli wanted to see his face again in case it really was the last time.

But her brain had shut down, whether from exhaustion or stress or trauma she wasn't sure, but whatever the reason she found she could no longer string a coherent sentence together. She didn't know how to ask for what she wanted. How to ask for Patrick.

But he was there anyway. He appeared beside her as if he knew what she needed almost before she did. His red uniform and dark hair stood out in stark contrast to the white surroundings. Seeing him immediately calmed her racing heart.

He came to stand on her left side and she instinctively reached out for him, unsure just when she had become so dependent on him but certain that he would take her hand. He would offer comfort.

'Hey.' He smiled and she relaxed. 'I hear you're in pretty good shape.'

He didn't tell her she looked better or brighter but he did take her hand. She could only imagine what she looked like. Bloodied, bruised and filthy. She would look like someone who had been buried alive for forty hours. She knew her blonde hair was matted and dirty. She could feel that her left eye, just under the cut on her forehead, was partially closed from swelling and she imagined it was turning purple. She suspected she looked like the victim of a mugging or a car accident.

'Melissa tells me you're stable enough to be transferred to Melbourne.'

'Melbourne?' She knew that but her brain was taking a long time to catch up to what she was hearing and even longer to process information. She was sure she wasn't concussed. She just needed to eat and sleep, then everything would be back to normal.

'The helicopter is on its way to take you to the Princess Elizabeth Hospital.'

'By myself?' She looked at Pat, waiting for his answer, knowing it wasn't going to be the one she wanted to hear.

Pat could see a cascade of emotions in her blue eyes. Pleading, longing, desperation, fear, worry and loneliness. He knew she was asking him to accompany her.

She was waiting for his answer but he couldn't do it. He was already breaking protocol by being at the medical centre. His shift should have ended the minute Charli had been extracted from the rubble. He'd worked overtime and he was supposed to be resting. He could argue that he was off duty, though he couldn't pretend he was resting. But he wasn't going to abandon Charli now. He'd stay with her until she was on the helicopter. Stay with her for as long as possible. He wasn't ready to say goodbye.

He saw Melissa glance at his hand, where Charli's fingers had entwined with his. Could Melissa tell that Pat was holding on just as firmly? Could she tell he didn't want to let her go?

'I'll give you a moment,' Melissa said as she turned and left the room. Leaving them truly alone for the first time.

He knew Charli had formed a bond with him while she'd been trapped. He knew. He felt it too. But if he was asked to explain it, he wouldn't be able to. It had to be fate that had put him in her path, or her in his. He didn't really know. All he knew was that she was important to him.

But he couldn't leave the mountain. He wasn't dismissed from duty. He would have to take his break and then get back to work. He couldn't go to Melbourne. He still had a job to do here. He didn't want her to go without him, he didn't want to say goodbye, but he didn't have a choice.

'I can't leave the mountain,' he told her. 'We still have work to do. Amy will go with you.'

She nodded. Her eyes were teary but the tears did not spill over. The moisture turned them a more startling shade of blue. He shouldn't be noticing things like that but he couldn't help it.

'Will I see you again?' she asked.

He nodded. 'I'll come and see you as soon as I can,' he said, and he knew it was a promise he would do everything he could to keep.

Charli had spent two days in the Princess Elizabeth Hospital in Melbourne staring at the walls. Two days with mostly only her thoughts for company. And her thoughts were far from pleasant. She was clean and she'd eaten and she was starting to feel more human, although she still longed for a shower. The nurses had tried but the pain in her feet was so intense she hadn't been able to stand or walk. They had tried to transfer her to a shower chair but even lowering her feet was too painful. She'd had to make do with a bed bath.

The nurses had put the television on yesterday but it had seemed to be showing a constant tale of the disaster in Wombat Gully and Charli had switched it off and had kept it turned it off. She couldn't bear to watch or listen to any more of the stories being told. The reporters had no idea what it had been like. They had no idea how it had felt to be buried alive, how scared she'd been, how cold, how lonely.

But she hadn't expected to still feel lonely. She wasn't good at being by herself.

She knew her fear of being alone stemmed from losing her mother at a young age, and usually she felt better if Amy was nearby. Amy was her someone, but even though her sister had made the trip to Melbourne and was keeping her company, it wasn't enough to keep the doldrums at bay. She missed Pat.

She knew he wasn't the answer, he couldn't fix her fears or dispel her depression, but she still hoped he'd come to see her as he'd promised.

He had said she would see him again but she had no idea if or when. Maybe he hadn't meant it.

She lay on her back with the sheets tented over her swollen and painful feet. She had her head turned to the wall, ignoring the door, feeling sorry for herself.

'Hey.'

She turned at the sound of a voice. *His* voice. She recognised it instantly. 'Pat! What are you doing here?'

'I told you I would come as soon as I could.'

She'd hoped to see him but as the days had passed she'd convinced herself that he hadn't meant it. He had a family to go home to. Why would he come to see her? But she wasn't going to pretend she wasn't pleased to see him. She couldn't believe he was here. And she couldn't stop the smile that was spreading across her face. She wondered briefly if she should be so transparent but she figured she might as well let him know she appreciated his visit.

He held two takeaway cups in his hand. 'I brought you the hot chocolate I promised,' he said, as he passed her a cup.

'I can't believe you remembered. Thank you.'

'There's one for Amy too. Isn't she here?'

'She's gone to the airport to pick up our father.'

Her tone was less than enthusiastic and Pat responded to it. 'Aren't you looking forward to seeing him?'

'Not particularly. I can't believe she rang him.'

Pat was frowning. 'Why wouldn't she?'

'I know you're close to your brother and I assume to your parents too, but it's not like that for me and Amy.

We're not at the top of his list of priorities. I'm surprised he's even coming.'

'But you're his daughters. Surely if you need him, he's there for you?'

'We don't need him. We haven't needed him in a long time. We've learnt to manage on our own.'

'What do you mean by that?'

'Our mother died when I was seven. Dad was never the same after that. I know he loved us, we had been the centre of their world, but after Mum died it was almost as though he couldn't bear to have us around. We assumed we reminded him of everything he'd lost. When Dad married Victoria we were sent off to boarding school. I was ten.'

'Ten! That's a bit young, isn't it?'

'It is, but it's not unusual in the UK, especially for wealthier families. Lots of children go to boarding school but it wasn't something that was on the agenda for us, at least it wasn't while our mother was alive. But Victoria isn't the maternal type. She is very career focussed and I don't think she ever wanted to be responsible for raising another woman's children and we were sent away. Our father had other priorities, his work and Victoria. We haven't spent much time with him for years.'

Charli's bedside phone rang, interrupting their discussion. She breathed a sigh of relief. 'Would you mind answering that?' she asked. 'I don't want to speak to anyone.'

She could tell from his side of the conversation who it was and she watched as Pat scribbled a note on a piece of paper.

'That was another news station wanting to interview me, wasn't it?' she said as he hung up the phone.

Pat nodded. 'Have you had lots?'

'Quite a few. I've told the nurses I don't want to speak to reporters. I don't have the energy and I can't imagine why they'd be interested in my story. I'm not even Australian. Surely they can find someone else to interview? I figured one of the other survivors might be happy to do it.'

'Charli...' Pat ran his fingers through his hair, making it spike up. He looked exhausted and she wondered how much sleep he'd had in the past few days. 'Haven't you been watching the news?'

'No. It was all about the landslide. I didn't want to relive it so I've kept the television off. Why?' she asked.

Pat rubbed his jaw. 'There weren't any other survivors,' he told her. 'You're the only one.'

'What?' She frowned, thinking she must have misheard him. 'I can't be. There were fifteen other people missing. You've found them all?'

He nodded.

'They're all dead?'

He nodded again.

'Oh, my God, those poor people.' Charli's eyes filled with tears but before they had a chance to spill over Pat was sitting beside her on the bed and had wrapped his arm around her. She let her tears flow as Pat rubbed her back. The pressure of his hand was firm but gentle. She didn't know how but, once again, he had the knack, either through his words or a smile or a touch of his hand, of being able to soothe her. She wondered when she would run out of tears; she had cried more in the past few weeks than she had in the past twenty years.

Burying her face in his shoulder, she let him comfort her until she thought she could speak without crying. She lifted her head and rubbed the tears from her face. 'I'm sorry.'

'It's okay.' He brushed a tear from her cheek with his thumb. 'You've had a traumatic experience. It's a normal reaction.'

But Charli was mortified. She couldn't believe she'd been whinging about her father when fifteen other people were dead. She was safe. Pat and his colleagues had risked their lives for her and she was being self-absorbed. It wasn't all about her. In fact, it wasn't about her at all. 'How are you and your team?' she asked. 'It must have been awful. Finding no one.'

'We found you,' he replied simply, as if that was enough. Maybe, under the circumstances, it was.

She smiled. 'Yes, you did.'

'What time are you expecting Amy?'

'Soon, I think. Why?'

'I have to go. I don't want to leave you alone if you're feeling fragile but I haven't seen my daughter yet.'

'You came here instead?'

He nodded.

'Why?'

'I wanted to see you and if I went home first I wasn't sure that I'd get away again, but if I don't go soon she'll be in bed and it will be another day that I haven't kissed her goodnight. After days like we've just had I really need to do that. For me, more than for her.'

He stood up and Charli noticed he was still in his uniform. She hadn't seen him in anything else so it hadn't seemed significant until now. She couldn't believe he'd come to see her first, before anything else. It was no wonder he looked exhausted. She needed to let him leave. 'You should go,' she said. 'I'm fine.'

As much as she didn't want him to leave, she knew she couldn't ask him to stay. She was resilient. She would be fine. His daughter needed him more.

'I'll come back tomorrow,' he told her. 'Is there anything you need me to bring you?'

She and Amy had lost everything in the landslide. Granted it hadn't been their entire possessions but all they had left was Amy's phone and wallet. All of Charli's belongings were gone.

'I need to do something about replacing my stuff,' she said. 'I lost my phone and passport. I can ring my insurance company but the policy number and all the details were in my phone. Amy will get me a phone but I need access to email.' Keeping busy, making a list of what she needed to do and ticking things off as she went would keep her busy for now.

'I'll bring in a laptop you can borrow. Would that help?'

She nodded. 'Thank you, that would be great.'

'Okay, I'll see you tomorrow.'

He leant over and kissed her on the forehead and Charli's heart flipped in her chest. She caught her breath and hoped she wasn't turning bright red from embarrassment. He had done it so casually she wondered if he'd even noticed, but she certainly had.

She waited until he left the room and then pressed her fingers to the spot where his lips had rested. She'd gone from feeling sad and lonely to elated and hopeful.

She lay back on the bed with a smile on her face as she counted her blessings. She was alive and so was

Amy. Her injuries were minor. Pat had come to see her and he would come back again. And he'd kissed her.

Maybe something good would come out of the tragedy. Maybe there was something to look forward to in the days ahead.

CHAPTER SEVEN

HE'D KISSED HER without thinking yesterday. Automatically. But it had felt entirely natural and she hadn't seemed to mind. But he hadn't waited around to find out. He was telling himself it had been a spur-of-the-moment thing but, in all honesty, he'd been wanting to kiss her since he'd first met her, since the night she'd literally fallen into his arms at the bar and he'd walked her home.

The feeling had only intensified as he'd talked to her through the hours that she'd been trapped and then when he'd joined her in her tomb-like space. He wanted to taste her, to hold her in his arms for a reason other than providing comfort or safety. A kiss on the forehead wasn't enough. All it had done was serve to whet his desire even more.

Wanting to take something further with a woman was a new experience for him. He'd been on a couple of dates in the past two years but neither of them had gone well. Friends had set him up and he'd gone along with their plans out of politeness, but he hadn't wanted to have a second date with either of the women and he'd discouraged any further suggestions from well-meaning friends and colleagues. But things were different with

Charli. His interest was definitely piqued. He'd only felt this sense of excitement and anticipation once before. When he'd first met his wife.

Was he being disloyal to Margie? To her memory? To the life they'd shared?

He waited for the sense of betrayal to hit him but there was nothing. No guilt, no recriminations. The life he'd had with Margie was over. He had Ella but that relationship, while precious, wasn't enough to sustain him. He needed more. He knew he still wasn't ready for, or looking for, anything serious or permanent but needed adult company, a physical relationship, physical intimacy, and Charli was the first woman he'd met that he could imagine taking that step with. That he wanted to take that step with.

If he hadn't come straight from Wombat Gully to the hospital yesterday he would have stayed longer with her. If he hadn't needed a shower and something to eat, if he hadn't needed to see his daughter. But he'd had to spend time with Ella and it was now late in the afternoon, almost tea time in the hospital, less than two hours until he started a night shift, and he couldn't wait to get back to see Charli again.

He was approaching Charli's room when a tall man with greying hair, an upright posture and a confident walk came through her door and headed for the nurses' station. His bearing was controlled and purposeful but Pat recognised sorrow in his eyes.

It had to be Charli's father. He looked like he was working hard to hold it together.

Pat watched him walk away before he continued on into Charli's room.

He pushed open the door and found her lying in bed

and she looked upset too. Immediately he wanted to comfort her, to take her in his arms and kiss her better, but he wasn't sure that he had that right. Yesterday's actions had been spontaneous but he couldn't presume that she would welcome any further violation of her personal space.

But something about her brought out all his protective instincts. She had an air of fragility about her but she wasn't fragile, she'd shown that throughout her ordeal, but she seemed delicate. Was it her appearance? Her enormous blue eyes, her porcelain skin or the circumstances of her rescue that bound him to her? He didn't know but she'd certainly got under his defences. He thought about her constantly but had no idea what could come of this attraction.

He looked over his shoulder, making sure the doorway was clear. 'That man who just left your room? Was that your father?' he asked. She nodded and he looked around the room. 'Did he come alone?'

'What do you mean?'

The room was empty save for him and Charli. 'Your stepmother. She's not here?'

'No. Apparently her doctor advised her not to fly, although I'm not sure she would have come anyway.'

He frowned. 'Why? What's the matter with her?'

'She's eight months pregnant. Eight months!' Charli's eyebrows arched wildly. 'Can you believe it?' She didn't wait for his response, which was just as well as he really had no opinion to offer. 'She's pregnant and this is the first I've heard of it.'

'Why are you so upset?'

Charli gave a heavy, exasperated sigh. 'I don't understand my father at all. He married someone almost half his age and sent Amy and me to boarding school. He couldn't wait to get rid of us and now he's starting all over again. Victoria didn't want children and now suddenly she's pregnant at the age of thirty-nine. It's crazy.'

'Maybe this is a good thing.'

She looked at him like he'd gone mad. She wasn't upset, he realised. She was angry. 'How can this be a good thing?'

He knew she was struggling emotionally after the landslide. It wasn't an unusual response after a traumatic experience, but maybe this would give her something to look forward to. A baby was the perfect distraction. He knew that from his own experience. 'A new life brings hope. This baby will be a half-sibling. This baby will be family.'

'One who is twenty-six years younger than me!' she countered. 'That's not a sibling. That poor child, having to be a part of our family, having Victoria and my father as parents. It'll probably be shunted off to boarding school too at the earliest opportunity, unwanted and unloved.'

'Are you sure you're not being a bit harsh?'

'No.' She shook her head. 'You don't know my father.'

Pat thought about the man he'd seen leaving Charli's room just minutes ago and the sadness he'd seen in his eyes. 'Don't you think he might love you the best way he knows how? He's flown halfway across the world to see you.'

'And he can't wait to get home again. He's already told me he doesn't want to leave Victoria alone for too long.'

'Things are rarely that black and white.'

'Oh, I think they are. I have spent years trying to figure out why I don't have a relationship with my father but I've got nowhere. I have loved my medical training and I can't wait to start the next stage towards becoming a GP, but one of the reasons I chose medicine was because I thought it might make my father proud of me. I thought it might make him take an interest in me but nothing changed.

'I know it was easy for Amy and me to blame our stepmother's influence but even if it was her decision to send us away, I can't really believe that my father, an intelligent, accomplished man, would have followed her lead if he didn't agree with her. At the end of the day he paid for our education but didn't put much time or effort into maintaining or even establishing a relationship with either of us. Even now, all he can think about is getting back home. He's not thinking about me or Amy, it's all about him and Victoria.'

'But he's here *now*. Doesn't that count for something?'

Charli was shaking her head. 'He's never around when I need him and so I've learnt not to need him, and I *definitely* don't need him now.'

Pat knew he wouldn't win any arguments with Charli about her family. He didn't know her father—he could have been imagining what he'd seen in his expression, in his eyes. He could have been projecting what his feelings as a father would be if Ella was lying in hospital. He knew he would be heartbroken, but he had to take Charli's word for her father's actions and feelings. At least for now.

He nodded and decided to change the subject. He opened the bag he'd brought with him, pulling out various bits of electronic equipment. 'I brought you my laptop. If I set you up a profile and a password, can you access your emails remotely?'

He saw her take a deep breath to regain her composure before saying, 'Yes, thank you.'

'I'm working night shift but I'll leave it with you.'

He flipped the laptop open and fired it up. His screensaver appeared. He was so used to it that he didn't give it a second thought until Charli said, 'Is that your family?'

The photo was one of him with Margie and Ella. He had taken a photo of the three of them in bed on Christmas morning. It had been their first Christmas as a family. Ella had only been eight months old, too young to understand Christmas, but he and Margie had been very excited about the next stage of their life together as a family, celebrating all these milestones with their daughter and anticipating the future. They'd been happy. Really happy.

Of course, they hadn't known then it would be their only Christmas as a family.

'Is that your wife?' He could hear the puzzlement in Charli's voice. 'Aren't you divorced?' The puzzlement was now an accusation.

'No, I'm not divorced.'

'You said you and your daughter lived in Melbourne. You told me you weren't married. You invited me for brunch!'

'I'm not married or divorced,' he explained. 'I'm a widower.'

'Oh, Pat, I'm sorry. I just assumed. You never said…'

Her tone was contrite and perhaps a little guilty.

'What should I have said?'

'I don't know,' she said with a shake of her head.

'When I asked if you were married, why didn't you tell me then?'

'I didn't want to talk about someone who had died. Not in those circumstances.'

'I'm sorry, I didn't know. I didn't mean to bring it up.'

'It's okay. I don't mind talking about her. I need to keep her memory alive for Ella and I'm getting used to being alone.'

'How long ago did she die?'

'Two years.'

'So your daughter would have been very young.'

Pat nodded.

'That must have been an awful time for you. How are you doing now?'

'I'm good. We're good, Ella and I.'

'Do you want to tell me about her?'

'About who?'

'Your wife.'

'Why?'

She shrugged. 'I feel like you know everything about me but I know almost nothing about you.'

What did she want to hear? What did she want him to say? He had never had a problem talking about Margie, it had been a way of keeping her memory alive, but he'd always talked to people who had known her. Talking to Charli would be different. But she was right, he knew far more about her and he didn't want Margie to come between them and whatever this connection was. Wherever this was going. And he was definite that he wanted this to go somewhere. He'd known his past and his future would collide at some point and it looked like today was the day. He took a deep breath and said, 'What do you want to know?'

'How long were you married?'

'Three years.'

'That's not long.'

'No, it wasn't nearly long enough.'

'Where did you meet?'

'In the UK.'

'She was English?'

'No. Her grandfather was but Margie was Australian. She was a nurse, from Melbourne. I was on a working visa as a paramedic and she was an ED nurse in one of the large hospitals. We travelled half way around the world to fall in love with someone from home. We used to laugh about that.'

'What happened to her? Was she sick?'

'No. She was perfectly healthy. She was in an accident.' He sighed. Her death had been so senseless, so unnecessary and such a shock, which had made it hard to comprehend and even harder to accept. 'Ella had just turned one and Margie had not long returned to work. She was on a late. Her shifts had to work around my roster but that was okay—we were used to the shift work and it meant someone was always there for Ella. She was in her car, stopped at traffic lights. The lights turned green but as she went through the intersection some kids in a stolen car ran the red light and crashed into her. She died at the scene.'

'Oh, Pat. That's so sudden. It must have been such a shock.'

He nodded. 'Margie always used to worry about my job and the associated risks. We always thought there was more of a chance of something happening to me because of the job I did, but it turned out it wasn't my job we needed to concern ourselves about. It turned out that no one is safe. I should have known that better than any-one. Margie was in the wrong place at the wrong time. I struggled for a long time with guilt. I save lives for a living but I couldn't save Margie.'

'But you're doing okay now?'

'Yes.'

'How long did that take?'

'A long time,' he admitted. 'Gradually I have made memories that don't involve her, which is painful at times, but slowly those new memories dull the loss and it becomes easier to cope with. Now there are things I can think about that don't automatically make me think about her too. I had to go on because of Ella but I've only recently got to a place where I'm looking forward to the future, where I can imagine a different future, one without Margie in it.'

'Have you dated since Margie died?'

'Not seriously.'

'Why not?'

'Lots of reasons.' Initially he'd felt he was betraying Margie's memory and as the dates had been casual he'd preferred to sacrifice the date rather than his late wife's memory. That had changed with meeting Charli but he wasn't sure how to phrase that without sounding like he was trying out a line. 'I haven't met anyone I really wanted to date or who I was prepared to introduce to Ella. She's already lost one mother, I need to think care-fully about how my actions will impact on her if things don't work out. Ella and I are okay as a unit of two.'

'I bet she was a good mother.'

'She was a fabulous mother. We were so excited when we found out she was pregnant. It's tough being a single parent but having Ella was the thing that really pulled me through after Margie died. I had to keep going, for her.'

'How do you manage? It can't be easy, especially not with shift work.'

'I have a *lot* of help. My parents and my in-laws live close by and Ella also goes to child care when I work. Speaking of which, I really have to get to work.' He hoped what he'd told her would be enough to satisfy her for now. He set up a password for her on his laptop and headed off, resisting the urge to kiss her again.

'You did well. How're you feeling?' Harriet said as she accompanied Charli back to her bed after her physiotherapy session.

Charli's feet were still heavily bandaged but Harriet had given her a pair of shoes made from pieces of foam and rubber, which cushioned her feet, and she was able now to stand with a walking frame and get herself to the bathroom. Her gait was still slow and she couldn't be upright for too long as her feet remained painful, but it was a nice change to be able to stand, even briefly.

'You might be able to get out of here in another couple of days, once I can get you on crutches,' the physio said. 'I'll bring you a pair tomorrow and you can try walking with them. Once you can manage stairs, you'll be able to be discharged.'

'When do you think I'll be able to fly?'

'Not for a little while yet. Your feet are still too swollen, and the risk of clots is too high. Why do you ask?'

'I haven't got anywhere to go once I'm discharged. I need to think about flying home.'

'Where is Amy staying?'

'She has to go back to Wombat Gully tomorrow. It's

the start of the school holidays and they need her for ski school.' Charli shrugged. 'I guess I'll have to stay with my father in the hotel.' That wouldn't be ideal as she and her father didn't have the easiest of relationships, but she didn't have another choice.

'I thought you said he wanted to go home soon?' Harriet queried, raising another obstacle. 'What if he leaves before you're ready to fly? Why don't you stay with your cute paramedic?'

'Patrick? He's not *my* paramedic.'

'What do you mean?' Harriet said. 'I thought you were an item. Are you just friends?'

Charli didn't know how to describe their relationship. She had spent quite a bit of time with Harriet over the past few days. The nurses bustled in and out, too busy to talk, but the physiotherapist had become something of a confidante to her, though they hadn't discussed Pat. 'I'm not sure what we are. I think he feels a sense of duty to me. He was the one who pulled me from the building.'

'I don't think he's here out of duty,' Harriet said. 'Have you seen the way he looks at you? I swear he wants to sweep you off your feet and take you away from here. He's your knight in shining armour. If he had a horse I could just imagine him riding in here on his noble steed.' She sighed. 'I've always wanted one of them.'

'A noble steed?' Charli smiled.

'A hero!'

'You've been watching too many movies.'

'No,' she said with a laugh. 'Reading too many books probably.'

Charli shook her head. 'I couldn't impose on Patrick like that.' She'd had the same fantasy of Pat as her real-life hero—he had rescued her after all—but that didn't mean he was about to sweep her off her feet and run away with her, and she didn't feel she could ask him to. She had no idea if they had that sort of relationship and listening to how he'd spoken about his late wife and daughter, Charli wasn't sure that he saw any sort of romantic relationship in his immediate future. She didn't want to put him in a difficult position, she was pretty sure that if she was brave enough to ask, the answer would be no. 'I'll discuss it with my father. He's meeting Amy and me here to take us to lunch.'

Just the mention of lunch with her father was enough to make her feel nervous. He'd suggested lunch and they were only going to the street-level coffee shop at the front of the hospital, but Charli suspected there was something her father wanted to discuss. She couldn't imagine him arranging lunch with his daughters for no reason.

'Let's get you changed.' Harriet grabbed a suit bag that she had hung behind the door when she'd arrived for the physio session. She'd offered to lend Charli a dress for lunch as the two of them were a similar size and Charli had absolutely nothing to wear. She could hardly go to the coffee shop in a hospital gown. She'd ordered some clothes online, using Pat's laptop and Amy's credit card, but, as yet, nothing had been delivered. It had been a surreal experience to be lying in a hospital bed, doing online shopping.

Harriet unzipped the bag and pulled out some new underwear, a navy wrap dress in a stretchy cotton and a white shirt and simple black jeans. She held them up. 'Will one of these do?'

'The dress,' Charli said. She would need to wear the shoes that Harriet had made for her and thought they might look less ridiculous with the dress, although any-thing was going to be better than the hospital gowns she had spent the past few days wearing. 'Thank you so much, Harriet.'

'Do you need a hand to get changed or can you man-age?'

'I'll be fine.'

'All right, I'll guard the door for you and then fetch a wheelchair to take you down to the coffee shop.'

As the door closed behind Harriet, Charli stripped off the hospital gown and left it on the end of the bed. She tossed the uncomfortable and unflattering dispos-able undies into the bin and replaced them with the pair Harriet had given her. She wrapped the dress around her-self, pulling the ties tight. It was a little loose on her—she'd lost weight over the past week—but it would do. She brushed her hair and tied it back into a ponytail. She couldn't do anything about her make-up, but it wasn't an occasion that warranted any.

There was a knock on her door. 'I'm decent,' she called.

'That's the worst news I've heard all morning. Should I come back when you're indecent?'

She had assumed it was Harriet knocking but the door had opened to reveal Pat.

He was grinning at her and her heart flipped in her chest as Harriet's words rang in her ears. Did he have feelings for her?

The idea thrilled her and terrified her at the same time but she couldn't deny she was attracted to him. Who could blame her? He was gorgeous. He wore a pair of bone-coloured cotton trousers and a grey shirt that highlighted his olive complexion and hugged his chest.

It was the first time she'd seen him out of uniform and, incredibly, he looked even more amazing.

She smiled, unable to pretend she wasn't excited to see him.

'You look good. Are you going somewhere?' he asked as Harriet appeared with a wheelchair and Charli tried to ignore the knowing smirk on the physio's face.

'Amy and I are having lunch with my father.'

He looked a little crestfallen and she wondered if he'd had other plans. For the first time he looked as if he wasn't going to work or rushing off to pick up Ella. Not that she minded, she knew his daughter came first and she couldn't begrudge that, not when it was exactly how she wished her own father had prioritised things. Ella was lucky to have Pat for a father, she thought, not for the first time.

'Let me help you into this chair,' he said as he slid his hands under her thighs and scooped her off the bed. Her arms automatically wound around his neck as he held her close. She breathed in, inhaling the scent of freshly washed skin and soap.

'You do know the hospital has a no-lift policy,' Harriet told him as he set Charli down in the wheelchair and she reluctantly unwound her arms from his neck.

'Good thing I'm not employed by the hospital then, isn't it?' Pat laughed as he spun the chair around to face the door.

Charli was still smiling when her father walked into the room.

'Charlotte! I thought I was meeting you here?' He looked from Charli to Pat.

'Mr Lawson.' Patrick spoke before Charli had a chance to and extended his hand. 'I'm Patrick Reeves.'

'Reeves?' her father said. 'I've heard your name before. You rescued Charlotte from the building.'

'I did.'

'Thank you.' He reached for Pat's hand and shook it. 'Please, call me Jack. You're a paramedic, I believe?'

Charli sat in semi-uncomfortable silence and listened to the easy conversation between her father and Pat while they discussed his job as he wheeled her out into the corridor towards the lift. Charli couldn't remember ever having an easy conversation with her father about anything.

'Would you like to join us for lunch?' Her father extended an invitation to Pat.

'Thank you, but I can't. Maybe another time.'

Charli wished he would. Maybe then she wouldn't have to endure a stilted conversation or listen to whatever bad news she was certain her father was going to deliver.

The lift arrived and Pat let her father take over, leaving Charli to wonder what the purpose of Pat's visit had been.

Pat was back at the hospital as early as possible the following day. He wanted to check on Charli. He'd sensed she'd been nervous about lunch with her father and he wanted to see her just to make sure she was okay.

He pushed open her hospital door and was confronted by an empty room. There was a travel bag on the bed, clothes folded and set in a pile beside it.

Amy came out of the bathroom, carrying a small cosmetics bag.

'What's going on?' Pat asked just as the door opened behind him. Harriet was holding it as Charli stepped through with the aid of crutches. Pat was surprised. When he'd seen her yesterday, she'd still been using a wheelchair.

'She's made good progress,' the physiotherapist commented when she saw Pat's expression.

'The doctors are ready to discharge me,' Charli added.

'You can fly?'

'Not yet. Walking with crutches is enough. Flying is not one of my superpowers.' She smiled and Pat was relieved. Maybe yesterday's lunch had gone well.

But his relief was short-lived. If she was recovering physically and emotionally and was ready for discharge, that meant she would be leaving. Leaving the hospital and one step closer to leaving Melbourne. One step closer to being out of his life. 'Is your father coming to get you?'

She shook her head. 'No. He's gone.'

'Gone where?'

'Back to England.'

Pat frowned. 'Without you?' He had assumed that Jack would stay until Charli was ready to fly. He'd assumed her father would travel with her.

'That was what lunch was all about.' Charli glanced at Amy. 'He was telling us he's leaving.'

'Why?' Pat was totally confused.

'My stepmother is having complications with the pregnancy. As usual, she trumps me. Us. Dad is concerned because, apparently, Victoria is having twins, which was a bit of information he neglected to pass on initially.'

He could hear the effort she made to keep her tone light but he knew she would be hurting. She'd said enough for him to know that her father's reserve bothered her, that she felt he had abandoned her on more than one occasion. But he wondered if her father's departure was as straightforward as Charli believed. All relationships were complicated and he wondered if she was expecting things to be black and white when in reality they were usually shades of grey. He'd seen Jack's expression when he'd visited Charli and Pat's opinion was that Jack was a man who felt things but perhaps had learned to keep his emotions hidden.

But Pat knew it wasn't his place to interfere. He didn't know their history. He'd only heard one side of the story. And that didn't change the fact that Jack had left, had returned to England, once again choosing his wife over his daughter, or, as he expected Charli would see it, abandoning her yet again.

He looked at the small pile of her possessions on the bed, reflecting the little she had left in her world. 'Where are you going to go?' He turned to Amy. 'Is she coming to stay with you?'

'No, I have to head back to Wombat Gully tonight.'

He looked back to Charli, who shrugged her shoulders. 'I guess I'll book a hotel room.'

'I don't think you're quite ready to be on your own yet, Charli,' Harriet said. 'I know you're mobile but you *are* still on crutches.'

Pat looked at the physio. 'Should she be being discharged then?'

'She meets the criteria and I think getting out of here would be good. The media are still ringing constantly, wanting an interview, so leaving might avoid that stress.'

He looked at Charli, making a snap decision. 'You can stay with me.'

'I couldn't do that.'

'Why not?'

'That sounds like a perfect solution,' Harriet interrupted. 'I'll let the two of you sort out the details and I'll let the nurses know to start your discharge paperwork.' She spun on her heel and left the room.

Charli was looking at him warily.

'What are your objections?' he asked her.

'What would you tell your daughter?' she queried as she sat on the edge of her bed.

'Don't worry about Ella,' he replied as he took the crutches from her and leant them against the wall. 'My in-laws have taken her interstate to visit her cousins. She won't be home. But I wasn't planning on taking you to my house. I have somewhere better in mind. My family has a house in the country. It's the perfect place for some R and R. There's no cell phone reception. It will just be the two of us.'

'I've seen that movie, *Wolf Creek*...'

'I promise I have honourable intentions.' While he may have entertained some less-than-honourable thoughts, his intentions were genuine. He wanted to help. They were friends first, and if she wanted to keep it that way he would respect her wishes. He wanted her to feel safe with him.

'Amy will know where you are. I have four days off. Let me help. What do you think?'

He stepped closer, making a pretence of adjusting the pillows on her bed. Charli wriggled backwards and he scooped her legs up, lifting them for her. She was wearing a pair of gym shorts and her legs were virtually bare. His forearm was under her thighs, skin against bare skin. He was deliberately testing the water, testing her reaction. He saw her pupils dilate. He knew she felt the same connection. Whenever he held her in his arms he never wanted to let her go. She was casting a spell and he was falling under it, fast. It was good for his ego to know he was having a similar effect on her too.

'Would you like to run away with me?'

She smiled and his heart flipped. He knew she was going to say yes.

'I think that sounds wonderful.'

'Pat?' Amy's voice surprised him. He'd forgotten she was also in the room. 'Could you give us a minute?'

Amy waited until Pat left the room but Charli could tell from her sister's expression that she was about to get the third degree.

'Do you think this is a good idea?' Amy asked.

'What?'

'Going to stay with Pat.'

'I don't see the problem?'

'You don't think this is another knee-jerk reaction?'

'A knee-jerk reaction? To what?'

Amy sighed. 'To everything that has happened. To you being trapped. To Hugo's behaviour. To Dad leaving so quickly. I worry that every time Dad disappoints you, you try to find someone who will stay by your side, but you have to admit your choices haven't always been great. Wouldn't you be better off coming with me? I'm going to stay with Daniel, I'm sure he wouldn't mind if you stayed too.'

'I think he might,' Charli retorted, 'but anyway I can't go back to Wombat Gully. Not yet. Maybe not ever. I don't think I could bear it.'

'I just don't want to see you get hurt again. I know

you're attracted to Pat but I don't want you to think he
is the answer.'

'To what?'

'To giving you a safe haven.'

'That's not what this is,' she replied. 'It's fine, it's not
for ever. I'm not *expecting* it to be for ever. I'm supposed
to be home to start my GP training in a few weeks.'

'Are you sure? You don't think you're putting yourself in a vulnerable position?'

'What does that mean?'

Amy raised her hands in protest when she saw Charli's
expression. 'Don't get me wrong,' she clarified. 'I really
like him, but he has plenty of baggage and so do you.
He's a single dad, he's got lots of other commitments
and responsibilities. You're still recovering from your
ordeal, physically and emotionally. Do you think staying with him is wise? Would you stay with him if you
weren't attracted to him?'

She knew she wouldn't but if she lied she also knew
that Amy would see straight through her. 'I'd probably
ask Harriet if there were any other options,' she admitted.

'Are you strong enough to handle things if they go
wrong again? I'm not saying they will, but you need to
at least consider that.'

Charli hesitated. Amy had a point. She *did* tend to
romanticise things—people and situations—but she had
spent a lot of time thinking about her life while she'd
been trapped. About her mother and father. About her
stepmother. About Hugo.

After her mother had died and their father had re-
married, she had felt as though all she'd had left in the
world was Amy. It had been the two of them alone. All

she'd wanted was to feel loved and cared for, to feel important to someone, and she had spent most of her life looking for that person.

She knew now that she'd thrown herself into her relationship with Hugo without stopping to examine if he was right for her. She'd been so desperate to belong to someone that it hadn't mattered whether or not he was perfect for her—all that had mattered was that he showed her interest and attention. But their relationship hadn't been enough for him. *She* hadn't been enough for him. She was never enough for anyone.

She couldn't believe she'd been so naïve as to think Hugo had been the one for her. She couldn't believe that it had taken this crazy situation to give her some perspective on her life and on her own behaviour. Because she couldn't lay all the blame at Hugo's feet. She had to take some responsibility or risk making the same mistakes over and over again. She had made a promise to herself while she'd been trapped that when she got out she would focus on her career. Hopefully that would be something she could control, and she would take a break from trying to find the perfect relationship.

'I'm not looking for someone to run off into the sunset with,' she said. 'This will just be for a few days. As soon as I can fly I'll be going home.'

She wasn't planning on staying indefinitely. This time *she* would be the one leaving, on her terms. She couldn't deny she was attracted to Patrick but she was convinced she could handle it.

Charli slept most of the way while Pat drove, and only woke up when he bumped over a cattle grate as he turned off the bitumen and onto a rough, potholed dirt road.

Sheep grazed in the paddocks on either side of the road and ahead of her a lake glistened in the afternoon light.

The view was breath-taking. Rolling green hills, plump white sheep, stately eucalyptus trees and the dark blue of the lake all nestled under a clear blue winter sky. '*This* is where you grew up?'

This wasn't what she'd expected when Pat had asked her to run away with him. This idyllic, secluded spot. Her heart raced with a mixture of nervousness and anticipation.

She had been on an emotional roller-coaster ever since the disaster, and her father's most recent abandonment to support his wife had reopened past wounds. She was exhausted, tired of thinking about her father, tired of being in pain, tired of constantly refusing interview requests. Even while she'd been forced to admit that perhaps Amy had a point, she hadn't been able to refuse Pat's offer of a place to stay.

Maybe it was a place to run and hide. Maybe running away was becoming a thing for her. She'd chosen a medical school far from home so she'd have to live in. She'd chosen to run to Amy rather than face a showdown with Hugo. Each time someone let her down, that was her response. But she enjoyed Pat's company, she enjoyed the way he made her feel, and she hadn't wanted to refuse his invitation. Maybe she was running away again but she'd made her decision. She was in Pat's car and about to spend a few days alone with him.

She wondered what the next few days would bring. Would it give them the time and space she wanted, needed, to explore the possibilities between them?

She swallowed nervously and took a deep breath as Pat nodded and turned in behind a weatherboard house that sat on a rise overlooking the lake. It was painted cream with a grey tin roof and wide steps led up to verandas which wrapped around three sides. Vines crawled up the veranda posts and a post-and-rail fence protected the garden beds from the grazing sheep.

'Are those your sheep?'

Pat shook his head. 'My parents leased the land to one of the neighbours when they moved to Melbourne. The sheep are his.'

He switched the engine off and Charli opened her door. Pat handed her the crutches as she swung her legs out of the car.

He had their bags in his hands. 'I'll come back for you and help you with the stairs,' he said. 'Just let me open up.'

'I can manage. Harriet wouldn't let me be discharged unless I could negotiate steps.'

She swung her legs out of the car and stood up. The air was crisp and cool but it felt good to be outside. It had been over a week and a half since she'd last breathed fresh air. Her feet were still swollen but the pain was manageable if she could keep her legs elevated. It wasn't far to the house. She'd put her feet up again when she was inside. She knew she wasn't able to be a useful house guest, given that she couldn't stand for long, but she'd try not to be a nuisance.

Taking the stairs slowly and carefully, she entered through the front door, which opened directly into a large, open living space with the kitchen at one end. The floorboards were strewn with large rugs delineating the different spaces—living and dining—and the windows all looked out towards the lake. Enormous, overstuffed couches sat in front of a large stone fireplace in the living area.

The house was cool but there were plenty of blankets draped over the couches and fresh logs had been stacked in the fireplace grate, just waiting for someone to strike a match. Bookcases were built in on either side of the fireplace filled with books, board games, old vinyl records and jigsaw puzzles. Despite the fact that the house was now only used for holidays and weekend getaways, it had a welcoming feeling. Charli could imagine that Pat's childhood here had been a happy one.

She followed behind him as he gave her a brief tour. Behind the living room were several bedrooms and a couple of bathrooms. He put her bag in the room closest to the bathroom. The double bed in the centre was easily big enough for two but Charli noticed, with some disappointment, that he took his bag to a second room across the hall. Maybe that was just as well, she chided herself as Amy's warning replayed in her head. After all, she had sworn off relationships.

He boiled the kettle for tea and directed Charli to a chair set beside the fire. The chair was angled to look out over the view through the large windows down to the lake. A wooden jetty jutted out over the water and a rope swing hung in a gum tree near a fire pit.

'What is the name of the lake?' she asked.

'Lake Eildon.'

'It's beautiful. This must have been an incredible place to grow up.'

'It was brilliant. My brother and I had an adventurous childhood. Swimming, fishing, water-skiing in summer and snow-skiing in winter. Wombat Gully is only an hour away.'

'This is the brother who gave you that scar under your eye? Is he older or younger than you?'

'Three years younger.'

She sipped her tea. 'How long did you live here?'

'Until I was twelve. We moved to Melbourne when I started high school.'

'But your parents kept the house here?'

'We spent our holidays here. Summer and winter. I'm glad they kept it. I have fabulous memories of growing up here and I want Ella to have the opportunity to experience this lifestyle as well. It's harder now, being a single parent, but I have a lot of support from my parents.' Pat struck a match and Charli tried not to stare at his backside as the denim of his jeans stretched taut across it as he bent over to light the fire. 'Are you okay there for a bit?' he asked as he straightened up. 'I just want to chop some more wood.'

'I'm fine, thanks.' There was a pile of magazines on a small table beside her chair and Charli flicked through a couple as she drank her tea but her concentration was interrupted by the sound of Pat's axe splitting wood.

The view through the windows was incredible but Charli was restless. She'd been in the car for a few hours and cooped up in hospital for days before that. She'd had enough of being inside and on her own. She wanted to be outside. She wanted to be with Pat.

She grabbed her crutches and went out and sat on the veranda. Pat had his back to her and she watched, almost mesmerised, as he swung the axe. Despite the cool temperature of the day he had stripped off his shirt and the muscles in his back and arms were slick with sweat, gleaming in the late afternoon light. She watched his hands where they gripped the axe and remembered when he'd held her with those same hands. How warm they'd felt. How safe they'd made her feel.

He split the last log and started to throw the smaller pieces into a pile beside the fire pit. He turned and saw her watching him. He winked at her but didn't stop. Charli felt her nerves settle. She felt like this was where she was supposed to be. Here, with him.

Behind Pat she could see the sun starting to set over the lake. The mountains were growing grey in the shadows and the water was turning gold. It was still and peaceful. Sunset was rapidly becoming her favourite part of the day. On the edge of one of the paddocks, in the shadow of a stand of gum trees, she could see animals grazing.

'Are those sheep?'

'Where?'

'Over there.' She pointed at the animals whose shapes she could just make out in the dusky light. 'By the trees.'

'They're kangaroos.'

Charli stood up and leant on the veranda railing, as if the few extra inches would improve her sight. 'Kangaroos! I've never seen a live kangaroo before. Can we go closer?'

'They're wild,' he said with a laugh. 'They won't hang around.'

'They are so cute.'

'Don't judge a book by its cover,' he said as he tossed the last log onto the pile. 'They're a pest.'

'Really?'

'Yep. They destroy the crops and compete with the stock for feed,' he told her as he climbed the steps and leant against the veranda post.

He was standing close beside her. She could smell his sweat—warm, musky and masculine. She watched as he wiped himself down with his T-shirt and slung it over his shoulder. She couldn't keep her eyes off him and she had completely lost her train of thought.

She straightened up, bringing herself even closer to him. He was watching her watching him.

He bent his head and she saw his eyes darken. Her lips parted; he was close enough to kiss her.

His lips brushed her cheek and Charli closed her eyes in anticipation. She felt his hand on her hip, felt it curl around behind her and cup her buttock as he whispered into her ear, 'Hold that thought. I need a shower.'

She opened her eyes in time to see him smile at her before he turned and walked away, leaving her all hot and bothered and barely able to stand on shaky legs. She leant back against the railing as she tried to work out what had just happened. And what would happen next.

She heard water running as Pat turned the shower on. She could imagine him, stripped naked, hands soaping his chest, head tipped back under the spray as the warm water ran over his body. She could feel herself blushing and she shook her head. She hadn't realised she had such a vivid imagination. She needed something to keep her busy.

Charli moved into the kitchen and looked in the fridge. Pat had said there was homemade soup for dinner. She ladled some into a pot and put it on the stove to reheat before putting bread rolls in the oven to warm.

She heard the shower stop as she ladled the soup into bowls and took the rolls from the oven. Dinner was ready but she couldn't manage to carry the food to the table while using crutches. She'd need Patrick's help.

She grabbed her crutches and hobbled into the passage to call him to the kitchen.

She rounded the corner and came face to face with Pat as he emerged from the bathroom.

Or rather, she came face to bare, muscular chest.

A few drops of water remained, glistening on his skin. He smelt of soap and she could feel the heat of the shower rising off him.

Without thinking, she lowered her gaze. He had a thick, fluffy, white towel wrapped around his hips and she knew he was naked beneath it.

Her heart was beating rapidly and she lifted her eyes and met his dark, intense gaze. She swallowed, suddenly and unexpectedly nervous, and swayed a little on her sore feet.

'Are you looking for me?' he asked as he reached for her, his large hands holding her by the arms as he steadied her. His hands were warm and gentle and her skin tingled under his touch.

'Dinner is ready,' she stammered.

One corner of his mouth twitched up in a smile. 'I might just put some clothes on.'

'Would you like some help?' The words passed her lips before she had time to think.

His smile widened. 'Do you think that's a good idea?'

Charli took a deep breath as she thought about what she was about to do. She nodded. 'I think it's a very good idea.'

His green eyes darkened and Charli caught her bottom lip between her teeth as she waited for his reply.

He bent his head and his words brushed over her cheek as he said, 'We won't be needing these then.' He eased the crutches away from her body and scooped her off her feet.

She wrapped her arms around his neck as he pressed her against his chest. She could feel his heart beating strong and fast against her. He was firm and hard in all the right places. She tilted her head and looked up at him. His lips were millimetres from hers. She licked her lips and watched as his pupils dilated. Her lips parted, a soft moan escaping her throat as he closed the gap and pressed his lips to hers. Her lips parted further as Pat's tongue slipped inside her mouth. She tightened her hold on him as she kissed him back. He tasted of mint, he tasted of desire and she couldn't remember ever wanting someone as badly as she wanted him.

His mouth broke from hers, leaving her lips swollen and lonely. 'Are you sure about this?'

She nodded. She was panting, out of breath, but she knew what she wanted. She wanted him. She wanted to taste him and feel him and let him take away the longing and the hunger that was eating away inside her and she couldn't think about anything else.

'I'm sure.'

She might have sworn off relationships but this could only be a fling anyway, this situation was only temporary. Besides, she was sure he was still in love with his late wife but she didn't care. It wasn't as though he could be unfaithful, neither was she trying to steal him away from Ella. What she wanted to do wouldn't affect anyone else, this was between the two of them, simply a physical relationship, not an emotional one. What was the harm in that?

Convinced there was none she made her final decision. 'I want you to make love to me.'

She didn't need to ask him twice.

CHAPTER EIGHT

HE PICKED HER up and she wrapped her legs around his waist as he carried her to his room. He kissed her as he walked. She had no idea how he negotiated the path but she didn't care. All she cared about was getting naked. All she cared about was finding out if the reality was going to be as good as her fantasies.

He sat on the bed and she nestled in his lap, her knees either side of his thighs. She slid her fingers into his hair. It was still damp and still unruly. She'd been wanting to touch his hair since the night she'd met him. She'd been wanting to do a lot of things. He was sexy and strong but gentle at the same time, and she had been longing to touch him for days.

She traced the scar under his eye with her thumb, lightly brushing the skin before letting her fingers move over his cheek and jaw. She ran her index finger over the ridges of his abdominal muscles, tracing them from where they began under his ribs, counting the bumps silently in her head, one, two, three, four, five…until they disappeared under the edge of the towel. Her fingers stilled and she saw him tense. He breathed out, a long slow breath.

She lifted her hand and placed it over his heart. She

felt it beating, hard and fast. His nipples were hard and she ran her thumb over one brown nub and heard him catch his breath.

He didn't say a word but his hands spoke for him.

His right hand moved from her hip, sliding under her top. It was warm on her skin and as his thumb grazed the lace of her bra she felt her nipple tighten under his touch. He lifted the hem of her top and she raised her arms as he slid her clothes from her. With a flick of his fingers he undid her bra. He bent his head and she closed her eyes in ecstasy as his tongue licked her nipple before his mouth closed over her breast.

He flipped her over, off his lap and onto her back, and lifted her hips as he slid one hand under the waistband of her loose trousers. She wriggled out of her clothes until she lay almost naked before him.

He lay beside her, stretched out on the bed. His hand rested on her thigh. She parted her knees and his hand slid up the inside of her leg, sending spasms of desire through her. His fingers found the edges of her knickers, found the warmth of her centre, and Charli trembled as her desire intensified.

She watched as he ran his eyes over the length of her. His gaze was dark and intense. Her body was still varying shades of yellow and purple as the bruises faded but under his gaze she felt beautiful. Under the touch of his fingers she came alive.

His fingers were teasing and taunting her. She had to touch him. She put her hand on his knee and slid it under the towel. His erection was thick and firm and warm beneath her hand.

'I want you to make love to me,' she whispered. She needed him. She needed to feel his warmth, his energy.

'I don't want to hurt you.'

'You won't.'

He rolled over and opened a drawer beside the bed. She knew he was looking for protection. And hoped he found some. She wanted to be joined to him. Wanted him to bring her to orgasm.

She watched as he stood up and retrieved a small packet. She reached out and flicked the towel from his waist. He was now completely naked and Charli couldn't take her eyes off him. He was glorious. Perfect.

She took her knickers off as he sheathed himself. He stood and watched her. Waiting. She bent her knees and spread her legs further, letting him see, inviting him in.

His dark eyes met hers as she reached for him, wrapping her hand around his length. 'I want you inside me.'

He moaned and removed her hand as he knelt on the bed. He held both of hers in his and pinned them above her head. He moved between her thighs and bent his head and it was her turn to moan as he covered one breast with his lips, sucking on her swollen nipple as he thrust into her.

Charli pushed up, arching her hips and back as he entered her, wanting, needing to take all of him in. She welcomed him in and let him fill her. Physically and emotionally he sated her. She was no longer an individual, she was no longer abandoned. He filled her physically and emotionally as she let him possess her.

She dissolved into a state of absolute pleasure. There was no room for any of the thoughts that had been swirling in her head for days. There was no time to think about what had happened, to her or to Pat. There was just the two of them at this moment. Together. Entwined. She wasn't going to think about the past or the future.

There was only the present and she was going to make the most of the moment she'd been given. She was going to enjoy the man in her bed.

She woke to the sound of kookaburras laughing as the sun streamed in the window. She was alone in the bed but there was a note on the table beside her, tucked under a mug of tea. She picked up the mug, surprised to find it was still warm, and read the note.

Pat had gone fishing and hadn't wanted to wake her.

Had he needed time alone with his thoughts?

Did she need to be alone with hers?

She'd followed her heart last night, followed her desire, and she didn't regret it. Not yet. Pat was not a good match for her long term, she had no intention of getting seriously involved with a single father, no intention of being cast in the role of stepmother, but that didn't need to stop her from having some fun for the next couple of days. It wasn't like they could have a long-term future. She had to go back to the UK at some point as she was due to start work and further training in less than a month. But this could be fun for a couple of days.

She showered and dressed while she relived the events of last night in her head. She smiled as she hugged her thoughts to herself. She had never really expected reality to outdo her fantasies but she was happy to discover she'd been proved wrong. Last night had been everything she'd dreamt of and more, and for the first time since the landslide she felt happy, relaxed and peaceful.

She scanned the shore of the lake, looking for Pat. The banks were empty and there was no one on the jetty. Had he gone out in a boat? Did he have a boat? Her heart skittered anxiously until she reminded herself that he had grown up here. He knew the area and the lake. He wouldn't have put himself in danger.

A fire glowed in the fireplace, Pat must have lit it before he'd gone out. Charli threw another log on to keep it burning while she settled down with a cup of tea and a book. She had one eye on the story and the other trained on the lake. Watching and waiting for Pat.

Eventually she heard an engine and saw a boat approach and tie up to the jetty. She watched as Pat leapt ashore, carrying a bucket.

'Good morning,' he greeted her as he stepped into the house. He was smiling and looked relaxed, and only then did she realise she'd been a little uncertain. Unsure of how he would be feeling today. 'Do you fancy fish for lunch?' he asked as he opened the fridge door.

'That sounds good.'

'And how do you feel about fishermen? Do you fancy them too?'

She grinned. 'I find the local fishermen irresistible.'

'Is that so?' he said as he came and leant over her sofa. 'Just how many do you know?'

'Only one but he's more than enough for me.' She reached up and grabbed a fistful of the soft, grey cable-knit sweater he was wearing and pulled him down to her.

He kissed her firmly on the lips. 'No regrets about last night then?'

'Of course not. Why?'

He squeezed in behind her on the sofa and pulled her back until she was lying against his chest. She could hear the beat of his heart under her ear. She snuggled in closer as he wrapped one arm around her shoulders. 'I was worried that I'd taken advantage of you.'

She laughed. 'I think you know I was more than willing. I have wanted you since the moment I first saw you and, even with everything that has happened since I met you in the bar, that hasn't changed. I'm a big girl, Pat, I make my own decisions.'

'Are you sure?'

'I'm positive.'

'I promised I had honourable intentions and the next thing you know I've got you naked in my bed. I wanted to help you. I wanted to give you time to recover. To heal. I thought you needed to escape, not just from the hospital and the media attention but from the world in a way.'

'And that is exactly what you are doing. Let's not over-think it, let's just enjoy the next few days. And each other. We can both recharge and be ready to get on with our lives when the time comes. I don't want to think. I want to feel. Last night was incredible. Shall we see if we can repeat it before lunch?' she whispered.

Charli arched her back as he slid his hand under her sweater. She felt her nipple harden in response to his touch and then there was no room in her mind for anything other than Pat.

Charli spent the next two days in a quiet bubble. She slept and read while Pat fished and did some minor repairs to the house. They shared wine and food by the fire and at night they shared a bed. They didn't discuss the outside world. For forty-eight hours it ceased to exist, and Charli was content just to be in the moment, away from the real world. She knew it was out there, waiting, but she was happy not to think about it for now.

On the last night they sat by the fire pit, bundled in thick jackets and blankets under the dark sky. She lay in Pat's arms as they shared a bottle of wine and looked at the stars. 'It's so beautiful. I wondered if I'd ever see the stars again when I was trapped. But I don't recognise these ones, your stars are so different.'

'Does it feel strange, lying under a different sky?' he asked.

'It feels like a dream.' She felt safe and comfortable in his arms and she could almost let herself believe that this was exactly where she was meant to be, even though she knew it couldn't last. 'It's almost impossible to imagine that in a few weeks' time I'll be back in London.'

'Are you ready to go back?'

'Yes.' And, no, she thought, but she didn't have an option. 'I've worked really hard to get into the GP training program, I need to get back. I need to be busy. I need to move forward.'

Going home was the safe option. She had a job, a career, a life waiting for her there. She knew she would take the safe option. What other choice did she have? She couldn't throw all of that away on the chance that Pat might be ready to move on. She wanted to be important to someone, she wanted to be special, and he'd made it clear that he wasn't looking for anyone special.

From the beginning their time together had been limited and while she could daydream about staying, it was only a fantasy. He had a daughter who needed his attention, one she was unlikely even to meet, and she wasn't sure she wanted to. That would be a dose of reality that she wasn't equipped to deal with. She was happy here, secluded in their own little world, and she wasn't naïve enough to think they could take what they had here back into their normal lives. Sexual chemistry wasn't enough to build something lasting on.

She would go home with her memories but, meanwhile, she would enjoy the last few hours with him. She'd made a decision to focus on her career but that didn't preclude her from enjoying this time with him. She wanted this interlude, a chance to restore some peace in her heart, even though she knew it couldn't last. Not the peace or the time with Pat. They both had complicated lives and she couldn't stay. Relationships didn't work out for her. She was always left alone. And she wasn't going to keep making the same mistakes. She would take pleasure in his company for as long as they had and then she would leave.

It was time to return to reality. They were headed back to Melbourne and the closer they got to the city the more Charli felt as though time was running out. They hadn't talked about what came next. She didn't want to be the one to raise the topic but it was becoming increasingly obvious as the kilometres ticked over that she would have to.

'Can you recommend a good hotel for me once we get back to the city?' she asked.

'A hotel? What for?'

'I need somewhere to stay. My review at the hospital is still several days away and I can't fly until then.'

'I thought you'd stay with me.'

'At your house?'

'Yes.'

'With you and Ella?'

'Yes. Is there a problem?'

'Does she know about me?'

'No.'

Pat had spoken to his daughter each day while they'd stayed at the lake. He hadn't tried to take the calls privately and Charli had been able to hear most of the conversation. She hadn't heard her name mentioned once and it had reinforced that Pat also had a different reality waiting for him when they left the lake house. He had responsibilities, not just to his career but to his daughter. Charli wasn't interested in playing happy families, she didn't know how to.

'So she'll come home to find a random stranger staying her house and you think she'll be okay with that?'

He'd told her that he had to think carefully about how his actions would impact on Ella. Was he ignoring his own advice now?

'She's three, Charli, her world revolves around her.'

'And your parents? What about them?'

'I have a spare room. You can stay in there for appearances' sake if you're worried.'

Perhaps he wasn't asking, or expecting, her to play happy families. He seemed quite content with his life the way it was.

Was this the end? She was under no illusion that things could continue between them long term but she hadn't actually thought about the end. She wished they could have stayed hidden away on the shores of the lake but that wasn't reality. For either of them.

'I'm not collecting Ella until after dinner tonight,' he said. 'It'll take us a few hours to get back to Melbourne. Why don't you think about it?'

'All right, I— Oh, my God! Stop. *Stop!*'

Charli flung her hands into the air and screamed as she watched helplessly as an accident unfolded before her. She'd seen the driver of a parked car open his door just as a cyclist was passing. The cyclist swerved to avoid the door but veered into the path of the car in front of Pat's.

Pat slammed on his brakes as the car in front of him swerved suddenly, and although Pat was able to avoid a collision the cyclist wasn't so fortunate. They watched, horrified, as the cyclist hit the bonnet of the car in front and bounced off the windscreen.

Pat switched off the engine, hit his hazard lights and leapt from the car. 'Check the driver,' he said to Charli as he ran towards the cyclist, who was now lying prostrate on the road.

Charli limped to the car in front. She didn't bother to grab her crutches, she was in too much of a hurry. The driver, an elderly gentleman, was conscious but obviously shaken.

'He rode right into me! I didn't have time to stop.'

'I know, I saw it happen,' she said as calmly as possible. 'Are you all right?'

'I think so.'

'I'm a doctor. Do you think you can walk? I can help you out of the car.'

His windscreen was smashed so a tow-truck would need to be called, and Charli knew the ambulance officers would want to check him out and give him the all clear.

She could hear Pat issuing instructions to other bystanders. Getting one to call an ambulance and another to direct traffic. The driver appeared to be okay and Charli knew Pat could probably use some help, but she needed to take care of the elderly man first.

'Do you have any medical conditions I should know about?' she asked as she helped him to the footpath.

'I'm on medication for my blood pressure and arthritis.'

There was a bus stop nearby and Charli assisted him to the seat. His knees shook as he sat down and Charli looked at him with some concern as his face went slightly grey.

'Are you feeling okay?'

He was rubbing his left shoulder with his hand. 'I think I might have strained my shoulder,' he said. His voice was breathless and, looking at him, Charli knew it was more than that.

He was having a heart attack.

'Pat!' she called. 'I need some help here!'

She caught the man as he toppled forward off the seat. She laid him on the ground and felt for a pulse. It disappeared under her fingers.

She started CPR.

Out of the corner of her eye she saw Pat run back to his car and when he got to her he had a resuscitation mask in his hand. He knelt beside her and Charli nodded, letting him know she needed him to breathe for the man. She counted out loud as Pat positioned the mask and pinched the man's nose. 'Twenty-eight, twenty-nine, thirty.'

She took a break as Pat breathed into the man's mouth.

He did two breaths and then sat back as Charli resumed compressions.

'Are you still on the phone to the ambulance?' Charli heard him ask one of the bystanders. 'Can you tell them it is now a category one, we have a patient in cardiac arrest.'

Charli and Pat continued CPR, alternating roles, until the paramedics arrived to take over. They hadn't managed to resuscitate the driver and Charli didn't like the ambulance officers' chances either. She had no idea how much time had passed but it had felt like many minutes.

She hobbled to Pat's car and collapsed into the passenger seat while Pat gave the crews a summary of the event. Eventually the two ambulances left the scene with their lights flashing and sirens screaming, and Pat joined her in the car.

'How was the cyclist?' she asked.

'He's pretty banged up,' he said as he pulled into the traffic, which was now heavily congested. 'He has a few broken bones, possibly a fractured scapula, collarbone, ribs and pelvis but it's internal injuries we were worried about. How are you?'

Charli was exhausted and her feet were sore. Kneeling on a hard footpath hadn't done them any favours and she suspected her efforts had all been in vain. 'Tired, and my feet are sore, but I'm in a lot better shape than either of those two.'

'This traffic is going to hold us up now. If you're in pain I think you should stay with me, at least for tonight. It'll be late before we get back to the city anyway. If you want to go to a hotel tomorrow, I'll sort something out then.'

Charli hesitated. She hadn't decided what to do and she was now too tired to think about it. She hesitated, but not for long. What would be the harm in staying with Pat for one more night?

Charli wandered through the house while Pat went to collect his daughter. She'd expected something comfortable and cosy, like the house in the country, but the house was sleek and modern. It didn't feel like Pat. She assumed his late wife had decorated it but she wondered what he'd changed in the past two years. She almost expected his wife to walk into the room, her presence was still so evident. Had Pat deliberately chosen not to change anything? Was this his way of keeping her memory alive?

Photos of Ella and of Margie with Ella dominated the shelves. Charli felt like an intruder as she picked up some framed photos but she couldn't resist. Ella was gorgeous. She had Pat's colouring, green eyes and dark hair, but her hair was a mass of ringlets and her face was a miniature version of her mother's. Margie was also dark with eyes that were bright with life and a smile that was full of laughter. They looked like they'd been happy.

She sighed as she replaced the photos. It was blindingly obvious that Pat was not ready to let go of his past.

She went to the pantry and searched for the tea, having decided she'd put the kettle on and take a cup of tea to her room. She probably should get off her feet and tea always made everything slightly more bearable.

Charli was still in the kitchen when Pat arrived home with Ella. She hadn't been able to decide where she should be. Hadn't decided how she was going to deal with meeting his daughter. Pat had assured her that Ella wouldn't have a problem with Charli staying. She was sociable child, used to being surrounded by lots of different people. He'd told her that he wouldn't have invited Charli to stay if he'd thought it would cause problems, but Charli was starting to feel uncomfortable now, although she had enough insight into herself to realise that her fears were based on her recollections of her own childhood and had nothing to do with Ella.

She took a deep breath as Pat came into the kitchen, carrying his daughter. She was overthinking things, there was no need to be nervous.

Pat set Ella down.

He rested his hand on top of Ella's dark curls. 'Ella, this is my friend, Charli. She's going to stay with us for a while.'

Ella stayed close to his side but looked up at Charli with her green eyes that mirrored Pat's, and Charli's nerves returned with a vengeance.

'Hello, Ella,' she managed to say. She wondered what she was supposed to do next. Should she squat down, bring herself closer to Ella's level, or would that be too confronting? She didn't know what to do so she stayed put, almost frozen in the corner of the kitchen.

'Remember, before you were born, Mummy and I lived in England?' Pat talked to fill the silence. 'Charli is from England.'

'Did you know my mummy?'

'No.' Charli shook her head.

Ella was looking at Charli's heavily bandaged feet. 'What happened to your feet?'

'I was in an accident.'

'My mummy was in an accident. She's in heaven now.'

'My mum is in heaven too.'

'Do you think they are friends?'

'I don't know.' Charli felt uncomfortable. She hadn't expected to be having this conversation with a three-year-old and had no idea how to respond.

Her phone vibrated and she snatched it off the countertop, relieved to have something to divert her attention. 'Can you excuse me, please?' she said as she left the room.

Pat watched her go, wondering what the hell had just happened.

That hadn't gone at all well.

Why was she so uncomfortable?

His parents-in-law had bathed and fed Ella before he'd collected her so he started her bedtime routine while Charli was on the phone. He helped Ella to clean her teeth and left her to choose a story while he went to speak to Charli to find out what was wrong.

Charli had finished on the phone but she spoke before he had a chance to.

'Can I talk to you?' she asked, and continued when he nodded. 'That was Harriet. The television stations are still calling, wanting to interview me.'

'We've had calls to Special Ops too.'

'You have? Why haven't you said something?'

'The journalists are only interested in an interview with us if they can interview you too. I told Connor you weren't keen, so he's shut them down.'

'Do you think they'll give up?'

'Eventually. Something else will come along that's more newsworthy.'

'If I agreed to give just one interview, do you think they would they be happy with that?'

'If you made it clear that's all you were prepared to do, I think that could work. Are you thinking about it?'

Charli nodded. 'Do you have a PR division as part of Special Ops?'

'We have a media liaison officer in the ambulance service. Why?'

'If the reporters were interviewing one of your team as well, do you think the media person could set it all up? I wouldn't know what to do.'

'I'm sure they could.'

'Would you do the interview with me?'

'Me?'

She nodded. 'I'd feel better if we could do it together. Do you think that would be a possibility or does the ambulance service have a regular spokesperson?'

Pat shook his head. 'Any one of us can give interviews. Sometimes we're briefed and sometimes it's on the spot at a scene. It should be possible to organise. I've got to read to Ella but I can make some calls after that. Unless you want to read to her?'

Maybe that could help break the ice. He hadn't expected Charli to be so reticent. Everyone loved Ella and he couldn't begin to fathom what the problem was.

'Me?'

He nodded.

Charli looked terrified. 'Can't you just ask tomorrow when you go to work?'

'I may not get time. Work can be a bit unpredictable, as I'm sure you can imagine. It's easier to do it now.' He felt a little bit guilty. Charli was obviously reluctant to read to Ella but he couldn't understand why. 'She's choosing the story now.'

Charli still hesitated. Maybe he shouldn't have pushed her but it was too late now.

'I don't think I can,' she said.

'Why not?'

'I'm no good with children. I don't know what to do. What if I do or say the wrong thing?'

'It's a story, Charli, all you have to do is read it.'

Finally, she nodded.

CHAPTER NINE

CHARLI HAD READ to Ella on the first night, thinking it was best to get it over and done with and knowing that, as Pat was doing her a favour, she needed to do one in return, but she hadn't counted on being asked to read *every* night. She had debated the wisdom of staying at Pat's but since Amy had returned to Wombat Gully her only other option, until she was fit to fly, was to book alternative accommodation, which would mean being on her own. She really *hated* being alone, so she'd stayed.

She been there for five nights and it was becoming harder and harder to maintain a safe distance.

Ella's favourite book was *Paddington*. Charli had loved that book too as a child and reading wasn't a problem, but spending this one-on-one time with Ella was. She was adorable, warm and open, and secure in the knowledge that she was loved, she had not hesitated to welcome Charli into her life.

But her open manner scared Charli. She didn't want to get attached to Ella, she didn't want to disappoint her. She knew she needed to maintain some distance, and didn't want to get too close or too comfortable, knowing it would make it more difficult when she had to leave. And she knew she couldn't stay. This couldn't be her life. She couldn't get too attached, to Ella or to Pat. It wasn't fair on any of them.

But Pat, or more accurately, Ella, seemed determined to include her in their lives and the more time Charli spent with them the harder it was to stay removed. She could feel herself being drawn in. They made her feel safe and secure. She was starting to feel like she was a part of a family and the feeling was addictive. It was what she had always wanted but was afraid of at the same time. She knew that loving people left her open to heartbreak.

But even knowing the risks, she couldn't avoid spending time with Pat and his daughter. If she was completely honest, she didn't *want* to avoid it. She had no issue with spending time with Pat behind closed doors but she was glad he hadn't suggested that she meet his parents or his friends. She didn't want to get more involved in his life as it would only make it harder to leave, but getting close to Ella was a different thing altogether and she was trying to limit the time she spent with her. Some things, however, she discovered, were not negotiable, which was exactly how she found herself agreeing to spend a day at the zoo with Pat and his daughter.

She'd tried half-heartedly to get out of the excursion, claiming that it would be too much walking, but Pat had insisted. Apparently the zoo had wheelchairs and he was happy to push her. She'd then tried to suggest that he might like the time alone with Ella but Ella was as insistent as her father and now here they were, all three of them, at the entrance gate.

'Where shall we go first, Ella?' Pat asked as he paid the admission fee. He knew what Ella's answer would be—it was always the same.

'The Butterfly House.'

Kept at a constant twenty-eight degrees, the butterfly exhibit was the perfect spot on a grey and drizzly Melbourne day, and Ella skipped ahead as Pat pushed Charli's wheelchair through the zoo. He and Ella had finally persuaded Charli to accompany them and he had a surprise organised for later in the morning but, knowing Ella's preferences, he'd allowed time for the butterflies first.

Charli had stopped looking so afraid when she was spending time with Ella but he hadn't been certain she would agree to spend the day with them doing one of Ella's favourite activities. He knew she was still holding back, fearful of engaging fully with Ella. It was odd. He'd thought she'd feel empathy with his daughter as they'd both suffered the same tragedy of losing their mothers at a young age but Charli seemed reluctant to get too close.

Maybe that wasn't a bad thing because she was only going to be in their lives for a short time, but if he'd thought for one moment that having Charli with them would have been at all disruptive for Ella, he wouldn't have suggested it. Ella was resilient and she enjoyed Charli's company like she enjoyed everyone's. When Charli left, Ella would have plenty of other people to fill that void so he hadn't thought it would be a problem. At least, not for Ella. But he'd come to realise that *he* would be the one who would be most affected when Charli left. He would be the one who missed her. Ella would move on, she was better at that than he was.

Charli had none of the same reservations about spending time with him, though, but she had insisted that they keep their relationship behind closed doors. Neither Ella nor his parents were allowed to know just what was happening between them but that was okay. Ella went to bed early and that gave him and Charli hours alone together.

But spending this time with her was complicating his feelings. He enjoyed spending time with her, physically and intellectually she stimulated him. He'd been attracted to her from the first moment and he'd been keen to pursue a physical relationship but he hadn't expected to connect any more deeply than that. He'd thought they could have some time together and then happily go their separate ways, but he liked having her in his life. He just wasn't sure how, or if, she could fit more permanently.

Did he want to go there?

She had a life in England, a career, and he had a life here, a career, a family, a daughter. Neither of them could give those things up. Timing was everything and he had a feeling their timing was wrong. It was too soon.

He couldn't worry about it now, he decided as he pushed Charli's chair through the double doors into the butterfly house. He'd enjoy the day and pretend he knew what he was doing.

'Sit very still, Charli,' Ella instructed, and Pat stifled a laugh. It was one thing for Ella to issue commands but quite another for her to follow her own rules. She danced from foot to foot and watched the butterflies. There were hundreds of them, looking like rose petals swirling in the breeze.

'Pretend you're a tree, Ella,' he said in an effort to get her to stand still. She stuck her arms out but continued to shuffle excitedly. Eventually the butterflies stopped fluttering and dipping and one landed on Ella's finger, to be quickly and unceremoniously frightened away when Ella's attention was caught by something else.

'Charli! You've got a butterfly on your head! Daddy, take a photo,' Ella ordered, used to having everything captured on his phone.

Charli had a butterfly perched on her head like an ornament. She was smiling at him as he took the photo and his breath caught in his throat and his chest went tight with desire. Another butterfly landed on her shoulder and he took a second photo.

'They like you, Charli!' Ella chattered. 'I think it's because you smell nice. Doesn't she smell nice, Daddy?'

He bent his head and smelt her hair. 'She does indeed, Ella.' Charli was blushing but her eyes were shining as he straightened up and looked at her.

'Maybe they like my hand cream.' She rummaged in her handbag and pulled out the tube. 'Why don't we put some on you, Ella?'

It was the first time in Pat's experience that Charli had voluntarily connected with Ella. Maybe she was getting under Charli's defences. He figured that her reluctance to get attached to Ella stemmed from her own childhood but Ella was irresistible and he didn't think it would do Charli any harm to spend time with her.

Charli rubbed cream into Ella's hands before dabbing a bit on the end of Ella's nose. Much to Ella's delight, a butterfly landed on her nose and Pat knew Charli had made a friend for life out of his daughter now. All that remained was to see how Charli felt about Ella.

They watched the butterflies feeding at the nectar tables until the glasshouse began to fill with people and Ella began to get restless. He pushed Charli out past the elephants to the platypus pool, where they laughed at the curious creature as it dived and twisted in a display of underwater acrobatics before they wandered through the Australian animal section to the kangaroo enclosure.

In typical Melbourne fashion, the sun had finally decided to make an appearance, pushing weakly through the clouds, but it was enough for the kangaroos to seek out the warm spots and lie basking in the sun.

People were milling around the enclosure as Pat parked Charli's chair near the gate and locked the brakes. 'We need to leave your wheelchair here.'

'What for?'

'We can't take it into the enclosure.'

'We're going in?' He nodded. 'With the kangaroos?'

'If you want to feed them you need to go in. They don't make a habit of letting them out.' He smiled.

Charli's blue eyes lit up. 'We can go in and feed them? Really?'

'Really.' This was the surprise he'd organised. He'd paid extra for the experience but he hadn't been able to resist. 'And pat them.'

Charli was out of the chair before Pat finished his sentence.

'That is amazing, thank you.' She flung her arms around his neck and kissed him on the cheek, possibly forgetting her own rules, but she'd dropped her arms almost before he'd registered her hug and held her hand out to Ella. 'Let's go.'

They listened quietly as the keeper gave a quick safety briefing, reminding visitors not to run or chase the kangaroos. 'Find a spot to sit quietly and let the kangaroos come to you. They are used to being hand fed, they'll be eager. Take some pellets and hold your hand flat, they'll eat off your hand.' She showed them how to hold their hands and then passed out small bags of pellets.

Charli and Ella chose a log to sit on. They sat side by side as the kangaroos fed from their hands. Pat took several photos as they fed and patted the kangaroos.

'They feel like velvet!' Charli exclaimed, as a young joey nuzzled her hand.

The joey turned and dived back into its mother's pouch, legs akimbo, and Ella giggled.

'Isn't it a bit big to be in the pouch?' Charli asked at the sight of its hind legs sticking out.

'They stay in the pouch for about six months,' the keeper said, 'but continue to go in and out of the pouch until they are almost a year old.'

Charli shook her head as she fed the mother and laughed along with Ella. Pat watched them together with a vision of what his life could be like with someone to share it with.

'Thank you, Pat, this is incredible.' Charli looked up and smiled at him and his heart skipped a beat and he knew, right then, that he was starting to fall for her.

'It's my pleasure,' he said, then pretended to check his phone. He didn't want her to be able to read his expression. He was terrified she would see what he was thinking and that it would scare her. He sensed it would be too much too soon for her.

'My food's all gone,' Ella said as she upended the bag to prove her point.

'Mine too,' Charli said. She took both bags and they had one final pat before they were ushered out of the enclosure.

'I want to be a baby joey. Can I sit on your lap, Charli?'

Charli held her arms out and Ella clambered onto her

lap. She curled herself into a ball and snuggled in. Charli tucked her coat around her, creating a makeshift pouch.

Back at the house Pat put a movie on the television and Charli and Ella fell asleep together on the couch. Ella had insisted on continuing with her joey impersonation and had refused to leave Charli's side. She lay curled up with her head on Charli's lap and Charli's arm was draped over her, holding her close. It was the most relaxed he had seen her with his daughter. Perhaps, with time, this could work out for all of them.

Charli barely recognised the face staring back at her from the mirror in front of the make-up chair. She hadn't expected the television station to bother with her make-up but now she was shocked to see that her bruises, which had been fading, had been accentuated by the make-up artist. She looked more battered than she had in days. Was that the effect they wanted?

She leaned in towards the mirror as the artist removed the white collar that had protected her clothes and started to clean the brushes.

Charli spun around in the chair, about to stand, when the door opened and Pat stuck his head into the room.

'All good?' he asked, before she saw him do a slight double take.

He crossed the room, coming closer. He put his fingers under her chin and Charli felt the now familiar frisson of desire with his touch, but that was quickly wiped out by Pat's frown. She knew what he was thinking.

'I was expecting to look better than I do in real life, not worse,' she said, trying to remain positive and make light of the situation.

'You're still gorgeous, but…' he turned her face to the side, examining the end result '…you look like you've gone three rounds with a prize fighter. I hope no one thinks I've done that to you.'

'I'm not sure why they've emphasised my bruises. What angle do you think they're going with?' She was growing more nervous by the minute and worried about what questions might be asked and how she would manage.

She'd agreed to the interview on the condition that Pat would do it with her, and she'd expected they would be interviewed together. She wanted to do the entire interview with Pat beside her but the producers, and Stacey, the show's host, had decided Pat would join in later. They felt it would be more dramatic.

She knew she was relying on Pat more than was healthy. It was so easy to let him take charge, to let him make the decisions. She didn't want to face up to the real world yet and suddenly she wondered if the interview was about to make her. Would she have to relive the entire disaster? She could feel her heart rate quicken and her breathing become more rapid. She reached for some paper towel to wipe her sweaty hands.

Things weren't going quite the way she'd expected.

'It will be okay,' Pat reassured her. 'Take your time answering the questions, there's no need to hurry. Take some deep breaths now,' he said as the door opened again and an assistant came to collect Charli. 'I'll be with you as soon as I can.'

Charli was escorted into the studio during an ad break. The interview was being broadcast live, which was something else she hadn't anticipated. She really hoped she didn't make a fool of herself.

A microphone was clipped to her collar and a battery pack tucked into her pocket before she was settled into position on a very small couch opposite the journalist, Stacey, who was in a chair. Fortunately, Charli was allowed to be seated when the interview began and didn't have to make her way to the couch using her crutches, although they had been propped next to the couch for effect.

Now that she was on set, under the glare of the lights and with no familiar faces, she wished she'd stood her ground. She could have done with Pat's moral support. She hoped the first part of the interview would be over quickly and then he would be with her.

She took a deep breath when she heard the producer start the countdown to the end of the ad break and mentally prepared herself as Stacey began the introductions.

'Here with me today I have Charlotte Lawson, the sole survivor of the Wombat Gully landslide that claimed the lives of fifteen people earlier this month. Welcome to the programme, Charlotte.'

Stacey's dark hair was styled and sprayed with hairspray, not a strand out of place. Her forehead was Botoxed and her lips plump. Charli found it quite disconcerting being interviewed by someone whose face was devoid of all expression. She wished she could tell what Stacey was thinking.

There was a large digital screen to Charli's left, positioned at the back of the studio, and on it Charli could see a photograph of Wombat Gully Resort with the big brown scar on the landscape and the rubble of the ruined buildings strewn down the mountain. She turned back to face Stacey.

'You were trapped, buried alive, for almost forty hours. You must have been terrified.'

She should have known the interview would go for drama and sensationalism. She'd watched enough of these interviews herself over the years. But, despite the dramatics, Stacey was right. Charli had been afraid.

'I was. I can't remember ever feeling so afraid. So alone.'

'Can you describe it to us?'

'It's hard to describe. It was so dark. Pitch black. I couldn't see anything. I had no idea what had happened, where anything was. Water flooded the floor and dripped through the roof. I could smell sewage. It was freezing cold. I was breathing in dust—it was so thick I thought it would choke me—and I was afraid I might run out of air. I tried calling out but no one responded.'

'Did you ever imagine that you might not be found?'

'Yes.' That had been her overriding fear. That she would die in a tomb, alone.

'How did you deal with that?'

'One step at a time. I was cold and thirsty and tired and that made it difficult to focus, to work out what to do. I tried to stay warm. I knew hypothermia and dehydration were the biggest dangers. There was nothing to drink. I tried not to move too much but I had to make noise, I had to try to get someone's attention.'

'And how did you do that?'

'I found a metal pole and when I could hear people nearby I'd hit it against the bed frame—but then everything would go quiet and I thought people were taking a break. I didn't know if they'd ever hear me.'

'But, in fact,' Stacey said, 'the rescuers called for quiet on the site so they could listen for noise, for a sound that might indicate there were survivors. They were, in fact, listening for you.'

'Yes. I had no idea I was working at cross-purposes to them. I was lucky to be found.'

'Yes, you were the lucky one. You were found by Patrick Reeves, one of a team of Special Operations paramedics, and he joins us now too. Wouldn't we all love to be rescued by someone tall, dark and handsome?' Stacey said as she turned to the side of the studio and watched as Pat came into view. 'Welcome, Pat. You're the hero in this story.' She stood up to shake Pat's hand and Charli could see the introduction embarrassed him.

'I was just one of hundreds of people searching the area,' he said as he sat beside Charli on the tiny couch.

'But you were the one who heard Charli's cry for help,' Stacey said, ramping up the melodrama. 'How did you feel? Talk us through the moment when you heard her voice.'

'I thought I was hearing things. I thought my imagination was working overtime initially. We'd been working hard in tough conditions, getting nowhere, and we were starting to think we wouldn't find *any* survivors. When I realised I hadn't imagined the noise, it was a huge relief.'

'And, Charli, that must have been a miraculous moment for you. Making contact. It's incredible to think that you could come through almost unscathed when there were no other survivors. Have you seen that before, Pat? You've been to lots of disasters. You've risked your life time and again.'

Visions flashed up on the large screen to Charli's left. The image of Wombat Gully Resort was replaced by photos of other tragedies. Charli knew the viewers would be able to see it. She could pick out Pat in a few of the photos, not all, there were a lot of media shots, but Stacey was talking about Pat's role in these other events—a train derailment in the Dandenong Ranges, some school students lost in the bush on an overnight hike, an airlift from a skiing accident.

'It's unusual to have only one survivor with something of this scale,' Pat admitted.

'And you were at the resort for a training exercise. Were you training for a landslide?'

'Not as such, but the processes are the same in any disaster.'

'Had you ever been involved in anything of this magnitude?'

'No. And I hope I never am again. We're in the business of saving lives and losing so many people was awful. It was an enormous tragedy.'

Charli knew he was thinking about the people he hadn't saved, the ones he'd heard calling for help minutes after the disaster, the ones who he'd known had survived the initial landslide only to perish from their injuries or from the elements before they could be rescued.

'But saving Charli must have given everyone hope.'

'It was unbelievable.'

The image on the screen changed again and a photo of Charli being lifted from the rubble appeared. She was strapped to the spinal board, filthy and dishevelled, but the setting sun cast a golden light onto her. Pat could be seen leaning over her and her eyes were fixed on him.

'Tell us what you were thinking in this moment, Charli.'

Charli remembered that moment vividly. She remembered not wanting to let Pat out of her sight but that revelation felt much too personal to share on national television. 'I was just so glad to see the sky. I was so relieved to be out of there and the sunset was spectacular.'

'Pat, do you think there was a reason Charli survived?'

'A reason?'

'Yes. Do you think this experience has brought you closer? Have you forged a relationship that will endure into the future? I hear you were a frequent visitor while Charli was in hospital. That's not normal practice for first responders or emergency personnel, is it? It's obvious there's a connection between you. Are you single? What about *you*, Charli, are you single?'

Charli wasn't sure where Stacey was going with this angle. She was completely unprepared for the question and she could only assume Pat was too.

'Oh, I've put you on the spot,' Stacey said. 'You're blushing, Charli. Is there more to the story? An addition to the happy ending?'

Charli realised, too late, that it had been a mistake to ask Pat to do the interview with her. Someone had obviously done their homework. She had no idea who Stacey had spoken to or who had done the digging, but the interview was taking a turn that she wasn't prepared for. Stacey was definitely going for drama but not in the direction Charli had expected.

She was suddenly aware of how close she and Pat were sitting. They had no choice on such a small couch but she wondered how it looked to the viewers. She didn't want to be the topic of rumours and innuendo. She shook her head. 'No, there's no more to the story.'

'You left hospital with Patrick on your discharge, though, didn't you?'

How on earth did she know that? Charli was afraid to ask, she didn't think she wanted to hear the answer.

Pat answered the question with one of his own. 'Charli is a visitor who lost everything in the landslide. Where was she supposed to go?'

Pat didn't sound as though he was going to admit to their relationship. And neither was she.

'To her sister's, perhaps?' Stacey said, before changing tack. 'I understand you're a widower, Pat, a single dad. It was interesting that Charli chose to go with you.'

'Interesting to whom?' Pat sounded annoyed now. 'Amy is back in Wombat Gully. Did you expect Charli to return there after everything that had happened?'

'No, not at all. I think everyone is curious about what happens next, though. That photo looks like the start of something to me and I'm sure everyone would love a fairy-tale ending to the tragedy. Charli?' Stacey was not backing down quietly.

'I think they're going to be disappointed,' she replied. 'I don't live here and when I am able to fly I will be going back to England.'

Charli loved the idea of fairy-tale endings as much as anybody but despite finding herself imagining a life with Patrick and Ella she knew it was impossible. She might love the idea of happily-ever-after but Patrick hadn't made any suggestions that he was feeling as though there could be a future for the two of them.

His house was still full of Margie's photos and Margie's touches. Charli was under no illusion that he was thinking about anything permanent. She needed to be careful. She couldn't afford to get in any deeper, to give her heart away completely. She would be leaving and she wanted her heart intact when she went. Giving it away twice, to Patrick and to Ella, would only cause her twice as much pain when she returned to the UK.

'There's nothing that would convince you to stay. A new romance, perhaps?'

Charli shook her head and Stacey turned to Pat. 'What about you, Pat?' Charli held her breath, waiting to hear if Pat would share his thoughts about her plans. Would he say he'd like her to stay?

But Stacey didn't ask him the question Charli hoped for. 'Is there anyone special in your life?'

'Only my daughter.'

Pain pierced Charli's chest at the implications of Pat's words. She knew Ella came first in Pat's life, that was fair and right, and she suspected that she was also further down the list than his late wife, but to hear Pat neglect to mention her at all was hurtful.

Pat's tone suggested that he wouldn't be answering any more questions and Charli was relieved when Stacey ended the interview. She was upset and she didn't want to break down on national television. Especially not in front of Stacey, who she knew would take great delight in asking her more pointed questions, or in front of Pat. She wanted to get away from the cameras, away from the scrutiny. The interview had been a mistake.

And perhaps the relationship with Pat had also been a mistake. Hearing him say he wasn't looking for anything serious hurt her more than it should have, given that she had been telling herself the same thing. But hearing him say it had made her realise just how invested she had become. How much she cared for him. How much she wanted to think this could be the real thing.

She was shaking as the crew removed the microphone

that was pinned to her shirt. She wasn't sure if she was angry or upset. Or both.

The drive back to Pat's house passed in an uncomfortable silence. Charli wanted to know what Pat was thinking but she was too much of a coward to ask.

He'd had ample opportunity over the past few weeks to tell her that she was special to him and he hadn't done it, and he'd made it perfectly clear tonight that she wasn't anywhere near the top of his list.

Would she have contemplated staying if he'd asked her to?

She shook her head in silent admonition. It was a ridiculous notion to entertain, it was obvious he would never ask. He had other priorities and Charli didn't need or want to compete with Ella and she couldn't compete with Margie.

How did you compete with a ghost?

She had only one option and that was to leave.

She went straight to her room and closed the door when they got home. She didn't want Pat to see her tears.

The pain in her chest was so intense she thought her heart might be breaking and for the first time since she'd left the hospital she slept alone.

'Thank you for meeting me.' Charli greeted Harriet with a hug. 'I wanted to say goodbye in person.'

'Goodbye?' Harriet let her go and stepped back. 'You're leaving?'

Charli nodded. 'I got the all clear to fly yesterday. I've booked my flight home.'

'But what about Patrick?' Harriet was frowning as she sat down. 'I thought things were going well... I thought the two of you... I don't know, did I get it wrong?'

'No, you didn't, but I think I might have.'

'What's happened?'

Nothing had happened. Or rather nothing had changed. That was the problem.

'Nothing' she said. 'Things just aren't quite what I imagined.'

Things had been awkward since the interview. Charli had waited, hoping that Pat might say something, anything, about his feelings for her, but he'd remained silent. She could only assume that his feelings were nothing more than superficial. That she was nothing more than a temporary person in his life.

'Are you sure?'

'I'm sure.' She nodded. 'I have to go.'

'You don't love him?'

She shook her head. It wasn't a question of her feelings for him. It was a question of his feelings for her. 'No.' She felt like crying but she had to stay strong. 'It doesn't matter how I feel.' She sighed. 'I don't think he can love me.'

'What does that mean?'

'I don't think he'll let himself love me. Or anyone. I think he's still in love with Ella's mother.'

'Has he told you that?'

'Not in so many words but I can hear it in the way he speaks about her and there are photos of her all over the house. She's everywhere you look. And Ella is a constant reminder of her too.'

'Charli, I saw the interview. I've seen the two of you together. Are you sure you're not in love?'

'I can't compete with a dead wife.' She wanted to be enough for someone. She didn't want to be second best.

She'd made up her mind. She had to go. This was the right decision. For all of them.

She couldn't risk her heart. Both Pat and Ella had got under her defences. Tears welled in her eyes as she thought of the little girl with her dark curls and mischievous smile, the way her warm little hand would slide into Charli's when she wasn't looking and not let go. She hadn't wanted to get attached, she'd been terrified she'd screw everything up if she did, but it had happened regardless.

'I can't stay. I have to leave before I get in any deeper. Before it hurts too much.'

Her heart was already breaking but there was no other choice.

Pat felt it as soon as he walked in the door. The air was still and quiet and the house was silent. Much too silent.

He called out to Charli but was greeted only by more silence and he knew the house was empty.

He went to her room. The door was ajar, her bed stripped bare, her sheets folded on the end of the mattress. On top of the sheets was an envelope with his name on it.

His hand shook as he opened the flap.

He didn't need to read the words. He knew what she would say.

She was gone.

He knew her flight left today but he hadn't thought she would leave without saying goodbye. He hadn't thought she would take a taxi to the airport to avoid saying farewell, but her letter told him that was exactly what she had done.

He sat on the bed and reread her note but it gave no

more clue as to what she was thinking. No more clue as to why she had left this way.

It didn't matter. It didn't change the fact that she was gone.

She had left him. And it was his fault.

But there was nothing else he could have done. Nothing he could have changed. He wasn't ready. Despite the fact that he was happy with her, he wasn't in a place where he could give his heart away again.

He'd been worried about getting too close. Worried about letting Charli into their lives, into his heart. He knew Ella had already opened her heart to her. His daughter was going to be distraught and that was his fault too. But there was nothing he could do.

He knew she couldn't stay and it wasn't fair to ask her to. He couldn't make a commitment or a promise. He couldn't offer her anything.

But he couldn't let her go without one last goodbye.

Saying goodbye was going to hurt but he would get over it. He'd got through worse.

He spotted her just as she was about to go through Security.

'Charli.' He resisted the urge to reach out and grab her, to physically stop her from taking another step.

She turned at the sound of his voice. 'Pat! What are you doing here?'

Her eyelids were puffy and the tip of her nose was red. Had she been crying? He wanted to pull her into his arms, to ask her what was wrong, but her posture was stiff and she had her arms crossed protectively over her chest. Was she protecting herself from him? He wasn't sure he could blame her.

He wanted to embrace her but instead he put his hand under her elbow and gently drew her out of the queue as he stepped backwards. 'Were you really planning on leaving without a word?' he asked.

'I thought we'd said all we had to say.'

'What about "Goodbye"?'

'You knew I was going. I'm no good at goodbyes.'

'What am I supposed to tell Ella?'

She shook her head. 'I don't know. Tell her I'm sorry.' She looked over his shoulder and he knew she was looking at the departures board. Was she really leaving? 'Pat, I have to go.'

I don't want you to. The words were on the tip of his tongue but he bit them back. Those words would get them nowhere. He couldn't ask her to stay.

She had a job to go back to. A life. A life that didn't include him.

He wanted to ask her to stay but the words lodged in his throat, choking him. He had nothing to offer her.

'Pat?' She watching him, her blue eyes big and bright. 'What are you really doing here? Is there something more you wanted to say?'

He wasn't ready but he was desperate. He took a deep breath. 'What if you stayed?'

'Stayed? Why would I stay? My future is in England. My career is there. My life is there.'

'Stay for Ella. Stay for me.'

'You said yourself there's no one important in your life other than Ella. We had fun, but we were always on a time limit. We were never supposed to have more than this.'

'If you leave now, we'll never know.'

She was shaking her head and he knew he was losing her. 'I can't be the person you want me to be.'

'What the hell does that mean?'

'I can't be Margie.'

'I don't want you to be Margie!'

'Maybe not, but I don't think you're ready for me or anyone else to take her place. You're still in love with her. You haven't moved on. You're not ready to move on. To let go.'

'That's ridiculous.'

'Is it? The house is like a shrine to her. Have you changed anything since she died?'

'No, but that wasn't for my sake or because I couldn't bear to. It was because I wanted to keep things consistent for Ella.' He hadn't been able to put away Margie's photos but he didn't even notice them any more.

'I'm sorry, Pat. I really like you and I did wish that what we had could develop into something more but I'm not ready and neither are you. There's no room for me. You told me you thought it would be you and Ella now, a unit of two, and I'm not going to come into your lives uninvited. I don't want to screw things up for Ella, like my stepmother did for me. I don't want Ella to hate me.'

'Ella loves you.'

He could make it all about Ella but they both knew that wasn't it.

'I'm not going to live in Margie's shadow. I'm not going to compete with her. You're not ready to include me in your life, not in the way I want.'

'What is it that you want?'

'I want what you and Margie had. I want to be somebody's special person.'

'Just give me some time,' he pleaded.

She shook her head. 'I haven't got time. I have to think about what is right for me. Ella will always come first in your life. Which is the way it should be, but I can't accept being anything less than second. And if I'm not going to be second then I'm not the right person for you. I'm not enough.'

He had to let her go. He had no choice. He couldn't tell her what she wanted to hear. The three words that he knew she deserved.

He'd been scared to love her in case it didn't work out, but he was going to lose her anyway.

The queue through Security was short. She stepped back into line and he watched her walk away. She didn't look back.

He'd asked her to stay and she'd shut him down.

It was over.

CHAPTER TEN

'HEY, HOW'RE THINGS at home?'

Charli kicked her shoes off and lay back on her bed as she answered her sister's phone call.

'It doesn't feel like home,' she admitted. She had been living with her father, Victoria and their newborn twins, her half-brothers, since she'd returned to England. It wasn't ideal but she'd been living with Hugo, now her ex-boyfriend, before she'd fled to Australia and she'd had nowhere else to go when she'd got back.

'No, I guess it wouldn't,' Amy said.

She and Amy hadn't lived at their father's house for years so she could understand why Amy would agree with her, but it wasn't the unfamiliar house that was the problem. The whole country felt foreign to her now. England didn't feel like home any more. She'd felt like she'd left home behind when she'd left Australia, even though she knew it wasn't the country she was missing. It was the people.

'You haven't had any luck finding something else?' Amy asked.

'No. I haven't had time to look. I'm working eighty-plus hours a week and studying.' She also hadn't been in the right frame of mind to look for alternatives. She knew she'd have to bite the bullet eventually, she couldn't stay at her father's indefinitely, but she didn't have the energy to do anything about it.

She was miserable, exhausted and lonely. She didn't *want* to start over with new flatmates, she wanted to be with Pat and Ella, but she'd mucked that up.

She missed Amy but she was missing Pat even more. Now that she was on the other side of the world she couldn't really remember why she'd left.

Nothing made sense without him.

Now that she was on her own she was acutely aware of the hole in her life. She supposed she would find something or someone else to fill it eventually, but she had come to the realisation that she didn't want to. She wanted Pat. She should have fought harder, been tougher, been braver. She should have given him more time. But none of those realisations were any use to her now.

'How are the twins?' Amy wanted to know.

'Good.' She couldn't pretend she didn't adore the babies. Despite her protests, she had fallen in love with Milo and Louis the minute she'd first held them.

'Victoria is coping okay with the whole baby thing?'

'I have to admit she's actually doing well but the nanny is a huge help. Maybe Dad should have employed nannies for us instead of marrying Victoria.'

'He did. We had a succession of them. Don't you remember?'

'No, I don't.'

'None of them stayed long. I think we were difficult and so was Dad. I don't think we can blame Victoria. She had a lot to deal with, a lot to sort out. But, tell me, how's work going?'

'It's okay.'

'Only okay?'

'It's pretty exhausting, to be honest. I'm really tired and finding it hard to focus. I feel a bit out of control.'

'I'm sure it's not that bad.'

'Adjusting to life back here *and* to work is a lot harder than I thought it would be.'

'Oh, Charli, give yourself a break. You've been through a lot of stress over the past few months—breaking up with Hugo, the landslide, leaving Pat, starting a new job—that's more than enough to deal with. Give yourself time to settle into the job, don't be so hard on yourself. Have you caught up with any of your friends?'

'I don't really feel up to it.'

'You should make an effort. I'm sure you'd feel brighter if there was something to look forward to other than work and going home. I wish I was there with you. I'd *make* you go out.'

'When will you be back?'

'I don't know. Dan has asked me to go to Canada with him. We talked about doing the winter there and he wants me to go home with him first to meet his family.'

'Really? That's great.'

She tried to be happy for Amy. Her sister had always been more adventurous, unlike Charli she'd never been afraid to take chances, but hearing Amy's plans just reinforced to her how alone she was. All she really wanted was someone to love her. Someone who wanted to share a future with her. She wanted to matter. She wanted to be the most important person to someone. But it hadn't worked out that way for her with Hugo or with Pat.

'Maybe I could come via England?' Amy was saying.

'No, don't be silly.' Charli didn't want Amy to change

her plans for her. She was a grown-up, she could manage. She'd have to manage. 'I'm fine. I'm just a bit sad.'

'What's the matter?'

'I miss Pat,' she admitted. 'Now that I'm here I wish I hadn't left.'

'Oh, Charli. You should have stayed. You *could* have stayed. Why didn't you?'

'I was scared.'

'Of what?'

'Of falling in love with him. He didn't feel the same way about me. He told me, more than once, that he and Ella were a unit of two, that he wasn't looking for anything serious, but I didn't listen.' She hadn't listened to Pat or to Amy or to herself. Instead she'd given her heart away again and hoped he'd change his mind. But he hadn't. 'I thought it was better to leave. I thought I'd get over him. But it's not getting better.'

'Why don't we make plans to meet up in Canada?'

'I've only just started work, I couldn't ask for time off.'

'What about stress leave? Surely with everything you've been through, that would be a reasonable request? You could come back to Australia. There's going to be a memorial service at Wombat Gully for the victims of the landslide. You could come for that.'

'No. I don't think so.' She couldn't go back.

'Are you sure? It would give you a chance to see Pat.'

'Will he be there?'

'I'm not sure but I'd imagine he'd try.'

No, she wouldn't go back. She'd made her position totally clear to Pat. Maybe fate had brought them together but it hadn't been for the reasons she wanted. Their timing had sucked but the ball had been in Pat's court. He hadn't been ready to move on and there was no reason to think he'd changed his mind.

Pat and Connor strapped themselves into their harnesses and double- and triple-checked the carabiners, lines and anchor points before abseiling down the side of the mountain. It was the first time they'd been back to Wombat Gully since the landslide and the memories were threatening to overwhelm him.

Work had been his saving grace over the past two months. Keeping busy kept his mind occupied, but he hadn't counted on being back in Wombat Gully, back where it had all begun.

He focussed hard to block out thoughts of Charli. The two teenaged snowboarders who'd got disoriented during a blizzard and had fallen into a crevice deserved his full attention.

His feet hit the side of the mountain and he bent his knees, absorbing the impact, before he pushed off again, swinging out and releasing the line, repeating the process until finally he was at the bottom of the gully.

They found the boys in good spirits considering their ordeal and, incredibly, with relatively minor injuries. The assessments were simple enough—one dislocated shoulder with an accompanying concussion and one fractured ankle.

The dislocated shoulder had been out of place for too long to be safely reduced in the field but Pat and Connor stabilised the broken ankle before calling for the stretchers.

They carefully lifted the boys onto the stretchers, securing them firmly before attaching the ropes and pulleys and calling for them to be winched up. Pat accompanied one boy, Connor the other, and once they reached the top a second team of Special Ops paramedics took over to transfer the boys down the mountain before they would be airlifted to Melbourne.

Pat jumped into an over-snow vehicle that would drop him and Connor off at the resort medical centre. He looked out the window as they drove past the site of the landslide. It was almost unrecognisable as the same place. The debris had been cleared and the slope was covered with snow. It was pristine and white. All traces of the disaster had been wiped clean but Pat could close his eyes and recall what it had been like. Just like he could close his eyes and remember Charli.

He opened his eyes as the over-snow transport vehicle came to a stop. As he climbed out he almost collided with Amy.

'Pat!'

The siblings were so similar that for a moment he'd thought she was Charli. He bit back his disappointment as she hugged him. He was surprised. He hadn't been sure of his reception given the way things had ended between him and her sister. 'Were you part of the rescue team?'

He nodded.

'I hear it went well.'

He nodded again. News travelled quickly around the resort.

'And how are you?' Amy asked him.

'Good,' he replied, even though it was a complete lie. He was barely coping. Charli had been gone for almost two months and he still wasn't used to her absence. He couldn't work out how a woman who had been in his life for a few weeks was managing to leave such a hole in his world.

He hadn't come to terms with the fact that he'd let her go. That he'd thought it was the best thing for both of them. That he'd thought he'd get over her quickly—after all, they hadn't had long together—but he hadn't been able to get her of his mind and he wondered how long it would take before he would stop thinking about her at all.

'How is Charli?'

The words were spoken before he'd had time to think and now they were out he wasn't sure if he wanted to hear the answer. What if Amy told him that Charli had met someone else? He wanted her to be happy but he didn't want her to have forgotten him. He didn't want her to have moved on already. She might have accused him of not moving on fast enough after Margie's death, and he knew that he couldn't compare what he and Charli had had to his wife's death, but, in many ways, he felt the loss just as keenly and part of him, selfishly, he knew, hoped that Charli was missing him just as much.

'She's sad. She misses you.'

'Did she tell you that?'

'Yes.'

'Why didn't she tell me?'

'I don't know. I think she was afraid.'

'Of what?'

'Afraid you wouldn't want her. She doesn't handle rejection well, she's been like that since our mother died, and it makes it hard for her to open up, to give her heart.'

Amy's words made sense. He had rejected her. He'd been afraid to let her in. Now all he wanted to do was to be able to take her in his arms. He wanted to protect her, to look after her. She'd gotten into his mind, his body and his heart, and his heart ached with longing.

No, it was more than that. His heart ached with love.

He closed his eyes as the realisation sank in. He loved her.

He opened his eyes as the pain sat heavily in his chest. 'I should never have let her go.'

'Maybe you should tell her that.'

He nodded. Amy was right.

He knew what he had to do. He just hoped he hadn't left it too late.

Charli signed out of her emails, closing Amy's latest message before she was tempted to make a rash decision. Amy had sent her the details of the memorial service to be held in Wombat Gully, asking her again if she thought she might return for it, but there was no way she could go. She couldn't go back.

She closed her laptop and went to check on the twins. The nanny had the night off and Charli had offered to babysit as her father and Victoria had a function to attend. It was a rare night off for Charli too but she'd had no other plans. She was too tired to go out and she wasn't really in the right frame of mind anyway. She wasn't feeling at all sociable. Wondering vaguely if she was depressed, perhaps suffering from post-traumatic stress disorder, she knew that really all she needed was time to get over Pat. What she didn't know was how *much* time she needed.

Babysitting wasn't affecting her plans at all. She climbed the stairs to the twins' bedroom. She'd check the boys and then put the kettle on, but her plans were abandoned when she opened the door and saw Milo's bassinette shaking violently.

'Oh, my God.' She sprinted across the room and peered into the cot.

Milo was convulsing. His little face was red and she could hear him gasping for air.

She had swaddled him in a light muslin wrap to settle him but it had come loose. She unwrapped him and stripped off his leggings.

He stopped twitching as she undressed him but then his limbs went stiff and his eyes rolled back in his head. His chest was still.

He'd stopped breathing.

Charli picked him up and he lay limply in her arms as she felt for a pulse. It was there, just.

She carried him to an armchair and laid him on her lap before she bent her head and puffed a couple of breaths into his mouth.

She pulled her phone from her pocket and dialled 999. Tears ran down her cheeks as she waited for the operator to connect her to the ambulance service. She tapped the speaker option and breathed for Milo again.

She heard the call connect.

'I have an infant who is having a seizure. Prem baby, four months old, adjusted age, eleven weeks. He is febrile, unresponsive and not breathing.' She listened to the ambulance operator's questions and then continued, 'I'm performing CPR. Please send help.'

She knew the ambulance would come quickly, infants were a top priority, but she stayed on the phone until she heard the siren. It was still faint in the distance when she managed to get Milo breathing again. She hung up the phone as she quickly checked on the still-sleeping

Louis, then, on shaky legs, she carried Milo carefully downstairs to open the front door.

She handed him over to the paramedics as she gave them his neonatal history and then she stood and listened and watched as they assessed Milo.

'Heart sounds normal. Left lung a little crackly. Oxygen sats ninety-eight. Pulse one hundred and forty-four. Resps thirty. Blood sugar sixty-six.' The paramedics rattled off Milo's stats.

She tasted salt on her lips and wiped her face, surprised to find the tears were still rolling down her cheeks. 'Is he going to be okay?'

'I think so.' One of the paramedics glanced up at her, a flicker of concern on his face, and Charli panicked. 'Why don't you take a seat for a moment?' he suggested, and she realised his concern was for her. She must look a complete fright.

'We'll need to take him to hospital for assessment,' the second paramedic said. 'You can come with us.'

Charli took a moment to process the information. As a doctor, she knew that would be the protocol but it seemed that when the patient was family her brain was having even more trouble than normal focussing. 'There's another baby.'

'Another one?'

'Another boy. They're twins.' She realised she wasn't being very clear.

'Is he okay?'

'He was sleeping when I checked him so I think so.'

'Where is he?'

'Upstairs. I'll need to get him. There's no one else here.'

She ran back up to the nursery and picked up Louis.

She was numb as she climbed into the ambulance holding Louis, but she managed to call her father and had got herself together by the time the ambulance pulled into the hospital emergency bay.

According to the attending paramedic, Milo hadn't had any further seizures and to look at him now he seemed perfectly healthy. The medical staff took over, taking both babies as a precaution. Charli paced the waiting-room floor, hoping it was nothing sinister, as she waited for her father.

'Where is he? Is he all right?' Victoria burst into the emergency department, her eyes wild.

'He's with one of the doctors,' Charli managed to say before of the nurses intervened.

Charli listened as the nurse calmly explained to Jack and Victoria what was happening. 'Your little boy is just being assessed. The doctors will try to determine the cause of the seizure and of his temperature. Hopefully it was just a febrile seizure, caused by his high temperature. That type of seizure is common in infants.'

'What about Louis? Is he going to have a fit as well?' Victoria turned to Charli. 'Where is he?' she asked, only just realising that he was missing.

'He's here. They're both with the doctors. Louis is fine, they're just being cautious,' she said.

'I'll take you through to them now,' the nurse said to Jack and Victoria.

Charli knew there would be a raft of tests. Now that her initial panic had subsided she could recall the protocols. While the chances of Milo's seizure being related to his temperature were high, the doctors would want to rule out other causes. They would order EEGs, EKGs, blood tests and possibly an echocardiogram. She knew they would also test for meningococcal disease.

The doctors and nurses would explain all of that to Jack and Victoria. There was nothing more she could do here except wait. Her father and Victoria had each other. They didn't need her.

But she couldn't go. Not just yet. She needed to know what was happening. She sat down to wait and eventually her father reappeared.

He seemed to have aged ten years in just a few moments. He collapsed into the chair beside her.

Charli put her hand on his. She wished they had the sort of relationship where she could hug him spontaneously, he looked like he could use a hug, but since her mother had died they had never been demonstrative. 'How is he?'

'The doctors have put him on precautionary antibiotics and they're waiting for test results but they seem hopeful that it's not meningococcal. Hopefully it's nothing more than a fever. I really hope so. I don't think I could handle anything more. Not on top of losing your mother and then almost losing you.'

Charli was momentarily taken aback. It was the first time her father had given any indication that past events had upset him.

'These boys are my second chance,' he continued.

'At what?'

'At being a decent father.'

'I didn't realise you had any regrets.'

'I have plenty of regrets, Charlotte, my girl. I was devastated when your mother died. I completely fell apart, I had depression for a long time. I was barely coping when

I met Victoria. She insists I *wasn't* coping. I was drinking heavily, it wasn't a healthy environment for the two of you. It wasn't a happy home. I needed time to heal and to recover. To learn how to cope. We thought boarding school would give you a safer, more stable environment. I thought I'd have time to make it up to you, to explain why I'd made that decision, but the years went past and I missed my chance. I thought I'd be able to be a father to you again but you'd grown up and didn't need me.'

'We always needed you, Dad.'

'I have lost a wife and lost touch with my daughters. I wish I could have my time again. I would do things differently. I love Victoria and I love the boys but I have never stopped loving you. I was distraught when your mother died, there went all my hopes and dreams for our future, but I appreciate how lucky I am to have had the love of two women in my life. Sometimes it still feels like your mother died yesterday. It's strange to think I've been married to Victoria for longer than your mother and I were married.'

Charli had never thought about her father's two marriages in terms of years of commitment. In her mind her mother was his first wife, which mentally elevated her status in Charli's opinion, but her father was right. His second marriage had lasted much longer. She should be glad that he'd found happiness a second time. She *was* glad.

Maybe it was possible to love more than one person.

She turned to her father. 'Can I ask you a question?' When he nodded, she continued, 'Did you love them the same or do you love Victoria differently?'

'The love is different in a way because your mother

and Victoria are different and because my life was different when I met Victoria. I didn't think I would fall in love again, I wasn't in the right place mentally for a long time, but when I met Victoria I knew she was my second chance and that I couldn't let her go. I was older, wiser, and I'd learnt the hard way to make the most of my opportunities. I hadn't expected to love again and I think I appreciate it more because of what I had already lost. But it's not a case of loving one more than the other. I love them both, but only one of them is here.'

'I'm glad you found love again, Dad.'

'And what about you, my girl? Are you happy?'

'No, not really.' Charli shook her head as she fought back the tears that seemed perpetually too close to the surface of late. 'I miss Patrick.'

'Why didn't you stay with him?'

'I had a job to come back to.'

'Surely you could have delayed your start date?'

'I suppose so but I couldn't stay. I didn't think he could love me the way he loved his wife.' But listening to her father talk, maybe she'd been wrong about that. Maybe she should have given him time.

'Do you love him?'

She nodded.

'Have you told him that?'

'No. I was afraid to.'

'It's not too late to tell him how you feel. You only get one shot at life but if you are lucky you get a second shot at love. If he's lucky, he'll get you.'

'You think I should tell him how I feel?'

'What have you got to lose?'

Her father was right. She'd already lost everything. She had nothing more to lose and everything to gain.

* * *

Wombat Gully was serene and still. The ski runs had closed for the day, the lifts were quiet, the season almost over. Most people would probably be glad for this season to end. The site of the landslide had been cleared and a pathway laid up the side of the hill, leading to the newly erected monument that marked the tragedy.

Charli negotiated the path, stopping at each bend to take in the views over the valley. The path had been built to encourage people to pause and look out, to look away from the mountain and out to the horizon. For Charli the view was a window to the future.

The memorial service was scheduled for tomorrow morning at eleven but Charli wanted to visit the memorial alone. At sunset. It seemed like the most appropriate time.

She needed some time to compose herself. Not for the memorial service but for the possibility that she might see Pat tomorrow. She had no idea if he planned to attend the service but if he wasn't there she would go to Melbourne next. She wasn't leaving Australia again without seeing him.

She hoped she might not have to leave again at all.

Charli reached the top of the path and stopped in front of the memorial. It was a simple structure made of stone and wood and metal. She ran her fingers over the fifteen names etched into the metal before sitting at the base of the monument. She turned her back to the path and faced west towards the setting sun.

'Charli?'

She almost didn't turn around, thinking she was imagining the sound of her name, but then she heard it again.

'Charli?'

She looked up, not quite able to believe what she was seeing.

'Pat!'

He was smiling at her and his arms were open. Before his smile had time to stretch across his face Charli was on her feet and in his arms. He scooped her up and she buried her face into the curve of his jaw, inhaling his scent. Tears flooded her eyes. It felt so good, *he* felt so good. He felt like home.

He set her down on her feet but kept his hands on her waist, keeping her close. She tipped her head back to look at him and lifted her hand to his face, checking that he was real. The dark stubble of his beard grazed her palm as he turned his head and kissed the soft flesh at the base of her thumb. Her stomach flipped as his lips grazed her skin. He was definitely real.

'What are you doing here?'

She had spent the hours of the long plane flight working out what she wanted to say but now that he was standing in front of her she couldn't remember how, or where, she'd planned to start. Her heart was pounding and her body trembled a little with nerves.

She looked up at him, at his familiar smile, and as she looked into his green eyes the fog that had surrounded her for the past few weeks lifted. Her world was suddenly brighter and her outlook immediately seemed more positive. She still had no idea how he did it, how he had *such* an effect on her and her sense of well-being, but just having him there, with his arms around her, made her feel as though there was light at the end of the dark tunnel she had found herself in.

He looked pleased to see her but was he ready to hear what she had to say? She had to take the chance.

'I came to see you,' she said. Encouraged by his smile, she continued, 'Getting on the plane to go back to England was the hardest thing I've ever done. I thought it would be okay because it was my choice, I thought it wouldn't hurt so much because *I* was the one leaving, but I hadn't counted on leaving my heart behind. I told myself I was going off to a new job, a new future, a new life, but it wasn't the future or life I wanted.'

'No?'

She shook her head. 'No.'

'What do you want?'

'I want you. I want us. I want a chance at being together, in whatever form that takes.'

'Are you sure?'

'I'm positive. And there's more I need to say. Even if it's still too soon for you or if you don't think we have a future, I can't leave things unsaid. I need to be brave. I need to know that I've gone after what I want. You might not want another wife. You might not want a stepmother for Ella but I want a chance to be a part of your life. To be with you. I love you.'

He cupped her chin with his fingers and tilted her face up to his. He bent his head and covered her lips with his. He wrapped his right arm around her waist and pulled her to him and kissed her firmly. She closed her eyes as she tasted him, as she melted into his embrace, surrendering to his touch, as everything came rushing back. He was so familiar. He was home.

God, she'd missed him.

Her lips were swollen and cold as his mouth left hers but his fingers traced the curve of her face. 'I can't believe you are here,' he said. 'Do you know, I was planning on coming to you?'

'To me?'

He nodded. 'I was just trying to work out the logistics of time off and who would look after Ella and then I was coming to find you.'

'Why?'

'To tell you I never should have let you go. I didn't realise what I was losing when I let you go. I want more time with you, time to make a new life, new memories, a future. I lost the chance to make something special with you and I had no idea how much it would hurt, what it would cost me to say goodbye. I will always love Margie, she's part of who I am, she's part of Ella too, but she's also part of my past. *You* are my future and I love you.'

'You love me?'

'I do.' He nodded again and wrapped her in his arms, his hug familiar, warm and comforting, and there was nowhere else she wanted to be. 'I should have asked you to stay but I didn't think I could. I didn't think it was fair to ask you to give up everything and take us on. I knew you had reservations about being a stepmother and I think you had reservations about me too.'

'I would have stayed if you'd said you loved me but I didn't think you really needed me. I didn't think I would ever be important enough and I didn't want to be second best. But I've regretted leaving ever since. It was a mistake. I missed you and I should have told you how I felt.'

'You're not second best.'

'It's okay. I'm happy to be second to Ella. She *should* be the most important person in your life, she deserves that, it's what I always wanted from my own father. I just need to be in your heart too.'

'You are definitely in my heart. I loved Margie and I love Ella but I also love you. Love isn't finite,' he said.

'I'm not afraid to love again. There's room in my heart for all of you. Do you trust me?'

'With my life. You saved me once already.'

'Then trust that I need you in my life. I fell for you the moment I first saw you and I started to fall in love with you and your courage and your spirit while you were trapped, and then I continued to fall in love with you a little more each day, but I didn't realise it until you left me. Until I was trying to live without you. I don't *want* to live my life without you. I love you and I want us to be together. I want you to share your life with me. And Ella. With us.'

'Do you think I can do it? Do you think I can be a stepmother? I haven't had a great experience.'

'I know you're worried about that but Ella adores you and she doesn't need a stepmother. She needs a mother. All you need to do is love her. She doesn't remember Margie and that's something that I had to learn to deal with, but I don't want her to forget you too. I don't want to lose you as well. I want to spend my life with you. I want a future with you. We'll figure it all out. Together.'

As the sun dipped below the mountains and the sky turned pink Pat dropped to one knee and held her hands. 'Charli, I want to give you the peace, stability, happiness and love that you deserve. Will you do me the honour of becoming my wife? Will you love me and Ella? Will you make us a family? Will you marry me?'

Charli beamed as she pulled him to his feet. She had tears of happiness in her eyes as she said simply, 'I will.'

She tilted her face up and kissed him, savouring the feel of his lips on hers. She'd had a million questions but none of them seemed important any more.

Patrick loved her. Nothing else mattered.

EPILOGUE

'ARE YOU READY?'

Charli heard her father's voice as he knocked on the closed door.

'I'm ready.'

Charli couldn't keep the smile off her face. She was getting married. Patrick was waiting for her at the edge of the lake. She felt as if she were dreaming. She could hardly believe that she could be so lucky. That this was actually happening. There had been no disasters. Everything had gone seamlessly.

She ran her hands down the front of her wedding dress, smoothing out the non-existent creases.

Harriet and Amy kissed her on her cheek and wished her well before leaving her to have a few minutes alone with her father. They had helped her to get ready, doing her hair and make-up and buttoning her into her dress. Butterflies danced in her belly as she thought about the person who would help her to undress later. She knew how lucky she was to be surrounded by friends and family, people who loved her, and she was so grateful. She was thankful that she'd been rescued and that Pat had been patient and taught her how to love him.

'Charlotte, you look beautiful. So like your mother.'

She knew she looked like her mother but today she was going to let that support her and give her strength. She was happy and ready for the next stage in her life. She had completed one year as a medical officer at the Princess Elizabeth Hospital, working with Harriet and the medical staff who had looked after her following the landslide. She was loving her career and had been accepted into GP training in Victoria but she was also ready now to become a wife and mother. With Pat beside her, she was ready for anything.

'He's a good man, your Patrick, and a lucky one to have found you. I know you'll both be very happy.'

Charli could see tears in his eyes. She wasn't going to lose it before she got married. Today was a day for smiles, laughter and happiness.

'Thanks, Dad.' She tucked her arm into the crook of his elbow and kissed his cheek. 'Shall we go?'

Pat's mum was waiting outside the door with a very excited Ella.

Charli stepped out onto the wide veranda of the lake house and looked down to the water. White wooden chairs had been set out in rows facing the lake and the guests had taken their seats. She was vaguely aware of Pat's father and Victoria in the first row with the twins who, amazingly for fifteen-month-old boys, were actually sitting still. Daniel sat alongside Victoria and Charli knew he'd have his eyes on Amy. She looked for Harriet among the hospital staff but saw her sitting with Pat's paramedic mates. Interesting, she thought with a smile.

The string quartet from the local high school began to

play and the guests all swivelled in their seats, turning to look at the bride, but now Charli only had eyes for Pat.

He was standing at the end of the grassy aisle on the bank of the lake under the wooden arch that she had watched him build. Heat flushed her cheeks as she thought about those late autumn weekends when he'd worked bare-chested in the sun, building the arbour.

He was flanked by his brother and Amy and he was smiling at her as he waited, and Charli had to stop herself from running to him and throwing herself into his arms. Looking at him now, she couldn't believe she had once been scared to love him. She was a different person from the one he had first met. She was confident, secure, loved and happy. He had taught her how to open her heart and how to love.

Ella was getting impatient. 'Now, Charli?' she asked as she tugged on her hand.

Charli nodded and Ella took off down the wooden steps and skipped along the aisle, scattering pink and white rose petals from her basket. Charli and her father followed at a slightly more sedate pace.

Pat scooped Ella up when she got to the arbour and gave her a kiss before setting her down at his side. Charli passed Ella her bouquet to hold and Pat shook Jack's hand before taking Charli's hands in his.

He was grinning at her, his green eyes sparkling with love. 'Do you want to get married now?' he asked.

Charli smiled back at him. 'I do.'

Pat leant in and kissed her as the celebrant cleared her throat. 'I think you're getting a little ahead of yourselves,' she said with a smile, but Charli didn't care. She was ready to marry Pat, ready to start their life together, ready to be a family.

'I love you,' she whispered to him. 'I will always love you.'

* * * * *

THE DOCTOR'S
MARRIAGE
FOR A MONTH

ANNIE O'NEIL

MILLS & BOON

This one goes to my editor Laurie,
who I've finally got to work with after she spotted me
in a *So You Think You Can Write* competition
many moons ago.

Thanks to her, my confidence grew enough for me
to keep on trying, keep on writing and
eventually get my very first contract to write books
for Mills & Boon/Harlequin.

Thank you so much, Laurie!

Your faith in me has led to a whole magical world of
book writing I never thought would come my way!

xx Annie O'

CHAPTER ONE

"No TAKERS FOR the Nocturnal Turtle Tour?" asked Isla MacLeay as she scrubbed at her face, hoping her father couldn't see that it was, as it had been for the past three days, stained with tears.

"Not tonight. I thought we had some takers, but…" Her father looked out at the huge expanse of beach before them. "I guess getting the sanctuary established is going to be a bit more of a task than I thought. Here you are, lassie."

She felt one of her father's soft cotton handkerchiefs brush against her hand. She took it with a smile she knew didn't reach her eyes as her heart cinched tight. It was the second time this week he'd acted like a "real dad."

If getting dumped a week before her wedding was all it took to get his attention, she would've faked a wedding years ago.

Before her father had found her she'd been sitting against a palm tree, next to the little tote bag that held her diary and her increasingly eclectic pen collection, almost enjoying quietly sniffling away as silvery moonlight bathed the idyllic crescent of beach, where palm leaves murmured in the light breeze as the warm Caribbean sea lapped and teased at the pure white sand.

She'd come a long way from her little Scottish home in Loch Craggen, but tonight the beach had been as far as she'd been prepared to go.

She had kissed her father goodnight when he'd pulled out yet another one of his huge folders full of plans for the El Valderon Turtle Sanctuary and, not being sleepy, had strolled to the beach for a bit of a sob, leaving the low-slung buildings of the sanctuary behind her, and losing herself to the beautiful cove which they surrounded.

The billowing foam arcing atop the waves surging in from the Caribbean Sea reminded her of a delicate glass of fizz, just about to overflow. Not that she was used to champagne being popped and poured at the drop of a hat. Her fiancé—her *ex*-fiancé—hadn't really been one to plump for that sort of thing. Not for her, anyway.

Remembering his words had fresh tears rolling down her freckled cheeks. Just in case she hadn't understood what *"I've fallen in love with someone else"* meant… he'd gone on to make it plain as day.

"How could I marry you? It wouldn't be fair. To either of us. Sorry, babes. Now that I've dipped my toe into the waters of life off Craggen it's plain as day. I'm a world traveler. And, as much as it pains me to say it, you're a boring, rule-abiding, science nerd. It's just not my scene, darlin'. Ciao!"

Ciao?

The man had only flown to Italy once. He'd not even left the airport and now he was fluent?

Pffft. That showed her for falling for pretty words and a handsome face. She saw it now. Plain as the hand in front of her face. Kyle had only wanted someone reliable until something better came along. The next man she met and fell for would be a nerd through and through.

"There's nothing wrong with being reliable as a mill-stone."

When her grandmother had said it, it had sounded like a good thing.

When Kyle had said it she'd instantly heard the bell toll for the end of their marriage plans.

She couldn't help but wonder how others might have reacted—what people who were perky flight attendants in Europe might have been inclined to say.

Not that she'd met Kyle's new girlfriend. *Girlfriend!* But the rumor mill ran stronger than the mountain rivers that flowed into the inky depths of Loch Craggen. Apparently the new girlfriend was absolutely *adorable* and *soooo* sophisticated.

What was wrong with corduroy skirts, woolly tights and hand-knitted jumpers? It was *cold* in Loch Craggen. Even in August.

Which was precisely why she had packed just about nothing appropriate for her last-minute trip El Valderon. Was there *anything* appropriate, apart from mourning clothes? She wasn't mourning Kyle, exactly. But she did feel she was mourning the loss of something intangible. Either way, she needed new clothes and had promised to take herself shopping. One of these days.

Pop! Pop! Pop!

Startled into the present, she stared with her father out into the inky darkness as the moon slid behind a cloud.

"What was that?"

Despite the late-night tropical heat, goose bumps rippled up Isla's arms, then shot down her back.

It wasn't a sudden chill she felt.

It was fear.

She pressed her fingers to her eyes, gave them a quick rub, then pinged them open, forcing herself to adjust to the inky darkness.

"Dad?" She couldn't see him. He'd been right beside her a second ago!

Fear clashed with an age-old anger. Had he run off toward the danger, instead of staying with her when she truly needed him?

She squinted out into the darkness.

The gunfire sounded again.

"Dad? Daddy! Are you all right?"

Where *was* he?

Her heart pounded against her chest. Isla hadn't called her father "daddy" in years. Decades, even. At thirty-one years old she was a grown woman. A *doctor*. But fear had a way of reducing a girl to her essential self. A little girl who'd come halfway round the world to seek solace from her father when her heart had been smashed into a thousand little pieces.

None of that mattered now.

An anguished male scream broke through the roar of blood in her head as rapid-fire Spanish was lobbed from one end of the cove to the other.

She didn't have to be a doctor to know the sound of pain, but she was thanking heaven that she was. It narrowed her focus. Pushed away the fear. Gave her something to do: *help*.

She spun round and saw a young man clutching his shoulder. Her heart lurched into her throat. She saw blood pouring between his fingers. Oh no. He'd been hit.

Everything slowed down, as if she were in a frame-by-frame film sequence.

The atmosphere at the oceanside cove had flipped from tranquil to chaotic in little more than the blink of an eye. One minute she'd been quietly sobbing her heart out about her wreck of a life and the next... Gunfire and shouting erupted from each of the two heavily armed groups facing off against each other.

So these were the men her father had said "might bear a bit of a grudge" against the sanctuary.

The man stumbling toward her must have been caught in the crossfire between The El Valderon Turtle Sanctuary's security guards and the tattooed, slick-haired members of Noche Blanca—the ragtag but reportedly vicious, mafia-type group led by the island's one notorious criminal: Axl Cruz.

He had been enraged when the owners of a large coffee plantation had donated the land to the sanctuary. Her father had hinted that there had been a rise in tension over precious turtle eggs. Precious to Axl Cruz because they meant money on the black market. Precious to her father because the sea creatures were endangered.

Instinct set her in motion.

Flashes of gunfire lit up the inky black sky. An illustration, if she needed one, of why the so-called gang called themselves White Night.

Her nostrils stung with the sour scent of spent gunpowder.

A volley of Spanish came at her from all directions as yet another round of gunfire broke through the night. When the moon reappeared she saw her father.

"Daddy!"

Why were they dragging him away?

"I'm all right, love." Her father's scratchy brogue carried across the cove. "Just stay calm. You'll be fine. They only want the eggs. They won't hurt you if you do what they say. All right, laddies. *¡Suéltame!*"

She strained to hear her father's calm, ever-scientific voice rising and falling, explaining something in Spanish as calmly as if the gun-wielding *pandilleros* had come along for one of her father's nocturnal sea turtle tours.

Ever since her mum had died the man had lived on another planet. How else could one unbelievably intelligent human think he could talk down a criminal gang intent on illegal turtle egg sales?

It was why her grandmother had raised *her* to be the sensible one. The reliable one.

The boring one.

She pushed aside her ex's cruel words and tried to follow her father's directions. As bonkers as he was, there wasn't a chance on earth she was going to lose him too. Not after the week she'd had. So she did what she was good at: following protocol.

There was a gunshot victim and he needed help. *Now.*

She astonished herself by offering a polite smile to one of the burlier men closing in on her. His pitch-black hair was pulled back in a tight ponytail. If he loosened his hair and put on a smile she could imagine him as a father or son.

He grunted and looked away.

Apparently smiles weren't going to help tonight.

Her father had told her that in a good year on the black market a family could live for a year on the proceeds of a single night's haul of the precious eggs. Little wonder some of the men had turned to crime when the land had become protected.

Not protected well enough.

Her father's project was meant to put an end to the

need for violence. Create a viable means of making a living on the island. Bring an end to the destruction of the endangered animals. An end to the violence. A way to legitimately support a family. But it would take time. Time these men didn't seem willing to give.

A tall, lanky man stepped forward and grabbed her arm as yet another unhooked a skein of rope from his shoulder.

Her vision blurred as reality dawned.

She was going to be held hostage.

She turned and caught a final glimpse of her father being manhandled toward the smattering of seaside bungalows where the sanctuary staff lived. Before he disappeared she heard him shouting something about calling for help.

An ice-cold flash of fear prickled along her spine.

Help? Which one of them was in any position to call for help? She'd only been on the island a few days, and those had largely been spent sobbing her eyes out over her broken engagement. The little girl in her wanted to scream with frustration. *He* was the one who was tapped into the local support network. *He* was the grown-up!

The male who'd been shot uttered a low groan as he dropped to his knees in pain.

And just like that she remembered she was an adult too. One with the power to help.

It felt as if hours had passed since she'd heard the first gunshots, but Isla knew better than most that only a few precious seconds had passed. Life-changing seconds.

The pony-tailed man shouldered an automatic weapon. She followed the trajectory of his gun as it swung to the far side of the cove.

He raised it to the starlit sky and fired. The sharp

rat-a-tat-tats sounded more like a signal than an attempt to get the turtle sanctuary's ragtag protection detail to run for the hills.

Her heart ached for the sanctuary security team. They were gentle men—cooks, farmers, bricklayers, fathers—whose sole desire was to see an end to the violence that threatened to taint their lives so cruelly.

Ire burnt and stung in her chest, then reformed as a white-hot rod of indignation. They shouldn't have to live like this. Fearing for their lives while trying to do the right thing by their families and their community.

"Everybody *stop*!"

Much to her astonishment, they did.

The moment's reprieve in the shooting and shouting gave her a chance to listen for anyone approaching or more instructions from her father.

Nope.

Not a living soul.

Just a chance to realize that her heart had stopped hammering against her rib cage as if it too were trying to escape.

Two weeks ago she would've been hiding under something right now. Most likely the big bed in her little stone cottage on Craggen. Not standing between two gun-toting groups of men with her arms out like some sort of bonkers traffic controller.

Was being dumped more character-building than soul-destroying? Or was the truth a bit more simple.

After the week she'd had Isla really didn't have time for this sort of ridiculous machismo.

She pushed her own issues to the wayside. Her father was here to *help* the community—not hinder. Nor had she faced up to a lifelong fear of flying only to get killed when she got here.

She was here to lick her emotional wounds, sulk a little. Wallow. Something she never did. And she was *not* best pleased to have to patch together gun-wielding turtle egg poachers just because they didn't see the sense in her father's big plan.

The same father, she reminded herself, who probably should've mentioned the fact that El Valderon was more akin to the Wild West of yesteryear than a restorative Caribbean spa.

Maybe he simply didn't want to see the dark side.

Her heart softened. For once, her father had been trying to do right by her. To give her a place to hide away from the prying eyes of Loch Craggen. Regroup after being deemed "the most boring girlfriend on earth."

Well, Kyle would've been boring too, if his mother had been killed and his father had lost the plot. *Someone* needed to be practical. *Someone* needed to look after Grannie. Someone had to *be there*.

Ponytail Man retrained his gun on her. She stared him straight in the eye. Here was her chance to show Kyle Strout just what boring looked like.

She looked down at the pure white sand currently soaking up the splatterings of very real blood, courtesy of the egg poachers and guards shooting at each other.

A swift shot of resolve crackled through her like a flash of unexpected lightning.

She wasn't boring.

Nor was she going to engage in all this mopey, weepy, victim of an ill-fated romance palaver.

She was going to save this man's life, then find her

father and help him make his dream of saving the sea turtle come true.

She squared off to Ponytail Man and fixed him with her fiercest look of determination. The type she would've given Annie Taggart's highly energized toddlers when she needed to take blood samples.

Yes, she'd show Kyle *precisely* how exciting "fifty shades of boring" could be.

Fury pumped through Diego's veins. He slammed his phone against the stucco wall outside the small hospital, not caring when the handset shattered.

If Noche Blanca were going to act like cavemen they could resort to smoke signals if they wanted his help.

But as quickly as the urge to tell them where to stick their call for help launched his blood pressure through the stratosphere, it crashed back down to earth.

A patient was a patient. Even if that patient was a class-A idiot. And this particular idiot was the son of Noche Blanca's take-no-prisoners head honcho Axl Cruz. If he died there was no telling the extremes Axl would take to exact revenge.

Diego picked up the pieces of his phone and shoved them into his pocket, shaking his head in utter disbelief. It was the third burner he'd obliterated in a week. Just yesterday, as he'd been stitching up one of Axl's *pandilleros* who'd lacerated his arm after putting his meaty fist through a window, he'd thought he'd made it crystal clear. The help would continue so long as they left the sanctuary alone.

Transition periods took time. And, sure, it depleted everyone's pocket money—which he knew was rich, coming from him—but the ultimate reward was peace.

A steady economy for all the islanders. That was price-
less. And it was why he'd instructed his family's company to gift the land to the sanctuary.

He swore as he strode into the hospital, not caring
who heard.

"*Amigo!* Hold up."

He whirled round as the small hospital's head surgeon caught up to him.

"*Que paso?* I didn't think you were on tonight."

The thunderous expression on Diego's face told Dr.
Antonio Aguillera all he needed to know.

He raised his hands and backed off. "I'll call in back-
up."

"I've got it," Diego growled, grabbing a fresh pair of
scrubs and a pair of surgical scrubs from a porter passing with a supplies trolley. "I'll bring them back to the
clinic."

They both knew what that meant. These patients
weren't on the right side of the law. The hospital was
stretched to the limit as it was, and Diego knew more
than most what happened when blood was shed and
Noche Blanca were involved.

"Just a bit short on supplies." He'd ordered some in
from the States, but, as often happened in developing
countries, things went missing.

"Okay, brother. Good luck."

Anton disappeared into a nearby supplies cupboard
and moments later handed Diego a jute coffee sack he
knew would be stuffed full of supplies. Supplies that the
hospital's administration would never officially hand
over to him, despite the number of lives he'd saved that
hadn't been linked to Noche Blanca.

Diego gave his colleague a slap on the back. One that communicated all the things he couldn't say.

No one will ever be able to replace my brother, but thank you for treating me like one. We both know luck counts for nothing when dealing with Noche Blanca.

"See you in the morning."

With any luck.

"Dr. Vasquez! *Momentito, por favor!*"

Irritation crackled through him. He didn't need to wriggle out of another administrative hoop. He wasn't on shift tonight.

He turned around.

Maria del Mar.

The woman was half siren, half business mogul. It was a shame she'd picked healthcare as her means of expressing the two sides of her personality.

Running the hospital was akin to a hot night in the sack for her. The life and death decisions… The status… The ability to play God… Or goddess, in her case.

The only reason he worked at the hospital was because he'd vowed not to hold the rest of the islanders accountable for one woman's idiot decision.

Sure. It sent a message to Noche Blanca. *You wield guns? Your problem.*

The only thing was, when it was your kid brother lines got blurred.

"No time, Maria." He tapped the face of his non-existent watch.

It was a ten-minute boat run to the turtle sanctuary. He'd thought with Professor MacLeay's plans to turn the turtle eggs into a legitimate commodity Noche Blanca might back off. That Axl would move on to another island, just as he had moved to theirs some fifteen years ago.

Maria wobbled toward him on her ridiculous high heels. Why the woman was even *at* the clinic after-hours was beyond him.

He snorted.

She has no life. Just like you.

No. That was exactly the point. He *did* have a life. Unlike his brother, who'd died just a few miles away from this very hospital.

Nico hadn't been a criminal. Wayward? Absolutely. But his heart had been pure gold. When some *bandilleros* from a neighboring island had tried to move in on El Valderon Nico had thrown himself between a bullet and the eldest son of Axl Cruz. On nights when he let himself think about it, Diego guessed his brother had thought *Better the devil they knew...*

In Maria's eyes the life-saving gesture had painted Diego's kid brother with the Noche Blanca brush, and Nico had bled out a handful of miles away as an ambulance idled in the hospital's parking lot.

Would going there have been scary? Sure. But that was what bullet proof vests and the police were for. And most of Noche Blanca weren't true criminals. They were weak men, intimidated and bullied into a life of crime by someone who promised them untold riches. Riches he had no right to promise them.

The only good thing about Axl Cruz was that he liked a clean shop. Not one other gang had ever gained a foothold on their small island nation.

Better the devil they knew...

"Diego Vasquez! Where are you off to with a bag of El Valderon coffee beans?"

She knew as well as he did that the sack he was holding wasn't full of premium roast.

He slung it over his shoulder and pasted on his version of a good-boy smile. "Off to help a citizen of this fair isle, Maria. Where else?"

He never saw the point in lying.

"That citizen had better not be inked up and wearing knuckle dusters."

He gave a careless shrug. "Won't know till I get there."

Her eyes narrowed. "Who made the call?"

"A concerned citizen."

He knew the drill now. Keep it vague, then she couldn't say no. Theirs was an unwritten agreement, but to all intents and purposes it was written in stone. So long as he could use hospital supplies to treat patients on-scene he'd continue to work at the poorly staffed hospital. The second she turned off the supply room tap it would be *Hasta luego, mamacita.*

"Meet up after for a drink? Maybe we can talk about putting you on the roster for a few more shifts?"

He laughed. He had to hand it to her. If she wanted something she went for it. Her husband must have one helluva spine. Diego was civil to her. Polite, even. But there wasn't a chance on God's green earth that he would be her friend.

"I've got to go, Maria." He swung the bag back round. "Duty calls."

He pulled the keys to his motorboat from his pocket and set off at a jog. He wasn't going to let Maria stand in the way of yet another life being lost.

Not on his watch. Not ever again.

CHAPTER TWO

ISLA HAD TWO CHOICES.

Give in to the nerves that were threatening to consume her alive, proving Kyle right for dumping her and moving on to someone with "a bit more pizzazz, baby." Or she could make her parents proud.

She chose the latter.

Sure, her mother was no longer here to see her, and her father wasn't bearing *actual* witness—not to mention the fact she was saving a human versus an endangered species—but there were guns, bullet wounds and angry faces holding ground over invisible turf lines. This was the stuff her parents were known for.

Besides… These goons had her father.

Losing one parent was bad enough. And when her grandmother had passed away a couple of years back she'd been devastated. No way was she losing her father as well.

She wasn't ready to be an orphan.

"Are you going to let me go to him or not?" Isla glared at Scarface—her new nickname for Ponytail Man who, now that he'd closed in on her, had revealed a raised scar running the length of his jawline.

There was some nice stitch work there for what

looked like a massively botched job in the old "assassination with one stroke of the knife" department'. It looked more jig-jaggy than one-fell-swoopy. Whoever had done the surgery had done their best with what must have been a pretty horrific wound. Not to mention offering Scarface the preferred end of the stick in the whole staying alive thing. She'd like to meet that doctor if she got the chance.

Scarface snapped something short and staccato at her. It didn't sound very nice, and suffice it to say her nerves were shot.

"That's not much of a way to speak to a lady. Especially when she has plans to help your wee friend, here."

She pointed down toward the shoreline, trying to channel the strength and courage her mother had virtually glowed with.

"I'll have you know if that young man has an arterial bleed…" She crossed her arms and gave him her best knowing look. "He'll be dead by now. *Muerto.*" She drew a line across her neck and made a dead face.

Scarface stepped forward, aimed his gun directly at her face and called the others to close in on her.

Oops.

She'd have to work on her communication by body language skills.

She shook her head and feigned world-weariness with a heavy sigh. "I am a doctor. *Médico.*" She pointed at herself again, hoping the word was an actual Spanish word.

She'd taken an oath to treat each and every patient who came her way. Even if they had been caught stealing turtle eggs for their alleged powers of sexual prowess.

Once Mr. Gunshot Wound was in Recovery, she'd

make it clear to him that the one thing these eggs *did* produce was *turtles*—not a hot night in the sack. Unless, of course, he was iron deficient, in which case she could recommend some supplements.

See? Sensible and *sassy.*

She turned toward the young man. Instantly all the guns were lifted a bit higher. A metallic reminder that her freedom was not her own.

"I need to examine him," she said, irritation threading actively through her voice as she met another one of the *pandillero's* dark eyes.

No response.

"If I don't get to him he's going to die."

The men stared at her.

She persisted. "He could drown. Look at him!"

The poor lad was sprawled on the shoreline, legs apart, hands clutched to his chest, and the tide was coming in without an ounce of pity for a young man whose life could be taken away. Much like the baddie now staring at her as if he were carved out of marble.

This was absolute madness!

She glanced toward the security men wearing El Valderon Turtle Sanctuary T-shirts. Their guns had been taken from them and they were being tied to palm trees by yet more members of Noche Blanca. *Terrific.* When had *that* happened?

"Any one of you willing to let me know why I can't help this guy?"

She stared at Scarface for answers. He pushed her further into the center of the newly floodlit part of the cove with the butt of his rifle.

"Hey!"

She rubbed the small of her back. *No one*—and that

included gun-wielding criminals trying to steal turtle eggs from idyllic beaches in the middle of the Carib-bean—was going to push her around. Had she mentioned being dumped this week? The cancelled wedding?

She wheeled on him. "I am a doctor," she ground out. *"Dottore?"* She pointed at herself, wondering why she was now speaking in Italian.

Maybe because you're a boring GP whose only access to the world is via your television.

She pushed Kyle's cutting tone out of her head. It was a heck of a lot better than getting access to the world via an array of flight attendants' lady gardens!

She gave the pushy gunman her best no-nonsense face. The one she always had to use with Mrs. Mac-Gregor when she refused to take her insulin. Scottish stubbornness was a force to be reckoned with. If she could get Mrs. MacGregor to listen she could do the same with these men.

"I can stop your friend from bleeding to death…" she pressed her hands to her stomach and then braved mak-ing her dying face again before looking him in the eye "…but you have to let me go to him."

She pointed at the young man again, speaking as calmly as she could. Difficult with her heart trying to launch itself into her throat every few seconds.

"I need to *help* him."

She kept pointing at herself and then the young man, feeling about as awkward as she did every Christmas when her aunties forced her to play charades.

Talking slowly didn't appear to be remotely helpful. The man stared at her entirely unmoved.

He would have been terrific at playing a tree in the

school play. She tried to picture the scene in an attempt to make him seem less scary. Miraculously, it worked.

So she did the only thing she could think of that would end this ridiculous stand-off while that poor man bled into the approaching surf. She ignored the man in front of her and began deliberately walking toward her patient.

No one moved a muscle.

No guns were raised.

No safety catches were unclipped.

Not that she really knew what that would sound like, but she was over-familiar with the crime show *oeuvre* and knew having the safety on or off was very important.

Was that what she'd done her life these past few years? Approach it with the safety on?

Well… Look at her now. Here she was in the middle of a crime scene, marching toward a patient as if the Hippocratic oath made her bullet proof.

At least if she died it would be in a blaze of glory. How very "MacLeay" of her. That would make the papers back home!

She looked down at her wrinkled eyelet blouse and crumpled A-line skirt. Her hand crept up to her hair. Her auburn curls had exploded into the equivalent of a comedy wig the second she'd stepped off the plane and she hadn't had the heart to try and wrestle them into submission. *Yet.* She'd given herself a week to cry and feel sorry for herself and she was only halfway through it.

Another reason to be annoyed with these *banditos*. How *dare* they interrupt her self-indulgent sob-fest when she so rarely took time for herself?

She gave her shoulders a little wriggle and kept her head held high. Looks weren't everything. Besides, she hadn't been shot yet, so perhaps dying in a scrappy skirt and T-shirt ensemble wouldn't be an issue.

She kept her eyes glued on the young man. A late teen at best. On the cusp of the rest of his life. He deserved a fighting chance to make some new decisions. Take a fresh path. And she was going to be the one to give him the chance. Then the *pandilleros* would free her, liberate her father, and everyone could get on with their lives.

Scarface shouted at her and then at another one of his *hombres* as the roar of a motorboat cracked through the thick night air. She heard the word *médico* somewhere in there, so thought the best thing to do was to keep on walking.

Finally! They were getting the hint. She was trying to *help*. And maybe the boat was the island version of an ambulance.

The waves were just beginning to shift the sand around the boy. She pulled off her light cardigan and moved his hands away from the wound without too much effort. His strength was clearly fading. She sucked in a sharp breath. The bullet had entered the lower region of his right shoulder. His breathing was jagged. She pressed her fingers to the pulse line on his throat. Accelerated.

Diagnoses flew threw her mind. Pneumothorax? Chest wall tenderness? Only an X-ray would give a proper read on the situation, but if that bullet had nicked the boy's lung on entry there was every chance he was suffering a hemo-pneumothorax. A potentially lethal combination of air and blood filling the chest cavity.

"Me llama, Isla."

He stared at her with glazed eyes and said nothing.

She silently berated herself. It didn't matter if he knew her name or not. What mattered was whether or not she could stop the bleeding and keep him breathing. The frightened look in his eyes sharpened her resolve to help him. Her heart twisted inside her chest as it hit home just how fortunate she had been as a child.

Okay, her parents had been away on research trips for the bulk of her childhood, but she'd had her grandmother. She'd known her parents would try their best to get home for holidays. They'd make a huge event out of her birthdays. She'd been clothed, fed, and she'd always known she was loved.

It was why she'd vowed to become such a solid rock for her father when her mother had died. She knew half of his world had been torn away from him that day and, like her grandmother before her, she was going to be there for him. Reliable. Dependable.

Boring.

She gave her head a shake. Boring or not, she had a patient.

"Isla," she repeated, pointing to herself. *"No hablo Española."*

Obviously. She'd hardly be prattling on to him in English if she was fluent in Spanish.

He said nothing.

"I'm here to help."

She did her best not to look horrified when she tore a bit of his shirt away to examine the open wound the bullet had made. You didn't get this sort of injury at her "humdrum fuddy-duddy" general practice on Loch Craggen. The worst she'd seen since she'd taken over from Old Doc Jimmy MacLean was an accidental impalement when a pitchfork-throwing contest had gone wrong.

She pressed her cardigan to the wound and as gently

as she could turned the young man on to his side, so she could see if the bullet had come out the other side. No.

That scenario came with its own set of complications. Her mind whirled back to her first posting after med school. A central Glasgow A&E department. The gunshot and stabbing victims there had the entire Imaging Ward at their disposal. X-rays to locate the bullets. CT scans to check for symptoms, and any indication of vascular damage or unstable vital signs.

The only thing she wouldn't need here was an MRI. If that bullet was close to any vital soft tissue structures Magnetic Resonance Imaging was the last thing you wanted with a metal bullet inside you.

She pressed her fingers to the young man's carotid artery. *If he loses more blood...*

She gave her head a short, sharp shake. His pulse was still there. He was obviously a fighter. *Good*. He was too young to die and, judging by the impressive array of ink on his arms, and the fact he wasn't wearing the sanctuary uniform, she had a feeling that if he lost his life on her watch things might not pan out so well for her father.

She was mentally kicking herself for not bringing her medical kit on the trip. The only useful things she had back at the bungalow were an extra-large box of tissues, the small bottle of tequila she'd spied on her father's bookshelf and so far refused to let herself pinch, and her ever-present pair of tweezers.

She might be boring, but her eyebrows were perfect. Not to mention the fact she could pull a sliver out of a little boy's knee faster than you could say *boo*.

What she wouldn't give for a wound-packing kit.

What this kid needed was a hospital. And blood. An IV

line chock-full of antibiotics. An X-ray and a chest tube to get the air out of his chest cavity and into his lungs.

As if on cue, a medium-sized motorboat roared into the isolated cove. A gabble of response burst from all the men who had been closing in round Isla.

When she clapped her eyes on the man at the helm of the high-tech boat—a man with inky dark hair, bone structure that would put a supermodel to shame and body language that belonged solely to an elite group of alpha males she'd never even dreamed of seeing in real life, let alone meeting on a tropical beach—one thing and one thing only popped into her mind: *You're not to be trusted. Not by a long shot.*

Diego took in the scene as quickly as he could. Eight men circled around something or someone on the beach. The reason he'd been called, no doubt. Paz "Cruzito" Cruz. Axl's youngest son.

The pointlessness of it all clouded his heart.

A young man shouldn't be risking his life so another could slurp down raw turtle eggs in a pint of beer.

Axl told them they were brave. *Revolutionaries.* Taking what was rightfully theirs.

Cowards. That was what they really were.

Cowards with guns threatening an already poor nation with civil unrest.

He jumped out of the boat in one fluid motion, the warm sea water saturating his trousers up to his thighs. He pulled the motorboat up to the shore by a thick rope, which he tossed to one of the younger men. He threw his keys to another. They knew the consequences if anything happened to his boat.

Prison. For the lot of them.

But as it stood turning them in wasn't on the agenda. Saving a life was.

"Dónde está Cruzito?"

The men parted and there he was. The son of Noche Blanca's head honcho. Bleeding out on the beach over a handful of worthless cracked turtle eggs. They would've brought him maybe ten dollars. Twenty if he was lucky. Hardly the "big pull" he knew the kid was trying to reel in to win his father's approval.

He'd met him before. Cruzito was no career criminal. He was a boy trying to make his father proud the only way he knew how. The sooner he learnt that winning his father's approval was nigh on impossible, the better.

Diego bit back the telling-off the seventeen-year-old deserved. He'd save his life first. *Then* he'd give him a telling off. And hand him over to his father for an even bigger one.

His eyes traveled to the pair of hands pressing a blood-soaked wodge of fabric onto the gunshot wound. A woman's hands. Delicate. Pale skin. Creamy white and soft as silk. His gaze slid up her arms and widened when he reached her face.

His heart slammed against his rib cage so hard it punched the air straight out of his chest.

She was unlike any woman he'd ever seen. Utterly bewitching. Like some sort of fairy creature. The type who emerged from enchanted woodlands in faraway countries covered in snow and ice and had the power to take a man's heart hostage if she chose to.

Not that she looked cold-hearted. Far from it. Nor did she look as if she needed his help. Quite the opposite, in fact.

Her heart-shaped faced was a picture of crystalized

concentration. Her cheeks were pinked up with exertion. Her richly colored auburn hair looked as though it was made out of a millions strands of coiled silk. Wild and untameable. When he met her bright blue eyes, sparking with life, he thought the exact same thing. Here was a woman who did things *her* way.

"Are you just going to stand there or are you going to use those long legs of yours to walk over here and help me?"

He absorbed the Scottish accent and connected the dots. Doug MacLeay's daughter. She had to be. Where the Professor had a *Let's all calm down and talk about this* approach, his daughter looked as though she were ready to spit fire.

Her eyes lasered across the collection of men who had now finally dropped their weapons. "No one here seems to have a polite bone in their body. I hope you're planning on breaking the mold. A medical kit and a fourteen or sixteen-gauge needle wouldn't go awry either."

He smiled. He liked being right. She *was* feisty. Just as quickly he sobered. Axl Cruz didn't give a flying monkey if the most beautiful woman on the island was tending to his son. She'd seen too much. Knew too much. Cruzito's wouldn't be the only life he'd have to save today. Just by being here this woman had started a clock to her inevitable assassination.

The tumble of curls masked her eyes as she tipped her head toward the shoreline. "Tell me that boat of yours goes to the hospital."

"No." He shook his head. "But I'm here to help. Diego Vasquez," he said, by way of introduction.

She rolled her eyes. "Well, get on with it, then. This

flimsy jumper of mine's hardly going to save the lad's life, is it?"

The corners of his mouth twitched. Not the usual response he got. Usually it was more fawning. Sycophantic, even. More the swinging of a hip and the heave of a bosom if it was one of the island's few socialites. A batting of the eyes if it was that petite curvy nurse in Pediatrics.

He kind of liked being huffed at. But he liked saving lives more.

He rattled through a swift set of instructions in Spanish that set the men running.

In under a minute a stretcher was pulled out of the back of the boat, along with a wound-packing kit, a catheter and a chest tube.

He switched to English. "You're a doctor?"

She nodded. "Dr. MacLeay. Doug MacLeay's daughter. Isla."

Isla. "A beautiful name for a beautiful woman."

They both cringed at the cheesy line, but he wasn't about to take it back. In just a handful of seconds she'd lit fires inside his gut he'd long thought dormant. Dead, even. Dead for a very precise reason. Relationships meant caring. And caring meant loss.

He didn't do loss. Not anymore.

"I hope you've got a wound pack in there. I can't tell if the bullet's hit anything. Increased blood pressure and respiratory rate indicate the lung's taken a nick, or perhaps a bit of bone from the rib cage is lodged in there." She gave her shoulders a little shrug up to her ears.

He knew the drill. All too well, unfortunately.

He pulled out a handful of gauze packs. His hands covered hers as they swiftly packed the wound together.

He ignored the fireworks shooting up his arms and arrowing south as he spoke. "I've got a couple of IV bags preloaded with antibiotics in my run-bag. Looks like he'll need them. *Now.*"

She dropped her lids to half-mast over those bright blue eyes of hers, sucked in a sharp breath and pulled her hands away from his, dousing them in the approaching surf. Neither of them watched the blood travel back into the sea as the wave withdrew into the ocean.

"First…"

She pulled an IV bag from his medical tote, squinted at the writing on it, nodded, then expertly inserted a needle into Cruzito's arm. She connected it to the removable plug, then filled the drip chamber as she held the IV bag pinched between her shoulder and chin while he continued to compress the wound. Once she'd purged the air from the line she opened the catheter port so the solution could begin to flow.

"I hope you have a supply of O-positive blood in that bag somewhere. And second—I'm not going anywhere without my father."

"It's probably best if you leave him out of it."

"My only living relative?" Outrage radiated from her every pore. "I don't bloody think so!"

Diego lowered his voice. "If he's hiding, just leave him there. It's safest."

Giving the family land to the sanctuary had seemed like such a good idea. Now it seemed like his worst.

Life is complicated. Peace takes time. Peace takes perseverance.

"Too late for that," Isla bit back. "Two of your mates strong-armed him out of here. I want to see him before I do anything else." She held up the IV bag. "An air embolism is a dangerous thing for a man already teetering between life and death."

Something told him there wasn't a chance on earth she would really compromise Cruzito's welfare. If she really would take a life for a life she wouldn't have been compressing his wound with five gun barrels pointing at her head. Only a doctor who took her vow of care seriously would be kneeling in the blood-stained surf, prepared to give life to a man who was responsible for her father being dragged away by armed gang members.

Diego knew he wielded enough power with the thugs that all he had to do was say the word and they would pull her away. Disappear her. But he couldn't load Cruzito into his boat and get on with things without his conscience bashing him in the head every five seconds. She was fighting for her family. And that spoke to him louder than anything else could.

He turned to El Loco. *"Donde esta el Profesor?"*

El Loco, the largest of the group replied. They had him "in custody." El Jefe had rung when he'd heard about Cruzito and wanted "a word".

Diego's eyebrows shot up. A "word" could easily be accompanied by a bullet, followed by a mysterious disappearance.

This was his fault. *He* should be the one having a word. He hadn't told anyone he was the one who had donated the land. Most people thought it was government property and, as such, would remain unfunded. Noche Blanca hadn't realized until he'd got here that Doug MacLeay had come with more than his heart on his sleeve. He'd come with money. And the means to change the power structure on the island.

"Hello? Excuse me?" Isla MacLeay was waving a

hand in front of his face. "I don't suppose you have any oxygen in that magic bag of yours? His respiratory distress is increasing."

Diego produced a small tank and deftly slipped the mask over Cruzito's mouth and nose.

"And can I get that fourteen-gauge? I don't think the chest tube can wait."

"I don't have any one-way valves on me. Just the catheter hub." He opened his case, his hand automatically going to it.

"Do you have a pair of gloves?"

"Yes," he said, passing them to her.

He watched as she deftly slipped the needle into the second intercostal space, then asked for a scalpel, surprising him when she cut the finger off one of the gloves, inserted it on top of the catheter hub and heaved a sigh of relief when it began to flutter as the air released and Cruzito's gasping eased.

Impressive. The woman knew how to improvise. It was one of his specialties and he hadn't seen that particular technique before.

Diego lowered his voice and tried to make it look as if he was speaking to Isla about treating Cruzito.

"Do you know how things work here? With Noche Blanca?"

"I'm getting a pretty good idea."

And she clearly wasn't impressed. What she should have been was scared. Her father's life was in danger. Hers too. There was nothing win-win about this situation. The only way he could keep her alive for now was to make her crucial to Cruzito's welfare.

"Help me bind this packing for the bullet entry wound and we'll get him on the boat."

It wasn't a request.

She met his gaze, seemed to understand what he was saying and gave him a curt nod. She put the IV back between her chin and shoulder, then wound the gauze round Cruzito's shoulder as Diego carefully raised him and held him steady so Isla could tightly secure the gauze in place.

He continued in a low voice. "Have you seen El Jefe?"

She shook her head no.

"He's The Chief. The man who runs Noche Blanca. This is his son."

Her shoulders stiffened but she continued to wrap. Most people would have run for the hills or broken down in tears. She took the information in silently.

She was obviously running on adrenaline. He knew the feeling all too well.

He'd been in her shoes seven long years ago, but he could still remember every second of that night as if it had just happened.

He swallowed back the memories and continued, "They've run the island for the past ten years or so."

"Is this a turf war? Are there other gangs they're fighting with?"

"No. It's… There's a complicated history on El Valderon. All of the islands round here—like tiny countries…" He paused and started again. "You know how a farmer likes to 'know' his fox?"

"What? Keep the fox sweet otherwise a meaner, bigger one will move in?"

"Precisely. That's how it works here. There are other gangs who are much worse over in Latin America. Much more violent. This…" He nodded toward the hodgepodge squad of henchmen. "This is small-fry."

He watched as she absorbed the information. Many visitors refused to understand. Couldn't comprehend how might ruled over right. Especially on such a small island with a population under a million.

But fear, power and a very clear identity were effective means of gaining control. It was the way they'd won over his kid brother. A reedy teenager who hadn't yet found his place in the world. They'd given him one. Then put him in the line of fire.

Diego didn't know who he loathed more. The hospital for not treating him, Noche Blanca for putting him in front of a bullet, or himself for not seeing what was happening and forcing his brother to work for the family business.

He'd turned his loathing into action. Volunteering to treat any victim of violence, wherever they were, no matter the circumstances. No matter the danger.

"Your father's ruffled a lot of feathers since he's arrived here." He met her solid gaze. *Damn.* He'd never known eyes to be so blue. Or so unwavering in their ability to meet his. "You don't look surprised. I'm guessing you're your father's daughter."

She huffed out a laugh. "Genetically? Yes."

An invisible knife plunged into his gut and began to carve upwards toward his heart. Isla shouldn't have to go through what he had. Endure the loss senseless violence could bring.

He tilted his chin up at El Loco—the universal man signal for *Hey, pal, tune in.*

In Spanish he asked if he could find out if El Jefe would bring Isla's father to the clinic. The one hidden away from prying eyes.

"Estas loco?" The enormous bodyguard who had been with the gang since he'd been a teenager looked shocked.

"Sí." He shrugged, as if asking for the impossible was just how he rolled.

It *was* crazy. But if Diego saved Cruzito, Noche Blanca would owe him a second favor. And he was going to call both of those favors in tonight.

"Call him."

He flicked his head at the other men and issued a few quick instructions. They began forming a chain to load Cruzito onto the boat. He fixed his gaze on Isla.

"You ready for the ride of your life?"

Her jawline tightened and she arched an eyebrow. "Ready when you are."

CHAPTER THREE

Isla was discovering new things about herself at a rate of knots. Riding in a motorboat and willing a gunshot victim who was patently on the side of the "baddies" to survive apparently did that to a girl. If this boy didn't make it… It wasn't worth thinking about. Seven years of medical training had brought her to this point. And the revelations were flying thick and fast.

First and foremost: she'd do anything to save her father's life. Including volunteering to help Diego with the young teen's surgery—a skillset she had proactively stepped away from when she'd moved to Loch Craggen.

Which was how she now found herself in a well-kitted-out surgical suite tucked at the back of an inauspicious bungalow. All right. She'd been asked to help with the surgery. And it hadn't strictly been a "request" as such—more like a *I'd strongly advise participating if you want to your father to survive this sorry mess.* But…all things considered…she hadn't done emergency medicine in ages and she was pretty pleased with how it was all coming back.

Like riding a bike, her father would have said. With scalpels and suture kits and heart-rate monitors, but yes.

On the flipside, with Diego always within a meter's

reach she didn't know whether she felt protected or as if she were being lured into another charming man's web of lies. Like a Caribbean Stockholm syndrome. The worst possible antidote to her broken engagement. Her shattered confidence. The terror careering through her frayed nerves.

She glanced at Diego. Most of his face was hidden behind a mask, apart from his espresso-brown eyes outlined with kohl-black lashes. Were those eyes to be trusted? Were they really the key to a man's soul?

There'd been a magnetic flash of connection when they'd met, and it hadn't been the kind that repelled. It had been a primal response that had felt completely out of her control. At this exact moment her body's heightened sensitivity to anything and everything Diego seemed the scariest part of this whole palaver.

And that started with wearing scrubs that were patently Diego-sized. Rolled up at the ankles. Super-roomy over the shoulders.

It wasn't simply wearing the man's clothes that had her body super-alert to the brush and swoosh of the cotton against her belly, her breasts. It was that they were meant for *him*. A man she didn't know was friend or foe. And she had literally put herself in everything but his shoes.

It was an entirely unwelcome intimacy and her body was squirming with discomfort. No one wanted to walk in the shoes of their father's murderer.

It definitely wasn't his fresh-off-the-runway looks that were disarming her. Not by a long shot. It was his ease with her. With *them*. With this whole situation.

Not creepy. Or scary. More…*caring*. Reassuring. It had to be a clever ruse to disarm her. Just as her ex had lavished her with praise for being solid, steady, reliable, and then at the first sniff of something more interesting left her in the lurch.

Trust, suffice it to say, was an issue with her.

And all of this was going on whilst she knew if the surgery didn't go well she was looking at becoming a headline for all the wrong reasons.

Ecowarrior and Heartbroken Boring Daughter Found Dead in Mystery Shooting!

She shuddered as the true reality of the situation soaked through to her very core. Unless she helped save this man's life she and her father could lose theirs.

A tremor set light in her hands.

"Everything all right?" Diego's eyes snapped to hers, his instruments frozen in mid-air above Cruzito's entry wound.

"Sí. Muchas gracias."

Why was she speaking in her paltry Spanish? And why was she lying?

She forced herself to hold her hands steady, even though she was the opposite of all right. She was lurching from utter terror because—*hello!*—this was pretty terrifying and then slipping fleetingly into that beautiful, calm, quiet place that was medicine, where she knew she was in control.

She gave Diego another quick sidelong look and saw he was diligently back at work, completely unaware of her internal boxing match. If she could pull her right leg off and know she could trust him to ensure her father would be safe she would.

"I think it's best to leave the bullet in," Diego said without looking up.

"Why?"

She could have kicked herself for questioning him. This was *his* operating theatre. *His* set of rules. His scary gang of men, with an ominous overlord lurking out there somewhere, hopefully not torturing her father.

A thought struck. What if Diego was actually Axl Cruz? And this was *his* son?

Her mouth went completely dry.

Through the roar of blood in her head she could just hear Diego explaining his reasons why in that tobacco voice of his. Though she doubted he'd ever smoked so much as a cigarillo in his life. His personal aroma was more cocoa bean and coffee, with a splash of wood smoke just to ratchet up the alpha aura about him.

"Have you taken one out before?"

She shook her head and forced herself to answer in a steady, even voice. "Gunshot wounds are pretty rare in Loch Craggen. Handguns are illegal and hunting accidents are mercifully rare."

Diego made a throaty *humph* noise. She didn't need a translator to know what it meant. It meant, *Lucky you.*

A sliver of hope that he might actually be on the right side of the law flared inside her. Perhaps he was some sort of medical Robin Hood, stealing medical supplies to care for men who... Men who were holding her father captive.

Medicine. Just focus on the medicine.

"Any chance of lead poisoning?"

"No." He shook his head and asked her to hand him the hot blade used for cauterizing blood vessels. "Blood poisoning has largely been relegated to the past. These days leaving a bullet in is only a problem if the bullets are soaked in biological weapons. A double-edged sword."

He tipped his head to the side, then returned his focus to the web of open blood vessels.

"Thankfully, things are not that advanced here. There's more risk for Cruzito if we take it out. Further blood loss."

His eyes flicked to the solitary bag of O positive hanging on a stand.

"He was lucky nothing crucial was nicked apart from the lung. If it had been you know as well as I do that we wouldn't be standing here operating on him. This is all we have for now, so if something goes wrong it's better to let scar tissue grow round the bullet. Apart from problems going through airport security, the scar tissue around the bullet will protect the body from most complications. If not." His shoulders lifted in a casual shrug. "They know where I live."

A shiver of unease shuddered down her spine on his behalf. Although was he double-bluffing?

Before she could stop herself she asked, "Are you... one of them?"

His eyes pinged to hers and little crinkles fanned out from the edges as she saw the huff of a laugh inflate his face mask.

Was that a no? She didn't want it to be a yes. Something deep in her gut told her it wasn't a yes. But it looked a whole lot more complicated than a simple no.

He didn't answer, instead continued to steadily cauterize blood vessels and clean out the wound.

She took the moment to steal another not so secret stare. His jet-black lashes punctuated just how dark his irises were. She hadn't noticed they were flecked with gold before. Like dark spiced rum shot through with sunlight. Equal parts powerful and forgiving.

She saw his face mask move a bit. In, then out.

In the course of the boat ride she'd noticed Diego had a habit of shifting his tongue along his lower lip when he was concentrating. Then he'd pinch that same full lip between his teeth and slowly release it as his brows tucked together and those long fingers of his shifted through his hair.

All of which, she was horrified to discover, unleashed a heatwave of desire deep down in her most essential self. The easiest way to douse that fire was to remind herself that her life and her father's were very likely in his hands.

One tense and, mercifully successful hour of surgery later, Isla had finally willed her fingers into submission. No more shaking.

She took the clamps Diego handed her and put them on a sterilized tray. "You must be tired," she said. "Why don't you let me close…? What did you say his name was?"

"His nickname's Cruzito. Little Cruz," he translated. "His Christian name is Paz."

"That's an unusual name. Does it mean anything?"

Diego's eyes flicked to hers and cinched tight. "It means Peace."

Isla couldn't help herself. She laughed. "Seriously?"

Diego's shoulder lifted. "His *papà*'s name means Father of Peace."

"Axl Cruz? His first name means Father of Peace? He's got a funny way of showing it."

Diego tipped his head to the side, his dark eyes clouding for a minute before he looked at her and said, "Why don't you go on ahead and close up?"

Okay. She guessed she wasn't going to get any more answers on that front. The situation was far more complicated than bad guys wanting money and power.

Diego stood back from the table, pulled down his surgical mask and began clearing the area on his side of the surgical table without so much as a backward glance. The gesture felt…*huge*.

He didn't strike her as someone who freely handed over the reins at the surgical table. Nor did she think he would whimsically dole out trust and respect. He was a man who expected people to earn it.

And she liked earning it.

She dropped her gaze down to the black stubble on his throat, and just below it to where a thin leather strap hung round his neck. Whatever dangled at the end of it was weighting the leather below the V-neckline of his scrubs.

Her fingers twitched with the sudden urge to touch it. A whirl of self-loathing swept through her. She'd never had this sort of primal response to a man before. And he was her captor, no less.

As if she needed to feel even *more* vulnerable.

"Where is my father?"

"In time, *cariña*." His eyes met hers again, with that same unwavering strength.

Cariña? Seriously? The word, which she knew to be a term of endearment, felt discordant given the circumstances. He was in charge of the situation, as far as she could see. The only man apart from Axl Cruz the *pandilleros* would listen to. He was taller than most of them. Lean, but not skinny. Fit. He moved with leonine assurance. And a confidence that meant he knew his body could handle whatever he threw at it. A confidence that spoke of the power many surgeons held in their hands. The power to give and take life.

She tore her eyes from his and slowly, exactingly, began to close up the incisions with a combination of sutures and staples until Cruzito was ready to go into the small recovery room Diego had pointed out earlier. Two men were called in and they wheeled the lad away.

As they began cleaning the surgical tools a new man entered the room, with a couple of gunmen in his wake. He wasn't physically intimidating, in terms of height or musculature, but he radiated an aura of power. One that came from using fear as his main weapon. This had to be Axl Cruz.

He looked at the space where his son had been operated on, then rattled off a few staccato words to Diego.

"What is he saying?"

She would have gnawed her own arm off if it had made her fluent in Spanish. Particularly as *she* seemed to be the subject of the conversation.

The two men would say something, look at her as if they were sizing up a racehorse, then launch into a volley of speech again.

The gunmen looked utterly unmoved. As if this were an everyday sort of thing.

The only thing keeping her upright was the deep-seated need to be assured that her father was alive and well. That was it. Whatever it took to make that happen, she would do it.

When the rapid-fire conversation escalated, then reached a crescendo, Diego slammed his fist down on a nearby table, causing all the instruments on it to jump. His entire demeanor spoke of a man who had given an ultimatum.

Isla swallowed.

Was he negotiating for *her*? For her freedom? There was no British Embassy or High Commission in El Valderon. She didn't even know an emergency number she could call for help. And even if she had she somehow knew that any such intervention would only throw more fuel onto a fire that was already raging out of control.

How strange that she felt as if Diego had her back on this. It wasn't something she was used to feeling. As if she were part of a team.

Her eyes pinged to Axl.

He gave a *whaddya want me to do about it?* shrug. He'd obviously given his ultimatum too. And it wasn't one that leant in her favor.

Axl turned and walked away, taking all the oxygen in the room with him.

Diego's hand moved to the leather strip around his neck as he asked the remaining gunman a question. It sounded like a taunt. Diego kept his eyes boring into the man, until he too shrugged and left the room.

Isla watched, transfixed, as Diego curled his right index finger round the leather thong and, with one swift tug, freed the leather strap from his neck.

"Take off your gloves."

"What?"

She shook her head, not understanding, but did it anyway. Heat surged from her fingers up her arm and swirled round her collarbone as he took her left hand in his. She felt something cool slipped on to her finger.

What she saw drew all the breath from her lungs.

A ring. A beautiful triumvirate of gold, silver and

platinum bands linked together. At the apex, nestled amongst the bands, was one of the largest diamonds she had ever seen.

"What on—?" Confusion drowned out her ability to think straight. She looked up and met his solid gaze. "What is this for?"

"Marry me."

Diego was as shocked to hear himself ask Isla to marry him as she looked to receive a proposal.

When she remained drop-jawed, he said it again. "Marry me, Isla."

His voice sounded alien to him. Thick with emotion. Urgent. Not conveying the usual cool demeanor he'd worn as armor since his heart had all but been torn from his chest.

Desperate times. Desperate measures.

Isla shook her head, as if it would alter the words she'd just heard. "I'm sorry. Does that mean the same thing here as it means in Scotland? Because where I come from it means become husband and wife."

"I'm pretty sure I've proved my fluency in English." He felt his features harden. A muscle twitch in his jaw. The opposite of what one would expect from a lovestruck groom. A narky comment and a thunder face.

Muchas gracias, Noche Blanca. Once again you've managed to bring out my better side.

"I don't understand."

How could she? She lived in a kinder world. One where survival wasn't an issue. One where a marriage proposal didn't sit at the polar extreme of *Romance 101*.

"Marry me. To save your father. To save yourself."

Axl had been crystal-clear. The only way he would

back off from the sanctuary was if Doug MacLeay was out of the picture. Permanently.

Diego could only think of one way to save Doug and Isla's lives. An old vow on top of a new one.

After his brother's death, Axl had promised safety for every member of his family. And there was only one way to make Doug and Isla part of his family. So he told Axl he was in love with Isla. A whirlwind romance neither of them could fight.

Axl's response had been immediate. "You say you love this woman? Fine. Be my guest. Marry her. *Tonight*."

Otherwise…?

This was where the infamous Axl Cruz shrug had come in. Otherwise they would both go. And not back to Scotland.

It was that simple.

So here he was standing in front of a woman he didn't know, praying she would agree to marry him.

A door banged in the distance, followed by a loud volley of men's voices.

"This is ridiculous. Surely now that Cruzito is all right they'll let us go?"

Diego shook his head. "No. It doesn't work that way. You've both seen too much. Caused too much trouble."

"Trouble? Are you kidding—?"

He held a finger to her lips, wondering if she felt the same heat he felt pouring through his hand. If it was searing straight through to *her* tongue, *her* throat. What was it about this woman that was making him behave like this?

He dropped his hand and crushed his physiological response.

"They will kill your father. No question. You…?" He

held his palms up. "You helped save his son's life. That might count for something."

For a millisecond he saw fear ripple across her features. An instant later it was gone. He recognized the same mask he so often donned. The one he wore when he told patients they had cancer. Told parents that their child had an incurable illness. The one he'd worn ever since his own brother had died saving the son of the criminal who all but held their island hostage.

She nodded that she understood.

"Put on a pair of fresh gloves," Diego instructed.

Insane or not, it was a plan that might work. Why or how he'd chosen this woman, this moment, to pull in a favor he would never have again was a question he couldn't ask himself right now. Axl could sniff weakness and lies as easily as you could smell the salt in the air.

"We have to convince him this is what we want. That we met when you first arrived and that we're already engaged."

"But I only arrived a few days ago!"

"Never heard of love at first sight?"

She flushed and looked away.

Did she…? Had she felt it too? That crackle of connection?

Don't be an idiot. It wasn't love. It was lust.

He believed in lust. Passion, even. But love? He didn't believe in love anymore. Couldn't. Not when he knew how the world really worked.

"When the men come back in again take the gloves off. They won't know they're a different pair. Make sure the diamond hits the light. They need to see the ring."

Isla pursed her lips, looked at her hand, then nodded, tendrils of auburn hair masking her expression. He pulled his fingers into a fist, willing them not to tease a few of those wayward curls into submission. This wasn't the time to go all *Romeo and Juliet* on her.

She sniffed and shook her hair back, as if she was annoyed at his choice of paint for their new living room rather than being thrown into a vortex of fear and confusion. Most people would have been annoyed if their lives depended upon marrying a complete stranger.

"Do you always carry engagement rings around your neck? Just in case?"

She met his gaze straight on, defiance crackling through her blue eyes where he'd convinced himself he'd see gratitude.

She began tugging it off of her finger. "I've got an idea. Why don't you take this ring and let me have a phone so I can ring the police? I'd prefer *that* type of ring."

He almost laughed. Isla's hair wasn't the only thing made of fire.

Being forced to marry someone against your will was not ideal. Even so... He genuinely couldn't see another way round this.

He took the ring and slid it back on to her finger. "The walls have ears, *amorcita*. Best to keep your voice low."

"Why can't we call the police?"

She pressed her lips together until they drained of blood, glaring at him until he explained.

"The police won't intervene. They let matters of this variety sort themselves out." Just as they'd refused an escort for the ambulance that might have saved his brother's life.

"What on earth does that mean?"

"Too many pockets are lined with ill-gained gold."

"Are you kidding me?"

It keeps their families safe.

Diego's gaze flicked to the door, then back to Isla. "The ring. It's my grandmother's. I have never put it on anyone's finger. Never wanted to."

He let the words settle between them, but the intensity of his delivery meant they might as well have been shot directly from the center of his heart.

It shocked him to realize how genuine his sentiments were. Did he *love* her? Of course not. Would he take a sacred vow to care and protect her? Without a doubt.

Why her? Why now?

He smashed the thoughts back into his Questions to Remain Unanswered cupboard and kicked the door shut.

"I need a reason to believe you," she said. "Just one."

"Your life is at risk. Your father's life." And he couldn't let what happened to his brother happen to another family.

Isla's blue eyes glassed over, then cleared. She pulled on a fresh pair of gloves, and both of them were glued to the sight of the sparkling diamond disappearing beneath the light blue Neoprene.

A man walked in. He looked tired. Disheveled. As if he was there under duress.

Isla's eyes widened as she took in the man's dog collar.

Trust Noche Blanca to rustle up a priest in the dead of night, thought Diego.

The black thought that he might have been brought in earlier to deliver the last rites to Isla and her father crossed his mind. He slashed the thought in two, reminding himself that the poor man was more likely to be there to do the same for Cruzito.

His expression told Diego the last thing he thought he'd be performing was a wedding ceremony.

A grim smile teased at the corners of Diego's mouth. This was Axl putting him to the test. The "big doctor man" claimed to be in love with this woman? Well, there was only one way to prove it as far as Axl Cruz was concerned. Follow his lead. He'd met and married his own wife in a whirlwind twenty-four-hour romance. So Diego would do the same.

"Why is he forcing us to do this *now*? In the middle of the night?"

"It's a test."

He heard the emotion in his chest transforming his voice into something he'd never heard come from his own throat. Low, gravelly. Urgent.

"He promised long ago never to hurt my family. If you want to get out of this unharmed we must marry. I told him you were my fiancée. That we met when you first got here and fell in love in an instant. That I couldn't imagine my life without you."

Isla clenched the edge of the table with both hands. Was there a glimmer in her eyes? Just a hint of wanting what he said to be true?

¡Ni en sueños!

He was reading into things. Turning this into something it very distinctly wasn't. If he let himself go down that path none of them would survive.

Caring, loving, mourning—allowing himself to feel that triumvirate of powerful emotions had got him where he was today. Trapped by his own vow always to serve. No matter what the circumstances.

None of it would bring his brother back. But doing this one thing might ease the pain.

He looked into Isla's eyes, drilling it into his brain that doing this was purely to save the Professor and his daughter. Nothing more. No matter what the blood careening round his veins was suggesting.

Diego reached across and cupped Isla's face in his hand as a lover would. "If you want to save your father you will follow my lead."

She shook her head. Whether it was a no or a response to his touch was unclear. He pulled her closer—not to control her, but to hide the panic in her eyes from the guards as they darted about the room.

This house, a mishmash of surgery and hideaway, was hardly a dream destination for a wedding day.

He could easily picture Isla wanting something informal on the beach. A simple dress. Bare shoulders, perhaps. Some flowers in her hair. A look of pure and unfettered love in her eyes…

An insane urge to promise her something else, something better once they got through this, launched into his throat, barely giving him time to bite it back.

The gunman and the priest were openly waiting for Isla to make a move. She had seconds, if that, to decide.

Isla closed her eyes as Diego ran his hand down her neck and cupped it, moving his other hand to the base of her throat, resting his thumbs on her collarbones. She knew what he was doing. Playing a role. An insane role to see through an insane plan. But at this juncture did she have any other choice?

Her eyes flickered open as he whispered her name. When she connected to his rock-solid gaze one last time he said, "Do this. Marry me."

His touch, the intimacy, the intensity of his request—

it should have felt threatening. Terrifying, even. Astonishingly, from Diego, it felt more...*protective*. Caring...

It was a gesture that, if seen by someone who didn't know them, would have made the onlooker think she and Diego had known one another for years. Had been lovers, even. The way she naturally leaned into his caresses made it appear even more so. Little would they know it was terror at her father's imprisonment compelling her to believe Diego. Believe there was a way out of this mess.

Can you do this? Marry this stranger?

Axl appeared in the doorway and began speaking to Diego in a low voice.

Diego held up a hand. *"Momentito, por favor, Axl."*

The temperature in the room seemed to drop as Axl held his ground.

She caught his eye as he turned to leave the room. He looked at her and smiled, but there was no warmth in it.

"You're a lucky woman." He tipped his head toward Diego. "This is the only man on this island that I trust as one of my own."

Isla was about to say her father was every bit as trustworthy as Diego, but felt Diego's fingers press into her shoulder.

Axl turned and left the room.

"Isla." Diego spoke urgently now. "Listen to me. *Marry me*. It's the only way to save your father's life."

Glacier water shot through her veins. For the first time since the gunmen had shown up at the sanctuary Isla felt genuine fear. And that was saying something.

All that had seemed surreal—dreamlike, even—now hardened into ice-cold reality.

She had to do it.

"Your father's work is very important, but these men are…they're *tricky* to negotiate with."

No kidding. People who wielded guns and threatened to kill folk often were.

She pulled back, her spine braced as new fear struck. "Will it be…? Will it be a *real* marriage?"

Diego's full lips thinned. His expression spoke volumes. He wasn't the sort of man to take advantage of a woman. "It's a means to an end. You need protection. If you marry me you will be family—just as your father will be."

"You'll be lucky." She spat the words more out of fear than venom.

Much to her surprise, Diego nodded. "Yes," he said. "Yes, I will be. You may need to stay here awhile, but if we go ahead with this now we can negotiate your father's release. Get him on a plane back to Scotland. Safe."

The words were a salve to her raw emotions. Even so… "How long is 'awhile'?"

He shrugged as if time meant nothing. In these circumstances she supposed it didn't. "Marriage is something they take seriously here. You must stay with me for at least one month before—"

"*One month?* Why?" The logistics of staying away that long crashed into her solid, practical side.

"It's the end of the mating season. For the sea turtles," he qualified.

As if he needed to. It wasn't as if he and she were going to be doing any mating during this…this sham marriage.

"I—" She stopped herself.

One month. It would save her father's life.

She swallowed the lump in her throat. She would stay

forever if it meant her father could live the rest of his life without fear of harm.

"Fine. A month." She wanted to quibble. Say it sounded to her like he was making things up on the fly. She said it again so he knew she meant it.

He continued to explain, masking their chat in that low, rumbling voice of his that might just as easily be lavishing her with compliments.

"In public we must be seen as man and wife. In my home—our home—" he corrected "—we will work out the particulars of how it will work."

"The marriage?"

"*Sí, mi amor.* The marriage."

She knew enough Spanish to know he was using another term of endearment. Was he coercing her or comforting her?

She sought answers in those dark eyes of his and found solace in them. Honesty. He wouldn't hurt her. She would be safe.

This was definitely something she would never be able to encapsulate on the postcard she'd promised to send Dougray Campbell, whose blood pressure she'd finally got under control. Not that any of this was doing much for hers.

She could hear the blood roaring around her head, her heart, but when she blinked and realigned her focus on Diego's dark brown eyes she felt safe again.

What had happened to him to make him sacrifice his own future this way? If these men were as violent as they seemed and he had one favor why was he using it for her?

It wasn't for *her*. She was a means to the end. Saving her father was the goal. He was promising peace and economic stability for the island. To a man who clearly loved his home and his profession, a prosperous, peaceful nation would surely be the answer to a thousand prayers.

When the priest cleared his throat Diego gave him a quick nod, then put his entire focus on Isla. "I know nothing about this is normal. I know you must be scared." He looked her straight in the eye. "But you can trust me. We can work out how we approach things later. How we untangle the net. But if you want to save your father we must do this. We must marry. Now."

"*Now*—now?"

The priest stepped toward them.

Well, that answered that, then.

At least her long engagement to Kyle had meant she'd been dropped before the wedding bells chimed.

A mad thought flew into her head.

Had fate thrown her into Diego's arms? Had things fallen to bits back in Loch Craggen because she was meant to be *here*?

One month…

A month she already knew was going to change her life forever.

She heard the clank of a gun against the doorframe as one of the Noche Blanca members entered the room.

Violence had thrown them together. Violence that wouldn't end if she didn't agree to this hare-brained scheme. This *life-saving* scheme.

Isla's brain was reeling so fast she felt dizzy.

Her father was the kindest, most gentle man she'd ever known. After her mother had died his compassion had doubled instead of evaporating. Not many men who'd lost a wife to senseless violence would have found it in their hearts to see her dreams through.

You might have thought a quiet life with his daughter, researching otters in the farther reaches of Scotland, might be enough for him. But, no. His passion to carry on with his wife's work with endangered species had become his lifeblood.

Isla knew more than anyone that her father would be the last one to save himself if it meant compromising an endangered species. Science and nature spoke to him more loudly than common sense. More loudly than his love for his child.

In her case blood was thicker than water. She was going to have to agree to this hare-brained plan.

At least she wasn't required to fall in love with him.

Say yes. Save yourself. Save your father. Figure out how to get out of it later.

What if you don't want to?

"How can I be sure they'll let my father go back to Scotland? Safely?"

Diego dropped his hands to his sides. She watched his fingers stretch, then curl into fists as he answered. "He gave his word."

She couldn't help it. She laughed. "So you're saying if I agree to marry you—bearing in mind they've been aiming guns at me and my father all night—they will let my father go back to Scotland unharmed?"

Diego nodded, not a trace of humor lighting up those eyes of his.

Something else was. Something indecipherable.

Pain? Loss?

"And if he refuses to go?"

"For now? He must. Until the end of the egg-laying season. It is the only way or they *will* kill him."

That answered that, then. "How do I know they won't kill me once my father's on the plane?"

"They won't." His voice was solid. He didn't blink.

"Why should I believe anything they say?"

He tilted his head to the side, eyes still glued to hers. It was a gesture that said a thousand things at once—including the one that counted the most.

You can trust me.

"When Noche Blanca make a deal, they honor it." He turned and shifted his gaze to the doorway, where a pair of men in black clothes were wheeling the gurney with Cruzito on it into yet another room where his father was waiting. "They owe me."

It was all she needed to hear.

"Fine," she said. "I'll do it."

CHAPTER FOUR

"Si, quiero." Diego now understood the phrase "going through the motions." Hardly what he had imagined his wedding day would be like. Not that he'd imagined it. *Ever.* Going through years of relentless family tragedy had a way of casting a pall over the idea of marital bliss.

He nodded to the priest.

So this was it. He was halfway to becoming a married man. There'd be some hoops to jump through to get... unembroiled...but it wasn't as if life hadn't prepared him for a bit of elasticity when it came to survival.

That was how it worked on El Valderon. You picked a system and went with it. Above the law. Within the law. Or his way. Skirting the perimeters of everything to help those who needed medical care. It was that simple.

There'd be peace one day. Justice. But for now...? He was strangely looking forward to a few weeks of seeing the world through the eyes of his fiery-haired wife. A woman who looked about as thrilled to marry him as Axl had looked when he'd agreed to let Isla's father travel back to Scotland with a guarantee of safety. A *lifelong* guarantee. It had come with the condition he'd presumed it would. Isla must stay here, with her *esposo.*

In just a few moments she would be Isla Vasquez.

Funny… He liked the sound of it. Being part of a team. Doing things on his own had its benefits, but to have someone by his side…

Alto! This was an arrangement. Not a love match.

Diego spun his finger round in a *speed things up* gesture—which the priest ignored. He seemed keen on fleshing out the ceremony. The man wasn't oblivious to what was happening. It was the middle of the night and gunmen were aiming their weapons at the happy couple. Foolishly, the poor man was giving her a chance to back out.

Isla stared at the priest, her lower lip clamped so tightly beneath her teeth Diego wouldn't be surprised if she soon drew blood.

He was tempted to lean down and kiss her. Just to give that lip some relief.

Dios. That was an excuse. He *wanted* to kiss the bride. *His* bride.

The doctor in him knew that adrenaline and testosterone were overriding common sense. It was why men could roar into battle. Fear masked as courage fueled by the body's biological will to survive.

He watched Isla as her brow furrowed and her eyes narrowed as she tried to understand the priest's extensive preamble to the very simple question *Will you marry Diego Vasquez?*

A blast of heat lit up areas he hadn't thought about in the same context as marriage. One-night stands. A handful of friendships with benefits. Those had kept him running through the years. And they would carry on doing so after Isla was safely back home—because, he reminded himself, none of this was real.

"¿Quiere a Diego Vasquez por esposo?" The priest gave Isla an expectant look.

Diego squeezed her hand and gave her a soft smile. "At this point you're meant to say, *Sí, quiero.*"

"I am not going to say anything I don't understand," she snapped.

Where he would have expected to feel a flare of irritation at the fact that Isla wasn't just going along with things, he felt his heart soften with compassion. Fair enough. This was being done under duress. In a foreign language. Most people would have tears pouring down their face now.

Not Isla. He could see her battling her fear into submission—and winning. But if she wanted to save her life and, her father's, she'd be wise to follow his cues.

This was foreign territory for him as well. He wasn't a "save the damsel in distress" sort of guy. Not that Isla seemed weak. But she did need help. *His* help.

"How about I translate?"

She gave him a nod. One that said, *I'm not happy about this, but I'll do anything to save my father.* His heart twisted tight at the shot of fear that flashed through her eyes. Twisted once more when he saw it turn to anguish.

He brushed the back of his hand against her soft, pale cheek and against the odds she leaned into it. The intimacy of the moment suddenly made the vows they were mid-way through exchanging feel that much more real. They were in this together. He wasn't the white knight riding in and saving her. They were playing equal roles in a dangerous game of survival.

"He's asked if you will accept me as your husband. I

have already accepted you as my wife. So now you say, *Si, quiero.* It means you accept."

For an instant he thought her veneer of strength was going to crack. In the next he saw her entire body fill with resolve. Determination. It was an extraordinary thing to witness. The power of familial love. It made him proud to have made the decision he had. The first hit of genuine pride he'd felt since Nico had died.

"Si." She gave his hand a squeeze as she confirmed. *"Si, quiero."*

The priest pronounced them man and wife, and before another moment passed Diego gave in to impulse, put his hands on Isla's waist, pulled her to him and kissed her.

He would have loved to say he was gentle. He would've loved to say that the very first time their lips met it was with the softest touch his reluctant wife had ever known.

But the emotion heating up his veins was the past colliding with the present. When his mouth reached hers there was hunger in his touch. And fire.

The next few hours were frantic with activity. So much so that Isla periodically forgot to be blindsided by the fact that she was now, in the eyes of the Catholic church and the El Valderon government, Señora Isla Vasquez.

The whole thing was so ludicrous it was impossible to register. In just a few short days she'd gone from being engaged, to dumped, to married.

She was a wife.

In name only. Obviously.

But...

Her fingers drifted up to her lips and traced them as if that would turn back time. What she couldn't forget was that kiss. She'd never in her life felt anything like the lightning strike of connection she'd felt when Diego had kissed her. It hadn't been an ordinary kiss. Not like anything she'd experienced before. He had been tasting her. Exploring her. *Possessing her.*

She pressed her eyes tight and an image of him instantly pinged to the fore.

Tall. Caramel-skinned. Mahogany eyes flecked with gold. Long fingers. Strong arms. A body that filled out clothes in a way only a man who possessed leonine grace could.

And an above par surgeon.

The man who had saved three lives in one night.

Paz's. Her father's. And her own.

Diego was the stuff of fairy tales.

The kind that didn't always end so well for the Princess, she curtly reminded herself. There was a reason those stories didn't venture beyond the wedding.

She held up yet another book to her father. "Staying or going?"

"That one *has* to come back to Loch Craggen with me."

She gave her father an exasperated smile. "Dad. You can't take them all. We've got to get to the airport in less than an hour and there's usually some sort of weight restriction."

As if following the rules mattered anymore.

Her mind pinged to her pathetic carry-on bag with its two skirts and two T-shirts. One of each was ruined now. And she was still wearing the scrubs Diego had given her.

Her shoulders shifted along the fabric. She was too aware of the broad shoulders that would normally fill them. Though he was her husband now, there was a part of her that wanted to claw them off. To demand that for once she be allowed to be her own woman.

Not the rule-follower. Not the good daughter. Not the pragmatic GP. A woman who made her own decisions. Chose her own path. Wasn't forced to marry a man at gunpoint because her father valued turtles over his daughter.

"There won't be a weight restriction on business class."

"Business class?"

"Your husband's way of making the transition less painful, I suppose." He returned her perplexed smile with a weary one of his own. "You picked a good one, you know."

"What?" *What on earth was he on about?*

"Diego," her father explained unnecessarily. "He will be a good husband for you."

"Father!" Her nerves crackled with a peculiar mix of indignation and something else. Hope?

She tsked away the thought. "I married Diego so that Noche Blanca wouldn't *kill* us. Don't you remember that part?"

Her father tipped his head from side to side, as if wedlock under duress might not have been the only option available to her.

Was he stark raving mad?

The little girl in her wanted to throw herself on the floor and have a proper tantrum. Couldn't he see what his actions had done? It was her mother all over again. Wading into the danger zone with no thought for the family she'd leave behind.

"Anyway…" She primly packed the rest of the books

into the box without bothering to ask. "It's only for a month."

"That's what he told you?"

Isla's heart-rate careened into a sprint. "Do you think he was lying?"

Her father feigned interest in a book he was about to put into the box. "Island time works differently. So does Diego Vasquez."

Isla was about to ask what on earth that meant when, as if on cue, Diego poked his head through the open front door of the small bungalow her father had been staying in. Then he looked back over his shoulder when someone called his name.

Her pounding heart launched into her throat and her fingers automatically flew to her lips, as if seeing him brought back each and every moment of that searing kiss. It was as if they'd been branded into her cell structure. *In a good way.*

She scraped her nails along her lips, begging the accompanying pain to tear the memory from her.

Diego entered the room and he and her father quietly discussed logistics as she tried to attach reason to her physical response to her husband. Fear and excitement often felt the same. It was why people loved watching horror films. The thrill of surviving something terrifying. A physiological response to something outside of your control.

How else could she explain the powerful connection she'd felt when their lips had not only touched, but had sought each other as if their lives depended on it.

Hers had.

His hadn't.

And yet...

She looked at him, filling the doorway in a non-threatening way. Protectively. It wasn't the body language she'd experienced when he'd pulled her to him after they had been pronounced man and wife. His kiss had had intent. His hands on her body had had the feel of a man claiming something. As if he'd finally claimed her after a hard-fought battle to win her heart. As if he loved her with every fiber of his being.

But when she'd pushed at his chest he'd let go of her as if she'd been made of fire.

Would you have pushed away or pulled closer if you'd married Kyle?

Was this the point when she would admit to herself that she'd always known they weren't meant for one another? That someone else was out there?

"You two are ready?" Diego waited a moment, then gave the doorframe a one-two pat, as if their lack of response was all the answer he needed. "*Ahora.* I'll be driving you, but don't be alarmed if there appear to be… escorts."

"Axl?" Her father gave his head a distracted shake, as if this were all perfectly normal.

The two of them began discussing a route to the airport that would draw the least attention.

"I want people to know the sanctuary is still that. A sanctuary." Her father met Diego's gaze and said solidly, "And I'm not just talking about the turtles."

It struck Isla that maybe this was her father's way of dealing with her mother's death. Providing sanctuary to anything and everything he could. Even if it came at the cost of his own safety.

He was a scientist. One who understood the "risk" part of "risk assessment" much more than most. She should too, with her medical background. Operations weren't always successful. A small fever could kill. One day—any day—a person's heart could just stop.

Science didn't make up for loss, though. Not in her book. The day her mother had been killed was the day she had become an "i" dotter and a "t" crosser. The one who was *there*. The one who could be counted on. The one who would marry a stranger so her father could live to save another living being that wasn't his daughter.

Diego shifted and turned in the doorframe as a man approached the bungalow.

Something stirred in her that took the edge off the waves of fear. *Gratitude*. She owed her life to this man Dr. Diego Vasquez. A total stranger to her yesterday, and today he was her husband. Her *esposo*. It was plain as the nose on her face that he was no ordinary man. Not here on El Valderon, anyway.

She checked herself. *Not anywhere.*

He seemed to wield some sort of invisible power over the islanders. Not the power of force. Or of cruelty. The power of...*vision*. A man who left change in his wake. A man who had the power to convince her father he needed to leave his project if he had any hope of it ever succeeding.

Little short of a miracle in her book.

"Isla?"

Her heart squeezed tight as she looked at her dad. She didn't want him to leave.

"What do you think if I miss the flight?"

But she did want him to *live*.

"No, Dad. Absolutely not. You are getting on that plane." It was role reversal of the strangest kind. The child parenting the parent.

They talked back and forth in hurried whispers as Diego continued to talk to the man on the patio.

"What good are you to the turtles if you're dead?"

That was her final argument. The one that eventually convinced him to unearth his long-legged trousers. His hiking boots. Woolen socks. The worn green backpack he'd taken with him near enough everywhere in the world apart from home to Loch Craggen.

"The key to the house is at the surgery. My locum is called Dr. McCracken. There's not much to know about the house, but don't be surprised if Miss Laird nips in to water the plants. I've not been able to get hold of her yet to tell her you're on your way home."

"Miss Laird?"

Her father had no memory for names. Especially for the women of Craggen. There'd been only one woman for him, as he'd said on the rare occasions when he let himself revisit the past, *"and she's gone now."*

"She has been on the island about four years now. You'll like her. Mary Laird," Isla continued, "She has a small animal rescue shelter near the surgery—dogs, mostly, I think, but she'll take on anything. Last I heard she was nursing a seal. She sometimes does reception shifts for us at the surgery."

Her father barely seemed to register the information and she didn't blame him. If his thoughts were pinging round from topic to topic like hers were his brain was mush.

When they'd put the last book that would fit into his pack and sealed it, they stood and faced one another. He looked more weary than she had ever seen him. At fifty-eight he was hardly old, but the fine lines she'd seen round his eyes were now creases. And the gray at his temples had shot through the rest of his dark hair, giving him more salt than pepper. It hadn't happened overnight, of course. But it felt like it. His exhaustion had been accrued over years, but she felt as though it was the very first time she'd actually seen how much his diligent work had aged him.

The lines, the gray hair, the slightly hunched shoulders… She now realized they weren't just from fatigue. This was what defeat looked like.

MacLeays weren't very good at admitting defeat. Maybe that was one of the reasons why she'd turned a blind eye to all the glaring problems in her relationship with Kyle? The varied interests. His late nights to her early mornings. His crumpets and jam to her plain toast with butter.

"What do you want me to tell folk back home?"

Her heart thumped against her rib cage for a whole new reason. It was the first time her father had called Loch Craggen "home" in years. If ever.

"What do you think we should say?"

"Oh…" He pressed a couple of tentative fingers to his eye, which was quickly turning black.

He'd told her he had fallen against a chair when he was "chatting away" with the Cruz family. She believed that about as much as she believed Diego Vasquez was in love with her.

"I think I'll tell them I had a bit of regrouping to do and that you agreed to stay on to look after things at the sanctuary. You will, won't you?"

She nodded. The run-in with Noche Blanca had scared him. It made her blood boil. Made her want to stay and see her father's vision through to its fruition.

Bring peace to the island and longevity to the welfare of the sea turtle.

Piece of cake.

Right?

She forced a plucky smile so that her father couldn't see that her insides were turning into liquid fear.

"I'll come back." He pulled her into his arms. "And not just for the turtles," he whispered into her hair. "I'll come back for you."

Her heart nearly exploded with a combination of grief and love. How she wanted to believe it was true.

For the first time in her life she had absolutely no idea what her future looked like. She'd spent nearly every school holiday with her grandmother, because her father, once again, had forgotten to collect her from boarding school. She loved the man to within an inch of her life. He was her father. But he wasn't so great at keeping promises.

Maybe that was why she'd said yes to Kyle's proposal. Hoping against hope that she might be enough for an obvious playboy to change his ways.

Served her right for trying to change a man. The only person she could change was herself.

Diego, who she was quickly realizing seemed to have a sort of sixth sense of when he'd be needed, appeared in the doorway again. "Everything all right, *corazón*?"

He lifted her father's book-heavy backpack to the car as the two of them followed behind, each carrying a box.

Diego drove them to the airport in an open-topped Jeep. As predicted, there were a couple of ominous SUVs with tinted windows following behind. The Noche Blanca crew were ensuring that Professor MacLeay not only got on a plane but on the right one, with only a one-way ticket to his name.

As she waved goodbye to her father, after one last hug, then watched him disappear beyond the security gates it shocked her to realize her gut instinct was to turn to Diego for comfort.

Diego reached across from the driver's side of his car, only just stopping himself from giving Isla's leg a light squeeze. Again and again he found himself reaching out to touch her, comfort her. Again and again he reminded himself he was not the marrying kind. He'd never wanted to be a husband or a father. Even so...he didn't like seeing her face look so drawn.

"He'll be safe now."

Isla nodded and wove her fingers tightly together, watching as the blood drained from them. She drew a sharp breath, as if to launch into a speech about how loathsome she found this entire situation, then reconsidered, and, after steadying her breath said simply, "Thank you."

The words were so heartfelt they sucker-punched him straight in the chest.

He reminded himself that her gratitude was solely for her father's welfare. Not for any heroics on his part. Or kissing. Or marriage. Or any of it. She would have done anything to save her father. Just as he would have to save his brother, if he hadn't been away at medical school.

"Of course."

"What's that old saying?" she asked.

Isla drummed her fingers along her lips. Lips he would resist kissing again if he had to drain the very marrow from his bones. Isla MacLeay was not his to love.

"Marry at haste and repent at leisure?"

He gave his thick stubble a scrub. "That sounds about right."

She gave her shoulders a shake and let out a huff of air. No doubt psyching herself into her new reality.

"Well!" She unwove her fingers, rubbed her hands together, then let them land in her lap with a clap so sharp he knew it must have stung. "I guess that gives us a month of leisure," she said, without a trace of joy.

He was about to correct her. Say he wasn't sure about the timing. He'd just been making a stab in the dark last night. Working with men who circumnavigated the law as if it were lethal nerve gas took care. Delicacy.

"To us and our month of leisure!"

Without a thought, he took her hand in his, drew it to his lips and kissed the back of it. It was a strangely natural thing to do. Just as it had been when he'd pulled her into his arms after her father had disappeared into the departure lounge, and then again when they'd watched his plane rise and soar off into the deep blue sky.

Though her eyes were hidden by huge movie star sunglasses, and he'd not seen her shed a single tear, he had little doubt there'd be shadows beneath them.

"You must be exhausted."

She looked down at their hands as if they were foreign objects, then tipped her head back against the headrest, letting the wind ripple through that amazing hair of hers. Lit, as it was, by the late-morning sun, it was flame-colored.

"You're right. It would be fair to say I could probably do with a wee bit of a lie-down."

"Not long now."

She pulled off her sunglasses and crinkled her brow in that endearing way of hers.

He looked away.

This is for show only. When she's safe you'll let her go. Just as you let everything in your life go.

"I thought your place was down past the sanctuary." She pointed in the opposite direction. "We only drove a few minutes to get to your surgery."

"That's my…" He sought his English vocabulary for the most neutral description. "That's a facility Axl kindly accepted on behalf of the community."

Diego had donated the land and bungalow after his brother had taken a bullet for Axl's eldest son. Axl owed him favors, all right. Favors that would never be paid in full.

"Axl Cruz? The leader of *Noche Blanca*?"

"That's right."

"He doesn't strike me as a community-minded sort of man. Unless…" The lightbulb went on. "The clinic is only open to members of Noche Blanca."

No getting anything past her.

He thought of the scores of knife wounds he'd stitched up there. The bullets he'd extracted. The children of men who had grown up alongside his own father who had lain on that very same table Axl's son had been on this morning. There wasn't a chance in hell he'd live in that place. Not with the ghosts it housed.

"Suffice it to say it is a convenience they are willing to pay for."

"A convenience that ensures anyone in Noche Blanca who is injured while they are committing a crime receives treatment?"

"*Sí.* The island hospital isn't staffed well enough to

treat everyone who needs it. And more often than not the people involved in those sorts of activities are nervous about going to the hospital, where they would risk arrest."

"Can anyone else use it? The farmers who live nearby? It must be convenient for them as the hospital is on the far side of the island."

"No. It is for Noche Blanca only."

"What if the victims aren't gang members? Would an ambulance come for them? One from the hospital?"

"Not if they have anything to do with members of Noche Blanca. Family, friends…any kind of connection."

Saying that out loud never failed to bring a twist of bile into his throat. He waited for it to pass. "How do you mean? A patient's a patient where I come from."

"Music to my ears, *cariña*."

He meant it, too. It was his credo. A patient was a patient.

He cleared his throat and spoke as if by rote. "Here on El Valderon resources are extremely limited. The island has never had a very settled democracy since it was liberated from its colonial past, and suffice it to say not losing their ambulance staff to Noche Blanca is a priority."

"Is that a nice way of saying the baddies beat the goodies?"

"No. Not so simple."

He ran his fingers along the edges of his steering wheel to stop himself reaching out to her again. Touching her was hardly a way to remind himself that the marriage was a fake. *Facts.* Just stick to the facts and the month would soon be over. Then he could get back to his one-man crusade to slowly restore balance on the island.

"Axl is one of many men who took advantage of the poor in a handful of newly independent countries here in the Caribbean. Many people—laborers, mostly—who thought they might finally get some financial traction are still poor. Axl and his kind took advantage of them, telling them they deserved to be a part of being rich. That they shouldn't let the few who became very wealthy without sweating for it stay that way."

He swallowed back the bit of family history he wasn't particularly proud of. Isla would find out soon enough that he was one of the privileged few.

"How did the wealthy get that way?"

"Sugar is a big crop here. Tourism would make more money—*much* more—if the island's reputation for crime could be beaten. Not literally, of course," he added with a wicked grin.

He'd forced himself to keep his sense of humor over the years. Even if it did lurch into darker realms from time to time.

"So why steal the turtle eggs if they know that eco-tourism would help?"

"Have you ever cried yourself to sleep because you were hungry?"

She shook her head.

"A lot of people here have."

"And the government doesn't help?"

"It does what it can. But with so few people able to pay taxes it takes its toll. On the police force, the municipal services, the hospital."

He'd do more—work round the clock if he could—but he was drawn again and again to his work "behind the scenes." Trying, day by day, to pay penance for not being there for his brother.

"Why don't you work at the hospital full-time? Wouldn't that help with the staffing problems?"

"I already do."

He left it at that. No need to pour out his family history in one fell swoop.

She kept her eyes on the coastal road they were traveling and quietly asked, "What about *your* family? How did this journey toward democracy work for the Vasquez family?"

"You're one of us now, *mija*. Don't forget you'll be painted with the same brush."

She bristled. "Then I guess you'd better answer the question. Where does your family stand in El Valderon?

"Depends upon who you ask."

She sucked in a sharp breath. "*Ay, papi!* That sounds mysterious."

As dark as he'd felt the moment before, light filled him, like the sun coming out from behind a dark cloud. He laughed a full belly laugh, sweeping some hair away from Isla's face only to discover her cheeks flushed an adorable hot pink.

"Where did you learn that?"

"What?" She looked utterly mortified.

"That saying. *Ay, papi!* Where did you learn that?"

She pressed her hands between her knees and scrunched up her lips as she tried to remember. *Damn.* That was adorable, too.

"Television?" She sounded embarrassed to admit it. Then grew indignant. "It's what you say when you're admonishing someone, isn't it? Like, *Come on, you obfuscator! Tell me the truth!*"

He tried, unsuccessfully, to disguise his second hit

of hysterics as a cough. "No. That's not what it means. It's a turn of phrase you should save for…"

He scrubbed his hand through his hair. *Did he really want to go there?*

"Save it for what?"

She looked genuinely interested.

Dios. He scrubbed his jaw, his mouth, trying to wipe off the smile.

"It's something you might say if we were in our early twenties." *And naked. In bed.*

"Thirty-one doesn't exactly make me geriatric." She gave him a blue-eyed *Don't pigeonhole me, matey* glare and shrug, clearly waiting for a better explanation.

How did he explain that if she were ever to say it—which he doubted—she'd be more likely to *scream* it. Howl it or growl it. Moan it out of sheer rapture when both their bodies were bathed in sweat, his hands on the lower swoop of her waist as his hips rose to meet hers and their lovemaking was just about to hit a crescendo.

He cleared his throat and shifted in his seat. This was all getting a bit too vivid. And why the hell was he being so coy? He stood up against armed *pandilleros* on a regular basis, for heaven's sake. And demanded things. Demanded safety. Protection.

He snorted as he remembered pushing the envelope just that little bit further this morning. A business class ticket for Dr. MacLeay on his journey home. He'd done that for Isla. Demanded it when he had seen the horror in her eyes as she'd tended to the cuts and scrapes her father had received during his "chat" with Axl Cruz. Suffice it to say the man wasn't much of a wordsmith.

Diego looked to the sky, praying for a way to explain

to his in-name-only wife that she had, to all intents and purposes, called him her "big boy."

You want to protect her.

He'd known what he was doing when he had casually talked her through the surgery she'd helped him perform.

Protecting her.

He'd known what he was doing when he'd told her to marry him.

Again. Protecting her.

He'd known *exactly* what he was doing when he'd kissed her at the end of that do-or-die wedding ceremony.

Giving in to an urge that had been building in him from the moment he'd clapped eyes on her.

So why the hell was he protecting her now? When they both knew their marriage was nothing more than a front to save her father?

He didn't want the answer. If he acknowledged the simple fact that his body was waking up from some sort of primordial freeze, he risked opening up his heart to this woman. And that was most definitely *not* on the agenda.

Two separate lives. One pretend marriage. And then they could both go their own ways and leave this insane incident where it belonged. In the past.

"C'mon. What does it mean?" Isla had half turned to him in her seat and prompted, *"Ay, papi!"*

He dove straight into the deep end. "It's something people sometimes say to each other when they are being…*intimate*. Intensely intimate."

Isla's fingers flew to her lips. Lips he had enjoyed tasting more than he cared to admit.

His eyes involuntarily ran the length of her. He would

put money on the fact that she didn't have much confidence in herself. The wrinkled skirt and stained T-shirt she'd been wearing when he met her didn't speak of a woman who maximized her appearance over what was inside her head.

Then again…seeing her slender figure in his scrubs…

Muy caliente!

To him she was utterly beautiful. Her left-of-center looks lit him up right where they shouldn't. From his head to his toes and everywhere in between. He was going to have to squash each and every one of those feelings until Isla was exactly where her father was. Safe and sound on a plane on her way to a country where Noche Blanca would never go. They didn't "do" cold. Doug MacLeay had that on his side. And neither did they risk run-ins with Interpol, whose pockets couldn't be lined.

Diego's eyes flicked to Isla just in time to see fatigue overwhelm her in a series of little head-snaps.

"Right. Time for me to take you home and get you in bed."

She stared at him in horror.

Nice job, Romeo.

CHAPTER FIVE

DIEGO PULLED OFF the scenic coastal road after another ten minutes or so of driving. A thoughtful silence cushioning the air between them.

Or, more to the point, a horrified one.

How had Isla managed to so wildly misinterpret that phrase she'd heard again and again on television? It was more proof, if she'd needed any, of how right she had been to leave Loch Craggen to regroup.

Not that ending up married to a too-handsome stranger with her father winging his way back to Scotland had been anywhere close to the road to recovery she'd envisioned for her battered heart.

Isla forced herself to pay attention to where they were going. Get her physical bearings seeing as her emotional ones were going to remain elusive.

The road they were now on wasn't paved, but it was lined with an avenue of alternating palms and flowering trees that suggested whatever was at the end of the drive had been crafted with care. With longevity in mind.

They turned a corner and she gasped as a beautiful traditional *hacienda* appeared, nestled amidst a sea of flowering buddleia. The building itself was a combination of smoky topaz-colored *adobe*, handmade bricks and some sort of wooden beams that had weathered to a rich burnt umber. The strong earth tones were accented by sunshine and a dazzling array of flower blossoms.

There was a large central archway which was framed by an unearthly-looking bougainvillea. The purest, most deep purple she had ever seen. It reminded her of the type of rich jewel colors a prince might wear. Or a king. It was both beautiful and powerful.

She wrapped her arms round herself and shivered. *Just what had she got herself into?*

Diego parked just outside the archway with a practiced flourish and flashed her a swoon-worthy smile. She silently offered her gratitude that she was sitting down.

"Are we visiting someone?"

He shook his head, a soft smile playing on his lips. "No, *amorcita.*"

He stepped out of the car, walked round to her side and held a hand out to her as he opened her door. The way a suitor would. The way her fiancé never had.

"This is your home."

You could have knocked her over with a feather.

"What? Here?"

He turned round to face the *hacienda* alongside her, his hand still encasing hers. "Do you not like it?"

She liked everything about it. It was the kind of place she would have hoped to find if she'd done an internet search for an idyllic Caribbean home.

Talk about a man who played his cards close to his chest...

Suspicion swept away her pleasure. "This isn't something you got through your work with Noche Blanca, is it?"

He huffed out a laugh. "No! No money exchanges

hands. *Ever.* But I can't say it's through anything deeply reputable. My family deal in the sugar and coffee trades."

He glared at the house, then turned away. She guessed that meant the subject was closed for discussion. Was he one of "the few who got rich" on the backs of other people's labor?

Something told her that was true. Something else told her it didn't sit well with him.

Diego went to the back of the Jeep and shouldered her bag, which sagged in the middle—bereft, as it was, of clothes.

"You travel light."

She bristled. "I wasn't strictly preparing for a month of captivity." She threw him a haughty look. "If I'd known I would've packed my ball gowns and tiara."

Diego arched an eyebrow. "I'm sure we can rustle up something slightly more appropriate for the wife of one of the island's most prominent doctors than ball gowns or scrubs."

She gave him an apologetic smile when she realized she'd been glaring at him. It wasn't his fault she had packed with her heart rather than her brain. Somewhere way in the back of her wardrobe hung a nice summer dress or two. She screwed her lips up tight. Not that she was dressing up for him or anything.

"Well..." Diego gave her tote a pat. "Your ability to take a trip so spontaneously doubles my respect for your...*resilience* under adversity."

He gave her a small courtly bow, then ushered her toward the covered archway, its edges lined with a few dozen terracotta planters overflowing with ferns and broad-leafed palms.

As she walked under the arch and toward what looked

to be a sunlit central courtyard her stomach tightened. Could this experience be something that might actually be *good* for her? A chance to reinvent the woman Kyle had found so boring? So dull? The exact same woman she knew had it in her to be strong, resilient, courageous. Weren't those traits to admire?

She let her steps fall just a bit behind Diego's as he led her toward a broad wooden stairwell that spiraled up to a walkway that ran around the sunlit courtyard in the center of the house.

"It's absolutely huge. I thought you said you didn't have any family?"

"I didn't mention it one way or another." He stopped, his long legs looking even longer as he leant against the thick wooden banister and gazed around him. "It's complicated. Would you like to rest first? Or shall we meet for a coffee on the veranda after you've had a chance to freshen up?"

She looked down at her hands as if they would give her the answer she was looking for. She didn't think she was sleepy anymore. Not with the adrenaline zipping through her body as countless new questions whirled round her mind.

She felt Diego's gaze upon her before she lifted her eyes to meet it. He was heavy-lidded. Not tired. Or judgmental. His long inky lashes barely contained the heat in his gaze.

A flame burst alight in her very core as his eyes slowly began to scan the length of her. She didn't know whether it was fury at being treated like an ill-gotten gain or... Was it pride? Pride that a man would look at her with such barely disguised admiration? Though he was a good meter or two away, his gaze felt...*tactile*. Intimate.

She looked down, shocked to realize just how scruffy she looked. Her scrubs were not only stained with the dark red earth that made up the bulk of the unpaved roads, they were stained with Cruzito's blood. She'd completely forgotten that the clothes she'd been wearing would probably be better off being incinerated rather than washed.

Kyle would have insisted she change hours earlier—

She stopped the thought in its tracks. *He's not Kyle. Diego Vasquez is in a league of his own.*

She openly met his gaze, hoping he could see the depths of gratitude she felt that he had saved her father. Saved her. And somehow, in the process of doing it all, hadn't made her feel beholden. Quite the opposite, in fact. He was making her feel as if they were in this together.

She almost laughed.

Imagine! Little Miss Goody Two-Shoes being in cahoots with an off-the-radar doctor for El Valderon's criminal element.

Diego clearly sensed her ricocheting thoughts. He quirked an eyebrow as he waited, the corners of that sensual mouth of his twitching toward a full blown smile.

"Perhaps you'd prefer to take a shower?"

He was teasing her now. She could hear it in his voice. Playful. Suggestive. All her fault for saying that stupid phrase. *Ay, papi!* She'd have to banish it from her lexicon.

"A shower would be lovely," she said. Much more primly than she'd intended, but there were lines that were not to be crossed.

And one did *not* think saucy thoughts about the man who was effectively her captor when living in his home. That was the rule. And she was sticking to it.

Diego had half a mind to scoop Isla up, carry her the handful of remaining stairs up to his own suite and show her just how satisfying a shower could be.

But he was in his family home and his mother—back when she had cared about such things—had taught him to be respectful of women. That, and he already knew that one hot, soapy shower would only be the start of things. Which was why it was better not to start anything at all.

Visiting medical staff. Tourists looking for a holiday fling. Anyone with a guaranteed departure date. That was what he was interested in.

Isla has a guaranteed departure date.

"Allow me to show you to your room."

She nodded, caught his eye just before he turned away, and in that instant he saw a flash of fear.

A feeling of defensiveness tugged at his chest. He wouldn't hurt her. *Ever.* This was his sanctuary. He loved it here. Valued it. The handful of flings he'd had most certainly hadn't been conducted here, in the family home. This was not a place where he brought people—and yet here he was, guiding in his bride. A woman he'd known half as long as he'd been married to her. Less than a sum total of twenty-four hours. Didn't that speak to the fact that he should never even *think* of laying a hand on her?

She's not here by choice.

"Oh! Señor Diego." The family's long-term housekeeper, Carmela, bustled out of the room he was about to show Isla to. "The room is fixed as you requested. Who was it you were—?"

She stopped abruptly as her eyes lit on Isla. In the blink of an eye her dark gaze took in Isla's scrubs. The blood stains. The shadows under her eyes. The tension in her shoulders. The ring on her finger.

A stranger wouldn't have noticed, but Carmela had known him since he was a boy, and he watched as she registered the peculiarity of the situation and chalked it up to Noche Blanca.

Ever resilient, and prepared to wage resistance against the men who had brought violence to her homeland, Carmela popped on a warm smile and turned her attention fully toward Diego. "What can I do to help?"

Diego could have hugged her. Carmela's loyalty to his family ran in his veins. He knew he could count on her to roll with the… Well, not with the punches, exactly. No one had died. On either side. He had a reluctant bride, and he wasn't exactly dancing with joy either, but big picture? It was a good day.

Bigger picture? He'd figure out a way to deal with Axl. He usually did.

Immediate picture? He needed to look after his wife.

Isla was visibly wilting. Exhaustion was beginning to set in to her slight frame as the clarity of her aqua eyes became shadowed with fatigue. But seeing she wasn't completely alone with him in the house seemed to have given her a sense of comfort.

In Spanish he asked the housekeeper, "Would you mind showing Señora Vasquez her room?"

Carmela didn't arch her eyebrows or suck in a sharp breath. Nor did she comment on the fact that this had been his mother's room. Or that he had addressed the stranger standing on the external balcony as his wife. Instead she did what she always did—treated him like the son she'd never had.

She glared at him as Isla approached the doorway to the suite. *"Que?"* She switched to English. "You're just going to let the poor girl *walk* across the threshold?"

Isla's eyes popped wide open even as Diego narrowed his, only just managing to stem a laugh.

If he was going to come home married and expect Carmela to play along then she was going to call a few shots.

"Of course not." He held out a hand to Isla. *"Mi amor?"*

"What the—?"

"Do you remember when I told you we take marriage seriously here?"

Before she could ask another question Diego swept her into his arms and carried her across the threshold into a room he'd not stepped foot in for over five years.

She wasn't pushing him away. Or struggling to jump out of his arms. So he strode into the room and headed toward the—

Everything had changed.

He'd expected a… Well, a mausoleum wouldn't be the exact word he would've chosen… But Carmela had clearly taken matters into her own hands long before he'd sent her a text message to "freshen up the second master suite".

"I think you're going a bit overboard on the newly-wed thing," Isla whisper-growled.

He looked down at her and smiled. "What? You don't like being carried around?"

Her cheeks pinked up. "Not so much."

A devil lit on his shoulder. "Enough to protest…or not so much that you'd refuse me carrying you to your bed?"

She pursed her lips at him. "I think I can manage on my own, thank you very much."

He feigned a short gasp of woe. "Carmela will be very disappointed in me."

"Yes, well…"

She began to wriggle enough for him to concede that it was probably time to put her down.

"I think you probably could've introduced us a bit more…truthfully. That would've been a good way to start. I have a name. A job. A purpose in life other than being your…your…*arm candy.*"

"Carmela understands the situation."

"What?" she whipped round to look at the door, which had discreetly been shut by Carmela. "Have you *told* her? How many people know, exactly?"

"You, me, your father and Carmela."

"And the whole of Noche Blanca?" She stared at him. "Right? That's what this whole charade was for, wasn't it? For Noche Blanca? Making sure my father was safe."

"Sí, amorcita."

She gave her head a sharp shake. "Please don't call me that."

"It's a term of endearment. Like you might use *sweetie* or *honey.*"

"Yes. Well… I don't really use those terms. And I think under the circumstances they are wildly inappropriate."

Her discomfort crackled toward him as if he'd cornered her and she'd morphed into a feral cat.

No. The opposite of feral. He knew because he was the same way when cornered. It was loss of control. She didn't like it.

Well, nor did he. It was why he'd snatched back control of a spiraling situation last night. But his knight in shining armor act had taken any sense of control away from her.

They were each trying to find a way to navigate the best path out of this mess, and he owed it to her to let her know that they were on an equal footing. That they were both on foreign territory. The only way they'd get out of this was if they worked as one unit. He huffed out a laugh. Oh, the irony. If they worked as husband and wife.

He took a step back. Gave her the space she so obviously wanted.

"What do you say we take some time to have a rest and then we'll talk everything through? You can ask me anything. Whatever you like."

"What if I'd like to call my government back home and tell them I'm being held under duress?"

A shot of something hot and fiery seared through his chest. "Is that what you think this is? Some sort of *fun* I've been having with you?"

She backed up and bumped into the bed. He'd frightened her. *Dios!* He clawed a hand through his hair, then held up his hands.

"Apologies. There's no excuse for lashing out like that." He dug his fingers into the back of his neck, only to feel knots on top of the knots he'd felt the night before. "Look. We are both exhausted. Why don't we—?"

"I don't want to sleep," she interrupted. "I want to find out what on earth this is all about."

"Good. Fine." He rubbed his hands together. "Compromise?"

She gave him a wary look.

"I need a shower. You probably do, too."

"What? Are you saying I'm *smelly* now?"

Steam was virtually pouring out of her ears. Isla looked absolutely indignant.

His heart… What was his heart doing?

It was aching for her. For this insane situation. For the fear she must be feeling for her father. For… Yes, he might as well say it. For feeling imprisoned.

He had two choices here. Sit down and talk things through right now—and most likely stick his foot straight in it—or walk away, regroup, and talk it through later like a sane person.

"You smell like a spring morning." She didn't have to know he actually believed it.

She snorted. "I'd have to shower for a week to smell anything close to spring."

An image flashed into his mind of silky warm water pouring through Isla's red hair, across her pale skin, over the shifts and curves of her body. Hot blood shot due south of his hips.

Those thoughts were not helping.

"Very well, then. Do as you please." He knew he sounded as if he was dismissing her, but he needed a shower of his own. An icy cold one. "If we meet in the courtyard in an hour, say? Carmela will bring some coffee and we'll have a proper talk. Would that be all right?"

"Perfectly." She gave him a crisp nod.

He turned and left so she wouldn't see his grimace. The foreseeable future was going to be hell.

Not just because of Noche Blanca. They were a nasty irritant but they could be dealt with. The hell would be in reminding himself that he hadn't married this woman for a single reason other than to do his version of taking control. He was showing Axl Cruz he'd met his match.

That life would be different now on El Valderon. That the land he'd secretly donated to the turtle sanctuary via a shell corporation was meant to be that. A sanctuary and nothing else.

As he closed the thick cedar door behind him he felt, for the first time in a very long time, that he'd finally met someone who just might truly understand him.

And it scared the hell out of him.

As she watched Diego disappear behind the intricately carved wooden door Isla's fatigue was overridden by her first lucid thought since the entire drama had begun.

There's so much more to him than meets the eye.

She wanted to find out what motivated him. What insane turn of events had pushed him to take these equally mad measures. Marry a stranger to save the life of another one? Her father didn't know Diego. Or at least he didn't seem to.

Seeing Diego interact with the white-haired, clear-eyed housekeeper had opened up yet another side to him she hadn't expected. He was gentle. He liked to make people happy. Carmela was obviously the housekeeper, and yet he treated her like a beloved grandmother, indulging her with that ridiculously old-fashioned carrying the bride over the threshold palaver.

How many more sides to him were there?

She'd seen Diego the hero. The surgeon. The negotiator. The groom.

A lava-hot whorl of heat swirled up from her core and lazily floated around as her fingers traced her lips again. She gave her hands a brisk rub. The kind that was meant to clear those types of thoughts from her head. He was her husband in name only. A means to an end.

And yet…

And yet nothing.

He was a man who picked up his bride and carried her into a *separate* bedroom then walked away. Because he was also a man of his word. He said he wouldn't hurt her. And she believed him.

Standing here on her own was just the reminder she needed that none of this was real. It was a fiction created to get her father safely off the island.

You didn't exactly invite him to stay and test the firmness of the mattress!

She scanned the huge old wooden bed, the richly colored fabrics, the abundance of pillows and a headboard she could imagine clinging to while—

No. She couldn't picture anything of the sort.

A shiver juddered down her spine. She wasn't cold. Quite the opposite. So this was what it felt like to have someone under her skin.

Her spine straightened as yet another niggle from her past leapt to the fore.

Her ex had *never* given her this feeling. In a good or a bad way.

In fact, this was the first time in the past few days she had thought of him without an accompanying sense of…hurt? Betrayal?

She checked her cheeks.

No tears.

She put her hand on her heart.

No pain.

She tried to picture Kyle and…nothing.

So why had she spent a week sobbing into her pillow?

The truth shot through her like adrenaline.

She didn't love him.

She wasn't mourning a broken heart. She was mourning the fact that her sensible plan to get married, have a couple of children and lure her father back home to Loch Craggen had failed.

Until now.

Until Diego.

But her father was there and she was here.

How about that for irony?

The silly part of her—the one she rarely tapped into—stood up and spread her arms wide.

If her life was a musical, she suspected this would be the part where she started singing a hugely inspiring song about seeing the world through fresh eyes.

It would be quiet at first. *A capella.* She'd describe the mind-blowing epiphany of discovering that Kyle *hadn't* driven her from her home. That there'd been no need for her to leave. That she could still hold her head high. That *he* was the liar and the cheat in this scenario.

But he *had* destroyed her ultimate goal. To lure her father back with the promise of a something…*someone*… he might love enough to come home for. *She* obviously wasn't enough. Never had been. But grandchildren? Who could resist grandchildren?

It was all so clear now. Sobbing and bashing her pillow into submission hadn't been heartbreak over Kyle. It had been frustration that her father had, once again, prioritized his work over her. Even when she'd come to him virtually carrying her heart in both hands, saying, *Look. It's broken. Fix it.*

She'd truly believed he would fix it by throwing in the towel and agreeing to accompany her back to Loch Craggen.

Pffft. Showed her.

Turtles: One.

Isla: Nil.

Or was it one point each to Noche Blanca and the turtles? Either way it still left her at nil.

The more she thought about it, the more she realized this song of hers was going to be *really* long. More like an epic Nordic saga, involving travels to strange worlds, battles with evil clans, and confrontations of the totally mind-boggling variety with a drop-dead gorgeous surgeon who appeared like a Latin Poseidon in the midst of a storm.

Or a very close variation on that theme.

Diego *was* disarmingly attractive. Not that she'd spent all that much time noticing when her survival had been on the line, but now that it was down to just him, her and Carmela…

Oof. This was going to be a long month.

She gave the room another scan. It was completely plausible that a movie star might live here. Or a billionaire. Or both. It was the total opposite of her plain Jane bedroom back home. White walls. White sheets. White duvet cover.

The floor wasn't white. There was that… But this room was everything hers wasn't. Both a riot of color and the most soothing place she'd ever been.

It was huge. The size of her entire wee house back home.

The walls were a rich, buttery yellow. Naturally aged beams that looked as though they had borne witness to more than a century of Vasquez family history spanned the length of the room. There were thick teak chairs cushioned up to the hilt with jewel-colored pillows, set beside a set of French windows that led out to a balcony overlooking a ridiculously perfect sea view. Fresh flowers nestled in thick ceramic jugs and scented the air.

It was the type of place she'd never even thought to imagine herself visiting, let alone calling home.

This isn't your home. This is temporary.

She pressed her eyes tight shut as she sank onto the edge of the huge bed. A large, dark wooden-framed number that could have accommodated an entire family. At the end of it was a huge wooden chest with thick cast-iron clasps. The type of chest a woman from another era might have put her trousseau in. Or her wedding dress… stored away to share with her daughter one day…

An image popped into her mind of Diego, a swarm of children and…oh, goodness…*her*. Right there. On the bed. With all of them. Laughing. Smiling. Tickling. Hugging.

She shoved the image to one side and brought up the much more real memory of her father waving to her as he went through Security and disappeared into the crowd.

"You can do this," he'd whispered to her during their final hug. "You can save the turtles."

She wasn't one to resent an animal on the verge of extinction, but…*really?* It had been a much greater emotional blow than she'd imagined. Perhaps that was why she was being so snappy with Diego who, in fairness, deserved nothing but kindness for all he'd done.

She'd picked up her heart, stuffed it back into her chest and only stiffened a little bit when Diego had tried to wrap her in his arms and comfort her. In all honesty, she was frightened. Frightened to let those pent-up demons loose. Once she began to cry about the parents who'd never really valued her she wasn't sure she'd ever stop.

A soft knock sounded on the door. "*Señora?* It's me… Carmela."

She reluctantly pushed herself away from the bed and opened the door.

Carmela came in with Isla's bag over one shoulder and a big box that looked as if it was from an old-fashioned department store over the other.

"Señor Vasquez has asked me to bring you your things."

Isla rushed over to help unload Carmela. She took the bag, and Carmela crossed to the wooden chest and placed the box on top.

"Erm…this isn't mine."

She winced apologetically. This was so weird. Worse than being caught at a boyfriend's house by his parents wearing nothing but her bra and panties. Not that it had ever happened to her, because she was incredibly cautious in that department, but she was pretty sure this was what it would have felt like.

Carmela, however, seemed completely unfazed. As if mystery brides were always showing up unannounced and in need of protection.

The thought made her blood boil. She could have got herself out this mess her own way, given half a chance!

No, you couldn't. You needed him.

"These are some things Señor Vasquez thought you might need." Carmela looked at Isla with more than casual interest. "Can I get you anything?"

Nineteen different responses crowded in her throat. Her father, for one. Her old life. Her patient roster. Her cozy little home by a very different sea, where a half-eaten packet of biscuits lay in her favorite tin alongside the hot chocolate. She could definitely do without Kyle.

Or any boyfriends/fiancés/love interests for the foreseeable future. But…

She swallowed them all down and felt a pang of discomfort in her gut as they landed.

Did she *really* want those things? Or was this crazy scenario something she'd needed for a bit longer than she cared to admit? A chance to challenge herself to become the woman she'd always wanted to be? Fierce. Independent. Worthy of being loved.

She shook her head. "No, thank you. Everything's perfect."

"He's a good man, you know," Carmela said.

There was no need to ask who she was speaking about. A prickle of tears began to tease at the back of Isla's nose. She nodded her head. She knew that. She owed Diego a debt she could never repay. The debt of her life.

How soon would she owe him the debt of her freedom?

Carmela gave her arm a gentle squeeze. One that said, *I'm here for you if you need me.*

"Diego will see you in the courtyard in an hour's time. Perhaps some rest will help."

Like the ever-obedient child she'd crafted herself into, Isla sat down on the bed as Carmela left the room. Exhaustion hit her like a speeding train the moment the kind woman gently closed the door behind her. The bedding was unbelievably soft to the touch. If she lay down for just one sleepy second…

Diego stayed for a moment. He knew he shouldn't. That watching someone sleep might be seen as intrusive, but… *Dios mio*, the woman's beauty clawed at heart.

And she wasn't just anyone. She was his *wife*.

In name only, idiota!

A shot of unease curdled his relief at finally being home.

Axl Cruz was hardly high on the scale of globally feared gangsters. He'd barely register as a tiny dot on Interpol's radar. But here on El Valderon... Diego's hand automatically moved to his chest. The emotional scars upon his heart were traces of just how close to the bone Axl Cruz and his so-called "mischief-making" could cut. The man had to be stopped.

He pulled a light blue throw from the end of the bed, put it and over Isla's shoulders. She didn't deserve any of this. Nor did her father, for that matter. But Isla was a true innocent. He reached out, giving in to the urge to sweep an errant curl away from her face. She shifted and put her fingers alongside his. Squeezed them as if she knew he was there to help, gave a soft sigh, then curled her hands together over her heart.

He knew then and there that he would do everything in his power to protect her. To help her. And then he would let her go.

CHAPTER SIX

ISLA BLINKED HER eyes open and wondered how the room had gone from being filled with the warm glow of filtered sunlight to cozy and gently lit by a standing lamp in the corner. She examined the blue blanket that was wrapped around her and tried to remember covering herself with it. Unsuccessfully.

She bolted upright, suddenly remembering where she was and from whom she was meant to be nailing down some actual facts.

She squinted toward the French windows as her brain registered that the sun was slipping below the horizon. She must have been asleep for hours, and she was meant to be insisting that Diego take her to an embassy. If there even *were* any. This country was so isolated. Its government so new.

"The walls have ears, amorcita."

It was what he'd said when she'd starting flinging insults about Axl Cruz, after they'd finished operating on his son. Not her finest moment, but…

She rose and immediately realized that a shower was going to be essential before she went anywhere or did anything. She went to her bag and pulled out her lone skirt and T-shirt.

Filthy.

She hadn't yet figured out where the laundry facilities were at the turtle sanctuary...*ugh*. At least she had clean underwear. She'd been thorough in that department.

She glanced out the window at the setting sun. Her father should be landing any time now.

Home.

How cruel that her father should finally be there while she was stuck here in this— Well... She'd landed on her feet in terms of enforced captivity.

Her eyes slid across to the large box. She lifted the lid and gasped as she saw a pile of clothes.

There were lovely light cotton and linen tops. Some with pretty flower patterns. Some richly colored in shades of blue and green. Pedal-pushers and cropped trousers in neutral colors. A couple of swingy shift dresses she would never in her wildest dreams have had the courage to buy herself.

She held one up to her shoulders and stepped in front of the long mirror in the bathroom.

She actually sighed at how pretty it looked. How pretty *she* looked. And she just about *never* thought of herself as pretty. She'd wear it tonight. Only because she wouldn't ever be wearing it again, seeing as she would be putting her foot down and insisting they sort out this insane situation and get her back home with her father, where she belonged.

One luxuriously satisfying shower later and she gave herself a final glimpse in the mirror.

She was surprised to see how vital she looked. How alive. The color green Diego had chosen—or whoever he'd asked to choose for him had chosen—suited her fair skin and dark auburn hair to perfection. The wrap-around dress was form-fitting, but not so much that she felt she needed to suck in her tummy or worry about any strange bulges that might have appeared on her thighs after a bit of over-indulgent chocolate consumption the night she'd found out that she had been cuckolded.

She'd never felt more humiliated in her life. Or more furious.

Reluctantly, she conceded that maybe her ex had had a point. She'd been so set on her vision of how the future had to be that she had forgotten how to be spontaneous. Her drive and ambition to become an emergency medicine specialist had been channeled into her girlhood dream of playing Happy Families in Loch Craggen.

But what if her family's version of Happy Families was actually what it *was*? Everyone free to pursue their dreams?

She shook her head. Too much to think about. Tonight she had to quiz Diego.

She took a quick glance in the mirror again and gave her hair a stern warning not to go feral in the warm sea air. She needed to be at her persuasive best tonight, and if that involved employing her disturbingly under-utilized feminine wiles, then…

She caught the flash of her ring in the mirror. The ring that had come just before the exchange of vows that had come just before the most passionate kiss she'd ever had in her life.

Her tummy flipped and little bits of her tingled that she hadn't realize could tingle.

Crikey.

She was going to have to pretend Diego looked like a frog when she spoke to him.

Frogs turn into princes. And princes turn into Beasts.

Reminding herself that she was an immensely sensible woman with a very clear agenda—departure—she walked to the outdoor patio, to find Diego looking towards the sea into the embers of daylight.

"Ah! Isla. Are you feeling well rested? A bit more relaxed?"

She was feeling *something*, all right, but she wasn't sure it was relaxed.

The golden remains of the sun highlighted his warm, caramel-colored skin and the shiny black of his hair—still a bit wild and disheveled, even though his change of clothes and freshly shaved face indicated that he'd showered. She caught her fingers in their first full-on act of betrayal. They were itching to touch his hair. Touch *him*.

Which was why turning around and leaving when she felt him all but devouring her with his eyes was the wisest course of action.

She pulled herself up short.

"Would Señora Vasquez like a glass of wine?"

Isla stared at Carmela, wondering how on earth she'd appeared on the seaside patio without so much as a whisper of a noise.

"Isla, please. *Por favor.* Please call me Isla." She tried to add a message with her eyes… *Could you also rescue me from this sexy man? My husband?*

"*Si, señora.* Would you like a glass of wine? Or some *sangria*?"

Her throat was scratchy and dry. "*Sangria* would be lovely," she croaked.

She glanced back at Diego and saw he was still looking at her through eyes cast down at half-mast. He wasn't judging—he was assessing. And when his lifted his gaze to meet hers she saw an insatiable hunger in them.

Why had she worn the dress? She should have worn the pedal-pushers and the one long-sleeved top she'd found in the treasure trove of new clothes.

He blinked, and when he opened his eyes again they were cool. Completely absent was the heat she was certain she'd seen burning bright in them not milliseconds ago. Ice-cold. As if she were little more than someone he was obliged to greet when they passed one another in the street.

"I trust you slept well?"

It was a simple enough question. Yet she found she was standing there like a mute idiot.

How stark a reminder did she need that Diego was someone who played by a different set of rules? Rules that knew justice wasn't always found at the bottom of a judge's gavel.

She dropped her gaze to his mouth. A mouth that could be cruel at the flip of a coin. And ridiculously sensual if it was crashing down on a woman's mouth and claiming her as his own. For example...

Well, she was simply going to have to ignore his mouth. And his hair. And every other damn attractive thing about him.

"Are you all right, Isla?"

Diego had the cheek to switch moods again. Act as if he cared. Well, he could just bloody carry on trying. She was immune to him and his chameleon nature.

She crossed her arms and nodded. Sure. She was A-Okay. Wasn't *every* woman who had just gone through one of the most traumatic events of her life and then found herself married and captive in an absolutely perfect *hacienda* by the sea?

He crossed to her and led her to a nearby oak bench, piled abundantly with peacock-colored pillows and cushions.

"Here. Take a seat. Carmela will be back with your drink soon. Would you like some water?"

He lifted a jug weighted with water, the cool beads of perspiration on the outside of the dark blue glass indicating it was icy cold. She had half a mind to grab it and pour it on top of herself. Or him. But all she could do was nod, silently thanking the heavens that he didn't know what was going on in her brain.

One glass of water later she had knocked some proper Scottish common sense back into herself.

"So…" She sat primly on the edge of the bench, which was all but begging her to lean back into its pile of cushions with a sigh and a smile. "I suppose we have a fair amount of territory to cover…"

Diego lifted one of his eyebrows, amusement dancing through his eyes. "That's one way to put it."

He glanced into the house, then took a seat on a deep armchair catty-corner to her. His knees nearly touched hers. She shifted in the opposite direction. If they were going to do this, he was going to have to respect her personal space!

"Right." She gave her lap a little pat with her hands. "I suppose you could start by telling me who you really are."

"Are we talking on an existential level or just bare bones facts?"

Diego enjoyed watching Isla's hackles fly up and then swiftly, as she clocked his dry tone, seeing her frown straighten into a *ha-ha, very funny* smirk. A swell of pride that he'd eased the tension in those two little furrows between her eyebrows needled his resolve to keep this entire conversation as neutral as possible.

"Facts will do perfectly well, thank you very much."
She gave a curt nod.

She was adorable when she was being prim. But he
wouldn't belittle her by more teasing. Heaven knew, the
woman had been through more than enough over the
past twenty-four hours. But by God he was tempted. Her
smile was far more rewarding than her frown.

"*Ahora.* Shall I start at the beginning? Or are you
happy if I give you a quick overview and then you can
ask questions from there?"

"Quick overview," she said, without a moment's hes-
itation.

"Don't you want any time to think about that?"

She shot him a look.

There went his vow not to tease her anymore. He quite
liked it—seeing the flash of frustration, the quick dawning of recognition, the sharp wit whirling away behind
those blue eyes of hers, the smile that brought out a tiny
dimple in her left cheek.

"Right—"

He stopped as Carmela slid cool drinks onto the tiled
table between them and left the semi-enclosed patio area
as silently as she'd appeared. He swore the woman must
have been a trained ninja in a past life. And a Michelin-
starred chef. He made a quick mental note to ask her to
cook one or two of his favorites for Isla. He'd love to see
her reaction to them.

He pulled his eyes away from Isla's lips as they parted
to draw in a cool draught of the *sangria* and forced himself to start speaking again. This wasn't business. But it
most distinctly wasn't—couldn't be—pleasure. Not only
would he feel as if he was taking advantage of Isla, he'd

be breaking a seven-year vow to avenge his brother's death with the one thing Axl Cruz would loathe: peace.

"Fifteen years ago the government of El Valderon changed. But the new government has struggled to hold on to power."

"What is the biggest problem?"

"It needs a strong leader who can guide the country away from its colonial past. The rich are still rich and the poor are still for the most part very poor."

He watched as Isla's eyes scanned the beautifully appointed courtyard. This place oozed old money. After his parents' marriage had fallen to pieces, in the wake of Nico's death, he'd quietly taken the reins and turned most of his family's enterprises into more community friendly affairs. Fairtrade. Co-ops.

But there were a lot of hurdles yet to cross before they were truly egalitarian. And not everyone was happy with his plan to employ known Noche Blanca members.

Memories ran long and deep on El Valderon. It would take generations before the Vasquez name wasn't accompanied by a sneer. Over the past few hundred years they had done much more harm than good.

Isla was looking at him. Silently. Expectantly.

"I don't think I need to say which side of the coin my family were on."

"The gold-plated one?" Isla asked with a glint in her eye.

He nodded.

"Well, lucky me." She didn't sound as though she felt lucky. "Landing the island's most eligible bachelor."

He barked out a laugh. It was obvious she was trying to be narky. Funnily enough, it felt refreshing to have someone not treating him like royalty.

"Suffice it to say that when we go out tomorrow you will be on the receiving end of—"

"Wait a minute," Isla cut in sharply. "What do you mean, when we go out tomorrow? I thought I'd be holed up like Rapunzel or Briar Rose for the next thirty days."

All signs of humor dropped from his face as he leant forward, elbows on knees, and looked her straight in the eye. "I know what happened last night might seem a million miles away—"

"On the contrary," she bridled. "It's all still feeling very real! This time last night I was destined for spinsterhood and a life of giving unwelcome lectures on the merits of a low-fat diet for the rest of my life, all the while wondering if my father was dead or alive."

There was a lot of information there. Spinsterhood? Fear for her father? Had she suspected he was somewhere dangerous? What had prompted her to come if she knew it was dangerous?

You would've faced a firing squad if it would have saved Nico.

He wasn't going to touch on her love-life. Too personal. That, and he didn't really like the idea of Isla with another man. He went for as neutral a comment as he could.

"He's a bit of an eco-warrior, your father."

Her eyebrows shot up as high as they would go. "That's putting it mildly. He's like a one-man army. If my mother hadn't—" She clapped her hand over her mouth, shook her head, then reached for her glass and took another long drink.

Had her eyes filled up? Whatever had happened with her mother, she didn't want to talk about it. Fair enough. Mothers was a complicated topic for him too.

His mother managed to appear here at the *hacienda* once a year at best. Usually with the pretense of giving him a surprise birthday party, though the dates never actually coincided. He knew as well as she did that grown men didn't really need their mothers to throw them birthday parties. And she never refused the transfer he always put into whatever international bank account she accidentally-on-purpose mentioned "in passing."

"Are you in touch with her? Your mother?" he asked Isla.

"No."

He clearly wasn't getting any more than that. Fair enough. This was supposed to be about her current predicament, not her past.

"I thought you should come with me when I go to work at the hospital tomorrow. Seeing as news will travel fast that you're my new bride."

"Wait… At the hospital? And how on earth will anyone know we're—?" She stopped herself as her ring caught the light of the stained-glass table lamp and threw a rainbow on her face. "The airport." She answered her own question. "We were together at the sanctuary and the airport. I still don't understand why Axl Cruz didn't oversee that himself… My father's departure."

"It's a power thing. He wants people to know your father was doing his bidding. Word would have spread about Cruzito and Axl would have seen taking no action as a sign of weakness."

"But my father wasn't the one to shoot him," Isla protested.

"No, but one of the security guards he was paying did."

She gold-fished for a minute, then asked, "So why do we need to go to the hospital?"

"One—because I work there. Two—I run a mobile clinic which I think you would find interesting."

"I can't believe the hospital employs you when they must know you also work for those...those *criminals*."

He felt the familiar wash of darkness cloud his heart. "I treat *patients*. Besides..." He heard his voice turn as crisply efficient as hers had earlier. "I don't work for Axl Cruz. Nor do I draw a salary from the hospital. As you can see, I have ample wealth. I want for nothing. I work for *me*. That's it."

She absorbed his tone, the stony features, the rigid set of his shoulders, and nodded. "Of course. I see."

He could tell that she didn't. That she knew there was something more. And that she was frightened enough by his dark mood-swing not to press.

Just tell her about your brother!

He took a long draught of his drink, then refilled both their glasses. He wasn't used to this. Having someone to talk with. Someone he could genuinely confide in. Carmela knew everything about him, making talking to her a moot point. Besides, she and her family were dependent on him. It automatically created a barrier between them.

Unlike that perfectly natural marriage at gunpoint you shared with Isla...

She'd not shown fear. She'd shown resourcefulness. And right now she was sitting here, waiting for him to give her a damn good explanation as to what had happened last night and why the hell he had plans to parade her around El Valderon.

So he told her the truth.

"Seven years ago my brother died. The hospital refused to send an ambulance when they heard he was the victim of a gunshot wound."

She sat forward in her chair and the space she'd obviously tried to keep between them dissolved. "You mean he was part of Noche Blanca?"

"No. It's more complicated than that." He drained his glass again. "When he was a teenager Nico had meningococcal septicemia."

"He was lucky he didn't die."

"He *did* die," Diego bit out. "That's the point."

Isla's brows cinched together as she waited for him to flesh out the story.

He drew a ragged breath, then continued. "Nico was the family favorite. He was a few years younger than me. The puppy I never had."

"Interesting analogy."

"Are you an only child?"

She nodded.

A wistful smile hit him, and left just as suddenly. "Suffice it to say, little brothers are like happy-go-lucky puppies with big dreams. Nico bewitched us all with his plans for the future. He was going to be an architect. Draw tourists to El Valderon with his whimsical creations. He was hoping he would open art museums and restaurants, showcasing local food and crafts. He was friends with everyone. Especially young men his own age who were…vulnerable. Easily persuaded."

"Easily persuaded by Axl Cruz?"

"One and the same. Long story short: Axl used to live on another island. He was big in the petty crime department there until a bigger man from a bigger island moved in. It's the way it seems to work. Turf-building. So Axl moved here, sensing a weak link as we moved toward democracy. A lot of the jobs that were manual had been mechanized or consolidated when the last government took over. Axl collected the unemployed, made them hangers-on. Then Nico fell ill and my world changed."

"That's when you decided to become a doctor?"

"*Sí. Exacto.* I had originally planned to follow in my father's footsteps. Run the family business. Provide for future generations of the Vasquez family and, of course, the people of El Valderon. I knew things were changing. My father didn't. But when Nico was ill I felt so powerless…"

His eyes caught and cinched with Isla's, but just as quickly he tore them away. He didn't want to feel vulnerable. Not now. Not ever.

In a monotone he continued. It was a painful story to tell and very few people tore it out of him. And by very few he meant only Isla.

"The meningitis damaged his brain. He was permanently a fourteen-year-old boy from that point on. He got mixed up with Noche Blanca, but not for the reasons most people thought. He was vulnerable. Wanted to be friends with anyone. Thought he could convince everyone to be friends with him. One day he got caught in the crossfire between Axl's oldest son and a shopkeeper. The boys were idiots. Untrained and wielding weapons they had no business having. There was too much chaos, and the hospital didn't want to risk the lives of their staff."

"So that's why you began to help Noche Blanca once you'd finished med school?"

How did she do it? See straight into his soul? As obvious as it was to him, not one single person had ever connected the dots. *Not. One.*

People had thought quite the opposite. That he'd become a lawyer. Go into politics. Anything that could help him wreak revenge. But he didn't want revenge. He wanted change.

"Got it in one."

"And has working with Noche Blanca helped?"

He shook his head. Some days he thought yes. Other days he didn't have a clue.

Isla's lips eased into a conspiratorial smile. "Keep your friends close and your enemies closer?"

He returned the smile. "Something like that."

"Fair enough."

Unexpectedly, she laughed.

"What?"

"Your situation reminds me of trying to get one of my patients to quit smoking. Dougray Campbell. We have a deal. Each year he'll take his daily count down by one."

"Slow and steady wins the race?"

She nodded. She was trying to tell him she understood. That she knew the changes he passionately sought wouldn't happen overnight.

He raised his glass. She lifted hers to meet his and together they drank. Their first toast as a married couple. To understanding how complicated the world was.

"So…" Isla put her glass down and looked him straight in the eye. "Seeing as you're keeping me even closer, what does that make me? A frenemy?"

"My wife."

Her flush of response pummeled any perspective he might have had on the scenario to smithereens.

"Right." Isla gave her lap a decisive pat. "If we're to go to the hospital for you to show me off, I'd like to make it very clear I'm not planning on lying around eating bonbons."

"Oh, no." If there was one thing he was certain about, the only way she'd be leaving this house would be under his watchful eye. And he couldn't do that at work. "You can consider yourself on holiday for the next month. Your honeymoon."

"Not without you taking precisely the same honeymoon, I'm not."

She could see from his gritted teeth that he wasn't going to be honeymooning anytime soon.

"I'm not just a show pony. I want to work."

"I see." He adopted a casual air, pulling his ankle atop his knee before leaning back into his chair. "And what is it, exactly, that you plan on doing?"

She ticked points off on her fingers. "I'd like to make sure the sanctuary stays safe. The best way to do that would be for me to be there. All day. Every day."

"No." She wouldn't be safe there. Not on her own.

She ignored him. "Turtles aren't really my thing, though, and, as such, I'd like to turn my father's bungalow into a health clinic."

"Absolutely not."

"Yes. Absolutely *yes*." She glared at him and made a *zip your lip* gesture. "I think this clinic should be about preventative medicine rather than emergency medicine. It should sending a message that I'm here to *prevent* bad things from happening—not cause them."

She would be sending a message, all right. One straight to the heart of a community that ached for peace.

"Don't you think you'd be better off doing this at the hospital?" He wanted her to say yes. *Needed* her to say yes. Not that he should care. He refused to let himself care about her.

Then why did you step in and marry the woman?

"No," she said.

He lifted his hands to the heavens. *Surprise, surprise.*

"As I said, I'd like to keep an eye on the sanctuary and it's the best way for me to do that."

"People will be frightened to go there right now. Perhaps if you start at the mobile clinic I run for the hospital and move over to the sanctuary once you've made your point it would be better…"

He left out the part about how much he wanted her close to him, where he could keep an eye on her. Protect her. He knew Axl would back off the land for a few days, but after that… He simply had no guarantees.

Her smile and casual shrug told him she'd take his advice under consideration. But ultimately He knew she was through being told what to do.

"I want to make a splash."

"Oh, you'll definitely do that." He downed the rest of his drink in one. "El Valderon won't know what's hit it."

CHAPTER SEVEN

Isla woke with a surprising amount of zing in her step.

Taking charge of one's own destiny and wearing yet another new dress that fit like a dream had a way of adding a bit of kick to a girl's attitude.

That, and—although she was a bit shocked to admit it—so was wearing sexy underwear she never ever would have chosen if left to her own devices.

Gone were the plain-Jane matching bra and panties sets she normally bought at the supermarket. The lingerie she wore today was in another league from her regular cotton panties and bra of dubious assistance. It was *lingerie*, not underwear. Sexy silk and lace lingerie, in bold jewel colors.

Was this how Diego imagined her? As a woman whose skin knew only silk and the finest of lace? A part of her was horrified to think he knew exactly what she was wearing under the dress. But another part... Another part felt emboldened that he saw her as a woman, rather than the boring old plod who always did the dishes and made sure her other half's dinner was hot, no matter what time of night he wandered in.

She shot a glare at her invisible ex-fiancé and flicked her hair. *See? Not everyone thinks I'm boring.*

She looked at herself in the long mirror and slid her hands along her sides, over her curves, more aware than she'd ever been of how *feminine* she felt dressed this way. How strong.

By choosing these clothes Diego was telling her he saw strength in her. Beauty.

No wonder she had extra zing.

And she knew where the bulk of that energy was going to go.

In showing Axl Cruz precisely what happened when you pushed around a woman from Loch Craggen.

She gave herself a silly grin in the mirror. As if she'd be doing it all on her own! Having Diego Vasquez as her ally—*her husband*—would make all the difference. Particularly as he'd made it more than clear that his entire aim was to bring peace to the island.

When she went down the outdoor staircase that curved into the internal courtyard her heart-rate sped up a notch when she saw Diego was already having coffee at a tile mosaic table.

He looked up. Heat flared in his eyes when they lit on her.

She swished her way down the stairs as if she were a movie star. Something about him made her want to show off a little. Make him proud to call her his wife— even if it *was* just a fiction.

Or was it just plain old chemistry? They hadn't stayed up half the night comparing medical school stories just because they cracked each other up. Well, they did that too. But she knew she'd stayed up talking to him because there was a huge part of her that was wondering if he wanted to kiss her as much as she wanted to kiss him.

A chaste kiss had brought the evening to a close when she'd no longer been able to hide her yawns.

The sparks that had followed and sent her running for her room had given "chaste" a whole new definition.

"That's a nice dress."

She gave him a twirl at the bottom of the stairs suddenly acutely aware that moves like this—girly, swirly whirls, making her vividly aware of the feel of the fabric on her skin—were incredibly out of character.

"You're fifty shades of boring!"

Not in Diego's eyes.

Meeting him had been like unzipping an ill-fitting suit and discovering there was a whole different woman inside her. A woman she could admire.

Her spirits sank as quickly as they'd risen. If only her father felt the same.

"You're up early."

She glanced at the large grandfather clock behind Diego. It wasn't *that* early. "Have you already been out?"

He rose from his seat and gestured at the chair across from him, waiting until she sat before continuing. "Paz Cruz. He needed his dressings changed. His medication."

Out of instinct Isla asked for his stats and then, as Diego rattled them off, realized she wished she'd been there too. She didn't like the idea that she and her father might have been discussed. Or that Diego might have undergone some sort of interrogation about his shotgun wedding.

Officially, of course, the marriage could be annulled. There had been no sex. Would be no sex.

She hid behind an eggshell-blue coffee mug and looked at the man who had saved her life by becoming her husband. He was honorable. Proud. With a core of courage and strength. Her father had been right. Of all the men in all the world to be in this particular one-in-a-gazillion scenario with Diego was the man she would have picked.

But she wasn't picking. And she wasn't developing feelings for him. She was going to be sensible and count down the days, then go home and never think about this again.

"When are we going to work?"

He gave her a dry smile and nodded at the cafetière, still half full of coffee. "We islanders like to properly fuel up before we tend to our sick." He indicated a hand-woven basket brimming with tiny pastries. "Want one?"

She laughed. "This is exactly the type of food I try and tell my patients to avoid."

He shrugged and placed it in front of her. "Indulge. You're on your honeymoon."

She pursed her lips but felt tendrils of heat creep into her cheeks in defiance of her cavalier *yeah, right* attitude. A reminder of the saucy thoughts that had kept her awake for far too long in her much too empty bed...

When she had finally nodded off she'd dreamt of him. Definitely something new to tick off on the old sexy bucket list.

Not that she'd ever had one.

Maybe she *had* been one or two of shades of boring...

She bit into a pastry, moaning with pleasure at the buttery hit of sugar, fruit and pastry.

"That's more like it," Diego murmured, his deliciously throaty accent sending her nervous system into overdrive. "Eat up, *mi amor*. We've got a big day ahead of us."

Eyes glued to hers, Diego scraped a crumb of pastry

off his lower lip with his tongue. How the man infused the most pedestrian of moves with sex was beyond her.

Her eyes pinged open as a thought occurred to her. If, by some insane turn of events, he were to kiss her right now she'd be powerless to resist. More than that. She wouldn't *want* to.

It was just as well Isla had said she wanted to check out a few things in the hospital foyer. The atmosphere between Diego and Maria was…prickly at best.

"And just who *is* that woman, exactly?"

"She's my wife," he repeated, doing his level-best to keep his tone neutral.

How the hell he'd become so defensive about his fake wife in front of his real employer was beyond him, but he knew one thing for sure. He didn't want anyone referring to Isla as "that woman". She had more integrity in her little finger than most people showed in a lifetime, so he'd be damned if he was going to let Maria shoot the idea down before she heard him out.

"Doug MacLeay's daughter. It was all very fast. Unexpected. But I am sure you will join me in welcoming her both to El Valderon and here at the hospital. She's hoping to make quite a difference in the mobile clinic."

The clinic he and Maria fought about endlessly. She saw it as wasted money. He saw it as an invaluable resource.

"I suppose she'll want to be paid?" Maria threw down her proverbial pair of aces.

"No. She's happy to volunteer." He trumped her with a royal flush.

A cruel man would have enjoyed the shot of fury in Maria's eyes as she absorbed the news. Diego took no pleasure in it. He simply wanted to go to work and keep Isla safe in the process.

He was about to embark on what he was certain would be an unwelcome monologue, flaunting Isla's merits, when—as if she knew he might go off-piste—Isla walked across from the entryway, where she'd been looking at some of the health notices.

Diego introduced them.

"It's a pleasure to meet you." Isla looked Maria straight in the eye. "I'm really looking forward to working in the mobile clinic."

Any pretense of charm Maria had been trying to maintain dropped away. "I'm afraid we really don't have the funding to cover your insurance. And, of course, you'll have to sit our medical exam. It's very rigorous. It'll take weeks, if not months to organize. And as you're newlywed I suppose time is at a premium for you?"

"Fair enough." Isla smiled brightly. "Seeing as that's the case here, I'm assuming it won't be a problem for you if I open up a wellness clinic out at the turtle sanctuary?"

Diego almost laughed. Isla wasn't just delivering a blow to Maria, she was giving *him* the proverbial heave-ho as well. Kudos to her for knowing her own mind.

"Wellness clinic?" Maria didn't even try to rein in her disdain.

"I run a similar program back in Scotland. Just a couple of low-cost clinics a week. I find a preventative approach to medicine cuts back on a lot of unnecessary trips to the emergency ward. It's a way to put a fast track on people prone to diabetes, heart disease, chronic respiratory problems—that sort of thing. Catching preventable diseases late proves very expensive for us, as it involves having to get patients back to the mainland via helicopter or boat. I suspect it's the same for you. I've found the clinic to be a most cost-effective investment. Not to mention its use as a means of catching various cancers early, and lung disease, hypercholesterolemia—"

"Fine. You've painted the picture." Maria glanced at Diego, visibly annoyed at Isla's commonsense plan.

If Diego hadn't been so keen to keep Isla within eyesight—or at least earshot—for the foreseeable future he would've applauded her.

"Turtles *and* people. *Aren't* you from an interesting family?" Maria flicked an invisible piece of lint off her shoulder.

"Diego certainly thought so." Isla smiled benignly. "Didn't you, *mi amor*?"

She looked up at him with a look so pure and loving he would have sworn she meant it. *¡Dios mio!* The woman could've been a politician!

Diego put his arm round his wife's shoulders, a smile twitching at his lips as she snuggled up almost conspiratorially beneath it. They'd make a hell of a team if she weren't here under duress. If she actually cared about him. About the island.

Then again, if this was Isla under pressure he couldn't begin to imagine what she'd be like unleashed.

"Maria, it might be worth considering the excellent PR that would come from launching such a forward-looking program in the mobile clinic. Of course I'd be busy seeing patients of my own there, but if you were to be happy using Isla's British medical license as sufficient evidence of her ability to practice medicine you could announce her intention to meet preventative care patients. There's more than enough room. And if there were any problems I would be on hand to help. Smooth over any transitional problems."

"Our diagnosticians are already overwhelmed with their work here at the hospital…"

It was a flimsy excuse and everyone knew it. The term *grasping at straws* sprang to mind.

"A press release would be brilliant!" Isla leant in to Maria, praising her as if the idea had been her own. "You can assure the press that I'm used to working with limited resources. A stethoscope, a blood pressure cuff and a thermometer work wonders. There would be zero draw on the hospital's resources."

Maria scowled, but didn't storm off as she often did when she and Diego discussed preventative care. She would be perfectly happy for Diego to run a similar clinic so long as he stopped helping Noche Blanca. The argument ended the same way every single time: *Not until we treat everyone the same.*

Maria gave Isla a cursory up-and-down eye-flick. She too operated a policy of keeping her friends close and her enemies closer.

"What if you have no patients and Diego is overloaded? Do you plan on sitting around filing your nails?"

Her hostile approach would have made many women run for the hills. He'd seen it before with Maria. Hackles flew up. Claws came out. Whoever she was speaking to would take their services elsewhere. To a different island, even. But not Isla.

Shrugging out from underneath his arm, she took a step toward Maria and solemnly shook her head no. "Absolutely not. It would be a privilege to work with my husband. Ease his burden. And, of course, help the people of El Valderon."

Diego had to stop himself from letting out a low whistle of approval. His wife gave as good as she got—but with kindness and fairness at the fore.

"Even plasters cost money—who will cover *that*?"

The crack in Maria's voice told him she was beginning to flounder.

"I will," he said.

Any profits Vasquez Corp made were plowed right back into the community, and he was pretty sure this counted. He made a mental note to call the head of the board—a woman who doled out fair solutions as rigorously and passionately as she worked picking coffee beans.

"Dropping money on vanity projects? Picking up wives in the course of a weekend?" Maria snapped. "It's all so easy for you, isn't it?"

Diego dropped any pretense of charm. "No, Maria. It isn't. The instant my brother died any sort of ease I had with the world evaporated."

The blood drained from Maria's face, and as she drew in a sharp breath to launch her rebuttal attack Isla stepped between the pair of them, instantly defusing the near-explosive tension with a quick nod and a clap of her hands.

"Right, then," she said. "If it's all right with the pair of you, I'd like to get to work."

"Well done, *mi amor*."

Isla gave Diego a cautious smile. She felt as though she'd held her own, but also that they had acted like a team. It was something she'd never felt with Kyle. There was exhilaration in the power of two. Even so...

"I would've preferred to work at the sanctuary."

Diego nodded. She saw that he understood, but that he wasn't going to budge on this point. Annoying as it was, she also felt that warm, glowing feeling that someone had her back. And not just any someone.

Diego.

If she didn't watch herself she'd go down the same path she had with her parents and Kyle. Seeking love and attention where it simply wasn't on tap.

"One step at a time, Isla. For now? You wanted to be useful and you will be. Consider yourself the victor. Maria del Mar is a force to be reckoned with."

"A force who would've preferred *she* was the one wearing this?" Isla held up her hand, shifting it until the diamond caught the light.

Diego nodded. "Perhaps. One day long ago." His eyes shifted to where Maria was disappearing around a corner. "She's married now. Happily, believe it or not. She generally just likes torturing people. I think it's a hospital administrator's mission."

Isla didn't press the point. There was clearly some sort of history there, but it wasn't as if *she'd* arrived on El Valderon with a clean slate. Well…it had been clean-ish…slightly muddied…

Whatever. Her entire world was different now. *She* was different now.

To have gone from a sobbing-into-the-pillow wreck to a woman who could hold her own against another woman so obviously used to coming out on top of the food chain felt amazing. Maybe it was still adrenaline. Maybe it was the fact that she had no one here expecting her to be a particular way.

She stole a quick glance at Diego and fought the warm glow heating up her belly.

Maybe it was having someone believe in her.

She stepped away from the hand Diego was about to put on the small of her back. "Why don't you show me the clinic?"

A few days later Isla's admiration for Diego had quadrupled. Every morning he ensured she spoke with her father via a video call, so they could each see the other was alive and well. The line usually broke up before either of them were able to say much, but it was ridiculously comforting to see her father in the little stone cottage. The same wee house he'd been raised in. But then once they'd changed into scrubs and climbed into the mobile clinic Diego treated her exactly as she'd been hoping he would: as a professional.

Seeing the island—Diego's homeland—this way also gave her a greater insight into the man who held her destiny in his hands.

He was generous. Almost to a fault. Kind. Patient. And he always had her safety in mind. She'd thought it would feel stifling...suffocating, even...to once again be filling a role she hadn't planned on: meek, over-grateful, reluctant, bride.

But it was quite the opposite. He expected nothing of the sort from her, and the feisty spirit she'd surprised herself by showing at the hospital that first day with Maria was something he not only enjoyed but encouraged.

This particularly bright morning he made the usual stop on their way out to the far end of the island and picked up Carmela's twenty-year-old granddaughter Sofia—"just in case the language barrier proves problematic".

It was his deft way of dealing with her minimal grasp of Spanish.

"Where is the next stop?" she asked. The mobile clinic had already stopped at a remote village and a tiny school.

"It's going to be a longer visit than the others. It's at the Vasquez Coffee Plantation."

"As in…?" She pointed at him.

He gave her a nod and a slow wink, which sent uninvited ripples of pleasure down her spine. She was going to have to find a tactful way to ask him to stop doing that. He was too…too *yummy* to also be flirty. This was work. She was *working*. Twenty-five more days and she'd be at home in the cottage, making her father hot chocolate.

A jag of discomfort blurred the vision.

Was that what she really wanted? To go back to the same old, same old? Had it ever been?

Diego, she abruptly realized, was merrily chatting on about the coffee plantation.

"It's a bit more diversified these days. When my father left and I had to take over the companies, I turned them into co-operatives. Fairtrade initiatives and the like. It's better for the workers that way. The co-operatives agreed to a pool of money going toward healthcare—which the hospital allowed to be used to fund the mobile clinic—and this way they can see, hands-on, that I care. And, of course…" he dropped her another of those steamy winks of his "…Maria isn't out of pocket."

Isla managed to ignore the wink and, because Sofia was clearly tuning in to their conversation, stemmed the questions she wanted to ask about his family and the businesses. Instead asked about the people they would be seeing.

"Poor, mostly. Laborers. They will likely never be rich." He sounded disappointed, but then regrouped. "They are certainly better off than they were when my father ran things."

"And he is…?" She left the question open.

"In Nicaragua. No doubt on his fourth or fifth wife and sixth or seventh business empire. Maybe both."

Diego kept his eyes glued to the road, his tone neutral, so Isla didn't press. She knew how complicated it could be to talk about parents. She still hadn't told Diego her own mother had died. That information felt like a precious secret that, if kept incredibly close and deeply private, might one day change the past.

A young girl's dream that would never come true.

After a few more minutes of driving in silence, he said, "My mother's in America. No doubt doing the same. With husbands. Not so sure about empires."

"I suppose everyone has their own way of dealing with grief."

"*Brava, cariña.* You're one of the few to see it that way. Most of the islanders think my parents are spoiled brats who left when the going got tough."

Isla looked out the window and swiped away an unexpected tear. "Let's just say my father didn't cope very well when my mother died."

Oops. So much for keeping her secret close and safe.

"Oh…?" he said simply.

It would have been so easy to pour out her life story. Tell him all the things she was sure he'd understand. How she'd become a doctor because it had been the one thing that might have helped her mother out there in the jungle. How she'd felt utterly powerless to keep her father safe, but loved him anyway. He was her *father*. How she'd become more and more conservative in order to counterbalance his recklessness. How she was wondering now if anything she'd done—her move back to Loch Craggen, her insane engagement to Kyle—had mattered.

Diego didn't press for more details, but he reached across and gave her leg a squeeze. He got it. Here was yet another layer of connection with this mysterious and wonderful man. She was really going to have to clamp down on her emotions if she was going to get through the remaining twenty-five days with her heart intact.

"Right!" Diego said eventually, pointing toward a huge wooden gateway that led down a beautifully manicured road to a series of low traditional stucco buildings. "Welcome to the plantation."

They parked up outside the cottages—which, he explained, were housing for the full-time workers. There was also housing further along the road, for people who had worked there their entire lives and were now retired.

"Like these houses? That's amazing."

He shrugged. "It's not much when you consider what their hard work has given my family."

And there he was in a nutshell. A man vividly aware of what he owed his community.

It didn't surprise her in the slightest when, just a few patients in, it became clear to see they adored him.

She'd never seen so many octogenarians fluttering their eyelashes, nor so much disappointment when they realized she was the one who would be taking their blood pressure.

"It'll be easier to get a more accurate read if you do it," he'd cheekily whispered in her ear as one elderly woman blushed when he showed her to a chair.

Isla had blushed too, when his hand had casually

shifted from her waist to her hip, then lightly grazed over the curve of her derriere as if they had been married for years. Such a casual but intimate gesture, and it was chased up by the shock of realizing that the feeling she couldn't put a name to when he dropped his hand was an ache for more.

Diego was seeing their last patient—a teenage boy—in the back exam room with Sofia when a knock sounded at the open door. Isla took the opportunity as a chance to try out her limited grasp on Spanish.

"Adelante, por favor!"

A beautiful woman, exquisitely dressed with a thick mane of black hair tumbling down her back, stepped into the small waiting area. Isla pushed her papers to the side of the table at which she'd been working and half rose. They hadn't been expecting anyone else.

The woman wasn't dressed at all like the other women they'd seen. They had mostly been wearing thick cotton work clothes or brightly colored traditional skirts and blouses. The fabric of this woman's dress was clearly high quality. Raw silk? A high-quality linen? The rings on her fingers weren't cheap knock-offs, either. The sheer luster of them spoke of their authenticity.

She shot a nervous look behind her, then came and sat next to Isla at the table just outside another small exam room.

"How may I help you today?"

"You are Isla Vasquez?" The woman hesitated, a well of emotion clearly building in her throat.

Isla handed her a tissue. She'd always believed knowing it was safe to cry made it easier to stop fighting the emotion. When she looked at the woman's face again she saw tears brimming in her dark eyes.

"I am Serena Cruz."

For a moment the name didn't register. Then everything came together so rapidly Isla didn't have a moment to put on her game face.

Serena reached out and put a heavily jeweled hand on Isla's arm. "Don't be scared. I am here as a mother."

"Well, then…" Isla held her head high. "I will listen to you as the daughter of a man hounded away from a place he loved. At gunpoint."

Serena nodded, visibly taking on board what Isla had said. "I want to thank you."

For what, exactly? Surviving the most terrifying experience she'd ever been through? Agreeing to marry Diego to save her father's life?

She couldn't exactly spell any of that out. Diego had told Axl they were in love.

Then again, if Serena knew where she was—knew she was Diego's wife—surely she also knew this whole charade was a ruse to keep her father alive. A swirl of bile rose in her throat as she reminded herself that this woman's husband had threatened to kill her and her father. She owed her nothing. She pressed her lips tight.

"My son is alive because of you. And, of course, Diego."

Isla forced herself to speak levelly. "The way I understand it, *both* your sons are alive because of the Vasquez sons."

Serena shot her a sad smile. "This is true. But I believe it is you who has made the bravest of sacrifices."

Isla bridled. "I don't think so. I'm still alive." She let the words simmer between them, then softened. Serena obviously wasn't here to fight. "None of this needed to happen."

Serena shook her head. "When I met my husband he was a strong, honorable man. He worked hard. When the government changed in our country his job was taken from him. He lost himself that day."

Something twigged in Isla. Diego had mentioned earlier they'd be heading toward a village where quite a few Noche Blanca members lived, including Axl. He'd already been out this morning to change Paz's dressings, but had made no mention of seeing Serena.

"Does he know you're here?"

Serena shook her head, no.

"Why didn't you want him to know you were here?"

A tear lost its hold on Serena's eyelash and slid down her cheek. "I want my husband back. The man I married. I love him. And I will stand by him no matter what. Do you understand?"

Strangely, Isla did. It was exactly what she'd always done for her parents. Stood by them, all the while trusting, believing, loving. An invisible trinity holding her together through the darkest of days.

"Do you want out?"

Serena shook her head again. "No. But I want *change*. I know Diego is doing his best, but…"

"Everything all right in here?"

Isla's heart skipped a beat at the sound of Diego's voice. Her tummy did an entire tango when she turned around and saw him filling up the doorway, all dark-haired and pitch-black eyes…protective. Protective of *her*.

Serena rose and nodded solemnly at Diego. "Señor Vasquez."

He nodded, his expression inscrutable. "Serena. What brings you here? You know we planned on dropping by later."

"Sí." She put on a neutral smile. "I was just extending my felicitations to your new wife."

Diego's eyes pinged to Isla. He didn't say anything. He didn't have to.

She held up her hands as if to say, *I'm fine. I will explain everything later.*

"How very kind of you." His voice was curt. Officious. "If that's all, then, we were just about to pack up and head out to Corona Beach. To see your son. The one with the gunshot wounds."

Diego knew he was pouring salt into a wound that would never heal. Knew Serena wasn't the one who should be on the receiving end of his verbal potshots. And, more than that, he didn't want Isla knowing there was this side to him. The side still seething with anger at the injustice of his brother's death.

Sure. He did his thing. He brought healthcare to the island as if he were a warrior and treating even the most vile of characters were his greatest pleasure. But seeing Serena here, on some sort of obvious power play with the woman he'd vowed to care for—that was stepping on territory he wasn't willing to give up.

He stepped to the side and showed her the door. "Do give Axl my very best."

Serena went to the doorway and then turned to him, nearly said something, reconsidered when he pushed himself up to his full height, and walked away.

After she'd gone he took two long-legged strides to where Isla was standing, her expression one of pure shell-shock.

He stroked her hair. Cupped her cheek. When he

dropped his hands to her shoulders she shrugged herself away from him, visibly annoyed.

"Why were you so rude to her?"

"*Que*? *Cariña*, I was protecting you, not being rude."

She snorted. "Where I come from that sort of behavior is considered rude."

He *had* been rude. And a boor. And for the first time ever he liked having someone in his life who would hold his own actions up to him for examination. For too long he'd felt like a solitary crusader. A man hell-bent on bringing peace to the island through means he wasn't sure would ever wholly do the trick.

Isla crossed her arms and glared at him. He had to bite back a smile. Minute by minute she was slipping under his skin, and he didn't feel like putting up any sort of roadblocks to stop her.

"Do you know why she was here?"

"I would say to lord it over you, but I'm guessing by your reaction to my caveman routine I might be wrong."

"Correct. You're wrong. As my grandmother would say, you went a bit *crabbit* on the poor woman."

No guesses as to what *crabbit* meant.

He took a step closer toward her. "You know, you have a lovely way of rolling your Rs. Not everyone who tries Spanish can do that."

He took another step in and lightly rested his hands on her hips. She arched an imperious eyebrow at him, but didn't shake him off. He shouldn't be doing this. Neither of them should. And yet here they were. Neither of them moving.

Isla adopted an imperious tone. "I wasn't speaking Spanish. I was speaking Scots."

"And you and Serena were holding an international peace summit, I suppose?"

"As a matter of fact we were. Well… We might have been if *someone* hadn't showed her the door. I believe she was here offering herself as an olive branch, and if you hadn't come in like some sort of big old swash-buckling hero I might've found out exactly what it was she wanted."

Isla shifted under his touch and, if he wasn't mistaken, arched in toward him. Was she enjoying their feisty banter as much as he was?

Isla didn't blink. "Don't you believe me?"

"When it comes to you, my dear, I could believe just about anything." He wove a hand through her thick hair and tilted her face up toward his. "But right now I'd like to talk about something else. In fact…" his voice lowered to a growl "…I'd like not to talk at all."

He closed the few inches between them, feeling the pulse of longing hit him fast and hard. Sofia had gone out. He kicked the door shut.

The minute his mouth touched hers, heat exploded in his body like a petrol bomb. Hot. Fast. Furious. It was as intense as their first kiss, but better. This time it was entirely by choice.

How did he know? He *felt* the difference. She'd responded to him before, but there had been so much adrenaline running through her system he hadn't been a hundred percent certain if she'd been expending her stores as a means of survival or acting on the same animal instinct that had made him kiss her in the first place.

This time he knew she was slaking the exact same

hunger he'd been feeling from the moment he'd laid eyes on her.

She was tasting him. Touching him. Her hands were round his neck. In his hair. Rucking his shirt up and out of his trousers. Feeling his hot skin against her slender fingers. When she slid her hand between them and felt the strength of his desire they groaned together. He scooped her up and wrapped her legs round his waist faster than you could say—

"Oh! *Lo siento mucho!*"

They both turned to see Sofia, standing, frozen, in the open doorway.

Diego slowly eased his wife down his front, well aware that if he turned around he would be betraying more than elevated blood pressure.

"I— Should I—? Perhaps…should I go?" Sofia looked as if she wanted to run for the hills and never come back, but couldn't because her feet were cemented to the ground.

To his surprise, Isla slipped in front of Diego, pulling her scrubs back into a semblance of order, and smiled as if being caught in the throes of a passionate liaison happened to her all the time.

"Not at all. Apologies, Sofia. You'll have to forgive us…" She brandished her ring. "Newlyweds."

When Sofia made some sort of excuse about having left something a very exact "ten minutes away and ten minutes back", and slammed the door shut behind her, Isla whirled round and pointed her finger at Diego.

"No," she said, her chest still heaving, lips bruised, two bright dots of pink lighting up her cheeks. "No more of that. I'm *not* your property!"

He wanted to protest. Say he knew she wanted him

every bit as much as he wanted her, but demons of his own stepped to the fore.

Isla muddied his focus. His drive.

CHAPTER EIGHT

ISLA WAVED HER patient off, took the stethoscope from round her neck, popped it into her ears and pressed the diaphragm to her heart.

Ba-bump. Ba-bump.

Yup! Still beating. Would wonders never cease?

Clawing her way through these last few days pretending she was completely immune to Diego was an entirely brand-new form of torture. Particularly when patients asked about their plans. Did they have plans for the sanctuary? Remodeling? Were they taking a honeymoon? Starting a family?

It was the plans for a family part she found particularly difficult to grapple with. She really wanted children. When Kyle had left her, her very first thought had been, *Tick-tock, tick-tock*. It had been then that she'd known the rumored biological clock was very real. And painful to live with, considering Diego was so at ease with telling everyone, "The more the merrier!"

She'd never realized emotional torture could be physically painful before.

Life after that kiss…*those* kisses…all the fictions… *Sigh*. It would be an uphill battle to keep her strict, blinkered eyes on the actual prize—leaving El Valderon.

Not to mention the fact that with each passing day the tension between the pair of them increased.

Pre-clinic kiss? Surprisingly light. Fun, even.

Post-clinic kiss? More…*guarded*. Intense. Driven.

It was almost impossible to figure out which one was the real Diego. Again and again she had to remind herself to fight her instinct to peel away the layers of this man who had unwittingly awoken something powerful and strong within her.

Today, in particular, as they worked at a remote mountaintop village school, Isla felt as though she were operating on a knife's edge—a totally different sensation from operating at gunpoint. This felt…insane, really. As if she'd been invaded by some sort of lust monster. A beautiful one. An Aphrodite. An insatiable she-devil. A *femme fatale*.

On a practical level, she knew she should be feeling fragile—terrified, even, given the fact her month in El Valderon was not even halfway done… But under Diego's gaze she felt empowered. Her entire body felt different.

Sure. She'd kissed other men before. She'd been intimate before. Felt the butterfly wing tickling of pleasure. But she'd never felt someone's unmasked desire invade her body like a nuclear-charged life force before.

"Isla?" Diego knocked on the doorframe of the tiny exam room where she was finishing up some paperwork.

He wasn't even touching her, and still…*fireworks*.

"Any chance I can borrow your lap?"

"I beg your pardon?" A rush of images jostled each other for pole position.

"For a child," he quickly explained, his expression neutral. "Sofia's nipped out. Would you be able to hold on to a four-year-old with some rather nasty splinters in her knee?"

"You need me to hold her?"

He tipped his head to the side, brow furrowed. "She's scared. Hurt. Her mother's not here, the teacher is busy, and I thought she could do with some comfort."

"But you're so good at that."

He shook his head. "Not with children."

"But I thought—"

"What?" An intensity she hadn't seen before radiated from him. "*What* did you think?"

"'The more the merrier?'"

Something bleak and painful darkened his eyes. "We tell people what they want to hear in public, *mija*. When it's just you and me I thought we'd opted for honesty."

Her heart sank. He didn't want children? Sure. On an intellectual level she understood why he couldn't have them right now, with her, but he was *great* with them. She'd seen him playing a game of hide and seek earlier and he'd been hilarious. Had had piles of children clambering all over him.

She rounded on herself. *This isn't about the two of you and your fictional future.*

"Isla? We need to get to my patient. Tick-tock."

Tick-tock.

"Of course."

She understood. It didn't sit well, but it wasn't as if having a real-life family was their destiny. She saw something in him relax. As if he'd been bearing the burden of his lies about wanting children on his own and now that she knew it was a burden halved.

"Right!" She stood up with as bright a smile as she could muster. "Let's go meet this little monkey."

A few minutes later Isla's every nerve-ending was at war with her common sense. Sitting there, in that tiny room, holding the most adorable little girl and watching Diego pull splinter after splinter after splinter from her knee...

It was like watching a man rescue kittens from a cliff-edge.

Utterly impossible not to go all gooey inside.

She let her cheek rest atop the little girl's head. It was so soft. For just a fraction of a second she allowed herself to wonder what it would be like if she was holding her own daughter, and Diego was the caring, loving father painstakingly extracting the remains of a log-jumping game gone wrong.

She lifted her gaze and met Diego's. He was looking directly at her.

Heat seared straight through to every part of her body it shouldn't. Every part of her body she had lectured each night about due diligence. An actual physical ache squeezed at her heart so tightly she could hardly breathe.

Was she falling in love with him? Her husband? Her captor?

He's not your captor. He saved you. And in two weeks he's going to let you go.

The flare of light in Diego's eyes was so intense she felt as if he was actually following her thoughts.

Just when she thought she couldn't bear it any longer, he dropped his gaze.

"*Ahora, mi muy linda niña.* That's you, all patched up." He lifted the little girl off Isla's lap and gave her head a little rub. "Let's let Isla go back to work now."

An electric tension simmered between them as Isla

rose and left the room. It wasn't anger. Not loss. Or fear. It was sexual. Hot, fierce, sexual desire.

Two broken fingers, one mystery rash, three diabetes check-ups, four general health checks and about nineteen blood pressure checks on herself later, Isla and Diego called it a day.

When they got back to the house Carmela had already gone home.

The nanosecond the large wooden door to the courtyard shut behind her Diego became a man possessed. An explorer with one quest. One mission. To find the Holy Grail. And when Isla looked into his espresso-dark eyes, lit from within by the flame of desire, she knew without a shadow of a doubt that he'd found what he sought.

Without a word, he closed the space between them, reached out, took hold of the small waist tie that held her dress together and pulled it.

The woman she'd been a fortnight ago would have been horrified. The woman she was today felt beautiful enough to stand before him and let him appraise her.

She even shifted her leg, so that the wrap-around dress fell to the side, giving him more than a sliver of insight as to what lay beneath the fabric.

She didn't have to be told he liked what he saw.

His pupils dilated. His tongue swept across his lips.

Almost against her will, she did the same with her own dry lips, wondering if he could see the pulse-point at the base of her throat pounding. She dropped her eyes, half tempted to step forward and see how quickly she could make short shrift of the buttons on Diego's dark linen shirt, which accented the warm burnt sugar color of his skin.

Instead she let her gaze drop further. A warmth infused her entire body, coiling hot and tight between her legs as she saw the length of his erection appear instantly.

She'd never known the power of arousing a man just by standing in front of him. Seized with a boldness she'd not known she possessed, Isla slipped her dress off first one shoulder and then the other, catching the sleeves on her wrists, still keeping the whirl of fabric in place around her waist and legs.

He made a move toward her, his eyes glued to her breasts. Her nipples ached with need. For his touch. For his caresses. For the hot, wet licks she knew he'd give her with his tongue when she finally allowed him to come close and take her breast between his lips.

She shook her finger back and forth when he made a move to step forward. "Not yet."

"*Cariña*, you are torturing me."

"Isn't a new bride allowed to be shy?"

Where on earth had she found this new coquettishness…? She looked up to meet Diego's hungry gaze. Well… No guesses there, really.

She checked herself. It wasn't shyness. This was no ordinary margarita-fueled holiday romance. She wanted answers first.

"Is this real?"

A ragged breath left his chest and he held out his hands as if presenting his whole true self to her. "*Si amorcita.*" He held out his wrists. "As real as what is flowing through these veins." He put his hands on his heart. "As real as what I felt the moment I first saw you."

"As real as this?" She held up her hand, showing him the ring he'd put on her finger.

Pain flashed across his eyes but he didn't blink. She knew it wasn't fair. Asking a man who'd married her in

an insane situation to paint a picture. There wasn't a cell
in her body that wanted to refuse him. That *could* refuse
him. But she wanted to hear him tell her that what they
were about to share was based on a fiction. That it *would*
end. That anything and everything that passed between
them was solely based on the here and now. Two hearts.
Two minds. Two souls. One undeniably carnal attraction.

Diego stilled, then spoke, "The first woman who wore
that ring—my grandmother—was the strongest, most
noble woman I ever knew. She stood for truth, honesty
and conviction. I vowed to her I would never put her
ring on the finger of a woman who stood for anything
less than she did. But as for what lies ahead for us...? I
can make you no promises."

Isla respected his honesty. It wasn't as if she could,
hand on heart, tell him she was in love with him. Did
she care for him? Absolutely. Did she respect him. Beyond a shadow of a doubt. Did her body crave his touch?

More than anything.

She stared at the diamond ring on her finger.

She thought of her own grandmother, who had been
her ballast during her childhood. With her parents constantly flying off to protect one endangered species or
another Isla might easily have felt neglected. Uncared-
for. But her grandmother had made sure Isla knew just
how very much she was loved. From the look in his eyes,
the ache in his voice, it was easy to see Diego's grandmother had been the same for him.

She didn't need to talk anymore. Quiz him. Push him
into false declarations of feelings he couldn't possibly have.
Not now. Not with so many questions left unanswered.

At this exact moment she wanted him. Plain and simple. The same way he wanted her.

She let her dress drop to the floor.

It had barely pooled round her ankles before she was in his arms, his mouth claiming hers more exquisitely than she would ever have imagined possible. His hands, broad and strong, spread along her back, her waist, her buttocks...all his touches and caresses leaving tendrils of heat in their wake.

As he drew her closer to him she reveled in the sensation of his shirt and trousers against her skin. The solid reminder of his ache for her. The warm, tropical air tickled like silk against her shoulders, between her thighs, on the soles of her feet as she went up on tiptoe to hungrily match his kisses.

Abruptly, he pulled back, his eyes burning with urgency and need. "You know this isn't real."

"This is." She put her hand on his pounding heart, then moved it to her own. "And this is."

"When this is over I will let you go."

She nodded. She knew.

"I'm not gone yet."

In one swift move, Diego scooped Isla up and into his arms and carried her toward the outside veranda—an enchanted sprawl of painted tiles, outdoor sofas and climbing plants, providing a private view of the sea and the setting sun just a few hundred meters beyond them.

Waves... The gentle shuffling of the palms... The shadow of the approaching moon... Apart from the elements they were completely isolated from everything and everyone.

It was his favorite place in the villa. Even more so now, as he watched his bride stretch out on the luxurious emerald and azure-colored cushions of the expansive daybed. He ripped the ties off the mosquito netting and watched as Isla disappeared behind the gentle billows of diaphanous curtains.

He stood at the end of the bed, open to the elements, and soaked in the vision that lay before him. She was dangerously beautiful, his wife. Her dark auburn hair fanned out against the pillows like rare silk, the sun's golden rays weaving through it for added luster. Her blue eyes were clearer than the sea behind him.

His gaze shifted to her kiss-bruised lips. To the pink on her cheeks that had come from the abrasion of his stubble. Fighting his desire for her had been like holding a savage beast at bay.

"I like it," she said.

"What?"

She pushed up on her elbows, the tips of her nipples straining against the blue lace of her bra. "Your stubble. It's not as rough as you think."

He knelt at the end of the bed and began to crawl toward her, until he was straddling her, taking the bulk of his weight on his shins.

"Where would you like to feel it next?"

A wicked look lit up her features, her tongue dipping out of her mouth to lick her upper lip. "Surprise me."

His gut told him this was all new to Isla. The sensuality. The bravery. The brazenness of her longing. She was offering herself to him. And it wasn't in gratitude. It was because she wanted him every bit as much as he wanted her. So he was going to take his time and give her every ounce of pleasure she deserved.

"As you wish, *amorcita*."

He cupped her face with his hands and drew a long, sweet, hot kiss from her. There was an added boldness in her touch, different from just a few minutes ago when she'd dropped her dress and bared herself to him. She was wielding every bit as much power as he did, and she knew it.

They'd been open. Honest.

She was here now. And in a fortnight…as agreed… he would let her go.

"Unbutton my shirt."

She wriggled out from under him and knelt across him. She reached out, her fingers touching his lips. He drew them in to his mouth, his tongue swirling round them. Her other hand skimmed along the fabric barely containing her breasts, then down along her belly, then teased along the edges of her skimpy panties. Lava-strength heat harpooned straight between his legs.

"Forget it," he growled. "I can't wait that long."

He pulled his shirt off in one swift move. Her fingers reached out and found his belt buckle, undid it quickly then pulled it free of his trousers with whip-like precision.

Her hands sought his erection, straining against the fabric of his trousers, and stroked along the length of it. The rest of her body arched toward him as a little moan of pleasure swept past her lips. It was intensely erotic.

He clasped her wrists in one of his hands and pulled them up and over her head. He put his other hand to the small of her back. "Lie back. I want you to let me pleasure you."

"Not until you're naked," she whispered, undoing the buttons of his fly one excruciating button at a time.

It was his turn to groan.

The moment she reached the bottom button he yanked his trousers off, then stretched out along the length of her. Unable to wait for anymore commands he cupped one of her breasts while his mouth took the other through the delicate lace. Her fingernails bit into his back. He sucked harder, his teeth lightly grazing against her nipple, until he couldn't stand having anything between them. He flicked the clasp at the center of her chest apart and slipped the bra off, luxuriating in licking, sucking and kissing her breasts.

The more he touched her, the more her hips shifted and arched toward him. He gently grazed his hand along her belly, then slid it between her legs, where he could already feel she was ready for him. He slipped in a single finger, then another when she began to press against him with a rhythmic pulsing motion.

"I want you," she whispered into his ear as her hands raked the length of his back. "I want to feel you inside me."

He yanked his trousers up from the side of the bed and pulled out a small silver packet. He'd snagged a couple of condoms from the mobile clinic's supply after he and Isla had been caught kissing all those days ago. They'd been burning a hole in his wallet ever since. Now he wished he'd grabbed a dozen. More. The entire box might not be enough to sate his desire.

He quickly sheathed the length of his erection, then pulled her close to him, whispering again and again, "This is real."

Isla's entire body was humming with anticipation. She drew in a breath as Diego's arm muscles corded, taking the weight of his body as he held himself aloft. She had no actual control over her body's response to him. It was as if magnets had been placed inside her and were uncontrollably drawing her to him. Not that she wanted to resist.

He put a knee between her legs. "Wrap them round me."

His voice was so thick with emotion she felt tears spring to her eyes. A whimper of pleasure escaped her lips as she felt his length slide between her legs, shifting along the soft folds he'd already brought to a heated pool of readiness. Slowly, excruciatingly slowly, he began to slide into her. Teasingly. To the point where he knew she would have to beg. And she did. There was no shame in it. No weakness. Only pure, unadulterated need.

He drew out the long, heated strokes until neither of them could bear it anymore and she cried out for him to take her. His hips began to move with a more fluid cadence, faster, stronger, more demanding, until finally she knew he was no longer moving with control but with undiluted, animalistic need.

And then, as one, their hips met in one graceful, powerful connection and pleasure poured through her as they shared a mutual release. She clung to him, simultaneously exhausted and energized.

After a few moments he lowered himself, then rolled over onto his back, pulling her to him so that her whole body was stretched out along the pure masculine length of him. The sensuality of skin on skin—hers soft, his warm, hairy in parts, smooth in others—threatened to reignite the fire of desire all over again.

A soft breeze was shifting in from the sea, blowing along her back. She shivered—but not because she was cold.

Diego tightened his hold on her. "Everything all right, *amorcita*?"

"Mmm… More than."

She pressed a hand against his chest and pushed herself up so that she could see his face. For the first time he looked relaxed. Happy. Not a changed man, necessarily, but more…*complete*.

"Want to talk about it?"

She shook her head and drew her hand along the soft bristles of his five o'clock shadow. "No."

He let it drop, but she could see by the look in his eyes that he wouldn't forget. That she would have to find a way to tell him about how much he'd changed her. How when she'd arrived here she'd not only been a man's second choice, she'd become his reject. That the life she'd lived before meeting him had been a life crafted out of little more than fear. Fear of change. Fear of loss. Fear of being alone for the rest of her life.

And now she was halfway in love with a man who she would have to willingly walk away from if she wanted to live.

Diego reached up and swept a lock of hair behind her ear. "You look very thoughtful, *amorcita*. Are you sure you don't want to talk about anything?"

"I'm sure," she lied. "Just thinking about how this is absolutely the strangest holiday romance in the history of holiday romances."

His eyebrows nearly shot off his forehead. "Is that what you're calling this? A holiday romance?"

She shrugged. "No! I mean… What would *you* call it?"

She looked away, not really wanting an answer. They both knew what it was. A fiction.

Instead of answering, Diego wrapped his arms around her and pulled her to him, dropping a soft kiss on her forehead as the warm night air enveloped the pair of them in an invisible cocoon of togetherness.

Maybe she should stop asking questions, trying to define things, and give living in the moment a go.

She'd never lived her life as if she didn't have a care in the world, and in a strange way that was what her life was right here and now. Her father was at home. Safe. Her clinic was being covered by a really talented locum. Her ex, so she'd heard from her father, had applied for a transfer to "somewhere with a bit more pace" than Loch Craggen.

The only person she needed to worry about right now was herself, because for the first time in her life she felt as though someone truly had her back.

She pressed her fingertips into Diego's shoulders and nestled in close to him. Medicine, marriage and passion. It was almost unthinkably perfect…

But her heart nearly ripped at the seams as she let the truth invade it. This…the luxurious house, the extraordinary lovemaking, the undeniably noble man…none of it was based in reality. *Her* reality, at least. And sooner or later Isla would have to own the fact that everything that was happening between her and Diego was little more than a mirage.

She hid the tears that sprang to her eyes, nestling in even closer to Diego's warm chest, and made a promise to herself. She'd live in the moment. And when she walked away she would hold her head high.

CHAPTER NINE

EACH NIGHT SINCE they'd first made love they had shared the night together. Today, fresh back from a shift at the hospital, Diego pulled open the large, carved wooden door leading into the interior courtyard and burst into hysterics at the sight that greeted him.

Carmela had Isla up on the box she'd used to make him and his brother stand on when she was making clothes for them and had her draped in fabric every color of the rainbow.

Isla looked across at him, her eyes brightening as they met and, ironically or not, struck a pose akin to the Statue of Liberty. "What do you think?"

"I love it."

He gave Carmela an approving smile. The woman was clearly putting her stamp of approval almost literally on Diego's choice of bride. If only she knew the details…

He quietly harrumphed. Knowing Carmela, she *did* know the details. And now she was making a point. *Don't do what you always do and walk away. This one's a keeper.*

"So…" He tapped his index finger on his chin as he imagined a fashion designer might. "Is this an everyday outfit, or for something a bit more special?"

"Diego!" Isla gave her hair a coltish flick. "With you *every* day is special."

He wanted to believe it. Knew he couldn't. So he played along instead—just as she was. The pair of them assuming roles to make the best of an insane situation.

As mad as it was, he could genuinely see doing this for the rest of his life. Being caught in this bubble of happiness that surrounded the two of them, empowering them rather than breaking them.

He made a mark for Team Vasquez on his mental scorecard and put a large nil under Axl's. So far there had been no more trouble at the sanctuary. And no more mysterious "meet-and-greets" from Axl's wife Serena. That visit niggled, though. She'd never approached him before and, if it was true he had been as boorish as Isla had suggested, she might not again.

Had he missed a trick?

Proof, if he needed any, that letting himself fall for Isla would cloud his judgment.

"So?" He touched one of the fabrics—a luminous green. "What do you have in mind?"

Something flashed across her eyes he couldn't quite put a finger on. "Maybe when the dress is done we'll know what to do with it. For now I'd like to get back into my scrubs. Get word out about Phase Two of the mobile clinic."

"Phase Two?" This was news to him. "I didn't realize we had a Phase One in place?"

"Absolutely. Ooh!" She pulled a pin out of a piece of fabric held atop her shoulder and handed it to Carmela. In Spanish, she thanked her, then continued, "Is it all right if we finish this up tomorrow?"

"Absolutely, *señora*," Carmela cooed indulgently,

throwing an unmistakable *I'm* her *housekeeper now* look at Diego. "Whatever you like. Shall I put dinner out for you at eight?"

Isla shook her head as Carmela began undraping the fabrics. "Don't worry. We can sort something out. Perhaps I'll make something Scottish for Diego. A bowl of Stovies? Or perhaps some clootie dumplings?"

Carmela gave her a dubious look, one that suggested nothing Scottish could match *her* cooking. It pleased Diego to see Isla laugh good-naturedly at the obvious slight. As if she were a part of the place.

She is *part of the place, idiota. You guaranteed that when you put that ring on her finger. A ring that saved her life.*

"Right!" Isla rubbed her hands together once her stint as a mannequin had finished and Carmela had disappeared into her sewing room. "You ready to hear my plan? Perhaps over a glass of wine out on the patio?"

"Sounds perfect." He dropped a kiss on to her soft lips, instantly knowing, as she arched into him, that a simple kiss wouldn't tide him over until he held her in his arms tonight.

Skin against skin. Legs and arms tangled together. Hearts beating as one. He pulled her closer to him and drew a long, sensual, heated kiss from her not releasing her until he heard that adorable little mew of happiness that meant they either had to go straight to bed or stop touching one another.

He pulled away. She wanted to talk. He owed it to her to listen.

"Come, *amorcita*. Let's hear this plan of yours."

"So that's the plan in a nutshell."

Isla was unsurprised to see Diego's metaphorical

brake lights go on. The thing was, she needed a project to distract herself from her looming departure date. She wanted to stay now, every bit as much as she'd wanted to leave when Diego had first slipped that wedding ring on to her finger. And knowing that was going to require some serious distraction.

"There is no way she will go for it."

"But surely Maria will see the plus side of having a blood drive that would benefit the hospital?"

"*Sí*, but…"

"But what?"

He sat forward in his chair, elbows propped on his knees. "You want half the donations to go to the mobile clinic?"

She nodded.

"It's a great idea, but Maria would know that the blood would be going straight to Noche Blanca and would nix it in a minute."

"So if Noche Blanca were no longer a threat, *everyone* could receive healthcare?"

"Yes."

"Good. Then I think it's time we sat down with Axl Cruz and had a nice little chat."

"Que?" The brake lights went on again. "*Amor.* Things don't work so quickly here." He tapped his watch. "Island time. Besides, I thought we'd agreed to let things settle before we approached Axl."

She hung quote marks in the air with her fingers. "*'We'* agreed nothing of the sort. *You* made an executive decision."

"One that *you* agreed with."

Isla shook her finger in front of Diego's face and made a *No, I did not* sound. "There is no need for these ridiculous flares of violence. There's hasn't been so much as a whisper of crime in the past few weeks."

Diego's expression was deadly serious. "The incident at the sanctuary was huge. There's always a lull after that sort of things. People lay low. But it will happen again. Some would say it's human nature, *amor*. To fight. To have conflict."

"That's a pretty bleak attitude."

He fixed her with a solid gaze. One that reminded her he was a man who had lost his brother to violence. "There will never be a world without conflict. Without crime. Without loss."

It didn't mean they should give up. Just because they each bore the scars of other people's fury.

"I think peace *is* possible on El Valderon. *And* I think we should do a blood drive. Remind everyone they have the power to save lives."

He reached out and tucked a stray curl behind her ear. "How did one small Scottish island contain all this energy?"

She looked away. He wasn't to know she'd been an entirely different person less than a month ago. A person so intent on finding somewhere safe, somewhere it was impossible to get hurt, she'd not even noticed the only person she was hurting was herself.

Diego reached out a hand, sensing her change in mood, and pulled her to him on the deep sofa. She nestled in under his arm and pulled the other one around her, feeling his warmth as he cinched his fingers together and held her tight. She pushed away the mental reminders that none of this was real, because what she was feeling now was ridiculously real.

She loved him. She knew that now. Heart and soul. Loved everything they did together…

It was the type of relationship she was sure her parents had shared. One in which they'd stood up for what they'd believed in. Passionately followed their dreams. Their callings. It was an extraordinary privilege, she realized, to have grown up knowing two people who drew strength from one another to do what they thought was right.

She wanted to tell Diego *that* was the gift he had given to her when he'd slipped that ring on her finger. The gift of belief. Belief that she was strong. Capable of making change. Not just for herself, but for others.

"We'll talk to Maria."

He kissed the top of her head, and when he continued she could hear that same determined resolution in his voice she'd heard when he'd told her to marry him.

"It's time we shook things up around here."

She squeezed his hands tight, but didn't dare look at him. This was no holiday romance. Being married to Diego Vasquez was the most life-changing thing she would ever be a part of. And, even though it would only last a few more days, she renewed her vow to do everything in her power to help change the community he lived in for the better.

Maria was in full lioness mode. Diego took a step back, having learnt from experience that the best way to defuse her ire was to let her roar.

"The only reason I am agreeing to let you and the mobile clinic do it is because we don't have the staff to do a donation day. We need blood. Stores are low. But mark my words, Diego—" Maria pointed her painted talons at him, then Isla "—if people get even the slightest *sniff* that this blood might go to Noche Blanca…" Her dark eyes bored straight into Isla's as she continued. "They will never come."

Diego knew better than to step in and "protect" his wife. She could hold her own and *wanted* to.

Isla nodded, letting Maria know she'd heard her. "Your generosity will not be forgotten." She pressed a hand to her heart. "And this is a *good* thing. For the hospital. For El Valderon."

Maria sniffed, gave her a top-to-toe scan without moving anything other than her eyes. She pointed at the donors' chairs Isla had asked if they could borrow. "I want those back in pristine condition."

"Absolutely."

She gave them a curt nod, then swept out of the room.

When they were sure she was gone, Isla turned to him and did a melodramatic swipe of her brow. "Whew! She is a tough cookie."

"You're not wrong there. She's made of steel."

"And ice."

Diego tipped his head back and forth. It was more complicated than that. "She's…she's not just defending the hospital." He saw the dawning light of understanding hit Isla's blue eyes.

"She's defending her decision not to send the ambulance out for your brother?"

A grim smile served as his answer.

Isla scanned the morass of equipment. "Do you think this is madness? Moving all this gear on to the mobile clinic only for no one to come?"

Diego held out a hand to her. "We'll give it a few days so we can get the word out. The mere fact that Maria is so cross about it means she will be telling everyone. I'll tell Carmela, and all the people who work at the plantation. We're bound to have a few takers. At the very least we'll get the message out that the we need blood."

"*El Valderon* needs it. The *people* need it!"

She looked like *she* needed it. Was she pouring all her energies into work to keep her mind off the one-way ticket back to Scotland he'd booked the night before? He certainly was. Booking it had been his way of reminding himself this was all temporary.

"You're preaching to the converted, Isla. We have to take things as they come sometimes." He hoisted himself up onto the donor table and reached his hands out to her.

She didn't take them. She crossed her arms over her chest and said, "You're being defeatist."

Her words were like a searing hot poker plunged straight into a barely healed wound.

"Is *that* what you think? That I have given up? Is *that* why I arrived in the middle of the night to help Paz? Help you? Your father?"

Tears sprang to her eyes but Isla stood her ground, tilting her chin in that feisty way of hers. The way that indicated she was about to say something she knew would push the invisible envelope even more.

"How about I give Axl Cruz's wife a call? Serena? She seemed open to change. Given the blood you provided saved their son, you'd think they'd be keen to donate."

Diego shook his head and scrubbed a hand through his hair. "They won't come. Shouldn't come. Dodgy tattoos... Some of them might be users... Even if they could help, they never would."

"*You* show up. You show up whenever they need you,

even though they took your brother." She held up her finger, where his grandmother's ring sparkled. "You helped a complete stranger. Why shouldn't they?"

"That's different," he deflected, trying to gather his thoughts.

"How? *How* is that different?" Isla pressed her hands to her heart. "Isn't it an innate instinct to help people?"

He shook his head, no. "I do what I do to make myself feel better. But the sad truth is it will never be enough. No matter how many blood drives we hold, or splinters we remove, or blood pressures we check, my brother will never come back."

Isla started to say something, then pressed her lips tight.

Diego felt an old idea resurface. The job offer he had made to Axl in the wake of his brother's death. The job Axl had refused. Perhaps enough time had passed to try again.

"We'll tell him about the blood drive. Axl."

"You will or I will?" Isla asked, her hands planted on her hips as she glared at him. When he didn't answer, she asked in a gentler tone. "What are we actually talking about here? Are we talking about bringing the people on your island together or ensuring they stay apart?"

And that was when it hit him. He'd been doing his absolute best to keep Noche Blanca away from everyone else. No one had gone to prison for what had happened to his brother. No one had had to do community service. *Nothing.* The only thing he had over them was the fact that they owed him. And by continuing to offer them medical care he was encouraging them to carry on with their "lifestyle choices."

He hopped off the donor table he'd been sitting on. "Leave it with me. I need to do this."

She shot him a dubious look.

He raised his hands. "I know. It's not like you don't have your own battles to fight with Axl. But mine..." He thumped his fist against his gut. "They live *here*. I'm asking you to trust me."

She quirked an eyebrow at him.

"I know." He put one of his hands on her shoulder, then tipped her chin up so that she could see straight into his heart. "I promise you I want the same thing you do."

"Well, then." She gave him an efficient little nod. "I guess you'd better get on with it."

After she had made sure absolutely everything was as organized as it could be, Isla pushed open the door. She was just about to unfurl the homemade signs she'd made when she looked out beyond the clinic's awning.

Her jaw dropped.

There was already a queue. Some thirty or forty people were standing outside the clinic, all waiting to donate blood. And the first ten were all people she recognized from Noche Blanca. Not the gang members themselves, but their mothers. Sisters. Cousins. Aunts. Uncles.

Her heart filled to bursting. Diego must have told Axl after all.

He'd been so quiet these last couple of days. So much so she hadn't even asked him whether or not he'd spoken to anyone, let alone Axl, about the blood drive. She had been so intent on distracting herself from her feelings for Diego, she was now worried she'd pushed too much.

The ring on her finger caught the morning sun. She'd

have to return it soon. The sting of tears tore at her throat. She swallowed. Hard.

All good things must come to an end.

"Right everyone!" she called out in her fractured Spanish. "Let's do this for El Valderon!"

The crowd cheered and applauded. It was an extraordinary feeling. Being part of a place. Part of a movement for change.

When she turned around and saw Diego behind her, instinct took over. She went up on tiptoe and kissed him. "Thank you, Diego."

He whispered something in Spanish she didn't quite catch, but when he squeezed her hand and beckoned the people in the queue to enter, she knew the ties that already bound them had been strengthened.

CHAPTER TEN

"RIGHT YOU ARE, my dear. I think that's you all bandaged up!" Isla smiled at ten-year-old Natalia, the young daughter of Gloria, who had worked for her father at the sanctuary.

The little girl had gone for a rather eventful swim with some of the baby sea turtles. She'd followed them all the way out to the reef and now had quite a deep cut on the top of her foot.

"Next time you go swimming do your best to avoid the coral reef, all right?"

Her eyes drifted to the beach. It was the first time she'd been to the sanctuary since the shooting. The blood drive had gone so well Diego had finally relented and let her unlock the gates to the beachside cove. They'd set up the clinic under a small copse of palms and had already seen a handful of people, including little Natalia.

"Do we need to do anything with Natalia's dressing? Change the bandages or anything?"

Gloria accepted the antibiotics Isla handed her. She had been in charge of the day-to-day running of the sanctuary since her father had left.

Isla shook her head. "Not for the next couple of days, Gloria. Unless she gets it wet. I know my dad—Doug—"

She grimaced, then laughed. "It's weird talking about my father without him being here."

She waved away the unexpected rush of emotion that came with mentioning her father. *He's safe now.*

"Anyway. He would have helped you change the bandages. But we can do it here now. The antibiotics are precautionary more than anything. I wouldn't start her on them unless she begins to complain it's still hurting. It was a pretty bad cut, so it isn't always easy to rinse everything out, but we don't like to throw medicine at things that stand a chance of healing naturally."

"What kind of symptoms should I look for? If I need to give her the medicine?" Gloria pulled her daughter close to her side and popped a kiss atop her head.

The gesture was so simple. So natural. Casual, even. Yet it twisted Isla's heart so tight it nearly took her breath away. She didn't have memories of such gestures from her mother. Not that she hadn't been loving. She simply hadn't been there that often. To the point that when they had been together Isla had always felt a bit nervous about pushing herself on her mother. Appearing needy.

She often wondered if her mother and father had really thought the whole "let's have a baby" thing through. As much as it pained her to acknowledge it, both her parents' true love had been their work. Being at opposite ends of the earth had never seemed to bother them.

It was pointless drawing parallels, but every day she buzzed with the anticipation of seeing Diego on the days he worked at the hospital. In just a few short weeks he had shown her just how amazing a relationship could be...and their marriage wasn't even real!

The sex is real. The connection is real. The love you have for him is real.

"Isla? Are you all right?"

"Yes. Of course. Sorry. I went off to la-la land there for a minute, didn't I?"

She gave her cheeks a little pat and smiled apologetically at the pair of them. *How embarrassing.*

"What we're really looking to avoid is septicemia. So she should stay hydrated. Drink lots of water. Keep the wound clean. If it becomes inflamed, swollen or tender—those are signs there might be an infection. Spreading redness streaking out from the wound… If you want me to take a look at it again we're back…" She scanned the calendar she and Diego had drawn up a week earlier. "We're back on Tuesday. Two days from now."

Just a few short days before her flight.

Gloria looked over her shoulder, then leant close to her. "We want you to know the fact that you are here— that you and Mr. Vasquez have opened the gates and brought the clinic here—has given us the strength to carry on with our work. Change doesn't come easy. But we haven't given up on seeing your father's plans through."

Isla reached out and ruffled Natalia's hair. Protecting Natalia's future was precisely why her father had fought so hard to put those plans into place.

"How about when I come on Tuesday you and I set aside some time to talk?"

Gloria smiled and nodded. "That would be wonderful."

Isla made a couple of notes on Natalia's patient file, then went into the central reception area in the mobile clinic—which was, in truth, about five steps away from the table where she'd just been treating the little girl. In reality, the clinic it was little more than a glorified ambulance, but it did the trick. For them, anyway.

The night before she and Diego had made up a wishlist of things they'd like to change or add if they were ever able to get funding for a "proper" clinic. An extra exam room…an additional pair of hands, maybe. It hadn't hit her until now that what they had been doing was planning for the future.

A future she wasn't going to be a part of.

She stared at the door of the room where Diego was treating one of the guards who had been at the clinic *that* night.

Funny, she thought, how quickly she'd accepted this life, this lifestyle, as her own. Her eyes moved to the calendar on the wall. It had been exactly a month now. Her ticket was booked. Her carry-on bag lay on top of a chest, waiting to be packed. Shouldn't they be meeting with Axl? Discussing some sort of truce? Leaving with things so undecided seemed wrong.

Her stomach churned. And churned even faster when she heard Diego laugh with his patient through the thin walls.

She didn't want to go.

It was a life-altering revelation.

She didn't want to leave. Not El Valderon. Not the people they'd been helping. And most of all she didn't want to leave Diego.

As if on cue, he stepped through the door, shook hands with his patient, saw him out, then crossed to her and kissed her cheek.

"Everything all right, *mi amor*?"

The term of affection did the same thing it did every time Diego used it when he checked in with Isla. She smiled as she tried to neutralize the fireworks going off in her belly, the skip of her heart.

She smiled up at him. "All good."

He pulled his laptop onto the counter and started to make some notes, then looked up when he noticed she was still looking at him. "What do you say we have dinner in town tonight? Somewhere special?"

She hadn't been feeling a hundred percent that morning, but he looked so keen. "Any particular reason?"

He feigned mock horror. "It's our one-month anniversary, *amorcita*. We can't let the good people of El Valderon think I am not still treating you like a *princessa*."

She smiled, but the comment hurt more than it salved her already jangly nerves. He was still playing a role. The lovestruck doctor in a whirlwind romance.

A *fake* whirlwind romance that had saved her life.

She had to admit she had put down half of the nerves and the churning in her stomach she'd felt lately to her increasing anxiety about when her path might cross with Axl Cruz's again. Would the invisible stranglehold he had on her life drop away? With Diego she felt safe. But when she was home again in Craggen…would the fear return in force?

Another thought struck so powerfully she felt numb.

What if this "date" tonight—this public show of affection—was actually Diego's way of telling the island it was over?

She looked at Diego, at his strong profile, his kind eyes… Would he really do that? Shame her in the same way Kyle had?

No. Not the Diego she knew. He wouldn't do that. Couldn't. Unless this whole time she had been the un-

witting pawn in a much bigger game. A game to out-
wit Axl Cruz.

She was just about to ask Diego if they could go to see
Axl—find him, hash out what had actually happened—
when there was a knock at the clinic door.

Sofia.

Isla smiled across at the young woman who had become a real asset for the mobile clinic. Not to mention
a bit more wary about entering the clinic unannounced
since that day when Isla had been so steamed up by
Diego's kisses she hadn't even bothered with feeling
embarrassed.

"Are you ready for your next patient?"

"Absolutely." Diego rubbed his hands together. "Who
do we have next?"

Sofia winced at him. "Paz Cruz."

"Ah." Diego drew his brows together, as if the news
had caught him by surprise. When he noticed Isla staring at him, he gave her a quick smile. "Good. Nice to
see he's up and about."

"Not at my father's sanctuary, it isn't."

Everyone stared at her.

Diego stepped between her and the doorframe, giving a quick signal to Sofia to stall Paz.

"You've seen him recently, haven't you?" Isla stood
and crossed her arms. She could see by the shift of his
eyes he knew she didn't mean Paz. She meant Axl.

"*Amor…* I haven't seen him. No one has."

She doubted that. Part of Diego's strength of character was his unerring quest to keep her safe and out of
the reach of Axl Cruz.

Well, being kept in the dark wasn't good enough. She

was going to have to get used to looking after herself soon enough, so why not start now?

She stared at Diego, a mixture of frustration, betrayal and love gnawing a raw black hole in her belly.

How could she have let herself fall in love?

"Fine." She squared herself off to Diego. "Compromise. If you won't tell me what you and Axl have been up to, let me treat Paz. If he's actually here for an appointment."

She wanted to look the man in the eye—the man whose life she'd helped save. See if he knew how much pain he'd caused her father.

Their daily video calls were…*complicated*. Her father would pass on reams of instructions, she'd pass them on to Gloria… But until today, when they'd finally felt it was safe to open the sanctuary, she'd been completely powerless to help.

Diego shook his head. "That won't be necessary."

"I think it will." She gave him her best *I'm not going to budge* smile. If she was going to leave this island with a broken heart, she was also going to leave it with her head held high.

"Different compromise," Diego parried, taking a step closer toward her.

Which was clever. He knew she got all wobbly-kneed the closer he was.

Her pulse quickened as she waited for this alternative compromise.

"We do it together."

She pretended to consider it and saw from the smile teasing at the corners of his mouth that he knew damn well she was vulnerable to that cheeky smile of his. This man… There was no staying cross with someone who made her laugh, made her feel protected, not to mention feel as if she were the only woman in the world he wanted to hold in his arms.

Even if it was all a lie.

Tick-tock.

"Right, then." She peeled her eyes away from his. "Let's see Paz."

"It looks good." Isla took out some fresh bandages. "No swelling. No discharge. You've clearly been taking care of it."

Paz nodded. He hadn't said more than two words since he'd entered the exam room with the pair of them.

Diego gave Isla a sidelong look. One that was trying to gauge if she was irritated because he was there or irritated because of their patient.

Easy enough to see she wished he would leave. *Tough.* They'd made a deal. The fact he'd insisted upon being there was... Well, he'd hoped it would be more reassuring than annoying. There wasn't a chance in hell he was going to let Isla be hurt. Not tonight. Not ever again.

This isn't a forever game.

A weight landed in his gut.

It wasn't a game at all.

He needed to talk with Axl. Clear the path for Isla to go home.

Don't let her go. Tell her how you feel.

A buzzing began in his ears. That was precisely the problem. He didn't *know* how he felt. Teasing away fact from fiction had proved too difficult. The only thing he knew was real was how perfect it felt to hold her in his arms. How well they worked together. How, as a team, he felt they could conquer anything they wanted to.

He looked at Isla, wondering if she felt the same. From the face of it, it was impossible to tell. She was a picture of concentration.

"It looks like the Steristrips have all done their jobs. Did they naturally disintegrate or did you take them off?"

Paz muttered something he couldn't quite make out. Diego could tell the lad was uncomfortable. Whether it was because of Isla's presence or his was unclear.

"I know you've met with my husband a couple of times since you received your injury." She nodded toward Diego, but didn't meet his eyes. "How did those appointments go?"

Again, Paz muttered something largely unintelligible. No overt thanks, but neither was there any hostility. Or bravura. One might easily have imagined him swaggering in here, making threats, showing his strength—*his* father had bullied Isla's father out of the country.

"You were lucky. This could have been much worse. I believe my father was always pretty clear with Security that if things ever turned violent he would prefer they not make full use of their marksman skills."

Paz shot her a look.

"You probably already know this, seeing as it's such a small island, but all the security guards here are ex-military. Men who know the true value of life."

Diego was about to jump in, smooth things over, but Paz wasn't bridling as he thought. Perhaps he could see what it was he hoped Isla was doing. Showing Paz the same amount of respect they had shown him and his family.

They'd saved his life. His own government had refused to do the same. Fair enough that she would want some common courtesy in exchange. She would be such an asset to the island's community. A true role model.

What's stopping you from asking her to stay?

"I presume Dr. Vasquez has already given you a time-line, but I expect we'll be able to take these staples out in the next week or so." Not that she would be here. "We wouldn't want them leaving any permanent marks, would we?"

"My father's dead."

Diego did a double-take.

Isla looked just as shocked.

"What did you say?" Diego asked.

"Axl. My father. He was killed three days ago, on an island off of the coast of El Salvador."

"What was he—?"

Isla's question remained unanswered as she and Diego silently listened to Paz explain how Axl had left El Valderon on the off-chance that Isla called the police or Interpol. When he'd arrived on a new island he'd tried to establish his authority in a place that had zero toler-ance for *pandilleros*.

Axl Cruz was dead.

"I want out," Paz said now. "I don't want to fill his shoes." He met their astonished faces head-on, shoulders back, eyes unblinking. "You saved my life." He held up his hands as they both began to throw questions at him. "I want to honor the sacrifices you've made in your lives by changing mine."

Tears sprang to Isla's eyes. "Do you…do you have a plan or—?"

Diego cut in, putting a hand on his wife's back in a form of apology. This was game-changing stuff. The son of the island's terrorist was doing an about-face and choosing peace.

"Does your mother know about this? Have you told her anything?"

Paz looked away, then back at the pair of them.

It struck Diego that the young man was addressing them as a couple. He hadn't seen them being married at gunpoint. Hadn't seen the fear in Isla's eyes when Axl had threatened to kill her and her father. He'd only known them to be two people brave enough to step between warring factions and save his life.

A bolt of understanding hit him with lightning-strike precision.

He hadn't cared about putting himself in the line of fire before because he hadn't seen any reason to preserve his own life. Did he have a death wish? No. But did he have a reason to live?

He looked at the woman who stood beside him. Fierce. Brave. Compassionate. Loving.

Yes. Yes, he did.

Dr. and Dr. Vasquez. A married couple. A couple who served their community the only way they knew how: *together.*

He channeled the man he wished his father had become when their lives had been torn apart after Nico's death. A man who absorbed grief and turned it into good. Genuine, goalless good.

"What do you want, Paz? How do you see yourself changing?"

"I want to study medicine."

Isla looked across at Diego. He saw she was thinking the same thing. This was clearly a turning point and they would be fools to let any momentum they'd gained fade away.

He heard commitment in Paz's voice. Strength. He saw the change in his body. A different type of voltage fuelling his path in life.

Diego was also feeling a fresh surge of energy. The same invigorating charge he'd felt the night he'd pulled his grandmother's ring from his neck and slipped it on to Isla's finger.

It was the energy of change.

Paz was clearly expecting to be laughed at. Mocked. Turned away. Instead Diego took his declaration seriously. He pulled up a stool and sat across from him. Eye to eye. Man to man. He sat taller when Isla came up behind him and swept her hand along his shoulders. They were a team now. An indivisible team.

"You'll have to go away to study if you want to become a doctor. The university here isn't equipped for anything beyond nursing degrees or emergency medicine for paramedics. You can go to the States or…elsewhere."

He pointed vaguely in the direction of Latin America. He began talking to Paz about school options, the courses he'd have to take, the subjects he'd need to study to put himself on track for a medical degree.

The young man was like a sponge. Absorbing it all. Asking questions. He was completely engaged in finding the best way to make his decision. The *right* decision.

"At that point you'll have to choose a discipline…" Diego pulled out a blank piece of paper and started writing lists.

Isla gave him a nudge with her elbow. "The poor man's eyes are glazing over!"

"It's a big decision. He needs all the information."

"True…" She drummed her fingers along her mouth.

Heat shunted through him at the memory of her hands on his body, her mouth kissing his. Each night they shared together was better than the last. The memory of those sensations was so powerful it took him a moment to tune back in when she started speaking.

"…an idea I think could work."

They both looked at her, a bit shocked as she had been so quiet before.

"Diego, you're working at the hospital these next few days, right? The accident and emergency ward?"

"*Sí*…" He drew out the word, unsure as to where this was going.

"That means I'll be on my own. So…why don't we park the mobile clinic up here at the sanctuary on a more permanent basis? It's near the villages, easy to get to. Paz can help me make it a sanctuary for people as well as turtles. I'm in if you are."

She put out a hand to shake on it.

Paz stared at it.

It was a big ask.

Everyone in the room knew it.

It would tell the island that they were united in their mission for peace.

"You want me to come *here*?" Paz sounded utterly flabbergasted. "To the sanctuary?"

Diego couldn't stay out of the discussion any further. "I don't know if it's wise, *amorcita*."

He knew his body language was defensive. Protective. Only this time he wondered if what he was really protecting was the status quo.

"If my father can't be here," Isla said, "*I* want to be

here. And who better to make this place a genuine sanctuary for the islanders than Paz?"

There were about a thousand different options he could offer here, but Diego was struck by the fire of possibility brightening his wife's eyes.

She crossed her arms and gave Paz a solid look. "I presume you won't be advertising free turtle eggs to your friends?"

He had the grace to look ashamed.

Isla pulled up the other stool so they were all sitting at the same eye level. Paz had obviously come here in good faith. He was trusting them. Isla was trying to do the same.

"What does your mother think about you being here?"

"She's the one who told me you might be able to help."

He was looking directly at Isla. The penny dropped.

This was why Serena had come to the clinic the other day. They *both* wanted change. *They* were frightened of Axl...or at least of who he'd become. And they'd been brave enough to ask for help.

"Do you think you being here on a daily basis, helping with the clinic, will provoke the other members of Noche Blanca?" Isla asked.

The question was a serious one. There was no chance this would work if it would bring more violence.

Paz looked them both solidly in the eye, "Without my father there *is* no Noche Blanca."

"Right, then." Isla gave Paz's arm a squeeze. "I'll see you here tomorrow. If you like we can get you some scrubs to wear. Make you look like part of the team."

She and Diego both smiled as Paz's eyes lit up. "Really? I can wear scrubs? That would be amazing! It'll be just like on TV."

"Better than TV," Isla corrected. "You will be helping real people in your community."

Diego watched his wife say her goodbyes to Paz with a warm hug and that big, beautiful smile of hers.

Just for that perfect moment he let himself believe it was all real. That they were a real married couple, making changes in their community step by proud step. And, just for that instant in time, he felt as if he could leave his anger from the past behind and face the future with a smile. With hope.

CHAPTER ELEVEN

DIEGO THANKED THE waiter for the nibbles and gave Isla's hand a squeeze. "Help yourself, *amor*. The meal shouldn't be too long." He popped a few salted peanuts into his mouth and then, after they'd both enjoyed the setting sun for a few moments, said, "I have to admit I'm still a bit shell-shocked."

"About Paz wanting to work with us? Or about his father?"

They'd each had a few hours to process and confirm the news. Axl Cruz was dead. For Isla it changed everything. She could go home now if she wanted to. Or, if she *really* wanted to drag her heart through the coals, she could wait until her father's inevitable return.

He'd not want to stay in Craggen anymore. Not now that he was free to work at the sanctuary again.

She watched as Diego's features softened into a philosophical expression. With every fiber of her being she would miss this man.

"I'm not surprised about Axl. Relieved, in a way. Saddened that he never had to stand up in front of a court of law, but to have Paz come forward the way he did… *Amazing.*"

He started to drop her one of those winks she had expressly forbidden, then stopped himself.

"I think it's a real credit to you that he chose you to work with."

She bit her lip. Why was he pretending it was going to be for anything more than a handful of days? Her plane ticket was booked.

"He'll learn every bit as much from you."

Diego reached across and squeezed her hand, then drew it to his lips and kissed it. Warm fuzzies blurred any lucid thoughts she might have had about how her leaving now was actually a *good* thing.

"What do you mean?"

"I'll be off soon, won't I?"

She said it casually enough, but the air between them grew taut with tension.

Diego's eyes told her everything she needed to know. He was ready for it. Ready for her to go.

Which was why it came as a complete shock when he said, "You could extend your stay. For a while."

And there it was. The final nail in the coffin.

She needed to go home. The sooner the better. Prolonging this agony of a love that was so obviously unrequited…it was too painful. Besides, Diego might have made huge strides toward making peace with his own demons, but being here had allowed her to push hers into a cupboard and do her best to forget about them. Disguise them with the adrenaline rush of survival. Of falling in love.

"Before I came here…" Her hands began to shake at the flood of powerful memories, so she set down her fork. "Before I came here I was engaged to someone else."

If she hadn't had Diego's full attention before she had it in triplicate now.

"And you ended it?"

"No. Quite the opposite. He chose another woman over me."

"Obviously the man is an imbecile."

She wanted to say, *Yes. Absolutely. A liar and a cheat.* Those were the facts. But the reality was she couldn't let Kyle bear the brunt of the responsibility that the clarity of hindsight inevitably allowed.

Instead, she said, "I probably owe him a thank-you card, to be honest."

"Que?"

She drew little gratification from Diego's indignation.

"Seriously. I could throw him to the lions, but...but I was probably every bit as responsible for the relationship being a disaster as he was."

"If anyone should thank him for being such a fool it should be me. I won the bride."

She shook her head. "No, you didn't. Axl did. Fear did."

"You think fear was what made you say yes? Go through with the marriage?"

She nodded. "Of course it was! I was fearing for my life. My father's life."

As she spoke, the memory of how she had really felt shunted through her every bit as powerfully as if she were reliving it.

"Cariña..." Diego protested. "Only a woman shot through with *bravery* would have done what you did."

She fought the bloom of warmth and strength his compliment elicited. "There was some courage involved. Courage I wouldn't have felt if it hadn't been for you."

She hesitated. "I *should* thank Kyle, though. I went back to Loch Craggen after my mum died because I thought if I had the perfect job, the perfect family, gave my father grandchildren..." She paused only just catching Diego's infinitesimally small flinch. "Like an idiot I thought grandchildren would be enough to make my father come home. Now that I've seen him here I realize he's doing what he loves. That he wasn't built for traditional parenting...whatever *that* is. So, yes. I do owe Kyle a thank-you."

"For what? Making sure you didn't have children?"

"No!" she snapped, a bit more grumpily than she'd intended. "For forcing me into a place so vulnerable I only had two choices."

"What were they?"

"To fight or to give in. Turns out fighting is a whole lot more rewarding."

And a crucial reminder of why she so longed to stay. She'd taken to this lifestyle. To these people. To Diego. She hadn't told him, but her locum had expressed an interest in staying on in Craggen for longer. Her father seemed different too. He seemed to have... Well, he seemed to have bloomed a little, and was spending quite a bit of time with Mary Baird.

She took a drink of water to give herself time to gather her thoughts. "Have I ever told you how my mother died?"

"Not in so many words."

As the sting of tears hit, Isla was suddenly grateful for the isolated table Diego had requested for them, out on the seaside patio. She was normally much better at controlling her emotions, but—*tick-tock*. She wasn't going to be here much longer. She might as well leave Diego with a full portrait of the woman he'd risked his neck for.

The woman he was rejecting.

She swiped at the tear careering down her cheek.

He pulled out a clean handkerchief and handed it to her with a gentle smile. The simple gesture tore at the fragile hold she had on her emotions. She stemmed a small sob, then buried her face in the handkerchief that smelt so perfectly of him until she could speak like a vaguely normal human being.

"For as long as I could remember my parents were devoted to saving animals as much as they were devoted to each other."

"And to you?"

She swallowed back the urge to tell him they had never loved her as much, but that wasn't true.

"I don't think they were designed to be stay-at-home parents. I know they loved me, but they saw their causes as bigger than them. More powerful."

A rueful smile hit Diego's lips. "I can relate."

"And because of that," Isla continued, "you've helped me understand my parents more. Helped me realize they did love me, with all their hearts, but the *way* they loved me was always going to differ from the way people who 'toe the line' love."

"How do you mean?"

"My mother was killed trying to protect a young assistant and an orangutan. Poachers. They were armed. She wasn't. The assistant was trying to protect the orangutan...my mother intercepted the volley of bullets.

Diego winced. He now understood just how similar their paths had been. But his response to tragedy had been so much more proactive than her own.

"When my father left his elephant project—"

Diego's eyes widened.

"I know, I know… There are a lot of endangered species. From my perspective, seeing as I'd already lost one parent, I felt I in danger of losing another. So I upped sticks and did everything in my power to make myself into a safe haven for him, back in my grandmother's house on Loch Craggen. But really I was making it a safe haven for *me*. Cocooning myself against all the scary things. I dropped my exciting life in London like it was burning coals. Took over the GP practice. Helped elderly ladies across the street. Drank hot chocolate instead of wine…"

"Became engaged to someone you didn't love?"

She gave him a grim smile. "Yup. And I hung around long enough for him to get bored with this…" she drew her hands along the length of her body "…and ended up here, sobbing myself to sleep every night until…until I met you."

"Why are you telling me all this? Not that I don't want to hear it… It's just that you've had all month to explain."

She was telling him because she loved him. Because she wanted him to know that as she confessed to him it was coming from a place that was honest and true. But she didn't think he'd want to hear that. Not if his invitation for her to stay was only "for a while."

She forced herself to give a self-effacing laugh. "I guess it's a really long-winded way of telling you that you're the one I really owe thanks to."

"I think you could safely say the feeling is mutual. Now!" He looked at the steaming plates of food the waiter had just set down between them. "Shall we enjoy our meal and then…" he dropped her a sexy wink "…have an early night?"

The warmth in her chest turned to fire. A fire that arrowed down to her body's most intimate regions. She hardly needed to be told what her body wanted. What she did need was for her brain to come to terms with the fact she would have to say goodbye.

"Absolutely. *Bon appetit.*"

She speared a prawn with her fork and raised it to her lips. The instant the scent hit her a swell of nausea roiled in her belly.

She looked up at Diego. Their eyes met with an electric, unbreakable connection as the fork fell from her fingers and her hands flew to her mouth.

In that instant she knew exactly why her body was behaving this way. The easy tears. The zig-zagging emotions. The nausea.

Despite their precautions, despite the fiction of their marriage, and despite playing their emotional cards as close to their chests as possible…she was carrying his very real child.

CHAPTER TWELVE

THERE WAS ONLY so much pretending Diego was up to. Isla had been in a dark mood ever since her bout of food poisoning.

"Everything all right?"

"Yes, thanks." She took a sip of herbal tea instead of her usual coffee.

He didn't like this. Pretending they were a couple who barely knew one another instead of a couple who had shared a bed up until a week ago. Shared a bed in a rather spectacular fashion.

He scalded his throat, downing his morning coffee in one, his eyes glued to his wife. "Do you want to talk about it?"

"Nothing to talk about."

It was the same line she'd used for the past two days. And tonight she would board a plane for Scotland.

She was proactively avoiding any and all conversations that didn't involve the clinic. Nor had she slept in his room. The gesture felt like a knife blade searing directly into Diego's soul. He wanted to push. He wanted to demand. He wanted, he realized with a burning hot resolve, this marriage to be real.

But she'd very obviously turned some sort of corner

and was set on going home. He could hardly demand she stay. Not after everything she'd been through.

He nudged the basket of baked goods toward her. "*Amor*... Try something. A bit of bread? You've hardly eaten all week."

He saw her fight a swell of nausea.

"Still not feeling well?"

She shook her head. "I have to get to the clinic soon. I'll eat something at the sanctuary."

"Why are you going to work? You're leaving tonight."

"I don't really need reminding, Diego," she snapped.

Fine. He'd try another tack. "Is Paz working with you today?"

She screwed her lips up for a minute and thought. "Yesterday was Sofia, so today is Paz."

"He seems to be taking to his volunteer role like a duck to water."

She smiled, despite the obvious discomfort she was feeling. Whether it was still the nausea or his presence remained to be seen.

"I can't yet tell if he simply likes wearing scrubs or if he's really taking to medicine."

"Maybe a bit of both?" Diego suggested.

She shrugged and looked away.

"Have you spoken with your father?"

"No." Her hands swept to her belly. "I... I send him emails. We're in touch, but..."

Diego reached across and took Isla's hand in his. "*Amor.* Talk to me. None of this is under duress anymore. I'm here. For *you.*"

Tears sprang to her eyes. She pressed her lips together, fighting the emotion he could see clawing at her throat.

"We can get through this—whatever it is. Together."

"That's just it!" The words came out in a torrent. "We aren't a *we*. Are we?"

She opened her arms wide and scanned the sunny courtyard where they'd taken their breakfast so happily for the previous few weeks.

The thought sickened him.

The idea of living without Isla was even worse.

"We can be if you want to be."

She looked at him as if he'd just spat at her. Her features twisted in horror. "What? Live a lie? Tell our child—?" She choked on the word, her hands pressing protectively to her belly.

He stopped her. "*What* did you say?"

"I said our child." She lifted up her chin. Defiance was pouring from her.

"You're pregnant?"

He felt as if he'd been hit with a wrecking ball. His vow never to have children was the one thing he had never questioned. The one vow he'd always believed he would keep.

"I wasn't going to tell you. I was trying to keep the little bubble of this lie we've been living complete so that you never had to know."

Diego bridled. "Is that what you think? That everything we've been through is a lie?"

"What would you call a marriage at gunpoint?"

"Love at first sight," he answered, without pausing to think.

They stared at one another, absorbing the power of the words he'd just spoken.

"Is that what you genuinely feel?" she asked eventually. "Love? Are you sure it's not some Messiah complex? A built-in need to protect vulnerable people after your brother died?"

He stared at her and said nothing. An instant ago, when he'd said "love at first sight", he'd believed it to be completely true. He'd been bowled over by her from the instant he'd laid eyes on her. Instinctually drawn to protect her. Care for her. Ensure she was—

Hell. She was right. He had been protecting her. But did he *love* her?

It was impossible to know. How did a man go about teasing apart fact from fiction?

He was surprised to see she was pushing back from the table—away from him. "The fact you're not answering is giving me your answer."

"Isla, wait."

"No." She shook her head and held out a hand in a *stay where you are* gesture. "I don't want you treating me as if I'm weak. Or vulnerable."

She looked up at the sky, blinked away a couple of tears, then met his gaze head-on.

"What I am is strong. Resilient." She pressed her hands to her heart. "I know now I'm a survivor. I don't need you to protect me. Or care for me. Or create some sort of cocoon for me to live in. Because loving you has changed me."

Her sob echoed around the sunlit courtyard as she dropped her face into her hands.

She loved him?

Instinct drew him to her. He pushed his chair back and tried to pull her into his arms but she pushed him away.

"I don't want this. I don't want you if you don't love me."

Why can't you just tell her? Tell her how you feel?

He scrubbed his hands through his hair. "We've got quite a few questions up in the air, don't we?"

She made a noise in her throat that told him what he already knew. That he was prevaricating. Being pathetic.

Loving her doesn't have to mean losing her. She's not your brother. This is not the same scenario.

"Isla." He reached out as she passed and grabbed her wrist. "If you're carrying my child—"

"Stop! Stop trying to control the situation. I gave myself to you. Heart and soul. Willingly. Do you how painful it is for me to know you won't do the same?" She turned on him. "You don't even want children, Diego. You made that crystal-clear. *I do.* So do what you do best and leave me to get on with my life!"

He reached out and grabbed her wrist. Things weren't going to end this way. Not with a fight.

She yanked her wrist out of his hand. "Don't!" She massaged her wrist and stared at him, appalled. "Don't you *dare* try and stop me."

She headed for the stairs then turned on him again.

"Do you know how much trust it took for me to fall in love with you? How much faith? To convince myself you weren't like *them*? That you were kind? Good? Someone who was doing his best to rise above and make a difference? Well, it turns out you're just like my parents. You love the cause much more than the people involved in it. I *won't* be a victim of that again."

Then she ran up the stairs and into her room, where it didn't take a genius to figure out she would be packing her bag and preparing to leave.

CHAPTER THIRTEEN

A KNOCK SOUNDED at Isla's childhood bedroom door. "Hot chocolate, love?"

Isla shook her head. "No, thanks, Mary. I'm all right with mint tea for now."

She held up the mug sitting on her bedside table as if it was proof that mint tea was the thing she most wished for in life. The magic potion that was making everything about being back in Loch Craggen pregnant, alone, and living under the same roof as her father and—*hello!*—his new girlfriend completely natural.

"How're you getting on with the job-hunt?" Mary leant against the door, clearly not planning on budging until she got an answer.

Isla smiled at her persistence. No wonder her father was cock-a-hoop over this woman. She was strong. Emotionally grounded. As mad about dogs and Craggen as he was about turtles. And she never pushed Isla to talk more than she wanted to.

"Well…" Isla pushed aside her laptop and crossed her legs. "I have applied for four posts in London, but being two months pregnant isn't really much of a lure to prospective employers."

"You're a sensible girl. You have savings. And of

course your father and I are happy for you to stay here as long as you like."

She didn't want to stay here. She wanted to go back to El Valderon, where her father was on a quick advisory trip. He'd handed over the reins of the sanctuary to Gloria, with the tacit agreement that he would come out during egg-laying and hatching season each year.

It was almost physically painful to think his path might cross with Diego's. She'd dreamt of Diego and of El Valderon every night since she'd left. Left in a whirl of outrage, refusing to listen to so much as a solitary word from Diego. She'd known that if she'd stopped and listened to him she might have done what she always did—tried to craft herself into yet another person she wasn't in order to make someone happy.

Her hands slipped to her belly. She had someone else to prioritize now. That number one place was well and truly taken.

Wasn't there room enough for two?

It was difficult to admit, but with each day that passed she missed him more and more. She realized half the accusations she'd flung at him had been to protect herself from the truth. Life wasn't perfect. People weren't perfect. He, like her, was fallible. He made mistakes. She made mistakes.

And she loved him with every cell in her body.

Mary tipped her head to her shoulder and gave Isla a sidelong look. "Did you speak with your father today?"

She shook her head. "Not yet, but, you know… We had some really good talks before he left. Going through everything we did has kind of forced us to be more open with each other. More honest."

"I think your father is definitely president of the Isla MacLeay Fan Club!"

"Ach, away!" Isla laughed as a flush of pleasure hit her cheeks.

She had never felt more close to her father than she did now. There had definitely been a strong hit of *déjà vu* when she'd returned to Loch Craggen in tears about a man, but this time—this time she wasn't questioning her personal worth. Wasn't desperate for her father's approval. She now knew she'd had it all along.

And now she'd had a few long walks along the bracing Scottish coastline with her dad she knew in her heart that she had always been loved. Her parents, as she had begun to suspect, simply hadn't fit the traditional mold.

"What do you say you come out and walk some of the dogs with me today? Give your eyes a rest." Mary held up a handful of dog leashes.

A bit of fresh air was exactly what she needed after two hours staring at the computer. And maybe an opportunity for the North Sea wind to blow away the cobwebs. Remind her that, with or without Diego, her future had changed for the better. Even heartache had its place in making a person better, and she was going to strive to give her child the best life she could.

She pulled on the cardigan lying on the end of her bed. "I don't suppose you have any top tips on how to become pack leader?"

Mary shot her a mischievous smile and beckoned for Isla to join her. "Plenty. How do you think I snared your father?"

Isla was still laughing as they rounded the corner. Mary's dogs were hilarious. She'd have to work a walk into her daily routine. And not only was her father's new girlfriend funny, she always seemed to have a new angle to look at a situation from.

Like the whole family issue. She'd suggested Isla remember that family came in all shapes and forms. Some were so-called traditional. A mum. A dad. Two-point-two children. And others…? Others were made up of people who loved and cared for you.

"Like Rufus," she'd said, pointing to her St Bernard. "He's always on hand when I need a bit of a blub. Never tells me to bog off. Never tells me I'm being an idiot. He just lets me cry out whatever it is I'm boo-hooing about and all he wants in return is a belly-rub."

Leaving Mary to wrangle the dogs, Isla turned toward home. Her hands slipped to her tummy—which gave an enormous flip when she looked up at the front door to the cottage.

"Diego!" Isla's cheeks, pink with the cold, turned pale. "What are you doing here?"

All six-foot-something of him turned around, his dark eyes making the same powerful impact on her they had the first time all those weeks ago on El Valderon.

"I've come to try and convince my wife to come back home."

Isla looked down at her bare hand. She'd left the ring on the bedside table before she'd stormed off in a sea of hormones and self-protection.

"Convince or strong-arm?"

He winced.

"I'm sorry." She shook her head. "I— This is—"

"I know. It's a bit of a shock. But I'm not here to force you to do anything. I was just hoping…hoping you might spare a weary traveler a cup of coffee?"

It was so good to see him. So difficult not to run straight into his arms. But her hands were clasped on her belly for a very specific reason. They were protecting the child she knew he didn't want.

Mary rounded the corner, holding a Chihuahua in each hand. They were her two "house dogs." The rest of the pack lived in Mary's luxury kennels just down the lane.

Her eyes widened when she saw Diego. "Isla? Everything all right, dearie?"

"Yes, I—" She threw a look at Mary. One that she hoped said *Can you just remind me of all of those pack leader tips again?*

"You know…" Mary's brow crinkled. "I just remembered I've got to go do a few things at the kennels. Is it all right if I catch up with you and your friend later? As long as you're okay?"

Isla looked at Diego, then back at Mary. She'd never been frightened of Diego. Ever. What she had been frightened of was her feelings for him. The powerlessness she'd felt when she had tried to change herself to make someone love her. She knew now that you couldn't *make* anyone love you. They either did or they didn't. And the fact that she was pregnant had been a game-changer for the pair of them.

"It's okay, Mary. We'll be fine."

A few minutes later, after a lot of faffing about with cups and kettles, coffee and her ever-present mint tea, Isla and Diego were sitting at the round wooden kitchen table in the window nook that faced out to the North Sea.

"If you threw a few palm trees about the place it'd be just like El Valderon," Diego said dryly.

"Ha! Yes. Exactly."

They both stared at their hot drinks for a moment, then as one began speaking.

"You first," he said.

"No, no. You've come the furthest." Isla lifted her steaming mug to her lips and nodded for him to go ahead.

"I—"

Dios! This was harder than he'd thought it would be. All the speeches he'd prepared at home, on the plane, on the drive here…were gone. Every last word.

"Diego?"

"I love you."

She pursed her lips. "That may be so, but you don't want a child and I do, so—"

He held up a finger. "Please. Hear me out."

"Did my father put you up to this? Tell you that you had to make an honest woman of me?"

"No." Diego gave an amazed laugh. "Quite the opposite, in fact."

"What?"

Pure indignation lit up Isla's features and Diego couldn't help but smile. There she was. The spirited woman he'd fallen head over heels in love with.

"Honesty is the best policy?"

Isla nodded, though a flash of concern blunted the purity of her blue eyes for a moment.

"I love you."

"You already said that, and I told you—"

He spoke over her. "And I want to be a father to my child. To our children…if you'll have me."

"Oh? So now all of a sudden, after one month on your own and an entire adulthood of swearing off procreation, you've decided you want to have a big family? What spurred this on?"

He could see it was bluster. That she was protecting herself. The child. *Their* child.

"Por favor, amorcita." He took her hands in his and drew them to his lips. "I promise—once you agree to marry me again, for real—you can lead all of our conversations, but...if you will let me... I'd like to explain why I was such a *huevón*."

"I don't know what that means," she said with a sniff.

"It means I've not only been an idiot but I dropped the ball when it was most important. To us. It isn't as if you got pregnant on your own."

"Or on purpose," she added.

Her hands swept across her belly and a soft, beautiful smile lit up her face.

"Whatever you're about to say, Diego, know this. I am over the moon that I'm pregnant."

She didn't look elated. But she did look determined.

"I *want* this baby," she said, her index fingers arrowed at her flat belly.

"And I want it too."

"But you were so adamant..."

"That was before. When anger and revenge fueled everything. With Axl dying the way he did—everything happening so fast—it was all too much to process. There were too many sea changes to make on the edge of a coin."

She fixed him with a *yeah, right* glare.

"I did change. From the moment I met you—"

"All soaked in blood and surf and dirt? Yeah. A real pretty picture."

"You were then and still are the most beautiful

woman in the world, Isla. And I would love for you to come home. To *our* home."

"Having a child is a huge thing. Particularly when you don't even want one to sit on your lap!"

It was his turn to feel sheepish. "She asked for you instead of me. I didn't want to admit it. I was so busy fighting the fact I was in love with you I just let her request fuel the lie I'd fed myself over the years."

"Which was...?"

"That I wasn't fit to be a father. That I was a man who couldn't be trusted to be there when it counted."

She blinked a few times, as if reliving a memory, then asked, "And what was it that changed your mind?"

"Paz."

Her eyebrows shot up. "Paz Cruz?"

"The one and only. Believe it or not, he and I have had quite a few heart-to-hearts over the past few weeks and it's got me thinking. If the son of a man who was so obviously on the wrong side of the law could raise a child who's so kind—so willing to give of himself— maybe I'm better equipped than I thought to take that risk. So long as I let go of my anger over my brother's death—the self-hatred that I wasn't there."

"And...?" Isla reached across to him, gave his hand a squeeze. "Have you done that? Forgiven yourself?"

He nodded. "Yes—and no. I will always wish I'd been there. There will never be a day that I won't. But..." He looked her straight in the eye. "Knowing I have you by my side would always give me strength."

For the first time since he'd reached into his chest and handed her his heart she smiled. That full, bright, cheery smile that lit her up from within.

"What do you think? Could you leave the wilds of Loch Craggen behind a second time?"

"For you?" Isla feigned having to think about it, then threw herself into his arms. "For you I would do *anything*. Well…" She pulled back and gave him a serious look. "I will never eat beetroot. I can tell you that here and now."

"Right. Got it. I promise." He crossed his heart. "No beetroot. Can I kiss my wife now?"

"You may."

The moment their lips met he knew he would do everything in his power to make Isla happy. To bring her and their children joy. Peace was still a fragile thing on the island of El Valderon, but it lived solidly and happily in his heart.

EPILOGUE

"I CAN'T BELIEVE how many there are!" Isla tucked her hand in the crook of Diego's arm and gave his shoulder a kiss as they stood side by side to watch the excitement on the beach.

"There are over three hundred, if the last count was accurate." Diego pointed toward the shoreline, where the baby turtles were being released into the sea. "Look at your father. He's absolutely over the moon!"

Isla laughed. "This is pure bliss for him. Having his family all together…"

She leaned toward the baby Diego had strapped to his chest in the El Valderon version of a baby sling and gave his dark curly head a kiss.

"Hola, mi amor!"

Her heart nearly burst with happiness as her brand-new son wrapped his tiny hand round her index finger.

Diego slipped his arm round his wife's shoulders and dropped a soft kiss on to her forehead.

"This is all because of you."

She pursed her lips together and laughed. "Rubbish! It was *you*. You and Paz, working tirelessly to bring peace and stability to El Valderon."

They both looked at Serena, a mother clearly bursting with pride as her son talked a large group of school children through the release.

Paz was wearing his paramedic uniform, his long trousers rolled up to his knees as he and the children each brought a baby sea turtle close to the shoreline and watched it make its way toward the sea.

Diego tipped his head to the side, his cheeky grin lighting up her insides every bit as much as seeing him the first time had. "Shall we agree that it is because of all of us?"

She gave him a light kiss. "I can agree with that."

Diego slipped his hand to his wife's back and gave it a light rub. Isla shimmied against it. His touch never failed to unleash a flight of butterflies.

"I love you, Isla." His voice was thick with emotion.

Another ribbon of heat twirled through her belly and swirled round her heart. "I love you, too." She meant it with all her soul. "Meeting you…albeit in some rather peculiar circumstances…" They shared a wry laugh. "Meeting you changed how I saw things. How I saw the world. Life."

Diego brushed the backs of his fingers along his wife's cheek. "You give me too much credit. Besides…" He protectively cupped his newborn's head with his hand. "I don't think I'd be a proud father of two, watching just about the whole of El Valderon come together to secure a peaceful future for everyone who lives here, without you."

Isla threw back her head and laughed. "We're in danger of becoming a mutual admiration society if we don't watch it!"

Diego's eyes dropped to half-mast as he swept his

hand along Isla's back, then gave her a saucy pat on the butt. "Oh, we are long past that, *mi amor. Long* past that."

Isla's lips parted in a wide smile. "I think we may have to find time for that *siesta* we spoke about this morning after all…"

Diego's tongue swept across his lower lip. "I think that is a very good idea."

Emilio ran up the beach from where he'd been standing with his grandfather and Mary—who, she noticed, was wearing an engagement ring. Isla crossed her fingers that she and Diego would be on the receiving end of a bit of a speech and a toast at their anniversary dinner tonight.

Two years! It had gone by so quickly that sometimes she thought she'd barely drawn a breath. And other times…when her husband pulled his fingers through her hair and lifted her face to meet his gaze, his lips… she felt as if she'd finally learnt how to make a moment truly stand still.

Emilio reached up and grabbed his mother's hand. "Mamá! Turtles!"

She scooped her son up into her arms and laughed. "You want to set one of the babies free?"

Her toddler nodded, his grin of anticipation nearly splitting his face in two. Of course he did. She did as well.

"What do you say we all go down and help?"

"Sounds good to me!"

Diego took his wife's hand and together, as a family, they walked to the shoreline to join their community as they celebrated the first successful—and peaceful—release.

* * * * *

MILLS & BOON

Coming next month

A SINGLE DAD TO HEAL HER HEART
Caroline Anderson's 100th book

'I can't offer you a relationship, not one I can do justice to, but I'm lonely, Livvy. I'm ridiculously busy, constantly surrounded by people, and I'm hardly ever alone, and yet I'm lonely. I miss the companionship of a woman, and I'd like to spend time with one who isn't either simply a colleague or my mother. A woman who can make me laugh again. I spend my days rushed off my feet, the rest of my time is dedicated to my children, and don't get me wrong, I love them desperately, but—I have no downtime, no me-time, no time to chill out and have a conversation about something that isn't medicine or hospital politics or whether the kids want dippy eggs or scrambled.'

His mouth kicked up in a wry smile, and he shrugged, just a subtle shift of his shoulders that was more revealing than even his words had been, and she forgot the coffee, forgot her foot and her common sense, and walked up to him, put her arms round him and hugged him.

'Scrambled, every time,' she said, her voice slightly choked, and it took a second, but then he laughed, his chest shaking under her ear, and he tilted her head back and kissed her. Just briefly, not long enough to cause trouble, just long enough to remind her of what he did to her, and then he rested his forehead against her and smiled.

'Me, too. Preferably with bacon and slices of cold tomato in a massive club sandwich washed down with a bucket of coffee.'

'Oh, yes! I haven't had one of those for ages!'

He laughed and let her go. 'I'll cook you brunch one day,' he said, and it sounded like a promise.

'Is that a promise?' she asked, just to be sure. 'Not that I'll hold you to it, and I'm not in a position to do a relationship justice either for various reasons—work, health…'

'Health?'

She shrugged, not yet ready to tell him, to throw *that* word into the middle of a casual conversation. 'Amongst other things, but—whatever you want from me, wherever you want to take this, I'm up for it.'

'Is that what you want from this? An ad hoc affair?'

She held his eyes, wondering if she dared, if she had the courage to tell him, to let him that close, to open herself to potential hurt. Because she'd have to, if this was going any further.

But there was nothing in his eyes except need and tenderness, and she knew he wouldn't hurt her. She nodded. 'Yes. Yes, it is, if that's what you want, too.'

His breath huffed out, a quiet, surprised sound, and something flared in his eyes. 'Oh, Livvy. Absolutely. As long as we're on the same page.'

'We're on the same page,' she said, and he nodded slowly and dipped his head, taking her mouth in a lingering, tender kiss. And then he straightened, just as it was hotting up, and stepped away with a wry smile.

Continue reading
A SINGLE DAD TO HEAL HER HEART
Caroline Anderson's 100th book

Available next month
www.millsandboon.co.uk

LET'S TALK

For exclusive extracts, competitions
and special offers, find us online:

 facebook.com/millsandboon

🐦 @MillsandBoon

📷 @MillsandBoonUK

Get in touch on 01413 063232

COMING SOON!

We really hope you enjoyed reading this book. If you're looking for more romance, be sure to head to the shops when new books are available on

Thursday 21st March

To see which titles are coming soon, please visit

millsandboon.co.uk/nextmonth